The Eyes of Tokorel
The Color of Emotion

Drew Bankston

Deb Alverson

1st Edition

Copyright © 2013 by Drew Bankston and Deb Alverson

ISBN 978-0-9886966-0-0

http://www.tokorel.com

Published by Star Painter Productions, LLC

PO Box 272228

Fort Collins, CO 80527

Cover design by Christi Bankston

Original images courtesy of NASA/JDL

Dedication

I dedicate this book to my family, who put up with long hours of writing, late nights of hearing the voices that called me to write and for their patience in listening to my excitement and ramblings even when they had no idea what I was talking about. And to my friends who, while visiting in the evening, would listen to me say how someday my book will be published. And to them I say, "See! Here it is!"

-Drew

To Mal, who taught me to dream and believe in the mystery of imagination. Thanks, Dad.

-Deb

CHAPTER 1

"You had me arrested!" Hot breath riffled through Permac Sudé's dark, full beard. Cold metal stung his neck. He knew the voice hissing in his ear. He suspected he knew the knife at his throat. It was probably the same one he planned to pick up when the door chime woke him. He jerked forward, not a smart thing to do with a sharp blade close to delicate skin, and any skin that close to a blade is delicate. No door chime. No knife on the table. *How the hell did she get in?*

He had survived thirty-four years of life without wounds or scars and had no desire to find out what it felt like now. She was skilled enough to expect his startled reaction and allowed the knife to follow his slight movement without doing any damage. Any allowance beyond that was unlikely.

"Don't move, Tokorellan."

The knife pressed into his flesh. Permac sat awkwardly in the chair, not quite reclining, not quite sitting up. "How..." he croaked.

"Quiet! And if you use your tricks on me, I'll know. Then, believe me; you'll never sleep peacefully again."

He doubted that he would do so anyhow. The muscles of his back complained, but he didn't dare move. Moving was important. He wanted to jump up, to pace, to run, anything to use the adrenalin surging through his body. He realized he was blinking furiously in the dim light. It was the only movement he could make with any degree of safety.

"I can expl..."

"I said do not speak."

The blade of the knife was no longer cold. The heat of his body had warmed it. Still, he felt a chill as it shifted again, not tighter but he was sure he felt it turn so that the edge would slice his flesh if either of them hiccuped. He hoped his racing pulse wouldn't make some critical artery expand into the blade. He hoped his shallow breathing wouldn't make him pass out and fall forward onto it. He hoped he hadn't been as stupid as he felt right now.

He concentrated on the woman. Had she wanted to, she would have killed him already. Although he felt no immediate murderous intent, the fury was apparent and so was something else. Amid the boiling wrath he sensed a curiosity, maybe even a twinge of desperation. Any of that could be gone in an instant, replaced by murderous intent. By no means did he feel reassured. A bead of sweat tickled his face. The tips of her clawed fingernails bit into his neck.

"I've spent an entire year thinking about this," she said. Permac stifled a groan as a muscle contracted. Her voice was directly above his ear. He hoped she was bending over and as uncomfortable as he was. "Sometimes I wanted to kill you. Usually I just wanted to hurt you. Never, NEVER did I think of you fondly, Tokorellan. Do you know what a Carratian prison is like? I'm sure you do. I'm sure that's why I was in one and you weren't. What the hell are you still doing here, anyway? Are you suicidal or just stupid?"

He sensed her anger rising to a new plateau and risked a whisper, "Linsora, neither of us was supposed to be there."

"And what was I supposed to do. Turn you in?" She snarled.

"Yes, damn it, you were!"

Permac acted on her surprise.

He reached up. Grabbed her hand. Pulled it away from his neck. She yelped in surprise as he put pressure on top of her hand, forcing her palm inward as her wrist flexed. Her fingers opened and the knife fell into his lap.

"No tricks, Linsora," he said, "just skill and patience." He pulled her forward, gripping her arms as he stood, his lean, tan frame rising before her.

"Maybe now we can talk in a civilized manner."

"The only way you'll ever be civilized is when you've gone to whatever serves for hell in your after world."

He sidestepped a kick intended for his shin.

"Do you really expect me to believe that you wanted me to turn you in?"

"Yes! You were supposed to turn me in. Anyone else would have," he snarled back at her. Of all that he remembered about her, he had forgotten just how much strength this short, slight woman possessed. At 6 feet tall he stood at least a head taller and over the past year he had ample time to hone his square Tokorellan frame into a sleek muscular shape. Leaning, as he did, toward the burly end of the physical build scale, he should have been able to hold her effortlessly, but she was like a wild creature, wriggling and unpredictable. Besides, Permac's mother had made a point of teaching him never to harm a woman. But his mother had never met Linsora.

"I expected you to. They would have released you, come after me, and found nothing. Then we'd both have gone about our lives. But oh no, you and your principles wouldn't have that. It's far too simple! You admitted you had the artifacts. And to make it worse, you refused to tell them where they were."

"At least I have principles. You, Tokorellan, have none." Linsora spat the name of Permac's race. "You and your mutant race are more despicable than…than anything I can think of. I should have killed you a long time ago."

He felt the muscles in her arms relax. He knew the tactic. She hoped to lull him into loosening his grip.

"I know you can use a knife," he said, not releasing her. "But don't compliment yourself by thinking you ever had a chance to kill me."

"Really? Because of your skill and patience? Your little mind games?"

Her next kick connected. With a muffled, "Ooof," he flung her across the room, his thin face winced in reaction to the sharp pain. She landed hard on the floor. By the time she regained her breath, Permac stood over her with the knife in hand. Besides not having any scars, he had never been in any kind of fight. He hoped just holding the knife, even without knowing how to use it, would be enough.

"Now we can talk," he said.

Permac gazed down at the woman on the floor. Her eyes blazed a brilliant green. People of his race don't have green eyes. Then again, neither did people of hers. Both Tokorellans and Khizarans were blue eyed. Her father, a green eyed Terran, had given her both her eyes and a stature shorter than most Khizarans, but no one who spent much time with Linsora thought of her as short. She extended her height with the force of her temper.

Still, the genetic combination had been kind to her, softening the angular Khizaran lines and, Permac never failed to note, somehow packing Khizaran proportions onto a shorter body, making her, well, just curvier than most. *If she wasn't so irritable and irritating*, he thought, also not for the first time, *I might...* He shook his head. He found her intriguing. And tiring.

He wiped his forehead. His thick, shoulder length dark hair stuck to the sides of his face and, he noticed for the first time, was wet with sweat. Stabs of pain shot from his lower back, the result of quick movement from a cramped position. His shin hurt. He could almost feel the outlines of a boot-shaped bruise forming.

Linsora's heavy auburn hair was purely Khizaran and, Permac noted, in a great deal of disarray. The usual single braid she wore was partly unraveled and stray threads framed her tanned face. He reached down to brush a strand from her forehead and she slapped it away as she would a buzzing insect.

"You're bleeding," she said. "Good thing the knife isn't as rusty as your skill and patience."

His hand was sticky. He touched his neck and found it sticky, too. With all the other aches, he hadn't noticed his neck was cut.

"Damn it, Linsora!"

She shrugged and offered a tiny smile.

Without taking his eyes off her, he fumbled for some kind of cloth on the table behind him. He yanked the entire tablecloth off, sending an assortment of cups and plates clattering to the floor.

"You won't die," she said. "The cut's already sealing. Better to leave it

7

alone than stick that cloth on it. When's the last time you washed the thing?"

"I don't need your medical advice." Permac stuffed the tablecloth under his chin. He pulled a chair from the table and sat with a thump. "Look, neither of us was supposed to be in that prison. You knew I had the artifacts. There was no reason for you not to tell them that."

"No? You honestly believed they'd have released both of us?"

"So you were protecting me?" Permac daubed the tablecloth at his neck. He couldn't quite remember when he had washed it. The cut had stopped bleeding so he tossed the cloth back toward the table, annoyed that she was right about the cut and his housekeeping skills.

"I was protecting the artifacts. How was I supposed to know that telling the Carratians you had them wasn't the same thing as handing the artifacts over on a plate?"

"Because I risked as much as you did to collect them," Permac said. "Did you let me help you just because I was convenient?"

"You offered to help. Why, I don't know. I'd have done it on my own."

"But you didn't send me away, did you?"

Permac thought the look on her face was somewhere between exasperation and amusement. "You think you're easy to send away? This isn't the first time I held a knife to your miserable throat. That's usually enough of a hint. But you were always there. And you're still doing it." She breathed heavily. "I hoped there'd be a trial. They accused me of theft. I figured they'd have to specify just what it was I stole. Then there'd be a chance for publicity and I'd have accomplished my purpose. But Carratian justice is convenient. I was charged and sentenced in a private court."

"They don't want the artifacts. They just don't want anyone to know about them."

"And that makes your argument pointless. Even if they had the artifacts, they'd still have to get rid of me. And if I told them about you, they'd be after your head, too."

"Maybe not. We can say anything we want. Nobody has much good to say about Carratians. Without proof, we'd be just a couple more people griping about their business practices."

"So, where are the artifacts now?"

"Sold."

She seemed ready to spring to her feet and Permac was assaulted by a wave of pure venom. He kicked her boot lightly with his foot, "Your turn to listen and not move. Yes, I sold them. Why do you suppose I'm here? Why do you suppose you're still alive?" He didn't wait for an answer. "When I realized you were going to insist on upholding your *principles* I made some contacts with parties at the prison. I do have friends in low but useful places. For a price, they agreed to look after you."

He leaned toward Linsora, "I do know what a Carratian prison is like and you were spared the worst of it. Trust me in that. I felt stupidly responsible for you although right now I'm not quite sure why. I stayed here, sold the artifacts quietly, and paid off the guards."

He felt a softening, immediately replaced with a renewal of ire. "You did this for a year? I'm not ungrateful, but what happened? Another two months and I'd have been released. I wouldn't be a fugitive and I'd have some sort of future. Instead I'm dragged out of the prison and brought here? To YOU!"

Permac exploded in frustration, "You would NOT have been released! You'd have disappeared!" He added more softly, "I had another plan in mind closer to your release date, but the guards I paid were being transferred. I had to arrange your escape now."

"I'm afraid those guards will have some bruises to explain. I don't react well to being kidnapped in the middle of the night. By the time we got to this building, they just gave me this and left." As she reached into a pocket on the sleeve of her jacket, Permac knelt and grabbed her ankle, bringing the knife close to her before she had time to react.

He thought she was about to stick her tongue out at him, daring him to use the knife. He didn't think he could. He was sure she believed he wouldn't. But she was raised in a knife-wielding culture where anyone with a knife was someone to be respected. He didn't blink. With exaggerated caution, Linsora retrieved a small box with a blinking green light. Permac recognized it as a field modifier, that's how she had gotten into his apartment. One swipe of that and the flimsy Carratian locks and security systems would be turned off. He let go of her ankle and returned to the chair. "They said they had done enough and that you were more than welcomed to me. After what I said when I learned where they were taking me, I don't think they wanted to witness our loving reunion." Linsora took a deep breath, "You could have let me know what you were doing."

"No, I couldn't. I didn't think you'd have welcomed the help. Right now, though, we have to get out of here. You're a fugitive and I haven't exactly felt secure. I've heard of a Terran exploration ship that's looking for crew. They're going so far out they'll take anyone they can get without a lot of questions."

"Permac Sudé, you have ruined my life," she muttered.

"And you haven't brightened mine any," he said with disgust.

CHAPTER 2

"That's all you have?" Linsora asked.

"I don't need a lot. Why?"

"What about weapons? The Carratian markets are full of …"

"Full of things I don't need and full of things that might attract attention. Don't think I've had a lot of fun this past year myself." Permac stuffed the last of his belongings in a pack and handed an empty pack to Linsora. "The markets are always open and we can find some things for you along the way. Let's go."

Permac cast one last glance around the tiny apartment. Bare essentials furnished two rooms. A path in the dusty floor showed his usual pacing route. "Funny, I hated this place but I feel odd leaving it. This is the first time in twelve years that I've been in one place for so long."

"Me too, but I'm not inclined toward nostalgia," she said. "How's your neck?"

"Fine. The cut's small," he said.

"Told you!" Linsora sniffed. "You said let's go, so let's go!

Permac shivered in the chill of the night air. Carratia, the capital and major port city of the Carratian planetary system, was in a temperate latitude. Never too hot, never too cold, but always damp with the wilted look of a four day old floral arrangement–still colorful, but showing definite wear. He considered putting his arm around Linsora, or at least offering her his cloak. He remembered that she had pulled a knife on him the first time they met. Even though he didn't think she had a knife now, he didn't relish the idea of a scuffle in the streets should she mistake kindness for pity.

"You warm enough?" he asked. Carratians don't provide prisoners with clothing. Linsora had taken only what she had on, a black flowing mid-calf length skirt, black shirt, and light jacket, all shabby from a year of wear and washing.

"I'm fine," she said. "Actually, no. Let's get to the shops. We should still have a couple of hours before the Carratians realize I'm gone."

Like most port cities, Carratia was bright, loud, and, if you didn't know your way around, expensive. More than most, though, Carratia was noted for its commercial and moral ease. The Mercantile Board that regulated all interplanetary commerce regarded Carratia as no more than marginally reputable. They followed the rules closely enough to retain their membership, since not having Mercantile credentials made inter-system trade nearly impossible on a large scale. They also skittered past the rules whenever they thought they could get away with it. Carratian markets offered items not seen in strictly regulated ports – artifacts that more properly belonged in a museum, weapons that belonged only on military installations, substances that appealed to a wide variety of races' idea of intoxicants – all were available. The Mercantile authorities knew, but looked the other way. Carratia was willing to establish mining operations on far-flung planets no one else would consider. Not to mention the small fact that Carratian funds managed to find willing pockets among the Mercantile establishment. Those who grumbled about Mercantile corruption were those who didn't know which pockets were open to favors.

Permac couldn't think of time when the city was closed. The port operated at all hours and the shops and market stalls accommodated the steady stream of customers. Transports from orbiting ships arrived and left, each on its own clock. Commercial vessels operated on the time schedule preferred by their captain. Even in the nighttime darkness of the city, some ships hummed with noontime lights and activity, some were dimming for evening, some warming in lazy preparation for the day.

Permac guided Linsora through the bustle and noise. Vendors called out to passers-by, each one offering the best, the strongest, the newest, the cheapest. Raucous singing filtered out of several taverns, each off note accompanied by the tangy reek of strong ale. People bumped into them with no offer of apology. Shrill voices argued, laughed, called out to acquaintances. Even the beggars asking for a few coins were loud. Most Mercantile crews looked forward to a liberty stop on Carratia, but Permac hated it. No sense of decorum here. Any behavior was acceptable except what he considered good behavior.

Permac pulled the hood of his cloak up. People had remarked that his blue eyes sparkled when he was amused, and right now, for the first time in his year of enduring these streets, he was highly amused. He pursed his lips, hoping the bushy beard would hide his erupting smile. He felt something like a parent taking his child out on a shopping spree. Linsora flitted from shop to shop, stopping to sniff the aromas of food that wafted from stalls and cafes. With each whip of her head, the loose auburn braid flew from side to side, allowing more wisps to escape. He had never seen her so animated in a positive way. She was simply delighted in her freedom to touch and sniff and move. He wondered how long it would last.

He steered Linsora into a less frequented side street. The patina of glitz became dull as soon as they turned a corner into the relative quiet of neighborhoods where locals shopped. Their first stop was not, as Permac had expected, a clothing shop, but several food vendors. They sat on low stools outside an ale shop, the table between them stacked with half-empty baskets of bread and meat.

"Didn't they feed you in there?" he asked.

Linsora pulled the last bit of meat from a skewer, "Mmm. Not like this." Her nose, aquiline from her father with a squarish tip from her mother, crinkled with satisfaction.

"What did you do for a year?"

"Ah ha! So you don't really know what a Carratian prison is like." She jabbed the skewer toward his face, making him flinch. "Didn't think so, you're not the type who ends up in jail."

"Well, no." Permac almost felt guilty for having had a law-abiding life. He thought about saying he'd just been lucky or smart enough not to get caught, but the truth was he hadn't knowingly broken any laws before arranging Linsora's escape. Making alterations to official records might not be completely legal, but that's not the kind of offense Linsora would consider sexy. "But I can imagine not all of it is fun."

"Carratians don't let convenient manpower go to waste. They had us working in a factory producing parts for their ships. Next time you serve on a Carratian ship, think about who had a hand building it. Amazing that they don't all fall out of the sky," she said. "And they were asses. The factory people only spoke to us in Carratian."

"Not Merc?"

"Nope. So, I can now proudly proclaim that I'm fairly fluent in four languages; Khizaran, Merc, Terran, and Carratian. How about you?"

Permac mentally ticked off the languages he could speak, "Um, five fluently, and a little of three more." Her whistle of respect was not the expression of withering scorn for Tokorellan educational standards he expected. Tokorel, more than most cultures, placed a high emphasis on languages. Generally, societies taught their own planetary language, possibly an ethnic language, and Mercantile Standard, or Merc, the universal language of commerce and travel. No matter where you were from, you could understand it and speak it, although since Merc was spoken with a wide variety of accents, Permac wondered if any real standard existed.

"Must be useful." She reached for another skewer of meat from the plate. "Any Carratian?"

"Only a little. Not much Khizaran, either."

"Really? That's surprising."

"Why? You think we're taught to speak Khizaran so that when we go back to conquer your people we'll be able to communicate?" He was only half kidding. From what he knew of Khizarans, that was an accurate reflection of their attitude toward Tokorellans.

"Possibly. But if you try to conquer Khizara, you won't have to communicate. Either you'll fail or all the Khizarans will die trying to stop you."

"Nice vision of the future."

"It's reality. Want this?" She pointed to the last skewer of meat. Permac shook his head. "This and more of that ale and I'll be all set. I saw a cloak back there that would be useful."

"That's not all you saw."

Linsora grinned. "True, I could use a weapon. Or two." She thumped the mug on the table and rose. "Don't look so dejected, Permac. Did you think a year in prison would reform me? The people of my homeworld and yours might be related, but mine don't have your little talents."

"You carry knives instead," Permac grumbled. "And what do you think is better? At least I don't make a mess." Permac reached into his jacket and handed her a knife. "Here. Since you'll be getting more anyway, you may as well have this back. One of the few things the Carratians didn't confiscate when you were arrested."

Linsora examined it, flipped it and caught it by the blade between her fingers. "Thought it felt familiar. Keep it. You never know when you might find it useful. Besides, I cut you and didn't clean the blood, so it's yours."

Linsora strode off toward the shops. By the time Permac caught up with her, she had chosen a long black cloak made of the soft skin of some large creature, boots, several identical skirts and shirts, two plain jackets all nondescript and utilitarian clothing and four knives of various sizes.

"That should do it. Is it too much?"

"For my wallet?" he asked. "No. Go and change while I haggle."

She appeared minutes later looking not much different than she had. Permac knew the knives were now in places she could reach easily. Given a little time, she'd probably sew concealed pockets in all her clothing. He shook his head.

"What?" she asked.

"Nothing. If you're happy, let's go. We don't have a lot of time."

"Why are you so bothered about my knives?"

Permac raised an eyebrow, "Because they're dangerous. Isn't that enough?"

"Exactly enough! Every Khizaran knows that every other Khizaran is armed. We're taught to use knives all our lives. It's part of our culture. Look at this place. If I'm a big strong guy, I can threaten a smaller guy out of his wages, or just push him out of a long line. On Khizara, if I'm a big strong guy, I know that any skinny girl is probably just as skilled with a knife as I am.

Probably more so."

"Why not guns, then? Why knives?"

"Proximity," she said. "Knives are personal; they make you think about what you're doing with them. You can't accidentally mow down ten people with a knife, can you? Just one person at a time."

"Not to mention that you can't carry a gun on board a ship."

"Well, there's that, too. One blast through the hull, and it's all over." Linsora looked over a vendor's selection of gloves, choosing a supple black leather pair. Permac fished more coins from his belt purse. "I remember hearing about that, way back in the early days of the Mercantile when all the space faring people were just getting to be aware of each other. That must have been a time to be alive! Imagine meeting another whole race for the first time. They all had their own ideas of how to conduct business. Lots of fights over trade routes and merchandise rights. Still, more ships died because of fights between crew members from different races."

"Did Khizarans carry guns back then?"

"No, only the military. It's still that way."

They had returned to the main market street and jostled through the crews of docked ships.

"A lot of people around tonight, more than usual."

"That's good for us," she said. "We can blend in."

"I suppose. It's just odd," he said. Permac closed his eyes, reached his mind out up and down the street. He shrugged his broad shoulders. He sensed the usual assortment of people, nothing disturbing. Still, he felt uneasy.

"What's wrong?"

"Nothing. Nothing at all," he said. He rubbed his hands together, "I should pick up some gloves, too."

"They won't check the cells for another hour, we still have time."

"I know, I just…never mind." Permac stuffed his hands in his pockets, surprised to find the knife there and taking care not to cut himself. "By the way, what did you mean back in my place when you said if I used my tricks you'd know it?"

"What do you mean? Doesn't everyone?"

"No. No one does. At least no one ever has."

"Fool," she said, stepping around a gray-faced man lying on the street who had made one too many stops at ale vendors. Permac wondered whom she was calling a fool, the man on the street or him. She went on, "Maybe… okay, let's look at this. Your ancestors were kicked off my homeworld about two hundred years ago, right?"

"Two hundred years, yes. Kicked off? I don't think so," Permac said. "My ancestors developed our mental abilities and scared your ancestors so much that they would have exterminated us if we hadn't left."

She shook her head, "Your ancestors wanted to control Khizara. I think that's some rationale for wanting to be rid of you."

"Our versions of history differ. Tokor discovered how to sense emotions in others..."

"And how to influence emotions in others. The leader of your ancestors and his gang were using that to control elections and to skew the power of the government." Linsora stopped walking. "Don't you think that qualifies as treachery?"

"Keep your voice down and keep moving. We can debate the details of history and politics later. We've established that your race and mine parted company. I'm interested in the little fact that you know when I'm influencing your emotions."

Standing on her tiptoes, her nose barely reached his chin. She tapped his cheek with a gloved finger, "Simple, your eyes turn purple."

Permac watched her turn and walk away. He concentrated, and sent a sense of calm toward her. The return emotion he felt was one of curious conflict. The calm he directed was layered with rage. He didn't see her stop. When she wheeled toward him, a small blade glinted in her glove.

"I said you were not to use your tricks on me! Not then, not now, not ever," she whispered. "You think you're so powerful? While you've been standing here trying to figure out how I knew, you were so preoccupied I could have killed you before you had a chance to trick me again."

"You can't kill me yet. You don't know which ship we're going to."

"That little fact hasn't escaped me," she said softly. "Why do you think you're still standing?"

"Yes, my eyes turn purple when I influence emotional states. Just now, though, you couldn't see my eyes. How did you know?"

The blade disappeared in the folds of her cloak. "That's a backgammon! Good for you," she chuckled. "Fine, I can taste it."

"Taste it? How? I mean, what does it taste like?"

"I don't know how. I just experience a sweetness. Not so much like a sweet food, well maybe like a sweet fruit. Just sweetness. Don't stare at me. It makes some sense, doesn't it? That's what I was getting at. Our ancestors are related genetically. Since your people have this ability, maybe there's something latent in my branch that makes me able to detect it."

"Just you, or do you suppose all Khizarans can?"

"No idea. I'm only half Khizaran, you know that my father was Terran. If I can, then I'd assume all Khizarans would be able to." Linsora shrugged. "How do you manage it, anyway?"

"Well, other than you, no one can taste the influence. People just seem to feel a little confused, but they generally accept the emotion for a while."

"No, I mean how do you do it without people commenting on the change of your eye color?"

"The change is brief. I just look down for a minute or so. And, like I said, people feel momentarily confused. Emotions are subtle and I don't read minds. I couldn't force a change of mind on anyone, but I can send a feeling of acceptance or rejection, that sort of thing, and hope it's enough." Permac smiled, "Useful, huh? It creates a lot less stir than holding a knife to someone's throat."

"With a knife you never have to hope it's enough. It either works or it doesn't."

"And when it doesn't, you end up in prison."

"At least it's honest," Linsora snorted. "What about on Tokorel? How can anyone stand not having anything private? No emotions that someone else can't detect?"

Permac returned her snort. "Sorry to borrow your phrase, but it keeps everyone honest. Something like your knives, it's cultural. We know when someone is tapping into our emotional state. We have rules about when it's okay and when it's considered rude." He didn't have to sample Linsora's emotions to know that her sense of delight had vanished into edgy wariness. He nodded toward the end of the street and walked off. "Still, I do wonder if anyone else can taste influences."

"I wonder if it makes any difference?" She scurried to keep up with Permac's long stride. "People from Tokorel and Khizara aren't likely to mingle much. You're the first Tokorellan I ever met. We're on each other's forbidden lists. Even the Mercantile recognizes that. I suppose the only reason we both ended up on the Carratian ship is because it was Carratian. They don't care who they hire, or what they destroy."

"Mmm, I suppose so," Permac mumbled. "I hadn't thought about it."

"You never thought it was odd? Are you truly that naïve?" Linsora spat, a sometime habit of hers Permac found especially distasteful. "What about the ship we're going to? Mercantile regulations prohibit Khizarans and Tokorellans on the same ship and all Terran ships I know of are Mercantile."

"No," Permac admitted, "I didn't even consider it. But, I heard the captain's desperate for crew."

"What about Mercantile ID? Your intake will be fine, but what kind of record will I have? I have no idea if the Carratians reported back to the Mercantile when I was arrested."

Permac shrugged, "Don't worry about it."

"What do you mean?"

"I said I have friends in low but useful places, and don't forget I'm an engineer. Whatever is done can be undone. Your Mercantile record shows you currently unassigned, that's all."

"And what about when the Carratians start looking for me? Don't tell me you've taken care of that, too?"

"No. I'm going on the assumption that they won't waste a lot of effort to find you. Besides, the Mercantile doesn't cover everyone. Don't tell me you expected to have a simple existence after nearly killing a guard in prison?"

"I expected to be dead and that's simple enough. You obviously didn't pay off all the guards. Let's just say he made several suggestions I didn't care for. I don't have your talents and I did have a knife." She glanced at him, "Yes, even in prison knives can be had. The original sentence for theft stood, but they offered amnesty for the assault if I signed a long term contract with them."

"What a blazingly brilliant future that would have been."

"Blazingly brilliant to consider a future on non-Mercantile ships, too. Scum of the skies. Better to be dead. It wouldn't have taken long to buy out of the contract anyway. They just wanted to be sure I didn't talk about finding artifacts on a planet they wanted to reduce to mining slag rubble."

"You think you would have lived long enough to buy yourself out? They don't fool around when a planet full of a valuable mineral happens to have some annoying evidence of ancient occupation. They don't fool around with a cocky archaeologist who wants to be principled, either. The Carratians just don't care." He wagged a clawed finger at her. "Can you imagine the stir if the Mercantile Board actually had proof that Carratia was ignoring that rule? All evidence of occupation has to be investigated before a planet can be mined and that takes years. The Merc would welcome a chance to skewer the Carratians. And that's something the Carratians do care about."

She sniffed and strode away.

"You're welcome, by the way."

"For what?"

"I'm acknowledging your effusive thanks for saving your life and offering you a future at all, blazingly brilliant or not. Even you have to realize that it's better to have some chance than to be dead."

"As I said, I'm not ungrateful. That's about as effusive as I get." Linsora paused. "I can appreciate why you did what you did. I suppose you have your own set of principles, in spite of your contempt for mine."

Permac smiled, "And as I said, you're welcome."

CHAPTER 3

The line moved slowly. Linsora and Permac spent the hours of darkness huddled in the middle of dozens of other people outside the doors of a house-sized single story building designated as the intake point for the *Dominator*. Several times, Carratian police strode through the small crowd, obviously looking for someone. Linsora made it a point to remain seated, pretending to be asleep. She wasn't unusually short, but short enough that it might serve as an identifier. Just before sunrise, a transport craft landed on the roof of the building and the processing of crew began.

"See, I told you they wouldn't look too hard," Permac whispered. "They're probably happy to be rid of you."

"And they probably think I value my own skin enough to keep my mouth shut," she said. "They don't know me very well."

Linsora and Permac inched toward a uniformed man seated at a small table at the back of the room. His yellow-blonde hair stuck up in odd tufts, as though he had run his hand through it too often. The crew intake terminal blinked red, indicating the wrong sequence of his prior entry for a crew member. He looked up at Linsora with clear, steady eyes.

"You're next." His voice rumbled in his chest. "I'm Captain Haavens. Before you ask, and you look like you might, yes it's unusual for the commander of a ship to be processing crew. Yes, I look tired and I'll probably never live to be as old as I look. And yes, I've been at this all morning or whatever the hell time it is here and this chair is eating into my backside as much as this whole situation is eating into my gut. And no, I'm not good at this so it's taking a while. Just an advisory. You don't look like the patient type and I'm not in the mood for complaints. Got it?"

Linsora moved forward with a shrug.

Exploration ships generally lost some crew at stations like this one. People grew tired of space, cramped conditions - and no matter how large the ship, eventually it felt cramped - and the unending sameness of it all. The long stretches of time in transit from one system to the next were filled with routine maintenance work. Then if you were lucky, the system would have a planet worth exploring. You might be collecting mineral core samples, water samples, or vegetation. Only rarely were other creatures encountered and even then they were, for the most part, best fit for a meal or two. In her fifteen years of service, The *Dominator* had yet to discover a sentient race. Capt. Haavens often felt his vessel was named as a joke. But still, it was well armed and could live up to its name given the opportunity.

This trip would take them to new and uncharted territory. That should have been enough to keep most of the crew signed on, especially since the jumping off point was Carratian. Piotyr Haavens didn't hold Carratians in high regard. He never knew anyone to do business with them and come out ahead. Still, they did make attractive sounding offers. *Maybe that's why half my crew went to work for them*, Haavens thought. He shook his head as he waited for the terminal in front of him to accept the next crew change entry. *Maybe, but I never lost this many all at once before.*

The terminal finally blinked green, "Entry Complete." Haavens looked up. "Name?"

"Linsora."

He flexed his hands and typed in the name.

"First name," he said

"That IS my first name. I am Khizaran."

Haavens glanced up wearily at her unsmiling face. Behind her was a tall, powerfully built man with shoulder length black hair, a full beard, and the blunt square features of a Khizaran. He looked at the man's hands and sighed. He had the thick claw-like fingernails of a Khizaran. *Two of them. And that cut on his neck looks new. Just what I need to liven up the ship.*

"Sorry. I know you don't use surnames, but I know you have one and I need it for the records," he said, correcting and typing again.

"Anselm."

"Occupation?"

"Archaeologist."

Haavens looked up again, surprise on his face. "Unusual occupation for a Khizaran."

"Yes."

"Any good at it?" Her name was somehow familiar. *Maybe*, he thought. *Must be.* He locked his stare with hers, "Or should I check with the Carratians?"

Linsora bristled. "Yes, I am good at it. Even the Carratians would admit that much."

"Probably so. I have no special fondness for Khizarans, but I don't like Carratia and I do need an archaeologist. You're in," he said. "Ship operates on a Terran schedule, 24 hours. Right now it's late afternoon. One day to adjust. Report to your duty station day after tomorrow." He motioned toward a throng of other new crew members standing behind him. "Wait over there. I'll assign your quarters when I'm done here." *Then I'll probably have to cook you all breakfast and scrub the latrines myself too*, he thought. *Just as well this happened in Carratia, at least there are as many people who want to leave as there are people who want to stay.* "Next!"

Permac Sudé strode toward the desk. Towering over Haavens he smiled, "Name's Sudé. And I do use my surname."

Haavens could only sigh again.

Linsora slung her bag over her shoulder. It was light, but filled with enough. She could pick up whatever else she needed along the way. Along the way to where, she had no idea. Just getting away from here was enough. Looking at the others in the group she joined, she thought they were all in the same position. Many of them had the vacant look of waiting for the next minute to happen without caring what the next hour might bring.

When Permac joined her, he whispered, "He'll probably figure out he managed to end up with a Tokorellan and a Khizaran on his ship at some point, but we'll be away from Carratia by then."

They waited in silence until Haavens began the next crew process.

"Anselm ... no, it's Linsora, right?" he said, not looking up to see her nod. "Science Department. You want your own quarters, or with the engineer?" He gestured toward Permac.

"WHAT!" Linsora roared, rousing everyone in the room from whatever reverie they had been enjoying. "Did HE suggest that? The quarters I want are as far from his as possible." Then she added, standing at attention, "Sir."

Haavens stood, nearly upending the table, and leaned forward, "Look, I want no trouble on this ship. If either of you has a problem, you are to keep it quiet. This is a civilian ship, but I run it with military order. Use your knives on anything other than meat and you'll end up in my brig. And my brig will make where you've been look like a vacation. Got it?"

"Yes, sir!" Linsora said.

"Fine, just bloody fine," Haavens said, sitting again. He muttered a deck and room number to Linsora.

As she moved away, someone bumped her and placed a steadying hand on her arm. She was startled to see Khizaran nails. The tall, slender man hadn't been part of the new crew group. She wondered if he was one of the other officers of the ship and noted his face for future reference. It wouldn't be hard to recognize him. A scar ran down the length of his face from just beneath his left eye arcing toward his mouth and ending at his jaw. He patted her shoulder and muttered an apology.

The man bowed and moved toward Capt. Haavens. "Captain, I will be taking my leave now. I thank you again for providing me passage on your ship, I know you don't usually take passengers."

Capt. Haavens stood and shook the man's hand, "Mr. Moragh! I hope you haven't been inconvenienced at our early departure."

"Not at all, Captain. I'm glad you've been able to find crew replacements so quickly." The man surveyed the room and its remaining people. His eyes fell on Permac Sudé for a moment. "I wish you great success."

"Thank you. Perhaps we'll meet again one day, Mr. Moragh," Haavens said.

CORNERSTONE

"I've just returned, sir. The situation is becoming critical."

The lanky man eased the door closed. He blinked in the dim light and wrinkled his nose. He wondered how many times he had made the same entrance. Hundreds? More? And each time the same, with his bravado wavering on the far side of the door.

He glared at the wall of candles on the far side of the room. No mid-day sun filtered through the draped windows. Just another of the old man's quirks. In the musty ambiance of flickering light, people tended to speak in the same hushed tones they would use in a sacred place. It was an atmosphere crafted to make hot tempers and hasty plans unwelcome. The younger man felt it was a waste of imagination.

The candles' tiny flames flickered, as though cringing and recognizing that he would snuff them out by sheer willpower if he could. He shifted his weight and the candles puffed sweet aroma into the room before resuming their confident glow.

"Sir?"

The old man sat where he always did, in an overstuffed chair with the wall of candles behind him. The younger man shook his head at the impression of a halo created by the old man's mass of white hair bathed in the candle light. More unnecessary theatrics.

"Sir?" he repeated.

The gray haired man looked up. "Yes, thank you, I'm fine. How are you?" He tapped a clawed fingernail on the arm of the chair. Blue eyes, more clear than his age should have allowed, shone in the dim light. "You never do spend enough time on pleasantries."

"I'm fine, sir."

"Well then, I have to ask, is the situation *becoming* critical? Or has it already become critical? The verb tense is important."

Even in the soft light, the younger man's lean face showed not-so-youthful lines and not-so-respectful annoyance. He bowed slightly.

"Would you like to review my report? You'll see it indicates that circumstances dictate a higher level of our involvement."

"You mince words. *Our* involvement is most certainly not what you intend. I sometimes wonder why you bother to report at all." The aged warrior breathed heavily and waved his hand in the air at his visitor's protestations. "No, no, no. I understand your motives, perhaps better than you do yourself. And I do trust your observations. You may be right. I would say that the time has come for you to become more personally involved, but you've already done that."

"Sir, I have only done what …"

"You have only done what you have deemed necessary. I know. I've heard the litany before. It is over used and not necessary now, and has all led here." The older man stood with a surprising ease and elasticity for one who appeared so ancient. "I understand it would have happened eventually. But trust me, I also understand that it would not have happened now without a fair degree of, how did you put it, involvement."

"Better now than later. You know that."

"Do I? Do you?" He carefully kept himself between his younger companion and the candlelight, speaking quietly. "Truly, do you? Our directive is to monitor and guide, not to create. Don't dismiss that lightly." He sighed, "And I know I've overused that litany. So, we're even. Well, that's no longer relevant. I believe you have several circumstances at critical points. Do what you must, but carefully."

"My own life means little, sir. I only serve the greater cause."

The older man burst into a short, static laugh. "You give yourself far too much credit. No one is altruistic. Not even you. Your eyes are not meeting mine. Are you afraid I'll see the ambition behind them?" He walked the short distance to young visitor. When they stood inches apart, the he reached up to trace the outline of a scar on the younger man's face. It ran the length of his face from just beneath his left eye arcing toward his mouth and ending at his jaw "When you're as old as I am, that scar and others will disappear behind the folds of age, but the memory of it will never leave you. The memory of the perils you've faced will never leave those who care for you. I care for you. Understand, and always know that. If you fail, the failure is only for now. Circumstances will present themselves again even without you. Think about what is necessary and what is simply expedient."

The younger man nodded. He would offer respect, but he had no intention of allowing circumstances to do anything without him.

CHAPTER 4

The *Dominator* had been under way for less than a day before Linsora received a summons from Capt. Haavens. Her small room was close to the science labs, two floors above engineering but still not far enough away from Permac Sudé for her taste. Ever since she first met him, a year and a half ago, their lives seemed to be tangled. They met on her 30 birthday, in fact, a day that would otherwise have been cause for celebration. *He's attractive. He's pleasant. He's funny. He probably saved my life. But he's still Tokorellan. Best to just put as much distance as possible between us*, she thought, *and get on with life.*

She decided to take her meals at odd hours to lessen the chances of running into him. She'd have a more solitary existence that way, but the other crew members who ate at odd hours might be solitary types, too, and more to her liking. After about a week, she'd adjust to the 24-hour schedule of dark and light. Her home world of Khizara had 26-hour days. Carratia had a 22-hour cycle. Ten years of serving on ships of various orientations gave her the attitude of work when you have to, rest when you can, and always have something to keep you occupied during the down times. The standard Terran shifts applied, ten hours in your assigned department for four days, one ten-hour day helping with whatever maintenance the ship needed, then two days off.

After a morning spent sorting through the *Dominator*'s collection of neglected artifacts and a protein-laden lunch, she trudged up the winding corridors to the top level of the ship where Haavens lived and worked. The Dominator had already taken two stomach-churning space jumps. Linsora didn't think Haavens would turn the ship around and return her to Carratia, but she didn't think the summons to see him was good news either.

"Linsora Anselm," Haavens was perched on the edge of a table that served as his desk. Linsora knew the small door to her left led to his living quarters. She had never served on a Terran ship before and was impressed with the creature comforts offered. Even the corridors were painted a different color for each floor. Most ships made do with gray throughout.

"Nice quarters," she said. "Nice ship."

"Thank you." He gestured toward a chair with dark green upholstery stretched over thick padding. "I hear you've been in the lab already. You're still off duty until tomorrow, you know."

"I'd rather be busy, sir," she said.

"Good, I like that. Have a seat. I thought your name sounded familiar and I've done some checking. Your history is fascinating. I've already had a chat with Sudé. I understand he is Tokorellan and not Khizaran. Apparently, he failed to correct my initial impression of him. Seems he's done this much of his career. Even his Mercantile record lists him as Khizaran."

Haavens paused long enough for Linsora to register his casual statement. She made a silent ohhh with her lips and leaned forward like a feral beast about to spring on its next meal.

"Don't go rushing to his cabin to kill him, remember I said I wanted no trouble. It's not just Khizarans who don't fully trust Tokorellans. A lot of captains quietly refuse to sign them, or find ways to get rid of them. He's made his way in life quite well. I'm sure you'd agree that sometimes you do what you have to."

"That's how we both ended up on that Carratian ship, then," Linsora said. "They thought he was Khizaran. He told me…well, it doesn't matter what he told me, but it explains a lot."

"Indeed. Sudé said he innocently introduced himself and you pulled a knife on him."

"And if the First Officer hadn't stopped me, I'd have used it." She settled back into the chair, relaxing into the soft fabric. "There's not a lot about Mr. Sudé that's innocent, Captain, except maybe his mistaken belief that everyone likes him. I only pulled the knife when he told me he was Tokorellan. That's not innocent–it's stupid."

Haavens clucked his agreement. He wouldn't exactly call the woman pretty, but in a rough Khizaran sort of way she was striking. Dark-red hair, green eyes, the Khizaran angularity somehow blurred, softened. Her clothes weren't bulky, but consisted of a lot of flowing fabric. He knew Khizarans carried knives. Looking at Linsora, he could see the function of her fashion. The clothing didn't emphasize her body, but offered ample space for concealed pockets. Still, Haavens had heard, and been part of, many discussions over many cups of ale about the relative merits of women from all the known humanoid worlds. Khizaran women ranked high. Humanoid women of any race throughout the Mercantile worlds came in all ranges of dimensions, but Khizaran women seemed to be generally well-proportioned. If you could manage to get past their general air of superiority, the Khizaran love of hearty emotion made them amazing in bed. The general consensus was that if they carried all those reputed knives, they had to be in good enough shape to use them.

Haavens wondered what was going on between this particular Khizaran woman and Permac Sudé. *The man's both lucky and unfortunate*, he chuckled to himself.

Sudé certainly wasn't stupid, but perhaps he did honestly think everyone might like him–even a Khizaran woman raised to believe Tokorellans are nothing more than physical embodiments of demons from hell.

The cabin lights flashed twice then dimmed. Haavens moved to his own chair to prepare for the next jump. The ship's jumps through space would be regularly timed for the first several days of the trip. Known space was easy to navigate. In less well-charted areas, the navigators would carefully study star charts and schedule jumps only when they were sure of safe coordinates. The *Dominator* shuddered slightly. Seconds later, everyone on board felt something like a punch in the stomach followed by a brief falling sensation. The energy required to create the wormhole in space was nothing compared to the energy it needed to keep the hole open long enough for the ship to get through. The faster a ship made the trip, the less energy was needed. No one had yet found a way to compensate for the sensation of such rapid acceleration.

Linsora rubbed her midsection as the lights came back on. "I hate that. I've hated that for ten years."

"Amazing that anyone travels at all, isn't it?" Haavens said.

"Captain, you didn't call me here to discuss the finer points of Khizaran and Tokorellan relations. I agreed not to cause trouble and I won't. I can't speak for Sudé, but I'll do my best to stay away from him. You said you recognized my name and you seemed to know something about my trouble with the Carratians. If you don't mind my asking, just what do my records say? And just why did you call for me?"

"To the point, then. Your official records indicate that you had been with a Carratian ship and that you're currently unassigned. Nothing about any trouble," Haavens said. "Which I find odd, since I know for a fact that you did have some trouble. Word spreads quickly in ports. There have been rumors about the Carratians stumbling on something important and then covering it up. And your name has been wrapped up in it all."

"So, I'm a celebrity. What does it mean to you?"

"I want confirmation of the rumors."

"You've got it," Linsora said, rising.

"I haven't dismissed you yet," Haavens said. "I want specifics. What was found? Where it was found? What happened?"

"Why?"

"Tell me what, I'll tell you why."

Linsora sat down. Her heavy nails sank into the upholstery. "I've been away from Carratia for, what, a day? They didn't exactly give me permission to leave."

"So I gather."

"And if I talk to you, or to anyone Merc, the next time I run into a Carratian, I'll end up in a grave instead of a prison."

Haavens poured a cup of water and handed it to Linsora. She waited for him to pour another cup and joined him in thoughtful sipping.

"You intended to keep it all secret?" Haavens said. "After all you've been through to safeguard the information, I wouldn't have expected that."

"No," Linsora said. "I just didn't expect to be talking about it as soon as this to someone I don't know. You were good enough to sign me on and I owe you, but..."

"But you don't trust me. You think I might turn you in to the Carratians for the reward? Oh, they're offering one, not officially, but it's out there. I deal with Carratia because I have to, but I'm Mercantile first. You want to talk to the Mercantile? Talk to me."

Linsora stared into her cup. It was as empty as she felt. A year in prison to protect artifacts that were sold to keep her safe while she was in that prison. A year in prison to safeguard information this man wanted. *My job is to gather information for the Origin Project*, she thought, *it shouldn't be as hard as this.*

The Mercantile's Origin Project required all exploration ships to include an archaeologist among the crew. Soon after wormhole technology became commonly available, space faring races clashed more often than they cooperated. But curiosity sometimes has a way of tempering greed. Many races were humanoid, many were aquatic, many were reptilian, but most were carbon based. All humanoid races could breed successfully, as could those of other species. The genetic similarities were too great for each far-flung race to have evolved in complete isolation. Long before the economic arm of the Mercantile was established, the diverse races agreed to share information that might lead to the discovery of an origin. 'The Origin Project' set strict guidelines for any discoveries and maintained a central database of information. Initial cooperative efforts eventually evolved into the current extensive reach of Mercantile economic and political influence.

No, it's not just for the OP. It's for me. I won't allow slime like the Carratians to think everyone is as corrupt as they are. She puffed her cheeks with a frustrated exhale. *And who knows what Haavens wants. For once in my life I wish I could read emotions like Sudé does.*

"The planet the Carratians found is full of benadiaum. If you want the minerals, you're a year too late. I'm sure the Carratians have reduced it to rubble by now."

Every space-faring race needed benadiaum; it was part of the energy soup needed to hold wormholes open. Benadiaum deposits formed deep within a planet. After extensive mining, not much of the planet's surface was left. The Terrans wouldn't mind having their own stockpile. And they weren't above using Carratian tactics to corner the market and drive the price up. Or, to flood the market and hamstring the Carratians, who up until now, had the largest supplies and set the prevailing price.

"Actually, I hear they haven't touched it. You did accomplish something, after all. The rumor is that whatever you found belongs to a race that abandoned the planet. Now that they know it's valuable real estate, they want to negotiate the rights. They don't care about history, either, but at least it bought some time."

Linsora allowed herself a smile of small victory.

Haavens continued, "And I don't want the minerals, if that makes you feel better. My charter is the same as yours, to bring back information. Pinpointing the location of a previously unknown civilization wouldn't hurt my career, especially if it annoys the Carratians. It's well known that they skirt Mercantile regulations whenever it's convenient for them. Probably why they hired you in the first place."

"Because they didn't expect a Khizaran archaeologist to take the job seriously?"

"Khizarans are better known as military types, not students of the gentler sciences. Mercantile regs require certification of an archaeologist that a planet is clean before they allow large-scale mining. I'm sure the Carratians thought they were paying you well enough to give them what they wanted."

"You have nothing to lose, Linsora," Haavens said. "The Carratians know where the planet is and could conceivably start to mine it anytime they wanted. If I wanted the benadiaum, so what? A slag heap is a slag heap no matter who creates it. You stand a better chance of preserving whatever it is you found with me, though." He ran his hand through his tufted hair. "There's more than just professional integrity and revenge, too. Present the Merc with evidence of a new race...well, it wouldn't hurt your career, either."

"I suppose so." Linsora shifted her weight in the chair and hoped it didn't look like she was squirming.

"Don't tell me you're not interested in boosting your career standing. Instead of taking a berth on any ship you can, you'd have them clamoring for you. You'd get to choose. Maybe even get some Mercantile funding behind you. You know it's not outside the realm of possibility. Your father made a name for himself as an archaeologist. He trained you. The Mercantile's not above creating good publicity by advancing the fortunes of a known name."

Linsora knew. She had dreamed of her own ship, her own choice of destinations. Every archaeologist did. She might not be the one to solve the humanoid origin question, but with her own ship, she could follow her instinctual leads and have more of a chance.

"All right. I did find evidence of settlement. There were some surface artifacts that I collected. The Carratians only provided rudimentary tools for me to work with, but I did sink a test probe. I found several levels of possible occupation at the site, meaning it had been occupied for some time by sentient beings. I also suspect that the location of the site was minor. There are probably larger settlement sites somewhere else on the planet."

"Why?"

"I found finely crafted tiles and sophisticated metal work that a small or isolated community wouldn't have produced."

"That's what the Carratians accused you of stealing?"

"The artifacts, yes. I refused to hand them over and insisted on reporting the find to the Mercantile so the planet could be investigated before it was destroyed. So, they charged me with theft to get me out of the way."

"That makes sense," Haavens moved to his chair again as the lights dimmed and the ship made another jump.

"Ooof," he said, stretching. "Well, that all makes sense. How the hell did Sudé get involved in it, though?

"I'm not entirely sure," Linsora said. "He just seemed to be there at all the wrong times."

"Wrong for him, or wrong for you?"

"For him," she admitted. "He helped collect the artifacts and get them back on board the ship. The Carratians never found them because Sudé had them all the time."

"Interesting," Haavens said. "Will you tell me where it is?"

"The planet? I have no idea. I only pay attention to star charts after I've found something and have to document it. I never had a chance to do that." Linsora cursed softly, "But I'm sure Sudé knows."

Haavens walked the short distance from his chair to the woman's. "He does. To his credit, and you should appreciate this, he won't tell me until you agree."

CHAPTER 5

Permac's sense of satisfaction didn't last as long as he would have liked. He had maintained the integrity the Khizaran woman was so fond of saying he lacked, refusing to help the navigators map out the course to the planet until Linsora personally assured him she had agreed to give Haavens the coordinates. Instead of the thank you he thought he deserved, she had brushed past him without making eye contact and he hadn't seen her since. But Permac refused to be excluded from the fun. He exchanged the location for an assurance that he'd be part of the exploration team, an unusual task for an engineer and not an assignment Haavens relished since it would place Permac and Linsora together.

The *Dominator* had been orbiting Brachen, as the planet was called, for several days. Permac noted that Haavens had taken an indirect approach to the planet, coming in from deep space and not from the direction of Carratia, adding several days onto their eight-Terran-week trip. Permac also noted that the ship was in a state of low level alert. He wondered if Haavens expected, or even hoped for, a challenge by the Carratians. So far, they seemed to be alone and the *Dominator* crew had mapped Brachen uneventfully. A good-sized settlement was found and this was the target of the exploration team. Surely the Carratians knew about this settlement, too, and had purposefully set their earlier team down on the opposite side of the planet. Permac knew that Haavens was building a case against the Carratians, but he wasn't at all sure the Mercantile would welcome it. The Carratians might operate just within the regulations, but their interests were extensive and their economic power reached into the highest political levels of the Mercantile.

Permac shrugged into a jacket. Before leaving his quarters, he popped the knife Linsora had given him into his pocket.

"You never know," he said to his reflection in the mirror. "It might even give Linsora a chuckle." The blue eyes of his reflection sparkled back at him. He brushed his dark, shoulder length hair back from his face. It wasn't stylish, but he liked it. He had always felt his square Tokorellan features were too sharp. The full beard gave him a more acceptable rounded look. He thought of himself as rugged, with the looks of someone who's been on the far side of a distant world for months, out of touch with popular trends but uniquely outstanding.

He made his way down the increasingly steep slope of the corridor to the bottom level of the *Dominator*. One seat remained empty on the ten-man transport craft, directly across from Linsora. Permac shuffled past three sets of feet and grinned at Linsora as he took his place.

"Haven't seen you for awhile," he said.

Linsora stared at him as though he had just sprouted a second head, with a mixture of disgust and disbelief at his casual remark. "Consider yourself lucky," she said.

Permac held his tongue during the short flight. When the doors opened to the first whiff of fresh air in weeks, he was among the first to scramble out of the transport. As Linsora emerged, he stepped in front of her.

"Linsora, let's settle this. We're both on the exploration team. We have to work together."

"We're both on this team because you insisted. Engineers aren't generally on the first transport. That doesn't mean we have to work together. Excuse me, I have things to do."

"Uh-uh. Not yet. I want to know what I've ever done to you that hasn't been helpful or polite."

Permac sensed rising anger. "Helpful or polite? Is that how you see what you've done? Look Sudé, if it makes you feel better, you can go about your life being helpful and polite all you like. Your polite help landed me in prison. Your people nearly destroyed the society of my home world and would probably be helpful enough to try it again, given the chance. I'm not interested in helpfulness. Now get out of my way and stay out of my way."

"So it comes down to the fact that I'm Tokorellan, then?"

"What the hell do you think? You can't possibly be dense enough not to realize that!" Linsora shouted.

Permac's eyes shifted from blue to violet as he sent a wave of tranquility toward her. He saw her relax, then spit.

"Do NOT do that to me again," she said slowly.

"Linsora," Haavens called from a clearing, "Over here!"

Linsora strode off. Permac gazed at her retreating figure and, with a sigh, turned his attention to the landscape. On the previous trip, they found no structures, just the tracings of possible foundations in the dirt. This place looked like a town. The buildings he could see were small, single story and, for the most part, not very sturdy looking.

Permac walked toward the largest building that still had a roof. He noted that the other buildings he passed didn't look worn down from the ravages of the elements over time, but damaged. Outside walls were pocked with ragged holes, the edges sharp and often charred. More like a battle zone than an abandoned village.

He rapped on the wall of the large building. When nothing stirred or fell, he ventured inside. The building had no windows, just two doors, the one he had entered through and another that was slightly ajar on the far side. He reached for the control on his belt that activated the bright light on the chest of his jacket. The interior was one large room filled with what looked like workstations, evenly spaced waist-high cubes. At one time, people would have been standing at these cubes to work on whatever it was they did here. Broken machinery littered the floor. Bits of metal and glass crunched under Permac's boots as he toured the perimeter of the room. Once back at the door, he proceeded to circle toward the interior. The farther toward the middle he was, the less damage was apparent. He wasn't an archaeologist, but he did know this was not some ancient civilization. The technology might not be up-to-date, but it looked sophisticated.

Linsora and Haavens' excited voices reached him from outside. He couldn't make out what they were saying. Permac walked toward the center of the room choosing his steps carefully. The floor was springy and didn't feel like it was constructed as well as the machinery in the room. The top of one of the workstations was shinier than the others. He turned his body so that his light shone directly on it. A panel of controls was on a shelf under the clear surface. Permac reached inside the shelf, placing his hands on the controls. The buttons and knobs felt comfortable to his hands. A little odd, most keypads weren't designed with Tokorellan hands in mind. The heavy claws tended to get in the way of delicate controls.

Peering down through the glass, Permac could make out dust-covered inscriptions.

"...no idea. Only a name." Linsora's voice called from outside. "Is anyone inside?"

The doorway filled with another bright beam from a jacket light.

"Hello?" Linsora called. "Find anything in here?"

The light approached Permac. "Yes, come look at this."

"Sudé? How the hell do you end up being everyplace I am?"

"Just lucky, I guess," he snorted. "Look at this."

Linsora picked her way through the rubble. "What is it?"

"I've found some controls here and some writing," Permac said. "I think I can bring up some power for this building!"

He squinted through the glare of his light on the glass at the controls, fingers pressing a sequence of symbols. Linsora arrived at his side, peered over his shoulder.

"Sudé," she shouted. "Don't push..."

The final motion of Permac's hand cut her off. A soft whoosh accompanied the close of the main door. Linsora reached out and yanked Permac to the floor. A blinding light filled the room and began to pulse.

"Don't move!" Linsora said.

"Why?"

"You want to stay alive? Don't move," she muttered. The light pulsed for several minutes then stopped. Permac sensed mounting tension from the woman and prepared to move.

"Not yet," she said.

Permac wondered for a moment if she could sense his tension.

"The flashing will start again," Linsora whispered. "Whatever isn't in the same location during each flash will be hit with an energy beam. Security system. Fairly standard in old Khizaran installations like this."

"Khizaran? How could this..." Permac felt her shift very slightly next to him.

"I found a name on one of the walls outside," she said, "written in old Khizaran script."

"But the..."

"Shhh. Move as little as you can. Turn off your light and look to the left. One of the doors didn't close completely. Next time there's a period of darkness, we have to..." the return of the pulsating light interrupted her. They waited. The pulsing continued for a longer period this time. It seemed to be looking for them, becoming impatient. Permac sensed a rising anxiety in Linsora. He focused on it trying to ease the tension.

"Damn you," she growled softly. "Whatever I'm feeling that you don't happen to approve of might be the only thing to save us from your stupidity. Should be soon. Get ready."

When the pulsing stopped, they stood and ran toward the tiny shaft of light shining through the far door. The ancient floor groaned beneath their pounding feet in the blackness. Several feet before the door, Permac heard Linsora yell. He felt a rush of dry air, then nothing beneath his own feet. He tumbled through the hole the floor. With a tooth-rattling thud, he landed on the hard surface of the building's basement.

"What was that?" he panted. "Another security device?"

"An old floor," she said. "Get away from that opening. Now!"

The pulsing began on the floor above them.

"Damn, my light must have broken when I fell," Permac shouted.

Wires connected to the machines above dangled in front of them and wrapped around their feet. They stumbled forward. The only light came from the hole as the pulses of light accelerated. Finally, as though with satisfaction, the hole in the floor was detected. The blast of an energy beam singed and widened the area surrounding the hole in the floor. That change would be detected in the next pulse and the hole would be widened further. They had to

34

work themselves as far away from the opening as possible.

"I'll call Haavens. Maybe he can break in and turn that thing off," Permac shouted.

"If you can. If everything's working up there, communications will probably be blocked," she said.

"Yeah. Just getting static. I think we're on our own."

Another blast and debris peppered their heads. In the silence and darkness that followed, both Linsora and Permac stopped.

"My light's not working, either," Linsora said. "I wonder if we can pull some of these wires down and maybe pull the plug on it."

They tugged on whatever wires they could reach in the blackness.

"There are hundreds of them," Permac said, feeling around. "Wait, here's something. Feels like a pipe. I bet it has a mass of wires inside it. Could be a main power source."

"You're the engineer," she said.

Permac banged on the pipe. He followed it and bumped into Linsora.

"Sorry," he said. He placed her hand on the pipe. "Follow this, at least it leads away from the hole. Maybe we can find where it opens up."

Permac heard a thump, followed by a string of Khizaran curses.

"What's wrong?"

"I just walked into a wall," she said. "The pipe goes through it."

"Let's head back, maybe we can follow it the other way," Permac said.

As he turned, a flash of light dazzled his eyes. The pulses were slow this time, the bright flash and total darkness created dizzying visual phantoms.

"Wait!" Linsora called. "We have to wait. The lights are slower, but the blasts will be stronger. Stay as far away from the hole as you can."

Permac heard Linsora pounding on the wall that had stopped her, followed by the rasp of metal on stone and more curses. An explosion from above them made him jump, banging his head on another low pipe hanging from the ceiling.

"Must have hit some of the equipment up there," Linsora said. "I'm trying to chip through the wall. Seems to be stone or concrete, though."

Another explosion and the hole that had been well behind them became wider and nearly overhead–a blinking, smoky eye gleaming with malice. Linsora and Permac hunched close to the wall. The wires they had just pushed through smoldered and sparked in a frenzy of light and smoke. Permac's heartbeat raced faster than the pulsing light, sounded louder than the blasts.

He didn't hear the sharp crack of the floor over them.

With a slow shudder, the gaping eye closed. The ceiling tilted. A slab folded down over them. The hard stone wall lost some of its support and toppled inward, leaving Permac and Linsora in a tiny triangular space. In the sudden profound darkness, even sound was muted. Permac only heard the roar of his heart. The air was full of powder, chips of wood, dust.

"Sudé! You alive?" Linsora called. "I can't see a damn thing. The ceiling fell!"

"Alive," he coughed. "You okay?"

"Fine," she whispered. "Just fine."

Permac fumbled with controls on his belt. "Can't connect with Haavens. How about you?"

"What?" Linsora's breathing was labored. "Uh ... no."

Permac sensed not rage but panic. "What's wrong? Are you hurt?"

"Small places... can't breathe," she struggled.

Permac sent a feeling of airy openness. He heard a tiny squeak of surprise followed by a relieved series of breaths.

"I didn't think Khizarans were prone to claustrophobia."

"They're not. My father was Terran," Linsora said in a normal voice. "I suppose I should thank you."

"You can start by calling me Permac. Isn't it an insult for a Khizaran to refer to someone by their surname?"

Linsora grunted. "Only if that someone is another Khizaran."

"Ah." Permac still wasn't sure if he'd been insulted. "Well then, I should thank you for your help up there. Have to admit I'm a little surprised you saved my life when you had a golden opportunity to kill me."

He could almost feel her eyes glaring toward him in the darkness. "If I was inclined to kill you, you'd already be dead. And having a machine do it would give me no pleasure."

Permac decided that a change of subject would be prudent. "Just what did I do up there to start all this? The characters on the keyboard looked familiar. I could read the word, similar to the word for 'go' in Tokorellan, I assumed it would execute a program."

"Oh, it did. That word in Khizaran means 'fire', as in fire weapons." Linsora took a deep breath, "This place was obviously in a state of war. Did you see the damage to the buildings? Whatever they used this building for might have been critical. I've seen the security system in Khizaran installations before. If someone forces entry, you just press the button and whoever entered won't live long enough to tell anyone else. Meanwhile, you've popped into some hidden escape door."

"If there's an escape route…"

"Why didn't I just use it? It could be anywhere up there."

"I meant, maybe we can still find it." Permac pushed against the fallen ceiling. The walls of their enclosure creaked, eliciting another gasp from Linsora. Permac calmed her and she grunted a wordless reply. Permac settled on the floor.

"All my life, I've been taught to be wary of Tokorellans and your mind tricks. Thank you for your help, but don't expect me to like it."

"And Tokorellans are taught to be wary of Khizarans generally." Permac smiled in the darkness then suddenly rose to his feet, banging his head on the fallen ceiling. The wall Linsora tried to chip through was tilted over them. He felt along its surface. "That wall toppled. I'm trying to find if there's a room behind it. Wait, here's the edge." He grunted. "I can get my arm around the side but can't feel much on the other side."

"These blasts can't go on forever."

"Eventually it'll run out of power, but it doesn't make sense for it to go on this long. A few blasts would kill anyone up there," Permac said. "It could be that some of the timing mechanisms have stopped working."

"That's cheerful."

"Realistic. We need to push the floor away."

The edges of the fallen floor gleamed with each new pulse of light. Permac and Linsora scuttled as far back as they could, shoulder to shoulder and forehead to forehead when a new blast created shuddering falls of dust. Permac wrapped an arm around her and she didn't protest. She buried her face in his chest.

"After the next flashes I want to push the ceiling away and pull that wall down. Might be safer back there. Maybe the air'll be better. Not so smoky." Permac coughed.

The machines above them seemed to hear the plan. Following the next flashes of light, an energy blast tore through the fallen ceiling. A hole blazed in the protecting wall. Permac and Linsora shielded their eyes from the sudden brilliance and heat. Stray embers attacked their clothing and exposed skin.

"Permac, pull the wall! I've got the edge here."

"Get ready to jump out of the way when it falls." Permac gripped a rough edge and tugged. "Damn! It's not moving!"

"Permac, where are you? I can't see anything."

"Here. Push up on the ceiling. It's wedged against the wall."

37

"Ceiling's wedged in, too. Not moving!"

"Get back. Now! Lights coming back," Permac said.

"I will not die like this," Linsora whispered. She squinted into the smoky light beyond the hole, illuminated between flashes by the still-sparking wires and the orange glow of smoldering timbers.

Permac felt her urge to run. He sensed she was tensing her muscles to propel herself into the inferno, to die while acting instead of being struck down while hiding. With no time to argue, he sent her a feeling of enclosure. She gasped, screamed, and slumped against the wall.

"I doubt you'll thank me for that one," he said. "I wish I could knock myself out, too. I'd rather not be awake when that beam hits me. At least this place is made of something that doesn't burn well. Otherwise, we'd be dead already. I just hope a little optimism is better than being dead."

He moved Linsora as far away from the opening as he could and hunched his body against the wall. He closed his eyes. *How many heartbeats do we have left?* he thought. *I wish I'd counted the time between the series of lights in heartbeats. Then I'd know.* He reached ninety-two.

Searing pain. His leg jerked, stiffened. Heat, pure pain shot from his calf to every other nerve in his body. A shrill wail escaped between Permac's grinding teeth. Nothing but pain everywhere. The floor bounced. Permac opened his eyes. The darkness was tinged with red. It was hazy. His eyes burned. The floor just beyond where the ceiling had fallen was on fire.

The lights flashed twice. A blast. Needle sharp shards of wood peppered Permac, some as hot as tiny pokers. The floor bounced again. In the darkness that followed, Permac wiped his burning eyes. The red in front of him formed a ring.

"The floor's gone! There must be another level under us. Don't know what's there, but it can't be much worse than this."

The air felt thick, hard to breathe. Permac tasted grit and dirt and charred wood. He shoved Linsora toward the hot concrete opening and pushed her limp body over the edge, tumbling in after her as next round of lights flashed.

He landed on hard packed earth inches from Linsora, jarring raw nerve endings in his leg. The air was lighter here. He breathed deeply to fill his thirsty lungs, to quiet his pounding heart, and to stop the edges of gray from overcoming his consciousness.

In the dim flashes of light, he watched wisps of smoke hovering overhead like ghosts. The boom of something exploding startled him back to full awareness. He inched away from the hole, pulling Linsora behind him. Once well away from the hole, he sat panting and rested his head against the wall.

Light filled the new basement level. Permac curled into a ball around

Linsora, waiting for the blast that would end their lives. He counted ninety-seven heartbeats. Ninety-eight. Ninety-nine. The light remained steady. Not bright, just enough to illuminate what seemed to be a hallway.

"It's just light!" He shouted. "Just plain damn light!"

Linsora stirred. She rolled away from Permac, ending up on her knees, blinking in the dim light. "Where are we?"

"Some kind of sub-basement," Permac said. "That last blast went through the floor up there."

"Why didn't you wake me up?"

Permac coughed, "Didn't think of it."

Linsora threw her head back and laughed out loud. Permac didn't know if he'd ever appreciate the Khizaran fondness for extreme emotion in any situation. He glanced up at the tiny space they'd escaped from. Pulses of light illuminated the charred edges of the hole.

"Permac, don't look so grim!" Linsora brushed debris from her clothing, creating a cloud of dust. "If you die, you die. If you manage not to die, celebrate! You're far too serious about your own mortality."

"You'd have run right into it up there!"

"Yes. And I'd have died when I chose to. When I was ready. We're not dead, though," Linsora peered up at the hole.

"We got lucky," Permac grumbled.

Linsora shrugged. "You believed enough in luck, in the possibility of survival to stop me, didn't you? You were right. We're alive! Smile a little at your good fortune."

"We're not out of this yet," Permac said. "We can't go back that way. I still can't reach Haavens. And who knows what we're walking into now."

He glanced down the corridor, empty except for dim lights near the ceiling.

"Some kind of hallway. It must lead somewhere, and it hasn't killed us yet. This hallway could be part of the escape route. Come on." Linsora grabbed Permac's hand and tugged him to his feet. He wobbled. "You look awful. Are you okay?"

"My leg was hit up there."

"Here, sit down again and let me have a look at it." Linsora ripped Permac's pants. She whistled at the raw seared flesh. "I think it looks worse than it is. Didn't hit the knee. Don't think it severed the muscle. Bet it hurts like hell, though."

"Astute observation."

"All I can do is wrap something around it, try to hold still." She cut strips from the cleanest portion of her skirt she could find and wrapped it around the burn on his leg. "Another advantage of living in a knife-carrying culture is that we're taught to care for wounds."

"Thanks," he said.

Linsora finished tying the last strip of fabric. She stood over him, offering her hand to pull him up. "We're even. I saved your life, you saved mine."

They walked in a direction that seemed to take them away from the building above. The hallway curved, making it impossible to see what lay ahead, but thick dust on the floor indicated that no one else had been through for a long time. Permac sneezed again and again. Linsora walked on ahead.

"Permac, stop sneezing and come here. Look! A door! I bet it leads to a passage to the outside." Linsora stood at a very sturdy looking door. She pushed it, pressed each of the panels on its surface, kicked it, pounded on it before treating it to a string of Khizaran curses.

Permac laughed. "Brute force not working so well this time?"

"If you have a better idea, go ahead," she said.

"I do. Looks something like Tokorellan design."

"What do you do, send emotional impulses to open it?"

"Very funny," he said. "There should be a panel in the wall next to it." He ran his hand along the outside of the door-frame until a small square began to glow. He reached in his pocket for the knife he had taken with him and pried off the panel. Reaching inside the hole, he pulled out several wires, stripped the ends and touched them together. The wires sizzled, and the door creaked open just enough for one person to squeeze through.

"Kind of unhandy if you're in a hurry," Linsora said.

"Only if you don't have the proper palm prints."

They wedged themselves through the opening. The other side of the door was a copy of the hallway they had just been in.

"We should be outside that building by now. Doesn't look like the floor is sloping upward toward the outside, though," Permac said.

"All we can do is keep walking," Linsora said. "I noticed your knife, by the way. I didn't think you carried one."

"Umm. I thought you might find it amusing," he said. "Have to admit it was useful."

"How's your leg?"

"Feels like something ate a chunk of me. I'll live."

"Want to take a rest?"

"No, I'm walking slowly enough as it is. I don't want to sit down in all this dust."

Linsora brushed her hand along the wall, smearing a layer of powder.

"I don't see any kind of sign. I hope we're going the right way. The way this curves around, I don't have a good idea where we are anymore."

"I wonder what happened here," Permac pointed his thumb behind them. "I really did mean it when I said the door design looked Tokorellan."

Linsora pulled his arm across her shoulders. "Lean on me. I'm stronger than I look, you know." She looked up and down the hallway. "The defense system is definitely Khizaran and I've never seen that kind of door. How could it be Tokorellan?"

Permac sneezed again. Each hop on his good leg sent clouds of dust billowing around them. "Tokorellan legends tell of my people settling somewhere, battling Khizarans, and leaving the ruined planet. It was the final Wandering before they settled on Tokorel."

"When Tokor left Khizara a fleet was sent after him. They never came back. Maybe they did find Tokor after all, but it seems unlikely that Tokor's people defeated them in a battle," Linsora sniffed. "You think this might be the ruined planet?"

"Why not?"

"This could just be a Khizaran outpost that..."

Permac interrupted. "A Khizaran outpost that has no record in your history? Does that make sense to you? Or do you only record the battles that your people win? Maybe that fleet went back to Khizara with its tail between its legs and never made it into the history books."

"You think I know the name of every Khizaran outpost ever established? You think we're too pig headed to admit that we don't always win?"

"Of course not." Permac stopped walking. "Sorry. I didn't mean to insult you. I'm thirsty, tired, and not exactly feeling great. I only meant that an outpost this far away would have been significant. I mean…"

"I know. I didn't mean to snap, either," she said. "It's just all so strange. How many races are out there? How many different cultures? What are the odds of us finding something out of both our histories?" Linsora shifted Permac's arm. "Can you lean against the wall? I need to pace while I think."

"You'll just kick up more dust."

"Lean and don't breath, then," she said. "Okay, you said your ancestors settled someplace before Tokorel. Isn't it odd that you don't know where this place is? Wouldn't that have been recorded as a famous place in your history?"

Permac shook his head, "History's not my field, but I'd think if this place was known there'd be some kind of museum here. Brachen's not even listed as a known planet."

"Tokor left Khizara two hundred years ago. That was before the technology existed to create jump holes and Brachen's not close enough to Khizara for them to get here within several lifetimes with the technology they had back then."

"Not close enough to Tokorel, either."

"But it's old. It's got indications of Khizaran and Tokorellan occupation," Linsora kicked at the dust, making Permac sneeze again. "I don't know what to make of it."

They continued forward in silence. Around the next curve in the hallway, the tunnel became straight, ending with another door. Permac opened it and Linsora squeezed through the narrow opening.

"Look at this!" she said. "Permac, hurry up!"

Permac squeezed through, groaning as his burned leg scraped against the frame. He squinted around a spacious room and whistled. A modified version of the Khizaran national emblem was painted on the far wall, with a semi-circle of chairs arranged around it, some of them toppled over. The room was dim and musty with stands of partly burned candles throughout.

"Not exactly yours, not exactly mine," Permac said. "You see anything around those chairs?"

"Come on, I'll help you over there. At least you can sit down."

As they neared the chairs, a beam of light shot out from the ceiling illuminating a circle in the middle. Linsora and Permac froze, waiting for the light to pulse. Instead, the image of a man began to form. He appeared to be a Khizaran, dressed in very old-fashioned clothes. He had no substance and was not very clear, more like a projection than a hologram. Their entering must have triggered some type of recording. Linsora and Permac remained motionless as the image began to speak.

"Whoever you are, for whatever reason you have come here, know that my people have gone. I leave this recording in the hope that someday, someone like you will find it and hear me. This is a recording of the events of my people. My name is Tokor. I am from Khizara."

Permac and Linsora exchanged glances and settled into the seats facing the image.

Tokor appeared to be collecting his thoughts. With a sigh he continued, "I do not know if my people will be known to you. If we have been successful, then you will know us very well. If we have not yet achieved our goals, you may not know of us at all.

"My people originated on Khizara. We differ from other Khizarans in

42

that we possess the ability to read and affect the emotions of others. We share the Khizaran desire for unity, but not only within the bounds of Khizara and her colonies. We seek unity of all sentient creatures beneath all stars. We also differ from our Khizaran brothers in that we do not intend to achieve this goal through physical conquest."

"Physical conquest?" Linsora questioned. "Khizara has no intention of going to war to conquer anyone!"

"If this is genuine, it was made two hundred years ago," Permac whispered. "That was before the Mercantile and before anyone could easily travel outside their own systems. Maybe Khizara was different then, too."

"Maybe," she said. "He's talking again."

"On Khizara, we gathered into isolated colonies devoting our energies to scientific investigation. Regretfully, not all of my followers were patient. Given time, my goal of Khizaran unity would have been realized. Some of my associates attempted to take control of Khizara by force. Understandably, the Khizarans then wished to be rid of us entirely. Let me just say that we arranged to leave Khizara. But, Khizaran ships followed to destroy us."

Tokor ran his hand through his mane of tangled gray hair. Dim as the image was, the lines on his face were clear as was the wry smile slowly forming.

"We could not have imagined that they would become our means of survival," Tokor said.

The image seemed to stare directly at them.

"I am a botanist. My life has been spent collecting and studying plants from all regions of Khizara and, in the last several years, other planets. On one planet, I met the Ghoranth. This planet, though not occupied by them, belongs to them. They have discovered a method of creating wormholes for their ships to travel through. Marvelous. The possibilities are staggering."

Tokor paced around the chairs. "I didn't share the information with Khizarans. Maybe I should have. Other than my followers, though, Khizarans weren't interested in anything I had to offer. We offered the Ghoranth a trade – we'd teach them to influence emotions and they'd give us enough wormhole devices to get us safely away from Khizara when we had to, and I knew that time would come.

"The transit through the wormhole was terrible. We expected to die, but emerged close to this planet. Apparently, the Khizaran ships entered the wormhole behind us but did not exit in the same location. These holes seem to be something like a whip, stable at the hilt with the lash moving. Several years passed before they found us. During that time, we had dismantled our ships to establish this city and our research facilities. I suppose we had begun to feel complacent, perhaps safe." Tokor shook his head. "We spent those years with the Ghoranth. I trained them as I would have trained any Khizaran, but they couldn't read or influence emotions. No matter what I tried, nothing worked. I can't blame them for thinking we'd deceived them.

"They attacked from the air. We can't yet send our emotional influence into space, only very short distances. We had no ships. Many of our weapons had been dismantled for use in the research labs. What defensive weapons we possessed, we deemed adequate to protect us from the Khizarans and they would have been. But not from the Ghoranth. It was during their second attack that the Khizaran ships arrived."

Tokor's image faded from view, eliciting a gasp of disappointment from the two viewers. For several minutes Tokor appeared and vanished repeatedly as he paced around the room. Suddenly, he stopped and faced them.

"If the Ghoranth had welcomed the Khizarans, I would not be recording this. Instead, they also attacked our brothers. The Khizarans returned fire sending the Ghoranth away long enough for the Khizaran transports to land. Although I cannot say we met as friends, we did meet as allies against two common foes—the Ghoranth and our new stars. The Khizarans had not been able to find a wormhole back to Khizara and were stranded with these stars and us.

"Knowing the Ghoranth would be back, we reached an accord with the Khizarans. They would provide defense and transportation away from this place. We would provide them with a way to get back to Khizara."

Tokor uttered a clearly Khizaran curse.

"For now, we can influence them enough so that they believe us. My people do not want to return to Khizara, to the life of persecution and certain death that we left behind. We also do not want information on where we settle to reach Khizara. They saved us, but..." Tokor spread his hands out to his sides, indicating his frustration at the position in which he found himself. "I believe that during our voyage away from here, we will win over the Khizarans to our way of thinking. They will all have our abilities before long. Once they do, well, returning to Khizara will be a problem for them. Besides, they are weary of travel and hungry for a leader. I will be that leader."

"Your saintly Tokor lied to the Khizarans in order to save his own skin!" Linsora said.

Permac hushed her.

"Our equipment is loaded onto the Khizaran ships. When the Ghoranth do return, they will find their planet empty again."

Another Khizaran whispering in urgent tones joined Tokor's image.

"I wonder if those Ghoranth knew about the benadiaum?" Permac said.

"Two hundred years ago?"

"They must have. I don't know of anything else that can hold wormholes open. Theirs sound unstable, but they did it."

"But the Leuhom people developed the technology first. They were the pioneers."

"Maybe they got the idea from someone else, along with benadiaum."

"Where are the Ghoranth now, I wonder?" Linsora looked around the room as though expecting someone to leap out of the shadows.

"Out there someplace. Didn't Haavens say the Carratians were talking to people who said they owned Brachen?"

"That's true. Wait, he's going to say more."

Tokor dismissed the Khizaran and turned back to face them.

"There is so much more I would like to say. With the time permitted, I will only say that our goal is to develop a weapon that will make this type of warfare impossible. Peaceful negotiation will be the only option. Not a weapon of offense but one that will disable all other weapons. One capable of making any weapon it encounters benign. If we have accomplished that goal, as I said, you will be aware of us."

Tokor turned and walked out of the image range. Several other figures entered and left, but none of them spoke. Finally, the images were gone.

"He said he tried to train the Ghoranth just like he trained his people. He said the Khizarans would have mental abilities, even though it sounds like they didn't want them," Linsora said. "How do you get your abilities?"

"I don't know. It's just something I could always do." Permac wanted to be comforted. His image of someone his culture idolized had been brought all too solidly to life. Someone he thought was completely pure of heart and motivation had just admitted to deception, as Linsora pointed out, to save his own skin. Linsora was in no mood to offer soothing words. Her image of Tokor had been proven accurate.

"What about that weapon? What are your people planning?" Linsora asked.

"I don't know. I honestly don't know."

Permac's belt controls crackled. "Sudé, Linsora. Can you hear ..." Haavens voice faded.

"The image of Tokor and the others walked off in that direction," Permac pointed. "Let's look there for an exit."

"Wait," Linsora said. "Everyone says that Tokorellans are secretive, that not many leave Tokorel to work with the Mercantile—or with anyone else. Is that true?"

"I suppose it is."

"How many Tokorellans are out there masquerading as Khizarans, like you've done?"

Permac's face colored. "I don't see what your point is."

Linsora spat, "My point is that Tokorel presents itself as a tranquil society full of scientists so involved in their noble work they probably don't know which way is up without a compass. Thing is, no one seems to know exactly what kind of science they're so busy with."

"Khizara has scientists, too," Permac said.

"We don't pretend to be a poor suffering society living in fear. Poor defenseless Tokorel at the mercy of the terrible Khizarans, saved only by the grand and glorious Mercantile." Linsora suddenly had a knife in her hand. "You don't seem like a cowering bookish type. How many Tokorellans are there like you? How many Tokorellans are wandering around? How many Tokorellans might be using your tricks to give Khizarans a bad name?"

"Put the knife away. If you kill me here it'll be fairly obvious what happened. Besides, where will you find another bumbling Tokorellan who might be able to answer your questions?"

Linsora looked sheepishly at the blade. "Oh, sorry. I didn't even realize I had it." With a fluid motion, the knife disappeared back into the folds of her jacket.

"Thank you," Permac breathed. "Thank you, too, for not placing me among the cowering bookish Tokorellans. I can't tell you how many Tokorellans are wandering around because I don't know. Can we get out of here while there's still some light in the room?"

Linsora nodded. An old door, barely visible, was in the corner. Permac's hand was shaking. He fumbled with the knife while prying the panel from the wall to find the controls. He snatched at the falling weapon, grabbing it by the blade. Blood gushed from his fingertips.

"Didn't your mother teach you how to handle a knife?" Linsora asked. "I don't have to kill you. All I have to do is give you a knife and wait. Wrap your hand in something, I'll get the door."

"My mother would be horrified to know I own one," Permac said.

On the other side of the door, a passageway stretched ahead and up. Sunlight was visible farther down the corridor.

"It looks like we're on the way out," Permac tried to sound cheerful. Linsora was silent. Permac stopped and grabbed Linsora's arm. "Do you believe me; about the weapon I mean? It's important for me to know."

"I believe you," Linsora replied. "He said if he'd been successful, we'd know. Obviously it hasn't happened yet."

"We have to let people know about this."

"Honesty is a dangerous thing, Permac. We have to be careful," Linsora said. "I have a good idea how Khizarans would react. What about Tokorellans?"

"It doesn't make me feel good, I can tell you that much." Permac touched his belt and spoke, "Permac Sudé to Captain Haavens. We are exiting an underground tunnel."

"Acknowledged," came the reply. "We're on our way. Stay where you are and we'll be there shortly. Haavens out."

"Your other questions, about how many Tokorellans have left Tokorel? I don't know. It's true that I have pretended to be Khizaran. It makes life a lot easier sometimes. If I had let you think I was Khizaran …well, things would probably have gone differently."

"Tokor said they couldn't send influences through space *yet*. What about…"

"Enough what-abouts, Linsora! I don't have answers for you,' Permac shouted. He looked around, as though he was embarrassed to have let his composure slip. He sighed. "You sound like your lab assistant. Denub never stops asking questions. Look, if you can keep your knives to yourself, I'm willing to try to sort this all out with you. Maybe between the two of us, and this new information, we can figure out what's going on."

"Fine. I'll keep my knives to myself, you keep your mind games to yourself."

"Fine."

CHAPTER 6

During the next several days, Linsora oversaw the collection of artifacts and mapping the settlement.

Permac found the process less than fascinating. Linsora was so preoccupied with it that her interest in any conversation not related to archaeology was negligible. He didn't regret his refusal to take the transport back to the *Dominator*'s infirmary. After two days his leg and hand no longer ached. He kept busy making minor adjustments to the transport craft's engines and being a general beast of burden for people wanting shovels, rakes, and various containers. Still, with archaeology being the order of the day, he felt his engineering point of view wasn't appreciated. His work involved schematics. Things operate according to specific laws and designs. He didn't sit around making conjectures about what this or that item might have been used for or how it might or might not be like something found on some other planet somewhere.

The high point of each day was when the entire ground crew gathered for dinner. At least he was sitting still and could look forward to a few hours rest. He found Linsora's animated discussions about occupation levels dull, but he noted that she was in remarkably high spirits. She even tried to include him in the conversations, explaining the importance of stratigraphy in so much detail he dreamed about layers of soil, rock, and pottery.

Permac suspected she was also basking in the prospect of the laurels she'd receive on Khizara for being the first to return with information on what she called the Lost Fleet. Linsora told him a major Khizaran holiday celebrates the bravery of the fleet sent in pursuit of Tokor. When Khizara first learned of the existence of Tokorel, they had asked for information but after more than a hundred years, no one alive remembered and nothing had been recorded. *The Khizarans probably didn't ask at all, more likely they demanded*, Permac thought. *And not much credit goes to Tokorel for the if-you-don't-ask-nicely-I won't-tell-you reply.*

The habitation levels she and Permac found on their earlier trip were not Tokorellan or Khizaran. She explained that they probably represented Ghoranth occupation. The planet had been uninhabited for a long time before Tokor and his people arrived. All the artifacts from earlier occupations were covered by centuries of blowing silt.

By the fifth day, most of the crew had taken time to watch Tokor's message. Whatever Linsora and Permac had hoped to keep secret would be common knowledge when the *Dominator* reached its first port.

"Do you suppose Tokor and his people went directly to Tokorel when they left?" Linsora spoke through a mouthful of the meat of some small local, and unlucky, creature. The ship's kitchen crew had been busy trapping and preparing the tasty creatures, putting a good deal of meat into storage for those times on the voyage when such delicacies became scarce. Tonight's meal was one of Linsora's favorites, lightly roasted meat seasoned with some of the local peppers and served like a picnic, under the stars and the two moons. One was full and yellow, the other just a tiny sliver of gold.

Permac nibbled at a bone. He ate meat when he had to, but preferred a diet richer in fruits. "Don't know. What history I know only mentions one place Tokor stopped before finding Tokorel. The location wasn't recorded, as far as I know. I mean, obviously, otherwise there'd be Tokorellens here already. I never questioned it. I guess I assumed they didn't want to reveal a place where Khizarans might be waiting or maybe they were in such a hurry they didn't bother." Permac shrugged. "Don't know. Honestly, I just never thought about it. I told you before, history was never my favorite subject."

"Wonderful," Linsora said. "How good are you navigating, then?"

"Why?"

"I want to look around farther away from the main settlement. I don't think it's worth the time of a large party. Tokor spent several years here. There might be other settled areas nearby."

"What are you looking for?"

"Nothing specific, just more," she said.

Permac tossed the bone into the brush. "I'd like more to eat and I do know quite specifically what. Let's go see what the cooks have and I'll make you something Tokorellan."

"I suppose it won't be meat, will it?"

"No, it won't be meat," Permac said. "Tell you what, you eat my cooking and I'll navigate for you tomorrow."

"Sounds like a nasty Tokorellan trick to me," Linsora laughed. "It's a deal. Meet me back at my place and I'll add something to the meal."

The weather had been balmy, even the evenings warm and clear. Most members of the excavation crew were camping in the roofless buildings left by Tokor. Only the doorways had been repaired to keep small animals out. Permac balanced a steaming pot in one hand, bowls and utensils in the other, as he kicked dust from his boots before entering Linsora's house.

"Here it is!" He announced proudly. "They had nearly all the ingredients for kirch'ta. No chikara, that's a Tokorellan fruit, but it should be good anyway. What's that?"

"Something that will make even your cooking palatable. Some brandy I

49

bought a few weeks ago on the ship." Linsora handed a mug to Permac in exchange for a bowl of kirch'ta. They each sniffed the other's offerings and nodded approval. Permac rarely refused a free drink and Linsora rarely refused anything with such a spicy aroma.

"I'm surprised!" Linsora scooped up the last bite of fruit and vegetable combination then scraped the remaining spiced sauce from the sides of the bowl with her fingers "You can cook!"

Permac poured more brandy for both of them. "S'th only time my mother let me use a knife. When I was helping her cook."

"Y'r family prob'ly only had one and you had to pass it ... back and forth!" Linsora slurred. She gulped the last of the brandy. "One knife! Pass it back and forth–no, that can't be right. You'd 've lost all y'r fingers by now!" She started to laugh, a deep chuckle that burst out of her like the unplanned launch of a missile. Even though the humor was at his expense, Permac grinned. Much like Linsora's involuntary reach for a knife when she was agitated, Permac didn't give it a second thought when he closed his eyes and caused Linsora to feel even happier. He liked to see people laugh and generally felt enhancing a good mood was doing a good deed.

He didn't take into account the Khizaran propensity for extremes. Nor did he consider the quantities of brandy floating around in their systems. Even though she was sitting on the ground, Linsora lost her balance and rolled on the floor. Unable to stop laughing, she held her stomach and roared convulsively, gasping for breath.

"Linsora, it's not that funny!" Permac shook her. The amusement she felt began to affect him. He laughed along but sent serenity toward her. Far too late he realized she was staring back at him, no longer laughing.

"You did this to me!" She lunged. Her fists pounded whatever surface of his body she could reach. He tried to curl into a ball, until she used her clawed nails to gouge the back of his hands. He yelped in pain.

"Enough!" Permac twisted, grabbed her wrists, and ended up sitting on top of her. "Yes, I did it. And you didn't manage to kill me–again."

"I don't use knives when I've been drinking," Linsora panted. She started to laugh again. "I don't know which was more annoying–laughing or stopping."

"Annoying? You think it's not annoying to be hit and scratched?" Permac shouted. "What's funny now? I didn't do anything this time."

Linsora dissolved into another fit of laughter. "You're angry! That's what's so funny. If you weren't so afraid I'd poke your eyes out, you'd let go and hit me. And you don't like feeling that way."

Permac's hands slipped from around her wrists to her clasp her hands. She returned the embrace, clawed fingers entwined in clawed fingers. He felt warmth from her, an odd openness, maybe affection. He leaned down toward her. His lips lightly brushed hers. He saw a flash reflected in her eyes just moments before the booming crash from a lightning strike made them jerk in opposite directions, banging their foreheads together.

"Storm!" she called suddenly.

Most of the buildings provided no protection from the sudden downpour. Linsora and Permac joined the rush of bodies running toward the one large building with a roof. As far as they could tell, the security systems had been dismantled. Still, no one ventured inside unless it was absolutely necessary. In the dark interior, the chest high lights from people's jackets made everyone look short and headless. Middle of the night grumbling accompanied curses over stubbed toes as people kicked away rubble that sometimes proved to be solidly connected to the floor. Linsora and Permac cleared spaces as far as possible from the hole in the floor they had fallen through. They settled into blankets, curled up next to each other.

Morning was a haze of drizzle and fog. The excavation team huddled in the shelter of the covered building, sorting artifacts, making notes, and trying to stay warm around small space heaters. Linsora nudged the bundle of blankets next to her.

"Anyone ever tell you that you snore?" she said. "Ready for a walk? It's a lovely day."

"It's not lovely. I don't feel lovely. I'm not ready for a walk," he mumbled. "I like to snore and I'd like to do more of it right now, so go away."

She pulled the covers from what she thought might be his head and waved the bottle of brandy under his nose. "Have a swig of this and some food," she said. "A little walk in the rain will be good for you."

He sniffed the brandy and groaned.

"I suppose you've already had a bath in the cold stream and gathered firewood," he said.

"What? No, I had a hot shower in the transport and carried some heaters back here," she said, missing his joke.

An hour later, they slipped away from the shelter. Their feet made sucking sounds in the wet soil and whatever fallen vegetation was on the path through the forest was slick. Permac shivered in the damp air. Even with the slug of brandy, food, and a hot shower, he felt fuzzy and out of sorts.

"You're annoyed again," she said.

"Only that I feel like hell and you seem fine."

"You need to drink more often, Permac. Brandy is made from fruit, you know."

"About last night," he began.

"What about it?" Linsora stopped under a dripping tree to adjust her hat. "We ate, we drank. We kissed and probably would have done more if the storm hadn't hit."

"Don't you think that's significant?"

"Not especially," she said. "And don't go reading my emotions to find out if I'm telling the truth." She tapped her foot in a puddle. "Look, we knew each other half a year before I was arrested. Whenever we talked, it was only about work. I don't know anything about you – your family, whether you like your tea sweet or bitter, if you ever loved a pet. I didn't trust you because you're Tokorellan, pure and simple. I still have my doubts, but I've come to trust you as a person. There are probably as many good Tokorellans as there are good Khizarans."

"And you're letting me navigate today," he said. "Although I don't know if that's a blessing or a curse, and it still doesn't address last night."

"Last night was last night. Don't think we have anything more than a working relationship, Tokorellan," she said, punching him on the arm.

They trudged along the winding, slippery path in silence. Linsora stopped at several clearings along the way, but dismissed each one.

"Nothing here," she muttered.

"How do you know? You haven't even turned a stone over!"

"I just know," she shrugged. "Like tasting your influences, I just know."

"Speaking of which, last night could you taste it when I made you laugh?"

"No, only when you made me stop," she said. "All I could taste at the time was your food and the brandy."

"Hmm." Permac shook like a wet animal, sending spray in all directions. "Look, we've been out here in this miserable weather for an hour. If we cut through the woods back there, we can be at the town in fifteen minutes. I'll even cook for you again."

"Not yet. There's something else out here. Another town, maybe. We've been following a path, too. It's overgrown, but it was used at some point to get from the town to somewhere else. You scouted the town, what's on the other side?"

"Three sides have forest, like this. The other side is swampy. This is the only path into the woods I know of. And, no, I am not going to wade through the swamp."

"And we haven't passed any obvious forks in the path. Let's go another hour."

"Only if still you have brandy back at the transport."

The winding path ended before the hour was up. Linsora stamped her feet in frustration.

"Linsora, maybe you're thinking about the other settlement we found when we were here with the Carratians."

"No, that was a Ghoranth settlement. Too far away from here anyway."

"They've found other occupation sites with equipment on the ship. You've been to most of them."

"I know, but if a site is small or covered by the forest canopy, it wouldn't be detected."

"Well, I'm heading back and I'm taking a direct route," Permac said. "If you want to spend two hours walking back along the path, have fun. Otherwise, stay with me."

"I'll go," she muttered. "It's just that I know Haavens wants to leave soon and I still have a feeling there's something else to be found here. I wish I knew what I was looking for. It's kind of like a tiny itch. Something waiting to be found."

They plunged into the forest. Low hanging branches brushed their faces and water from swollen streams crept into their boots.

"Now you're annoyed," Permac grinned.

"The path is farther around, but it's there for a reason. It seems to follow the stream instead of going through it. We'll be crossing the path again soon. I think I'll take it back."

A break in the foliage appeared ahead at about the same time the rain stopped. Linsora picked up her pace toward the relative ease of the path. Permac grabbed her arm.

"Shhh. Wait. Someone else is out here."

"Probably people from the *Dominator* looking for us."

"No," Permac said softly. "Not unless we have Carratians on board, and I don't think Haavens would hire a Carratian even if they offered to pay him."

"Carratian? How do you know?"

"I just know." Permac allowed a smile.

Through the trees, they could see movement on the path and hear voices.

"They have to come back this way," one said. "Did you put brush over the path down there?"

"Days ago," another growled. "There's no other way back, unless they went through the woods."

"What did they say?" Permac asked.

"They made it look like the path ended!" Linsora whispered. "They've been waiting for someone to leave the camp."

"Lucky us," Permac said. "I'll call in, warn the people back in town. Maybe we can go back into the woods and get around them until the others get here."

Permac touched his belt and spoke softly. Before he was finished with his report on their location the Carratians pointed into the woods.

"Over that way! I picked up a transmission from one of them!"

"Damn," Linsora spat. "Did anyone besides the Carratians hear you?"

"I don't know. Come on, follow me."

Permac backed into the forest, keeping an eye on where the Carratians were entering. The three had fanned out and were looking for any sign of movement. Linsora and Permac hunched down and slid behind a stand of thin trees. Permac sensed Linsora was ready to make a fight out of the situation while his own first instinct was for flight. The Carratians' voices were closer.

"See anything? Remember we need one alive. Shoot, but don't kill them both."

"They want one of us alive," Linsora translated.

"Linsora," Permac spoke softly with shallow breath. "We don't have guns, they do. We have to get away. Understand?"

Linsora nodded. She pointed in the direction of the town and held up three fingers, then two, then one and both took off running. The blast from a weapon seared the branches over their heads. Permac clutched Linsora by the hand and changed direction. They plunged through underbrush, around trees with the calls of the Carratians getting closer. A thick stand of tall brush was ahead of them. Permac ran through it and nearly bumped into a Carratian waiting on the other side.

He shoved the Carratian backward, using the heel of his hand to strike the man's chin up and back sending him into a back flip and to the ground.. Permac turned to Linsora in time to see another Carratian emerge out of the brush, his weapon pointed directly at them.

CHAPTER 7

"Why don't you do something with that *power* of yours?" Linsora spoke in a whisper, "And be careful what you say, this place is probably monitored."

"I think I have a broken rib," Permac rubbed his ribcage. "It's not that simple. It didn't work before."

The Carratian Permac hit had taken his revenge by punching Permac in the stomach before they were all marched down the path. Where the path had seemed to end, the Carratians cleared away brush revealing a trail that soon forked into two possible directions. Following the rightmost, the five hiked a short distance to a rough encampment. Two temporary huts stood in a newly cleared area next to a large transport. Linsora and Permac were relieved of the most obvious of their weapons and shoved into a locked room on the transport.

"All the way here, I tried to influence them. Admittedly, I don't usually do it to more than one person at a time, but it seemed to have no effect at all."

"Maybe it's something about Carratians?"

"No, they're usually as easy to influence as anyone else. Something else is going on."

The door swung open. Two men in dark brown Carratian uniforms aimed weapons at them. Linsora and Permac followed them out of the transport. The storm had left behind a foggy mist that the midday sun couldn't quite break through. After the warmth of the transport, Linsora's clothes and saturated boots felt cold and clammy. She didn't think the Carratians would dare detain two crew members of a Terran ship for long, but Carratians were likely to dare anything if it served their interests. There was a chance, too, that she would be recognized and hauled back to Carratia. Even if Haavens found them, he'd have little to say about that. She shivered. Two more uniformed Carratians took up the position behind them. The parade marched across the clearing into the largest of the huts. The room was bright and held only a few tables and chairs. A woman with insignia of command on her brown uniform sat at the end of a long metal table. Linsora noted her pinched features, beak-like nose, drab brown hair pulled into a bun and small hands. Carratians liked their high-ranking officers to look the part. For a non-physically imposing woman to be in command, she had to be a lot tougher than she looked. None of this was good news.

"I am Captain Barthis of the Carratian Fleet. I have a few questions, then you can be on your way," she spoke in heavily accented Khizaran and addressed herself only to Permac. "Or you can die. The forest can be a dangerous place full of unfortunate accidents. Depends on you."

In his best Khizaran, Permac answered. "We were just looking for food to take aboard our ship."

A very slight sweet taste filled Linsora's mouth. She stepped forward, trying to create a diversion so that Permac could work his magic. She also wanted to stop Permac from telling ridiculous lies. Scouting for food would have taken a day at most, not six. She made a mental note to instruct Permac on how to handle himself during an interrogation. Saying nothing was smarter than telling tales. She hoped they'd live long enough to have that lesson.

"You're not the one the only with questions!" Linsora shouted, reverting to Mercantile Standard. "What is the meaning of hunting us down like dogs out there? What is the meaning of laying an ambush, disguising the path? And do you think we're stupid enough to believe you'll let us go after all of that?"

"Silence!" the woman said. "I am speaking to him and have no qualms about eliminating you."

With a motion stronger than her size indicated possible, Linsora brushed one of the guards aside and strode toward the captain. The guard stumbled but recovered quickly enough to reach out and pull her back to a position next to Permac. She shook the guard's hand from her arm.

"You are also speaking to me!" Linsora stepped back toward the captain slowly. "Who are you to violate Mercantile protocol? Did you forget the little step of contacting the captain of our ship? Oh, but wait, you're Carratian, aren't you? Bypassing rules seems to be part of your charter."

Barthis raised an eyebrow. The corners of her mouth turned up in something approaching a smile. "Well then, just what are you? You don't look like a typical Khizaran, although you act with the brainless bluster of one."

Linsora spat back. "You should know as well as I do that size and position don't go hand in hand, or did you win your rank in a poker game?"

She was not as prepared as she might have been for the blow. The back of Barthis' hand knocked her sprawling into Permac and left the unpleasant taste of her own blood in her mouth.

Barthis wiped her hands on a towel, as though touching Linsora had soiled them. "I might also ask what kind of Khizaran you are, sir. You do nothing while your pet rants? And, if you'll forgive me, you speak Khizaran no better than I do."

"He defers to his superior officer!" Linsora shouted.

"Enough!" Barthis said, her face a stony mask. "Now then. I know you are from the Terran ship orbiting this planet. You and the others have been trespassing here for days. I want to know why." Pointing at Permac, she said, "You!"

"Captain Barthis, no beacons indicate this planet is private property, so I don't believe we've been trespassing. If you wish to know why we are here, you'd be wisest to speak to the captain of our ship." Permac reached down to his belt. The guard nearest to him brought the butt of a gun down on the back of Permac's hand with a crack.

"If I had wanted to speak to your captain, I would have done so by now," Barthis said. "I am asking you and it is fast becoming tiresome. I want to know what you've been doing, what you've found, and what your captain intends to do. For that, I'll trade you your life. Maybe even hers." Barthis laughed.

Another man in Carratian uniform entered the hut, walked to Captain Barthis and spoke briefly. Barthis glanced at Permac and Linsora, and nodded to the newcomer.

"Seems you'll have some time to think about it," Barthis said. She motioned to the guards to take them away. "We'll meet again later today."

When Permac and Linsora were again in the cell, Permac exploded. "What do you think you were doing? You could have gotten us killed!"

"Just trying to give you some time," Linsora said, quietly adding, "Better to be killed sooner than later in some circumstances."

Permac leaned against the wall. He could sense that two guards had remained outside. His eyes turned a deep violet for a moment. He shook his head.

Linsora paced. "Pet! Your PET!" she snarled.

Permac laughed, "Defers to his superior officer? Where did that come from?"

"I suppose we're even," Linsora shrugged. "How's your hand?"

"Deft change of subject. My hand is fine. Bruised, but not broken. You know, before I met you I didn't have any scars. I'd never broken a bone. No one had ever hit me. I'd never been ambushed by machines or people. Have you ever had a quiet month? Have you ever known anyone who survived being associated with you?"

"Permac, I…"

"No. Sorry, just being grumpy again," he said. "How's your mouth?"

"Swollen, but fine," she said, running her tongue around the cut on the inside of her cheek. "And I do have the occasional quiet month – usually when you're not around."

"That's comforting. What about that rank thing?"

"I was in the Khizaran navy a long time ago. I outranked most engineers. I thought maybe she'd have some respect for a fellow officer." Linsora shrugged, "I guessed wrong. You shouldn't be surprised, most Khizarans do spend some time in the military."

"Most of them aren't officers," he mumbled. "I wonder what came up that gave us a reprieve."

"No idea. Could you sense anything?"

Permac settled his frame on the bench at the far end of the cell. Linsora perched on the edge next to him. They spoke in hushed tones. "Only that she was surprised," Permac said. "I can sense their emotions, but have no influence on them. It's frustrating."

"We should get some rest while we can."

"I suppose," Permac said. He added with a smile, "Since you are my pet, shouldn't you curl up on the floor?" Linsora spun around, but Permac caught her arm before it made contact. Permac pulled her close to him. He whispered, "Did you notice the arm band that they're all wearing? It's not standard Carratian uniform issue."

"Never saw them before. I'm too tired to try to figure out what they mean," Linsora sighed.

Linsora's breathing became shallow and regular. Permac was amazed that she could fall asleep so quickly in the middle of such a terrible situation. He knew their chances of getting away from the Carratians were slim. That dangerous forest accident Captain Barthis mentioned was far more likely than their release. Still, the level of fear he should feel as a prisoner with no chance of rescue wasn't there. The roiling emotions assaulted his senses, but included only a muted feel of menace directed toward the two of them. It was heartening but wrong. He wrapped an arm around his fellow prisoner and noted that this at least did not feel at all wrong.

Permac woke with a disoriented start. For a moment, he didn't know why two men in brown Carratian uniforms were pulling him to his feet. He pulled back from them and in the process of the brief struggle Linsora was dumped onto the floor. She sat up and stared at them, looking as confused as Permac felt.

"Captain Barthis wants to see you," one of the men said to Permac, "but not her."

"Oh," Permac said. His head ached, his ribs were sore, and his hand hurt. He remembered exactly where he was.

"Permac! I can taste som…" The cell door closed with a thump, cutting Linsora off. Permac heard her banging on the door. Looking at the two men, Permac knew he could go along quietly or be dragged. He rubbed his temples and decided on a friendly approach.

"Lead on."

"Shut up and move."

"Uh huh."

Permac was led the short distance from the cell to the bridge of the transport. Captain Barthis sat at the control panel. Through the front screen, Permac saw that the huts in the clearing were being dismantled.

"Mr. Khizaran," Barthis swiveled around to face Permac. "I never did get your name, but it doesn't matter. As you can see, we're leaving."

"Do you expect me to go back and report that Carratians were here, but have all gone away?" Permac asked. "You think anyone would believe that?"

"I didn't say you were being released, did I?" Barthis said. "I still want the same answers to the same questions. You're being turned over to someone better able to get those answers. I'll even be gracious enough to feed you first."

"Providing a last meal, Captain? How kind," Permac bowed slightly.

"Indeed," Barthis grinned. "I will even be willing to feed the woman, but she will not be released. I believe the Carratian authorities might be interested in her. Say your farewells over dinner."

"Captain, you …"

"That is all!" Barthis turned back to her work and the guards took hold of Permac's arms. Permac was strong, but no match for two equally strong guards. And, even if he did manage to break away, there was no chance of getting out of the encampment. He fought against the guards out of outrage and to preserve his dignity.

As they steered him past the cell, he tried to clear his aching head to sense if Linsora was still inside. He didn't think so. The earliest moon was just rising over trees shrouded in ghostly fog. Permac realized they had been away from the town since morning and would surely have been missed by now. He glanced toward the edges of the clearing, hoping that a rescue party from the *Dominator* was lurking in the darkness. With a sinking feeling, all he sensed was more darkness.

Permac was shoved through the door of the last remaining hut. Blinking in the sudden bright lights, he saw Linsora sitting alone at the end a table. In front of her was a plate heaped with food. It looked like most of the transport's crew was enjoying their last feast of fresh food, too. Permac made his way through the crowd and took a seat next to Linsora. Her plate was filled with stewed chunks of meat floating in a thin brown sauce. The aroma of heavy spices assaulted Permac's nose.

"How can you sit here calmly eating?"

"Rest when you can, eat when you can," she said. "You should do the same. It takes time to eat, you know. Fill your plate and come back, I have something to tell you."

Permac examined the offerings and placed mounds of the local vegetables, also stewed in some kind of brown sauce, on his plate. As a nod to balance, he placed a chunk or two of meat on top of it all.

"You should eat more vegetables," he said as he sat next to Linsora, turning the chair so that his back was to the throng of Carratians.

"I have a few plants, you have a little meat," Linsora popped a chunk of meat into her mouth and winced as the spices hit the cut on her cheek. "Not bad. Anyway, Permac, I have to tell you something. When I woke up, I felt groggy, like I'd been sleeping a very long time, but I don't think we had been. More than that, I could taste something. Not something sweet, though. It was … I can't describe a taste very well. But in a way it was similar to when you influence my emotions. When you were trying to influence the Carratians, I caught a slight taste of the sweetness from your influence. This other taste was different."

Permac chewed. "Do you still taste it?"

"No, all I can taste is the food right now. It went away soon after you left the cell."

"Odd. I've had a headache ever since I woke up. I don't usually have them. Any headache?" Linsora shook her head no. "I have something to tell you, too. Barthis said she was leaving and that she was releasing me to someone. I don't know who. She also said she was taking you back to Carratia. Must have figured out who you are somehow."

Linsora paused with a forkful of meat halfway to her mouth. Permac didn't have to sense her emotions–the color drained from her face. She replaced the fork on the plate.

"Sorry," he said. "I don't know what we can do."

"Neither do I. I suppose Haavens and the crew must be looking for us, but this camp is pretty well disguised and the rain would have washed away all our footprints." Linsora reached for a mug of water. "Wait, I can taste it again. Not the food, the other taste."

Permac reached out to her mentally. He was suddenly struck by a sense of assurance that didn't come from Linsora. Just as quickly, it was gone.

"No, now it's gone," Linsora said, eating again.

"I felt something, too," Permac said. "What the hell is going on?"

"I don't know, but keep eating. We need to take as much time as we can."

Permac glanced at the mass on his plate, squared his shoulders, and ate with as much gusto as he could muster. As he chewed he opened his mind toward Linsora again. "You're actually enjoying this aren't you?"

"What? Watching you eat?" she asked.

"All of this. The raw emotion of this situation invigorates you, and that's not from any kind of outside influence."

"Invigorate maybe," Linsora chewed. "Enjoy, not really."

A roar of laughter from the Carratians at the next table interrupted their conversation. Permac pulled his chair closer to Linsora.

"...seems stupid, unless the damn Tokies have their brains in their armpits," someone said.

Other ideas about where the "Tokies' brains might be located followed amid more laughter.

"You think the captain buys it?"

"Dunno. She wears one. Sure as hell, I'm going to wear it next time I'm in a poker game with anyone who looks Tokie." The man patted his armband. "Can't bluff if someone's reading your emotions. If these things stop that, I say it's worth it. I lost a bundle a couple years back. Thought the guy was Khizaran. Damn sneaky if you ask me."

"Shut up, we're supposed to keep this quiet."

"What? You worried about those Khizarans? They're not going far."

More laughter and the conversation at the next table went on to an exchange of poker tales.

"You know those guys?" Linsora whispered. "One of them lost money to a Tokorellan in a poker game. They say the armbands will stop anyone from reading their emotions. You can still do that, though, can't you?"

"Uh huh, but I can't influence them."

"So they don't completely work. Where'd they get them?"

"No idea." Permac reached across the table to grip Linsora's hand. "Believe me! I have no idea."

Before Linsora could reply, the muffled sound of an argument outside the hut silenced all conversation. Feet scuffled as most of the Carratians went to the door. Permac gripped his head. A stab of pain flowed through his brain like a stream of molten lava.

Two figures filled the doorway, the taller one spoke loudly, "That's right, both of them. I don't care what your previous orders were. Now step aside." The tall man waved a gloved hand, dismissing the other. He walked into the hut and approached Linsora and Permac. His gloves matched the deep brown of his jacket and pants, the same color as the Carratian uniform, but the cut and cloth were obviously civilian.

"You've both been released to me. Come along," he said.

"We haven't finished eating." Linsora turned her attention to the meat.

"Let's go," Permac whispered. "I have a feeling he's the only one who can help us."

"And who'll rescue us from him?" Linsora answered. "I'd rather face my fate here."

"You don't have a choice," the man said. "Look at me."

Linsora turned her head. The tall man had a scar running down the length of his face, starting beneath his left eye and curving down toward his jaw. She dropped the forkful of meat.

"Maybe you're right. Let's not waste an opportunity."

Permac sensed curiosity mixed with distrust alternating with flashes of relief. The swiftly changing emotions made his head throb even more. He was the last to move. Linsora's sudden change of heart disturbed him. By the time he left the hut, Linsora and the tall man were waiting for him at the edge of the clearing. They were having a vigorous discussion, which appeared to end with the man drawing a gun and pointing it at her head. Permac wondered if her first impression of their savior might have been right. He approached them slowly.

"My transport is this way. As I said before, neither of you have many options and if you don't hurry up, the option I'm offering is going to expire," the man said. "I'll explain later." He pointed the weapon at them. "Straight ahead."

The trio followed a narrow trail a short distance through the woods. The chest jacket lights were designed to illuminate a wide area, on the narrow trail the beam dissipated into the brush making the walking surface murky. Permac hoped the man with the scar wouldn't trip and fire his gun right into them. Not soon enough, the light glinted off something solid and they crashed through the last low branches into another small clearing.

"Get in," the man said. "We're taking a short flight."

He waited until Linsora and Permac had strapped their seat belts, then entered and locked the cockpit door. The engine hummed, roared, then fell silent once they were airborne.

"What's going on here?" Permac asked. "First you refuse to go, then you want to go, then he's holding a gun on you!"

"This man was at the dock when we boarded *The Dominator*," Linsora said. "He was a passenger just leaving the ship. He bumped into me and I saw that he was Khizaran. I recognized him back there in the hut."

"Khizaran? Are you sure? My headache had gone, but now all of this is threatening to give me another one."

The craft landed with a bump.

"He has the hands of a Khizaran, I know that much. I asked him who he was, what he was doing here, how he happened to be with the Carratians," Linsora smiled. "Maybe I asked too much. Maybe I have been around Denub too much. He told me to shut up and pulled the gun."

The man emerged from the front, still pointing his gun at them.

"It was also a useful gesture to impress the Carratians," he said.

"You can put it away now," Permac said.

"Not yet," the man said. "Allow me to do the introductions. You are Linsora Anselm, Khizaran archaeologist. And you," the man casually nodded toward Permac, "are Permac Sudé. Tokorellan engineer."

"How do you know us?" Permac locked eyes with the tall man. "I've seen you before, too. Not on the *Dominator*, though. There's something…" Permac stared for what seemed like an eternity before a sense of understanding hit him. "You're not Khizaran, are you?"

"My name is Moragh, and no, I'm not Khizaran," he said. "I'm Tokorellan, but not Tokorellan enough that I won't use this weapon."

Linsora fumbled with the latch of the seat belt. She wanted the option of mobility if a good opportunity arose. Moragh glanced at her and she slumped forward.

"She's sleeping," Moragh said.

"How did you do that? Your eyes!" Permac stared at Moragh.

"That's right, my eyes don't change color. As for how, I influenced her to feel calm to the point of sleep."

Permac's eyes became violet as he tried to counteract Moragh's control, but she remained limp. "Wake her, Moragh."

Moragh laughed, "She'll wake in a moment. You don't trust me, do you? Are you as poorly versed in reading emotions as you are at shielding your own? No wonder they let you go out on your own. You would be no threat to anyone except yourself!"

Linsora stirred, "Just who the hell are you? I didn't know Tokorellans were trained to shield their emotions."

"Neither did I," Permac said.

"No? No, I suppose not," said Moragh thoughtfully. "Read my emotions, then. Do you sense that I'm a threat?"

"No," Permac said. "But if you can shield your emotions, how can I tell?"

"Puts you in the same boat as me," Linsora said.

"And you automatically assume danger instead of assistance?" Moragh asked her.

"When someone is holding a gun to my head, I don't automatically consider that person a friend," she said. "Besides, if you can simply put me to sleep, why do you need it?" Linsora completed the unfastening of her seat belt. "Unless...hmm, unless you're really pointing it at Sudé. That's it, isn't it? You don't know if you can influence him so easily. A battle of the Tokorellan brains, this should be interesting."

"I don't enjoy sarcasm," Moragh said. "But you're not far from the truth."

Linsora settled back into her seat.

"Yes, I was on the *Dominator* as you were boarding. I was, to a large extent, responsible for the fact that your poor Captain Haavens lost most of his crew at Carratia. A few suggestions here and there, and ample openings."

"Why?" Linsora and Permac both asked. Moragh raised his hand.

"Left on your own, do you think you'd gotten out of Carratia alive? Either of you? Just the fact that you stayed there for so long, Permac, and that you're living as a Khizaran..." Moragh shook his head. "I knew the *Dominator* would be landing at Carratia around the time of your scheduled release, Linsora. I also suspected that Mr. Sudé here would play some role in ensuring that release. I was prepared to delay the *Dominator* long enough for you to board."

"Still doesn't answer the why part. What's the problem with my living as a Khizaran?" Permac asked. "You obviously do the same thing. It's not easy for a Tokorellan to get hired, you know."

"That's the whole point!" Moragh said. "Tokorellens aren't trusted. And that needs to be changed! Look, didn't you ever think it odd that your family let you leave Tokorel so easily?"

"No," Permac said.

"Did you know other Tokorellans who left?"

"No," Permac shifted uncomfortably in his seat.

"Why did you leave, then? Didn't you have a bright future on Tokorel? Weren't you safe and secure? Part of an influential, well off family?" Moragh demanded.

Permac glanced at Linsora, as if expecting another outburst from her that might save him from answering. She only raised an eyebrow, indicating her own interest. He hunched his shoulders and trudged into his past. "Spending my life safe and secure sounded boring. My parents are both scientists. Their work is satisfying enough to them, but their lives are predictable. I wanted, well, just more, I guess. They never protested."

"No, they didn't protest. In fact, they encouraged you didn't they. Subtly, but they did."

"Still doesn't answer the why part," Permac said, "or the problem with seeming to be Khizaran."

Moragh thumped himself on the chest. "I represent the necessary evil end of the spectrum. The Tokorellan that everyone expects and distrusts, with the scars to prove it. Yours is the face that Tokorel will present to the masses. The face of naïve honesty. Parading around as a Khizaran doesn't let anyone see the positive side of Tokorellans."

"What was I supposed to be? A one-man good will ambassador? What do you mean, naïve honesty? Is that face a lie?" Permac hissed. "Was I groomed to deceive everyone?"

"No! Not deceive, rather to represent the goals we all share. As trite as it sounds, the goal of peace throughout all systems. We must be trusted before we have any hope that our peace will be accepted."

"Your peace? You mean your weapon, don't you?" Linsora stood and backed toward the door.

"I mean the instrument of peace," Moragh said hotly, then added with a glance toward the Khizaran woman that sent searing pain through her head, "and I would advise you to remain where you are."

Linsora gripped her head and dropped to her knees.

"I am not your enemy," Moragh continued, "Look, let's just say that you weren't dissuaded from leaving Tokorel, Permac. You make yourself liked, generally, even after people know you're from Tokorel. And, you're not the only one. Some are more successful than others."

"And who are you?" Permac asked.

"Someone whose job it is to keep you safe. Keep you alive long enough to do what you do best, continue to make yourself liked."

Linsora, still holding her head, grunted a laugh.

Permac shot her a warning glance. "Protecting me? You haven't done a stellar job of it. We could have been killed in that building."

"I can't be everywhere," Moragh shrugged. "I can't protect you from the results of your own decisions. My job is to ensure that you continue, that you don't disappear."

Permac slumped forward, rubbed his eyes. "So you've been following me since I left Tokorel. Others, too." Permac looked toward Moragh, his eyes were at the same level as the muzzle of the weapon. "Are you saying that some of the Tokorellans you were supposed to protect have disappeared?"

"Some. Yes."

"Your everyone-loves-Tokorel program has critics? How shocking." Linsora eased into a sitting position on the floor.

"I still don't appreciate sarcasm," Moragh said. "The point is, dangers exists. I want you to be aware. No more, no less."

"What kind of dangers, Moragh? Am I supposed to look under my bed and sneak around corners?" Permac said. "People disappear all the time. Maybe some of your ambassadors just got tired of being followed. Have you thought of that?"

"A known danger, even a mysterious one, is better than a surprise, Permac." Moragh said. "I don't know why people have disappeared. I can't describe the danger. I can only warn you that it exists."

"What if you're the danger and this is a ruse to make him trust you?" Linsora lifted her head. The pain was gone but any movement made her queasy.

"I would have left you to the Carratians in that case," Moragh said.

"You gave them the armbands, didn't you?" Linsora asked.

"They told you about them?"

"No, but I do have ears," Linsora said. "Anything the Carratians have will be on the open market as soon as they reach the next port, so if secrecy was important you chose the wrong race to confide in. They think the bands stop you from reading them, but they don't. You going to become the richest man in the universe by letting Tokorellans get into more poker games?"

Moragh looked confused, "Poker games?"

"Poker. Tokorellans aren't welcomed into poker games. With those bands on, people will believe you don't have an advantage anymore," Linsora said. "But somehow I don't think poker is your game."

"No, it's not. Too much chance based on cards. I prefer games I have more control over," Moragh tilted his head, as though considering what to say next. He took a seat across from them. "All right. The Carratians know this place has something to do with Tokor and, like most people, aren't terribly fond of Tokorellans. I told them the armbands would protect them from Tokorellan influences, from anything Tokor might have left behind."

"Carratians aren't stupid, Moragh!"

"I offered them for free, in exchange for their allowing me to poke around. Anything free appeals to them. The bands do work, but not as the Carratians think. They actually permit a sort of emotional broadcast. I can influence several people within a short range."

"I don't believe you," Permac said. "I couldn't influence any of them."

"The device can be, well, tuned to accept only specific influences."

"I still don't believe you," Permac said. "No device has ever been found that can boost mental influences."

"No device that you know of," Linsora said. "I told you I could taste something. And your headache—maybe the broadcast of all those emotions affected you, too."

"Taste something?" Moragh stood suddenly.

"When Permac influences my emotions, I can taste it. Back there with the Carratians, I could taste something, but it was different than Permac's," she mumbled.

"Really!" Moragh stared at Linsora. He exhaled with something close to a whistle. "I've heard that you can find sites, that you're drawn to just the right place to find artifacts. Is that true?"

"Sometimes. How do you know that?"

"It's unusual. Your tasting influences is unusual."

"You seem impressed. Don't be. I can't take credit for any of it. It just is," she said, "and it hasn't kept me out of trouble."

Permac rubbed his temples. "You told them about Tokor's connection to Brachen, didn't you? How much have you done? Did you tell them about the benadiaum here? Did you tell Haavens about Linsora? You know damn well the Carratians aren't likely to keep something like the armbands secret. They'll be trotting off to Tokorel for more of them. Then what? They'll be encouraged to hire more Tokorellans? The Tokorellans will influence them and end up controlling the Carratian economy?"

"Nothing that crude," Moragh said. "Let's just say the Carratians know they have to go through me to get the armbands. As for what I've done, well, a few hints to the right people can go a long way."

"So you and whoever your people are, are deceiving everyone?" Linsora asked. "If the Carratians go to Tokorel, no one will know anything about the armbands, will they?"

"Again that word deceive. Again I say no. People on Tokorel are not being lied to. They are just not being told everything."

"And that's not deception?" Linsora spat. "I don't understand any of this. If you can tune those things to specific people, who decides who's trustworthy enough to have the power? You think you're morally superior enough to play god? You're not. No one is, Moragh. Why tell us, anyway?"

"Because you've both become involved. Now that Brachen has been found and Tokor's message has been revealed, it's even more important for Tokorellans to be trusted."

"If you knew about the message, and I take it you did, why not just destroy it? Then you could skulk around and no one would be the wiser," Permac said.

"Because he wanted it to be found," Linsora said. "Moragh here seems to be playing a little game with fate, aren't you? Nudging things along a little when you can. Dropping your little hints. Wouldn't be surprised if he arranged for you to be on the Carratian ship that found Brachen in the first place. Why the surprised look? Didn't you think a mere Khizaran could figure that out?"

"You're both free to go. The path directly outside will take you back to your camp in half an hour," Moragh still held the gun. "That means this discussion is over."

"Aren't you afraid we'll tell the Mercantile what you're up to?" Permac asked.

"No, he's not," Linsora said. "Who'd believe us?"

Moragh motioned toward the door. "Trust your instincts, both of you."

Moragh watched the couple until they disappeared into the forest. He thought of the old man in the candlelight. Maybe he was right about having too many elements working. He'd want to see her. Two weeks to Cornerstone from here. Two weeks with an unhappy Khizaran on board didn't sound appealing and he had other matters needing attention. The old man wouldn't be pleased that he'd told them so much but he didn't have to know everything. Moragh was contacting all the Tokorellens. They had to know a little. Just enough to be prepared. The *Dominator* is heading to the nearest Mercantile port. If the old man wants her, Moragh thought, I can meet her there.

CHAPTER 8

Her father told her that she seemed to hear voices from the past. Although Linsora thought this was too eerie to be taken seriously, like seeing ghosts, she knew most archaeologists feel a connection to sites and artifacts. Hers was just stronger than most. She didn't see ghosts or hear voices, she felt the presence of ancient people, an echo of their energy. She found the Ghoranth artifacts on Brachen a year earlier, much to the Carratians' displeasure. Now, even with the *Dominator* preparing to leave, she still felt something calling. A disquieting feeling that there was something else.

Moragh's advice to trust their instincts seemed funny to her. She had spent her life doing just that. Thirty-one years of living by her instincts had gotten her here, on a backwater planet with two companions; her lab assistant Denub who never stopped asking questions and a Tokorellan. She thought about Permac far too much. She had even wished, fleetingly, that he was Khizaran. He was right in saying that if she didn't know he was from Tokorel, things would be very different between them. Still, she couldn't imagine living her life any differently than she had nor would she take back any decisions she had made along the way. Now her instincts were pulling her toward some ancient presence calling from centuries past.

Since their encounter with the Carratians and the mysterious Tokorellan, Haavens ordered no further excursions into the surrounding area, especially unescorted and unarmed. The Carratian transport had flown toward the farther of Brachen's two moons where the main ship was probably docked. No other transports were detected, but there could be other Carratians still on the surface. He had allowed Linsora an escort to walk the forest path and examine the forks in the road. Both paths led to what had probably been cultivated fields.

As a nod to completion, he agreed to provide Linsora with an escort to the far side of the swamp. Another small clearing was found, but it seemed to have been temporary as no buildings or foundations were evident.

Her escort party jumped at every rustle in the bushes.

"Come on, Linsora," one of them said. "My feet are wet and I want to get back across that swamp before they dry out again. I only want to be miserable once."

"I know, just a minute." Linsora kicked at a pile of dirt. Something glittered, broken glass. She pulled on a glove and scooped up all she could find, placing them in a small pouch. "Help me pick these up and we'll go back."

Linsora clutched the edge of the lab table as the ship took a jump. Her stomach lurched. She wished she had some kind of schedule for the jumps so she could be sure not to eat just before they took one. The bits of broken glass had shifted only slightly. Linsora picked up a handful. They shone like gemstones. By themselves they were worthless; to the people who made them, they were utilitarian bits of daily life; to the people who would have them later, they might be priceless artifacts from a vanished civilization. But, right now, they were work. The shards had to be sorted, counted, cataloged and carefully packaged. Nothing about these artifacts was meaningful and she began to feel as if her instincts had finally let her down. But, she had collected them and it was her job to catalog them.

She counted: ten small brown pieces, eight large brown pieces; she entered the data into the console, twelve small bright blue, six large. It became a rote activity. The glittering bags on the counter top grew. She had cataloged three packets of green shards before she noticed the oddity.

"They all have one!" She ripped open the sealed packets and called to her lab assistant. "Denub, come and look at this!"

The short, round woman ambled to Linsora's workstation. A broad grin crossed her face. Denub liked to think of herself as a collector of people and information. She had never worked with a Khizaran and, after some initial fear, had grown to like the energy surrounding Linsora. The Khizaran woman launched herself into work with the fervor of a warrior going into battle. More than once Denub had to remind Linsora to sleep, although the slender Khizaran never seemed to miss a meal.

Linsora was one of the last remaining crew members on the ship who could still tolerate Denub and Captain Haavens was surprised at how well the two of them interacted. Denub, in her zeal to collect information, pestered everyone within earshot with endless questions. Haavens reasoned that they were, in a sense, kindred spirits, since Linsora had her own propensity for questions.

"Remember all that glass we found on Brachen? Look at the green pieces. Each one has a tiny plant embedded in it." Linsora laid several pieces out.

Denub picked up several of the green bits of glass. They were of varying sizes, most about the size of her thumb.

"Do you know what the plants are?" Denub held a piece up the light.

"No, but they didn't get there by accident," Linsora said.

Denub peered through the glass at Linsora. "Do your people use greenhouses to cultivate plants?"

"What does that have to do with anything we're doing now?"

"Nothing," Denub said. "just curious. I wonder if we could break it apart and examine the plant's chemical structure."

Denub gently tapped on the small glass piece in an attempt to break it without disturbing the plant inside. Nothing happened. She tapped harder. Still nothing. She gave it good whack! The piece bounced off the tabletop and struck Linsora on the side of the head.

"What are you doing?" Linsora roared.

"Sorry!" Denub began to brush the side of Linsora's head where the stone had hit.

"Stop that!" Linsora said, pushing Denub's hand away. "I'm fine, really. Just be more careful."

"All right," Denub said. "Do Khizarans teach their people medical procedures?"

"What?" Linsora whirled around and glared at Denub. "We all know medical basics, just like anyone else."

"Just asking," Denub said. "Here, let's see if we can get some kind of analysis of this. It's not glass."

"I'll do it," Linsora said.

Denub spread the green pieces out and began to move them around, placing the smallest pieces in the middle. Her stubby fingers shifted them around, making patterns.

"Linsora!" Denub called.

"Not now, I've just about got the analysis of this." Linsora tapped on the console. It didn't make the results arrive any faster, but she wasn't at her best waiting and some activity was better than standing still. "Odd, it can't identify the plant. There's also some kind of unknown microbe, maybe a plant disease of some sort. Probably just as well we couldn't break it open. You collected plant samples, find anything unusual?"

"No," Denub grinned broadly. She was always excessively pleased when someone asked her a question. "I haven't tested all of them, though."

"Well, let me know when you do. These leaves have little red veins, should be easy to see if you found anything that matches."

"Okay, but come and see this. The little pieces fit together."

"Fit together? Let me see."

The pieces formed a little picture, splashes of color separated by black from the edge of each piece. One small section was missing. Linsora picked up the piece she had been working with and fit it into place.

"Look at the plants!" Denub said. "It's a pattern, it's..."

"It's a solar system," Linsora said. "The large plant there could be a sun. The smaller ones could be planets. And this one," Linsora pointed, "this one could be Brachen – look at the two moons."

Linsora then pointed to a line that went from Brachen to the edge of the picture. "This could be some kind of flight plan. We need more of the picture. Empty the rest of the bags."

CHAPTER 9

Permac went back to his quarters after a long shift. He took off his boots and threw them across the room in frustration. He was restless. The work was routine and the prospects that awaited him at the next port were uncertain. On top of that, Linsora was always too busy to see him. He didn't have any answers for her. Worse, he now had the same questions she did.

He prepared himself a fruity Tokorellan drink. He wished again for some Tokorellan chikara. He sat on the edge of his bed. Moragh had opened avenues of thought he preferred not to visit. He wondered what his parents might know. He had always trusted them, but he usually trusted most people until they earned his distrust. Then there was Linsora. Hadn't she done enough to earn at least a small amount of distrust? Or had he done enough to earn her distrust?

His door buzzer sounded. Permac pushed himself up from his slouch and lumbered to the door.

"Am I interrupting you?" Linsora asked. She wore a green dress, the color of a summertime forest. The fabric flowed around her, not quite flimsy but assuredly not demure. Her hair was not in the usual braid but flowing.

"No. Come in," Permac said. "I thought it might be someone with an invitation to a poker game."

"I prefer backgammon myself," she said. "Ever play double boards?"

"Never heard of it."

"You have two boards. You play the opposite color on each board, but use one dice roll. When you roll the dice, you take the roll for your color on one board and I take the roll for my color on the other. Then I roll the dice, same thing."

"What's the point?"

"Makes people more honest with the dice for one thing. Increases the bets, too."

"Hmm," Permac said. "Tokorellans can't influence dice, you know."

"Just like you can't shield your emotions?"

"Okay, if you came here to start a debate, I'll tell you right now I'm not in the mood," Permac said. "What do you want?"

"Your Khizaran ancestry is showing," Linsora grinned. "See? You can be surly, too." When Permac failed to grin back, Linsora shrugged. Permac slumped on the edge of the bed. He didn't have to open his mind to sense her excitement. Something had grabbed her attention and he had a feeling he wanted nothing to do with it. "To business, then. I've been studying some artifacts from Brachen, the ones I found on the other side of the swamp. I think I've found a star chart."

"And?" Permac leaned forward, resting his elbows on his knees.

"And it doesn't lead to Tokorel. Remember I asked you if your history had anything about Tokor and his people going anyplace before they found Tokorel? Maybe some of the Khizarans who didn't join Tokor did go someplace else."

"They couldn't have had a lot of time, they arrived while the Ghoranth were attacking. Maybe the chart shows where the Ghoranth went, did you think of that?"

"I did, but the clearing wasn't Ghoranth. The other artifacts we found with the glass were recent, not as old as the Ghoranth site. And the glass isn't glass – it's a polymer the Ghoranth sites didn't have."

"Why tell me? You seem to have figured it all out."

"Don't sound so hurt! I thought archaeology bored you."

"Everything bores me right now," Permac stretched. "I'm sorry, I don't mean to be surly."

"Surly is okay. Petulant isn't," she said. "In other words, don't whine."

"And don't insult me. What's your point?"

"The point is I want to follow the star chart."

"Have you told Haavens?"

"Yes. He's hell bent on advancing his career by spiking the Carratians and won't change course for what he calls a 'dangerous enterprise'."

"Well, can't say I blame him. The Carratians wouldn't mind at all if this ship never got back to a Mercantile port."

"It's Haavens they want to stop this time, not me. Not you," she said. "I know the ship has a couple of skiffs. I know how to pilot, you know how to navigate."

"You want to steal a skiff from the *Dominator*? Have you lost your mind?"

"Not entirely. Look, we told Haavens about Moragh, but not everything. Only that he helped us, not how. He doesn't seem to be associated with anyone on Tokorel, does he? Maybe this place shown in the star chart will have some answers. Maybe we can trade something for a skiff. Maybe Haavens will be happy to get rid of us, too!"

"Wait wait wait!" Permac shouted. "You're saying you want to take off on a two person crusade full of maybes? Through deep space in a skiff? Following something you *think* might be a star chart? Did you listen to

Moragh? He's been behind all my moves for years. Who knows, maybe yours, too. Do you think he just let us go on our way without a reason? Don't you think he might know about this so-called star chart and wanted us to find it?"

Their discussion continued throughout the night. At times, the volume of their voices carried beyond the walls of Permac's quarters and bounced through the corridor. More than one passer-by considered summoning security but reconsidered when the voice of the second party to the conversation became clear. Amid the rumors surrounding the relationship between Permac and Linsora one fact was clear, whatever their relationship may be it was stormy and stepping into the middle of an argument would not be wise. By midnight, most people were avoiding that particular stretch of hallway and didn't hear the crash as glassware shattered against the walls inside.

"I did not come here to convince you of anything," Linsora hissed. "I came here to tell you what I plan to do. You can choose your own course. You can choose to let Moragh follow you. You can choose to be a target to whoever he says is a threat to you. Or you can choose to disappear on your own, make a move that he hasn't engineered. Maybe he did want us to find the chart, but I don't think he expected us to follow it immediately."

"You cannot just take off, on your own, looking for phantoms," Permac said. "A one woman crusade to track your Lost Fleet? I don't think you have my safety in mind. You'd risk your life, and mine, for the glory of a big homecoming parade! To have your name next to your father's as a great archaeologist? That's it, isn't it? You can't stand to be someone ordinary, can you?"

As he paced, broken glass skittered across the floor.

Linsora roared. She reared up, making ready to fling whatever happened to be at hand. Permac halted his pacing, reached out and stopped her arm.

"Please stop throwing things," he continued pacing. "I ask you again, what about weapons? Money? Clothes? Food? And the small point of what happens when we get there? That kind of trip in a skiff would be one way."

"What you mean is, what about Mercantile backing?" She rumbled, "Are you so afraid of being without that support? I don't think you can stand being someone a little outside the ordinary. You said you didn't want a boring life! Well, surprise, you've got one now anyway."

He shouted in wordless fury and seemed ready to strike her. Instead he picked up one of the remaining glasses and hurled it toward the wall.

He turned toward her. She met his glare with a steady gaze. He bared his teeth and stepped toward her. Her eyes glowed. He knew she could have broken the moment just by looking away. Instead, breathing heavily, she bared her teeth in answer. Two hundred years was not long enough to separate the most basic intimate signals of their two races.

He knew if the passion of the moment continued, he would be committed to following her. Although there never had been a question of his going with her - not really. If he had managed to talk her out of it, then her resolve would not have been strong. And if she had not been determined, she wouldn't have come to him in the first place. This night was more about convincing himself. And not only about her plan. Had she not found a reason to be in his quarters before *The Dominator* reached port, he would have found a reason to be in hers.

Two steps forward. He reached for her hand, raised it to his mouth, and gently bit the side of her wrist.

"What about Denub?" Permac asked later, gingerly lowering his bare feet to the glass-strewn floor. "She'll have to find someone else to question."

"You've decided?" But she already knew.

"No plan, no resources, no backup." Permac shook his head. "Sounds great to me. Let's have a look at your star chart."

"Do you realize what you're asking?" Captain Haavens wasn't surprised at the request for the use of one of his skiffs. He hadn't expected either of them to serve out their contracts. He was very surprised, though, to find the two of them asking together. "I don't just mean taking off through deep space in a skiff designed for short hops. I mean Carratians. I mean ports of call. And frankly, I wonder about the two of you, together in a small ship for weeks." Haavens waved his hand in the air, "Most of the reports I've had about you two involve quarrels and threats." Haavens looked at them carefully and smiled. "Not to mention broken glass and flying cutlery."

"Uhh, yes sir," Permac said. "We have, uhh, we've resolved, some of those, uhh, issues. At least the flying cutlery ones."

"Ah, well then," Haavens cleared his throat. "Have you verified the chart, Permac?"

"I have. It's an accurate map of this and some neighboring systems. And the leaves inside the polymer pieces looks like a plant I thought was native to Tokorel. It's called tejina, that's where Tokorellan chikara fruit comes from and I didn't think it grew anyplace other than Tokorel. None was found on Brachen, but it's another indicator that the chart points toward a place some of Tokor's party went."

"If they're still on this planet, don't you think they'd have made themselves known to Tokorel or Khizara by now?"

Linsora took up the argument. "The destination on the chart isn't listed as any known inhabited planet, just like Brachen wasn't. Maybe they're not there anymore. They had to go there, then come back to Brachen in order to leave the chart, though. Even if no one is there now, who knows what they might have left behind?"

"I agree the prospect is intriguing," Haavens said. "I'd be interested in following the chart after presenting the Brachen evidence to the Mercantile. I offered that to you when we spoke yesterday, Linsora."

"Sir, you have your personal mission to accomplish, and it's not one that's been specifically chartered. You have your evidence against the Carratians. You once asked me if I would be willing to testify. I can provide you with my testimony before we leave. More to the point, we have our own personal mission now. From here, we can use the skiff to follow the star chart. And, besides, presenting the evidence to the Mercantile could take months," Linsora said.

"Not to mention the little fact that you're not eager to run into Carratians again," Haavens said. "Are you offering your testimony in exchange for a skiff?"

"Anything I can do help your case against the Carratians, I'll do. And, no, I'm not eager to do it in person. I'm simply stating my case. Our case." Linsora tried not to look guilty, "I suppose you might say I was offering testimony for a skiff, but I'd testify even without the skiff."

"Captain," Permac said, "The Khizaran Prefecture wasn't happy when Tokorel began to venture into space. They treat us like enemies. And, I admit, we're not any friendlier toward them."

Haavens nodded.

"Linsora told me that her history says Tokor himself tried to take over the government, that he led an attack on their capital. My history says that the Khizarans attacked Tokor and he barely escaped with his followers. Both versions are wrong. If we can show that the history on both sides is mistaken, there's a chance for some reconciliation. Otherwise, a future war between the Khizaran Prefecture and my people may be unavoidable. This would force several sectors to choose sides. I'm sure that you can see that a war spanning the area of space between Khizara and Tokorel would lead to difficulties for Mercantile ships. Borders would close, planets, even dead ones, would become off limits, and your corporate backers would dwindle. Our efforts might prevent a war. It is, therefore as much in your interest for us to find the truth as it is for us to pursue it."

"A pretty speech, Sudé," Haavens laughed. "If you honestly believe correcting history books will change current attitudes, and if you honestly believe you can do this on your own, well, I have to admire your ambition. But, in a way, it's not unlike my own ambition to bring the Carratians down a notch or two. Unlikely, but well worth a try." Haavens' fingers played over the console on his desk. "I've cancelled the next few jumps. That will give us time to take your testimony, and time for you to finish loading the skiff. Meet me back here in an hour. I'll have witnesses ready. Log that star chart into the system, too. We'll pick you up when we can."

Linsora waited until the door to Haavens' quarters closed before grabbing Permac's arm in a grip that made him wince.

"*Finish* loading the skiff? What did Haavens mean?"

Permac wrenched his arm from her and took a step backward. "What's your point? We have transportation and supplies."

"So you already had arranged for a skiff?"

"Well, yes actually." He started walking down the ramp. "I didn't expect to stay with the *Dominator*. I had noticed the old skiff in the shuttle bay and asked about it. Haavens planned to dump it. So, I offered to fix it up, paid him a little money I had saved, and he said I could take it when my time on the ship was up. I have the title and all necessary papers back in my quarters. It's ours." Permac felt the heat of her fury radiating towards him.

Linsora stepped in front of Permac, hit him on the chest with her fist. "And you never told me?"

"I didn't know if he'd let us take it now," Permac said. "Besides, I was hoping you'd find it pleasant surprise."

"I don't like surprises," she said.

"I do," he said. "And if you don't, then maybe you should find yourself another navigator."

Linsora strode ahead, muttering Khizaran curses. Permac picked up references to his parentage and his possible blood relationship to some kind of sea creature.

"Greasy what?" he called.

"Slimy!" she answered, "Slimy sea scum!"

"Yeah? Well, your brother is chikara fertilizer!"

She stopped, whirled around to face Permac. "Is that the best you can do? Fruit fertilizer? Trust me, if you knew Yokosh you'd come up with worse than that."

"You don't know what they use for chikara fertilizer!"

Linsora laughed, "Fine, you can be my navigator under one condition."

"And that is?"

"That you learn some respectable curses."

In the hangar, Linsora and Permac completed the loading process. They argued about what food to take, finally settling on a mix of meat and fruit that pleased neither one of them but gave them some satisfaction in their ability to cooperate. Permac didn't argue about taking up space with weapons. Linsora

78

didn't argue about using space for replacement parts.

"Did your family travel much?" Linsora asked.

"You sound like Denub!" Permac said. "A little, but only on Tokorel. We didn't leave the planet. Did you spend much time on Khizara?"

"Quite at bit. I lived with relatives, but traveled with my parents when I wasn't in school. Leaving on a trip was always the best part of being alive."

"You didn't like your relatives?"

"I didn't like my brother–you know, the fruit fertilizer guy. Come to think of it, that might be the only thing he could be good for, except anything growing in his soil would grow already rotten." She handed him a box that indicated clothing. "Here, put this somewhere."

"I didn't know clothes clanked," he said, shoving it under a seat.

"Mine do," she said.

"Your brother must be amazing. The only other people I've ever heard you talk like that about are Tokorellans."

"My half-brother, actually. Son of my mother's first husband. And in terms of dislike, I'm a lot more tolerant of Tokorellans than dear Yokosh." She punched Permac lightly on the arm, "Especially one particular Tokorellan."

Permac punched her arm back softly. It wasn't a gesture he was familiar with, but it implied a sort of camaraderie. He'd learn to curse and punch, but he had decided not to take up spitting.

"I think we're ready to go," Linsora said. "Haven't lost your nerve, have you?"

"No," he replied. "Just taking one last look at stability."

"The skiff's stability?"

"No, the stability of life in general. I have a feeling we won't see it again for a while."

Permac stretched his tall frame. The skiff provided ample room for movement, but the prospect of spending an extended period in such a small ship still made him feel cramped. He spent one final moment questioning the wisdom of their enterprise.

Once settled into the navigator seat, he busied himself with pre-launch preparations. The skiff moved out of the shuttle bay, becoming part of the glittering canvas of stars. Linsora extended her hand to him. With a surprising gentleness of touch and an equally surprising softness of voice, she said, "I want to fly around her once. I don't know if we'll ever see the *Dominator* again and I don't want to forget her either."

CHAPTER 10

The first weeks in the skiff were routine: system's checks, computer analyses, and course charting and corrections. Once the preliminaries were taken care of, the skiff could almost have flown itself, leaving ample time for whatever recreation they could think of.

Permac taught Linsora the finer points of poker. Khizarans are known as one of those races of people who are utterly miserable poker players. They tend to be exuberant about all emotions, making the delicate maneuvering of the poker bluff impossible for all but a few. Linsora tried to stifle her grins at good hands, but never succeeded. Even when she tried, Permac could see the gleam in her eye.

Tokorellans, on the other hand, were excellent poker players but often found it difficult to join a game. It was assumed that they would sense the emotions of the other players and know who was being honest and who was trying to bluff. Permac had to admit they were right. He had won a lot of games during his time as "that quiet Khizaran."

What he won from her in poker, he lost playing backgammon. She taught him the double board game and never hesitated to double the bet when she saw the slightest advantage. And, for some reason, she was good with the dice.

They had divided up the daily maintenance chores by whoever had the most affinity or the least tolerance. Linsora couldn't stand clutter and accepted the job of tidying up with no complaint. After she made a meal or two, though, Permac gladly accepted the role of cook. She considered a meal cooked if she served some nearly raw meat with a pepper or two tossed on top. Permac said if she continued to cook such spicy food they'd run out of water before they were anywhere near their destination.

They spent time talking, discovering each other's family, friends, and history. Permac was astonished that the Khizaran definition of family included a large extended collection of relatives. They lived not in the parent-child homes common on Tokorel, but in large several-house enclaves with several generations mingling. Linsora though the small family homes of Tokorel sounded lonely. Since that night on the *Dominator*, they shared a bed and discovered that Khizarans and Tokorellans aren't so very different at all. When physical delights began to march toward genuine affection, though, their conversations became strained.

"Linsora, how about kirch'ta for dinner?"

"Sure." She poked her head into the small galley area, "Why, though? You only make that when you're feeling serious."

"Do I? I suppose so. My mother always made it when we had family discussions."

"Family discussions. Hmm, my father usually cooked. You'd have liked him, he felt the same way about Khizaran cuisine as you do. Family discussions usually consisted of my mother stomping around yelling."

"What did your father do?"

"He'd just wait for her to calm down. He was a patient man. They cared for each other, but the combination of Terran and Khizaran temperaments couldn't have been easy."

"What about your brother?"

"He's only three years older than I am, so we were usually in the same household complex. We never got along. You can imagine what that is like in a Khizaran household. Haven't seen him in nearly five years."

"I always wished I had siblings," Permac said, stepping around the corner with plates.

"Not if you had one like Yokosh. He's Khizaran and as emotional as any of us, but he's always gravitated toward the negative emotions. He never learned to lose at anything." At Permac's smirk, she smiled. "I know I tend to be extreme, but he enjoys creating discord. If he can make someone else miserable, he'll do it. Know that scar on my side? That's from a fight with him."

"I wondered about that. I don't know what the Khizaran protocol is for asking about scars, so I never did."

"It's fine to ask, most people are happy to tell you long tales about how they got them." Linsora took a filled plate. "Smells good."

"Mmm, when we find chikara you'll be amazed."

They ate, Permac deftly spooning the stewed fruit, Linsora picking up bits with her fingers.

"You slurp," he said. "Did you know that?"

"What? Does it matter?"

"Maybe." Permac scraped up the last of the sauce with a piece of bread while Linsora licked her fingers. "You said you thought it was difficult for your parents, being Terran and Khizaran. But they managed it. You said they cared for each other."

"Yes, they did. They had the same sense of humor, I think that saved them. She died only a few months after he did. I always thought she just didn't find life alone much fun."

"What about us?"

"About our sense of humor?"

"About everything," Permac said. "You were willing to spend months alone with a Tokorellan. And I was willing to do the same with a Khizaran. And it hasn't been bad. In fact, it's been very not bad."

"Very not bad at all," she agreed. "You're not at all what I thought a Tokorellan would be like."

"You're pretty much what I thought a Khizaran would be like," Permac laughed, "but I like you anyway. That's my point, Linsora. I care for you. Once we get to wherever it is we're going, I want to…I mean, I don't want to…I mean. Oh hell, I mean I don't want to lose you."

Linsora blinked, for once in her life at a loss for words.

"This calls for some brandy," she finally said. She poured smoky liquid in their cups. "I slurp. You snore. You create messes. I insist on being neat."

"But that's not a Tokorellan-Khizaran problem. I think most couples have to deal with that kind of issue," Permac drank the brandy in two gulps and gasped for breath. "On Tokorel we have a ceremony, Sealing the Oath, that binds people together."

"We have the same ceremony," Linsora swirled the brandy in her cup and stared into the murky vortex. "It's a serious thing, Permac."

"I know. That's why I'm bringing it up. Once we get back to Tokorel or Khizara, I don't think it would be easy to arrange, but if we've already Sealed the Oath everyone will have to accept it."

"By everyone, you mean your family?"

"And yours. Don't say you have no family. You still have relatives on Khizara, you may not be close to them, but they're still important."

"I suppose," Linsora tried to imagine their reaction to having a Tokorellan in the family. "I wonder who would object more, my side or yours? Oh Permac, why complicate things? We've only been together here for a few weeks. Before that…"

"Before that, we were together even though we didn't admit it," Permac said. "We worked together to get the artifacts away from the Carratians. You didn't send me away and I didn't leave you alone even when you hinted I should. I waited for you while you were in prison. Don't sniff at that. Yes I felt responsible, but I cared about you, too. And when you were taken out of prison, you didn't have to come up to my place. You could have just wandered off. You're resourceful enough. You could have managed on your own. I don't think you really wanted to kill me."

"I thought about walking off. I was shocked to find you were still on Carratia, to tell you the truth. I was mad, but I was curious, too. And, I'll admit, I was relieved to find someone waiting to help me. A friend." She stared out of the front viewport, watching the thousands of dots of light blinking in space. "And I wouldn't have asked you to come along if I didn't like you. I care about you, too."

"What about Sealing the Oath, then?"

"What about witnesses?"

"Look out there, millions of stars, millions of planets, millions upon millions of people. We'll ask all of them to be witnesses," Permac said.

"What about...well, Sealing the Oath implies permanence - a home, a family, or children? We're not exactly secure in our plans for the future."

"No one ever is," Permac announced. "I can be insightful once in a while, too, you know. People might have plans, might feel secure, but no one really is. Fate always plays a card or two to change plans. We're probably better off than most. We don't have any expectations. Everything ahead of us clearly uncertain. I can't promise you anything."

"Oddly, that makes sense," Linsora smiled. "Okay, where will we live out our old age? Khizara or Tokorel?"

"Both! We'll have a nice comfortable house on Tokorel and a damp dingy hut on Khizara."

"Damp dingy hut?"

Permac laughed, "Whenever I'd complain about doing household chores, my mother would say that I should be happy to live in a nice comfortable house, not a damp dingy hut like Khizarans have. She said Khizarans might not be so mean if they had nice houses, too."

"She said what?" Linsora laughed along. "Someday, I want to bring your mother to Khizara so she can visit our damp dingy huts."

"Will you Seal the Oath with me, then?"

"Permac, you know me, but you don't know everything about me. My relationships in the past never went well."

"If either of us had been successful in relationships, we wouldn't be here now. I care about you. What else matters? Will you?"

"Yes, I will."

The Sealing Ceremony for Tokorellans and Khizarans was nearly identical. Permac was concerned about the blood oath part, but Linsora assured him only a tiny drop of blood was needed. The phrase, "Your enemies are my enemies," had also been dropped by Tokorellans, but Permac was happy to include it. They both choked over the Tokorellan addition, "We will work for the betterment of all." Tokor's and Moragh's messages gave the phrase new and sinister meaning. But, they included it. The betterment they would seek might not be what Tokor or Moragh meant, but it was a noble purpose nonetheless.

Permac again lamented their lack of chikara. Besides being a dietary staple, the Sealing included a ceremonial sharing of especially sweet chikara, something Permac had always found touching. Linsora sniffed and lamented their lack of Khizaran ale. They compromised with some fruit from their supplies and brandy.

Facing the viewport and their millions of witnesses, Permac and Linsora exchanged vows and blood. When they were done, they recorded the event in the log of the skiff, making it at least somewhat official. There were no fanfares, no thumps on the back from friends. When it was over, they were still alone in the middle of an unknown part of space.

They stared at the specks of light for a long time. Nothing was different. Everything was different. Permac poured more brandy and they retired to the sleeping chamber, to seal their commitment properly.

CORNERSTONE AGAIN

The old man's den was filled with even more candles. Moragh coughed in the sweet but musty air. He had always wondered where candle wax went. Candles melt and what's left doesn't have the same mass as the original. He suspected that a good deal of it was lodged in his lungs.

This afternoon, though, the soft light provided little tranquility for the older man. He paced around the desk, stopping only to glare at Moragh.

"You're sure?"

"Yes. She said she could taste influences."

"And you let them go off together? What were you thinking? Obviously you failed to think at all!" he said. "You know damn well who she is!"

"Excuse me, but you sound like I've purposely allowed the greatest criminals ever known to escape! She experiences influences as a taste. That struck me as interesting enough to mention to you, but not disturbing!" Moragh crossed his arms. "Combined with her talent for finding archaeology sites, well, like I said, I found it interesting. I thought they'd stay with the *Dominator*. I only learned they'd gone off on their own after I talked to Haavens at his first port stop. They're just two people who have blundered into…"

"Moragh! They haven't *blundered* into anything! They've been pushed. If you'd simply found it clinically interesting, you wouldn't have mentioned it all. I know you well enough to realize you only tell me what you're afraid I'll find out from someone else anyway." The old man rubbed his eyes. "And they're both a long way from ordinary." He walked away from the candles to a bookcase-lined wall. The bindings of most volumes were worn from frequent use. He ran his thumb down two rows, finally choosing a small black-bound book. "Here it is. It hasn't been such a long time since your childhood. Remember this?" The old man read,

> "The universe has eyes and ways
>
> To touch your heart and mind.
>
> Beware the lowly and obscured
>
> Whose soul with bile is lined.
>
>
> They'll make you run in circles,
>
> They'll turn you inside out.
>
> Always trust your instincts

To see you through, throughout.

Six to none to five to none
Between not six but five and one.
A taste in mind and on the tongue.
A mix of blood and wars begun.

Then two uniting in the sky
Will five and one to six apply.
Six by four to multiply.
Makes one, makes one, makes one, say I.”

Moragh stared. “It's a nonsense rhyme. Children play a clapping game with it. They spin around, flap their arms and cheer at the end. Except for the first two verses that always seemed rather poignant, it never made a lot of sense to me. So?”

“It's most definitely not nonsense. Trust *my* instincts on this one. It's far more than a game.” The old sage held up six fingers. “Six – those are the spires in Khizara. The six spires of the capital building. One spire for each of the founding tribes. *Six to none* – the spires and the building were destroyed two hundred years ago in the war just before Tokor left Khizara. *Six to none to five* – since Tokor's tribe was banished, only five were rebuilt. *Between not six but five and one* – five on Khizara and one on Tokorel. *Six to none to five to none* – hasn't happened yet, but what does that imply?”

“You can't tell me you believe it's some kind of ancient prophecy!” Moragh threw up his hands.

“*A taste in mind and on the tongue* –she can taste influences. *A mix of blood* – she's Khizaran and Terran. He's Tokorellan. *Two uniting in the sky* – well, look where they are now. They're alone in a small ship and the trip will take months. What do you think they'll do, read to each other?”

“Not exactly.” Moragh stifled a laugh. “What about the lowly and obscured, the running around in circles?”

“Don't be condescending to me!” The old man spoke with whispered menace. “Think about where they're going, who they'll meet. Think about your travels of late.”

“So you think the 'five and one to six' means some kind of reunion between Khizara and Tokorel?”

"That comes after the part about the war."

"Six by four." Moragh raised his eyebrows. "Six spires on each of the four Cornerstones?"

"After the part about the war," he repeated. "Do you think we're ready for all that?"

"I think you've put an interpretation on that rhyme that's somewhat fantastical. Admittedly, when she told me she could taste influences, I was curious. Maybe I did remember something about the rhyme, but Linsora and Permac as the embodiment of legend? I don't think so. Where did that rhyme come from anyway?"

"From Tokor himself." The old man returned to the wall of candles. He sniffed, then filled his lungs, as if inhaling the savored sweetness of life itself. "Whether you choose to believe it or not is immaterial. Separate them. I'm not saying I believe in the prophecy either, but I'm not willing to tempt fate. If I place them in the rhyme, others might do the same. Heroes are created by circumstances. If they're apart, the circumstances you've said are critical might be put off. We need time, Moragh. Maybe more time than either of our lifetimes will allow."

"Sir, I have disagreed with you in the past, but always followed your directives. You know that. I don't see the point of risking further involvement to…"

The old man exploded, "You are telling me *you* don't want to risk involvement? Time and again you've created situations to meet your own views. You've called it 'taking advantage of opportunities'. But you created many of those opportunities. I don't think the Carratians found Brachen by accident."

"I may have hinted at the worth of the planet, but you know I had nothing to do with the two of them being on the Carratian ship."

"Really? I wonder at that, too. Other than the Carratians, who'd be interested in mining benadiaum? Practically no one. The effort is too great. If the woman hadn't been on that ship, do you think the Carratians would have worried about artifacts or about Tokor?"

Moragh shifted his weight, "I knew she was a reputable archaeologist. I thought the Carratians would land at Tokor's settlement. Who better to find it than a Khizaran? If a Tokorellan, had found it, the Khizarans wouldn't believe it was genuine."

"A Khizaran who happens to be Yokosh Kohl's sister!" The old man paced furiously in a circle around the room. "Irresponsible, dangerous, and very stupid!"

"Half sister," Moragh mumbled.

"Even if she was a distant cousin, she's still related! You know who he's consorting with. Gordek is a lot smarter than Yokosh and, if possible, even less principled. They aren't the kinds of people who look for any kind of peace. You've thrown a hot-headed, principled woman into the world he occupies. Before this she had all but forgotten him. You think she'll walk away from trying to stop him? You think he won't take advantage of any chaos he can?" His halo of white hair seemed to vibrate with outrage. "And what about Permac?"

"Permac? I was surprised that he joined a Carratian crew. His previous ship was in dry dock for repairs when he signed on. Officially, he was listed as Khizaran, but he never kept it much of a secret that he's Tokorellan."

"She might have killed him, did you consider that?" The old man glared at Moragh. "He's one of the best ambassadors out there!" He sighed. "He doesn't particularly like the role, does he?"

"No, he doesn't like it at all. I wish…well, of all I've done I wish I hadn't mentioned anything about that to him. Just made him more curious. Most of the others seemed pleased," Moragh said. "I only learned he had signed on to that Carratian ship after it was gone."

The old man slumped into a chair. "Unfortunate, but done. I can accept that. Sometimes surprises come from all sides at once. No one knew the star chart they found on Brachen existed either. Any other surprises you'd like to tell me about?"

Moragh considered the armbands he had given the Carratians. The old man would learn about them soon enough. Research and development was one thing, but eventually all devices required a testing phase outside the laboratory environment. The old man's timeline had no endpoint. His leadership lent no sense of urgency to the research. How perfect did perfect have to be before something was deemed usable? It reminded Moragh of a toy maker crafting masterpieces – toys too precious to be given to any child. Well, some secrets were best left secret.

"No, sir," he said.

"Well, that chart is probably leading them to Hakai."

"Most likely."

"In an old skiff, too." He stared into the flickering candle flames. "If they survive the trip, get them both away from Hakai. Karak, his daughter, and these two…it's not good, Moragh, not good at all." He smoothed the pages of the book. "Your choices are the misguided decisions of youth. The small ripples you created to achieve your ends are becoming waves you can't control. I know you believe in what you are doing, but my patience is wearing thin. And not just mine. Ambassadors have disappeared. Many of our people have disappeared. Don't become one of them." Closing the book and the conversation, he said. "Separate them. Bring her here. He's an engineer? Take him to Binsar Polinad at the research institute. They might find each other interesting."

CHAPTER 11

The skiff was sound but slow. They had planned for a trip of several months, since the small ship had only enough power for three jumps a day and the worm holes it created were short. Three a day was just about enough, though. Each one was a bone jarring, stomach churning experience. What protection a large vessel might provide was not possible in a skiff.

Slowly, the skiff began to show its age. After nearly every jump something failed. While they had expected to encounter difficulties, nothing could have prepared them for the unending series of problems they ran into. Permac was able to make repairs and he knew the ship would be fine in deep space. The rigors of entering an atmosphere worried him.

The farther along the star chart they were, the more serious the problems became. It seemed almost as though they were being warned, advised to turn back while they were still able. More than once Linsora had asked Permac if he could sense anyone out there. At first she had been joking, but before long they began to feel like a mouse being followed by an invisible cat. Permac felt no presence near them, yet he was uneasy.

They had sent a message to the *Dominator*, estimating it would reach their former ship before it was out of range. Their last message was sent desperately to anyone who might be able to receive it. Not a distress call, just one last gasp by the communications system before it failed irreparably in a cloud of smoke.

Now their goal loomed in front of them, and the guidance system had failed.

"Get the computer off line, we have to take it in manually!" Linsora screamed toward Permac, who was on the floor under the main control panel of the skiff. Sparks surrounded him for a moment singeing his beard and the ends of his long hair. He disabled the computer and struck his head on the control panel as he rose in the rocking ship. He muttered one of the many new words he had learned from Linsora during the trip, eliciting a wry smile from his teacher.

"Computer is off. Take her in," he said. "Still a few minutes before we enter the atmosphere."

"You sure of the trajectory?"

"I know we won't come down in the water. Aiming for that plain," Permac pointed. "Can't say how smooth the ground is, but it's the largest expanse of flat land I could find."

"All steady," Linsora said, as the ship began its precipitous and rocky descent toward the surface. Permac recited instrument display readings as

Linsora struggled to maintain a course. A cloudless blue sky surrounded the ship, giving them a clear view of the hard brown ground coming up fast.

"No trees, that's good," Linsora said.

"Get the nose up!" Permac shouted. "We can still glide in to land. Hang on, it'll be rough."

"Permac, I'm sorry," Linsora whispered as she grasped the console for support. The view screen showed brown earth, then blue sky, then brown earth, then nothing as the skiff touched down and tumbled end over end before coming to rest with its nose buried in a mound of dirt.

"Ralain! What was that?"

Gordek held his hand up to shield his eyes from the rising twin suns. He and Ralain stood at the mouth of a cave high up over the plain where the skiff crashed. They had been busy since well before dawn in the silence of darkness and the isolated location. The nearest village was on the opposite side of the hills.

"Two people aboard. They're alive."

"Interesting," Gordek said. "The skiff is Mercantile. I wonder why they've come back?"

"I don't know," Ralain said. "I'll have our people go down to them."

"No. Maybe Karak's expecting them. Even if he's not, he has the biggest stake in greeting outsiders. He'll send someone." Gordek brushed dust from his jacket. The fine fabric and intricate tailoring were never intended to withstand the rigors of manual labor. "Let's get this done."

Permac opened his eyes slowly, wondering if the skiff was still spinning or if it was just his head. After glimpsing the window, he decided that it was his head. The skiff was nose down and tilted. He tried to orient himself. He remembered the crash, foam spurting all over to cushion the impact. His clothes were damp and sticky. His head throbbed. A shooting pain burned in his leg. The rear door was wide open.

Linsora must be outside. She has to be...

He climbed out of the skiff. Pain shot through his entire body as his feet hit the ground. The edges of his vision blurred. *Got to stay conscious*, he thought.

Through hazy vision he saw another ship not far from the skiff. He heard footsteps behind him. He was turning when something hard stuck his head.

"Permac? Permac, wake up." The voice was familiar, comforting, soothing. It was Linsora.

"Where...are...we?" He managed to force the words from his throat. The gravely voice didn't sound like his own.

"I woke up here. I don't know who this ship belongs to. I've wandered around, but I haven't seen anyone else. When I came back here I found you. Looks like someone's tended to your leg. Is that the same one that was burned?"

"Of course," he said. "It feels better now. My head hurts more. Someone hit me after I climbed out of the skiff." Permac closed his eyes. He was thirsty. "Anything to drink?"

"No. I'll see what I can find," Linsora said. "Wait, someone's coming!"

When the door opened, Permac could have felt the heat of Linsora's rage even without being able to sense her emotions.

"You!" she shouted. "You made the skiff crash, didn't you? Are we really so hard to kill? If you want to get rid of us, just do it. Did you have to hit Permac in order to get him here?"

Permac struggled to sit up and managed to do so with some difficulty. "Moragh?"

"One and the same," Moragh bowed. "I've bought you some food and drink. It's not fancy, but it will give you strength. I hope you like it." He set plates down in front of them on a table. "If I wanted to kill you, I wouldn't feed you. The concept of a last meal for the condemned always struck me as a waste of food. And no, I didn't cause any trouble for your skiff. It's actually something of a tribute to both your skills that you made it this far in a craft that old. In fact, I'm the one who should be angry and ask what you were thinking when you took off in it. And, I didn't hit Permac. Whoever did that ran away when they saw me coming back to the skiff. Now please, sit and eat. You both have been through a lot and need to regain your strength."

Linsora sat at the small table and sniffed the food.

"I will be happy to taste the food for you to show that it is not poisoned. I have no reason to harm you." Moragh fingered a piece of fruit and popped it into his mouth. He filled a plate and handed it to Permac.

"Chikara? It's fresh," Permac said. He noticed Linsora eating the fruit and felt a pang that she was getting her first taste of it under less than ideal circumstances. He had envisioned presenting her with red ripe slices of chikara with great ceremony, to make up for not having any at their Sealing. "Moragh, the last time we met you told me to trust my instincts. Right now, my instincts are screaming. What are you doing here?"

Moragh paced the length of the room. "I told you I couldn't be everywhere. And I also don't know everything. I didn't know the remains of a star chart had been left behind on Brachen. Once you were on the way, I couldn't stop you. The most I could do was meet you here. From here, well," Moragh spread his hands, "there's a Tokorellan saying, do you know it? *The universe has eyes and ways to touch your mind. Beware the lowly and the obscured. They will make you run in circles and will turn you inside out. Trust your instincts and your heart.* It applies to you more than you know."

Permac glanced at Linsora. She was listening to the conversation, but seemed oddly detached. Permac realized she couldn't taste influences while she was eating and the chikara was especially sweet.

"It's nonsense, Moragh. You're the most lowly and obscure person I know. Are you telling me to beware of you?"

Moragh sat at the table, across from Linsora. "Permac, the story is a long one. For now, I can only tell you that this place isn't safe – for either of you. It's in your best interest, and hers, to leave with me now."

"Why isn't it safe?"

"I could have taken off with both of you on board, but I haven't. I want you to come with me willingly," Moragh said. "Have you heard of the Central Research Facility on Tokorel?"

"I have and I don't care. I want to know why this place isn't safe."

"I think you might be interested in some of the work they're doing. I'd like to take you there."

"You won't tell me what's not safe here. You think it would be any safer for Linsora to go to Tokorel?"

"She must go elsewhere." Moragh glanced at Linsora. "We...I mean, I believe she could benefit from some time...elsewhere. Your purpose is best accomplished on Tokorel. Besides, don't you think your life would be less, complicated, without her?"

"*What?* You can't possibly think I'll go to Tokorel and have Linsora go with you to some unknown place," Permac said. "If you want to protect me, Linsora is part of the package now. If you think there's something of value to me on Tokorel, she can come, too. If you think there's something dangerous here, we should have our own option of staying or leaving, together. You tell me I'm some kind of ambassador for Tokorel, that I should be prepared. Now you say my purpose is best accomplished on Tokorel? You don't tell me a damn thing about what I should prepare for or what my purpose is. You think that's not obscure?" Permac focused on Moragh.

"Don't try to influence me, Permac," Moragh growled.

"Why not? Don't you like having done to you what you do to everyone around you?" Permac asked. He concentrated all his attention.

Moragh reeled slightly. "Not bad, but you have no concept of the power you could have with my training."

"Not interested," Permac said. He stood and tested his weight on the injured leg. Good enough to walk on, he thought. A tingle at the base of his skull accompanied a wave of weariness. He sat down again. "What do you really want?"

"You will go to Tokorel. I'll take her where she'll be perfectly safe. That's what I want and that's what will happen. The whys will be answered later." Moragh moved toward the door. "Your belongings are being collected from the skiff now."

Permac cleared his mind of all emotion. He narrowed his vision to include only Moragh. When he was young, he and his friends had played power games. Generally the point was to make your opponent feel sick enough to puke. Permac had been remarkably good at the game. He was usually able to steer influences to a different part of his brain, someplace where it wouldn't affect his equilibrium. Tokorellans know when another Tokorellan is influencing them. Permac thought of it as a brain buzz, something like a tickle that, with practice, could be shifted. It had been a long time since he had the chance to practice and, in his lifetime, he had never had a need to use the skill seriously. What he felt from Moragh was no ordinary brain buzz. It felt more like tiny sparks flickering all over his head, not localized enough to deflect. He tried to ignore them. All of his energy and conscious attention was directed at Moragh. He didn't even try to send a specific emotion. He only wanted to make an impression.

For the first time, Permac saw Moragh's eyes change color to a glowing deep violet. The tiny sparks inside Permac's head burst into flame. His head was engulfed. He felt like his body was on fire. Knowing it was a trick of his brain didn't help. He could feel his skin melting. He howled in agony and rolled to the floor, an automatic reaction to douse the flames.

"You're not being harmed, Permac," Moragh said, "You can save yourself. Find a way."

Permac's focus, now, was only on pain. He couldn't find any way around it. He couldn't speak. He reached out toward Moragh trying to indicate he didn't understand what he had to do.

"Permac! What's wrong?" Linsora upended the table and chairs. Food bowls clattered to the floor and the remains of her meal splattered against the wall. As she rose, she pulled a knife from her boot. She didn't know what had happened. She remembered a far off conversation between Moragh and Permac while she was eating - something distant and not interesting. Suddenly, it seemed like a fog lifted and Permac was screaming. She looked at Moragh. His eyes were purple. The battle of Tokorellan minds she had joked about on Brachen was happening and it was most certainly not amusing. Permac rolled toward Moragh, his hands outstretched as though to grab him. Moragh's eyes blazed, a deep indigo. His attention was fully on Permac, who writhed in pain at his feet.

Linsora stepped forward. In a swift fluid motion, bumped her left elbow into Moragh's shoulder, and smashed the butt of the knife into his throat. He gurgled and staggered backward, clutching his throat. As he slumped to his knees, gasping for breath, she brought her elbow down on the base of his skull. Moragh fell to the ground, sliding on spilled fruit. The pink slices of chikara smeared the floor, like Moragh's blood would have if Linsora had trusted her first instinct to use the blade instead of the handle.

Permac sat up. The flames were gone, the pain stopped. Linsora stood in a fighting crouch near the door. Permac felt sick and weak. He inched along the floor toward Moragh. The tall man was alive, his breath ragged. Blood dribbled from the side of his open mouth.

"I didn't trust my instincts, Moragh. My instincts were to kill you," Linsora hissed. "If I live to regret it, so will you. Cross me or Permac again, and I will take your advice." She shoved the unconscious man aside with her foot. "We have to get out of here. Can you tell if anyone else is on this ship?"

"No. I mean, I don't know."

"Come on. A ship this size must have crew somewhere on board."

Several doors opened onto corridors before they found an exit. They stepped out into the bright light of the twin suns. Before their eyes could fully adjust to the light, a dark shadow loomed over them. They looked up to see a ship flying directly over them. It seemed to have come from the direction of the downed skiff.

"Do you recognize it, Permac?" asked Linsora, watching as the ship flew away, then banked sluggishly, turned, and came back toward them.

"It's not Tokorellan, if that's what you mean. Moragh did say he had people collecting our things from the skiff."

Linsora spat at the mention of Moragh's name. "Can you believe anything he said?"

Permac knew that Linsora hadn't heard what Moragh said. The part about how, with training, his mental abilities could be increased. He was afraid her mistrust of Tokorellans would be rekindled if he told her. He decided, though, that he was more afraid her mistrust of him would be rekindled if he did not. She wasn't telepathic, but she didn't have to be to know when he was hiding something. Before he could find a way to put any of this into words, Linsora was pulling him down onto the ground.

The ship approached their position. It was larger than the skiff, silent and bristling with what seemed to be weaponry. As it neared their position, it slowed then stopped, hovering above them. One of the bristles poking out from its side began to emit a shrill whine.

"It's going to fire on us!" Permac said.

Linsora and Permac ran to the side of the ship, away from the hovering craft.

"Permac! What's wrong?" Linsora called when Permac suddenly stopped. He seemed to be listening to something.

Permac stared at the ships. "Something. I..."

He was cut off by a deafening roar. The ground beneath them shook; the ship trembled, and the volume of the roar increased. It was not the sound of a weapon, it was the rumble of engines. Permac felt a tingling in his head as a sense of calm tugged at the edges of his mind, promising relief from all the strain he felt and beckoning him to surrender to it. Whoever was inside seemed to be calling them back.

He clenched his teeth and muttered, "No. Not this time," as his eyes shifted to violet. The small, heavily armed ship remained in position. Either it hadn't noticed them or something else far more interesting held its attention, or its occupants were being influenced, too.

"Linsora, run! Now!" he yelled. "Head toward the skiff."

She pointed to her ears. She couldn't hear him over the roar. He pointed to the skiff, grabbed her hand and began to run toward it. They had cleared the double shadows cast by the setting rays of the twin suns when the force of the engines knocked them down. Linsora sat up, her face smeared with dirt and hair tangled with dried vegetation. She clutched Permac's arm. Moragh's ship shimmered, glistened as though sprayed with a fine sheen of oil, and vanished. The roar, however, continued. The other craft had not moved. It hovered just to one side of the ship's location. Shielding their faces from the searing heat generated by the take-off of the invisible ship, Permac and Linsora saw the small craft tumble through the sky and plunge to the ground as though it had been flung aside by a hurricane wind.

Within seconds, only dust and silence remained.

"What happened?" Linsora asked, rubbing dirt from her eyes.

"I don't know," Permac said. He rubbed his arms and legs. "He influenced me to feel burning. It felt real, Linsora. That ship, that kind of power. He's not Tokorellan. He can't be. He's some kind of monster." Permac shook Linsora's comforting hand off his shoulder. "I will kill him," he shouted. "The next time we meet Moragh, trust me, I will kill you!"

"Permac, stop!" Linsora matched the volume of his shout to get his attention, "Be careful what you promise."

They surveyed the flat plain. Their skiff was some distance from them, in a direction opposite the setting suns. The downed craft lay in a shattered heap.

"It'll be dark soon," said Permac. "Let's see if we can salvage anything."

The suns warmed their backs as they walked.

Permac had developed grudging respect for Khizaran reasoning during their time together. He had learned how to carry concealed weapons himself, how to access them and admitted their value. Still, he didn't always appreciate his companion's blunt nature, her willingness to act first and consider later. They walked in silence until Permac became aware of a smoldering anger in Linsora. He felt some annoyance in that. If anyone should be angry, he had more claim to the emotion. He was angry at the continuing interference of Moragh in his life. He was angry at being unable to learn more from Moragh. And, he was angry with himself for wanting to kill Moragh. He felt as guilty about the desire to kill as he would if he had already accomplished the deed. Permac stopped.

"Maybe Moragh should be dead," Linsora muttered.

"Why are you angry? Because you didn't kill him?"

"Because you want to. Taking a life isn't a simple matter, Permac. Neither is making a vow to take one. I said I could kill. I have killed. I never said I enjoyed it. If the same end can result in disabling an opponent as by killing, I'll opt for disabling."

"Didn't you tell me once that I took mortality too seriously?"

"Your own mortality. You don't have the same luxury with other people's. I didn't kill that guard in the Carratian prison. I could have, but he deserved a warning, not death. I didn't kill Moragh because I owed him. He saved us on Brachen. Next time we meet, though, there will no debts." She tried not to snarl. "Are you disturbed that I can attack so easily? That I can leave a man bleeding on the floor and trust his life or death to fate? I did what I had to do. It's just that simple. And once done, I don't suffer guilt. I was trained not only to kill, but to assess situations quickly and act."

"Trained? When you were in the navy?"

"When I was a child and when I was in the navy, and in school. I'm Khizaran," she said. "I don't kill lightly, if I killed everyone who ever annoyed me, I'd be on some prison colony that you couldn't get me out of right now."

Permac smiled at her, "Mmmm, and I'd probably be dead!"

She returned the smile. Placing her hand on his chest, she said, "Your heart is Khizaran. Only your conscience is Tokorellan."

They embraced briefly, four shadows becoming one. Darkness had fallen over the plain by the time they reached the skiff. Moragh had been telling the truth about one thing, someone had been in the skiff, but not to collect belongings. Instrument panels had been ripped out, storage bins ransacked, the controls blasted. If they were ever to leave this planet, it would not be on the skiff. Linsora retrieved some supplies, instruments, and weapons from a hidden compartment. She estimated they had less than a week's worth of food. They decided to head westward in the morning, toward the nearest of the low hills surrounding the plain.

"Permac," Linsora whispered sleepily, "Do you think Moragh's ship

97

might still be there? It disappeared, it sounded and felt like it launched. Even if it did take off, it could come back. How powerful is he?"

"I don't know," Permac said. "I do know that something about this planet is important. Did you hear what he told me?"

"No, I don't remember much after Moragh walked in."

"He didn't say a lot. Just that something about this place isn't safe, but…" Permac pulled a blanket up around his chin. The night chill of the desert permeated the shell of their skiff. "He wanted to take me back to Tokorel."

"Why?"

"To work at the Central Research Institute. He wanted to take you someplace else, though. Someplace not on Tokorel."

"I'm not going anywhere without you, Tokorellan." Linsora yawned. She rounded her body around Permac. "Wonder why he didn't just take off with us on his ship?"

"He wanted us to go willingly. I think he was…maybe afraid that he couldn't control us during the trip."

Linsora mumbled something about Tokorellan magic. Permac listened as her breathing became measured and deep. Before long she'd start to snore. Permac smiled. She complained about his snoring but never believed him when he told her she snored, too. Still, he'd rather sleep with a snoring mate than sleep alone.

Across the desert at the mouth of the cave, Ralain had been watching intently. Gordek, who had witnessed only the last part of the chaos on the plain below, joined him.

"Ralain, whose ship was that out there?" Gordek peered across the plain.

"I honestly don't know," Ralain said. "Did you see everything?"

"No."

"That big one landed, well not landed exactly - it just appeared not long after the Mercantile skiff crashed. Someone carried a woman from the wreck over to the big ship. Then, before he had a chance to go back, some of our people who were nosing around knocked the man out."

"Idiots!" Gordek exploded. "If they…"

"It's fine, Gordek," said Ralain. "They just wanted what they could salvage. The man is alive. The same person who took the woman carried him to the big ship. I think the man in the skiff is Tokorellan. Oddly enough, I think the woman is Khizaran. Whoever is on that ship, though…"

"What?" Gordek was alarmed at the tone of awe in Ralain's voice.

"I have the impression that he's Tokorellan," Ralain said. "But no ordinary Tokorellan. The outside of his ship must be lined with kagamite, did you see how it seemed to vanish?"

"Two Tokorellans? How could he have kagamite?" Gordek stared out onto the plain. "Months of quiet, then two Tokorellans and a Khizaran land. I wonder what's going on."

"Maybe nothing," Ralain said.

"I don't believe in coincidences. Three Terrans, three Darubians - that might be in the range of normal. This is not normal. I wonder what the Tokorellan and Khizaran are doing traveling together."

"They ran from the big ship. Could be the Tokorellan in that ship isn't pleased with them."

"Could be, but why did they come here?"

Ralain shrugged. "They could be useful."

"Perhaps. If they've found us, we may need to hurry." Gordek began to pace. "What about the other Tokorellan, the one in the bigger ship?"

"His abilities are impressive. As far as I can tell, he's gone."

"You said the woman is Khizaran? Curious."

"What will you do now?" Ralain asked.

"I need to talk to some people in the village," Gordek said. "Meet me there in two days."

CHAPTER 12

The first sun colored the eastern sky with brilliant shades of red as it prepared to rise above the horizon. Linsora stirred from a troubled sleep. She gazed at Permac, still sleeping soundly. She wondered how much Permac really knew about all of this. Trusting anyone completely was not in her nature, but she had no one else. Even if a Khizaran fleet was orbiting this planet, she would still trust this man, still care for him. With another smile, she curled up next to him. As she drifted back to sleep she realized that she never seemed to choose mates wisely, but she always chose well.

Bright sunlight streamed through the broken door of the skiff. Permac placed a warning hand on Linsora's lips, waking her, and nodded toward the window. As they watched, a shadow accompanied by the sound of footsteps blocked the incoming light.

"Hello? Is anyone here?" The voice was soft and high pitched. A tall, broad-shouldered woman stepped into the skiff. Permac waited for her to take another step. She turned to examine a ruined panel. He leapt to his feet and clamped his hand on her forehead, pulling her head back. His other hand held a knife to her throat.

"Who are you? What do you want?" Permac realized with some surprise, that he was honestly prepared to kill.

"I could answer you better without a blade at my throat. Do you welcome all visitors like this?" Permac relaxed his grip. The woman turned and slowly lowered her hood. "That's better," she said, "don't you think?" She was tall and lean with long, flowing, black hair. Her hands had thick claw-like nails.

Linsora stepped from the shadows of the ship. She casually walked over and stood next to Permac, her hands in her pockets.

"So," the woman said, "there are two of you. One pure bred..." she looked at Permac, smiled, and slowly ran the tip of her tongue across her lower lip, "...and one, what exactly are you?"

"She is my mate," he said. He knew Linsora was reaching for a knife and probably had two of them in her hands already. "If you've come here to pillage the skiff, you're too late. I think your friends were here last night."

"What?" The stranger seemed genuinely surprised. "No, the Others were here. I am Tayla, of the Hakan people."

She smiled again. Permac could feel Linsora becoming calm but not through his influence. The woman was sending emotions to both of them, urging them to trust her, but her eyes did not change color. As the feelings became stronger, Permac resisted. His eyes blazed a bright violet.

Linsora spat, but the taste in her mouth remained. She felt too relaxed to do more than spit again.

"Who are you?" Permac whispered.

The woman's smile had become strained. She nodded to Permac as if to indicate the match had been a draw. Her influences vanished. "As I said, I will be happy to answer your questions. I saw another crashed ship farther west. It looks like one of the Others' and they'll be back before long. I prefer not to be here when they arrive. You may come with me, or you may stay here," she said. "But I am leaving."

Permac glanced at Linsora, who shrugged. Whoever these others were had certainly not offered to help them. "We'll go with you," he said.

As they left the skiff, Tayla continued, "We heard about your crash. I was sent to check for survivors. We can provide food, supplies, and a place to stay and rest until you feel strong enough to travel on. Although you definitely look strong enough," she said reaching out to place her palm on Permac's chest. Her hand was intercepted by Linsora's clutching fist.

"We're both strong enough!" Linsora growled.

Permac stifled a smile. He hated to admit it, but he found the attention of the two women enjoyable.

"Who are these others?" Permac asked.

The woman spoke as she walked. "You're the ones who crashed on my world. I should be questioning you, not the other way around." She waved toward Permac, "I take it you are Tokorellan. She must be Khizaran," she nodded toward Linsora. "Odd combination to find traveling together. And to call each other mates...well, just odd. My father will answer your questions."

The three climbed into a land craft. Tayla sat on a cushioned seat, next to Permac with Linsora on his other side. She spoke to someone in a language that sounded somewhat Tokorellan to Permac and somewhat Khizaran to Linsora, although neither could understand it clearly. Portions of the craft became clear that had previously been dark. They moved at high speed across the dry plain leaving a plume of dust in their wake.

"Thank you for helping us," Linsora said.

Permac's head whipped to the side. Linsora didn't usually exhibit diplomacy or expressive gratitude, but he couldn't sense that she was being influenced.

"You have the hands of a Khizaran," Linsora continued, "but I take it you have Tokorellan abilities. Is this place a Tokorellan outpost of some sort?"

"Not exactly," Tayla glanced toward Linsora. She, too, seemed uncertain of the short woman's intentions. "Why do you think I have Tokorellan abilities?"

"I can taste…" Linsora cursed to herself. Permac said her talent was unusual, she didn't want to give away more information than she had to.

"Taste what? Influences? That's odd." Tayla shrugged.

Linsora was relieved that Tayla didn't seem as interested as Moragh had.

"It's just that, well, we have Sealed the Oath. And, as you might imagine, neither of our families are pleased," Linsora said.

Permac understood. Linsora was trying to weave a tale to explain their presence. They hadn't discussed how they would handle themselves once they found the planet on the star chart. They had both assumed they would make an ordinary landing, perhaps in some busy port city or on a deserted planet. Crashing on a backwater world hadn't been part of the plan. Pretending to be a wayward couple running from their families wasn't that far from the truth. Still, he didn't know how to explain how they came to be here. Linsora had instructed him on how to behave during an interrogation after the unlikely tale he told the Carratian captain, but he wasn't sure that same principle applied to people who seemed to be friendly.

"I can imagine, indeed," Tayla said. She pointed toward the horizon, "The city is just ahead."

"How does your transport do that? Change from dark to clear, I mean?" Linsora asked.

"Kagamite," Tayla said. "It's a mineral unique to Hakai."

A swath of green at the edge of the plain appeared. Directly ahead of them, buildings were becoming clear. What Tayla called a city; Permac and Linsora would call a village. The buildings seemed to be no more than two or three stories tall. They all shimmered, as though painted with sparkles.

Tayla stopped the craft outside a house at the edge of town. At close range, the houses all looked almost like adobe constructions painted with metallics that made them glitter. A man was waiting in the doorway. He walked to the craft and embraced Tayla.

"Father," she said, "These are the people who crashed in the desert."

"Welcome," he said. "I am Karak. I'm pleased to see you survived!"

"Thank you, so are we. I'm Permac Sudé, this is my mate Linsora Anselm."

Permac thought Karak blinked a few too many times, hesitated a bit too long before his next cordial word. Permac knew it was well beyond the courtesy of a visitor to check your host's emotions, but he thought he felt a great deal of surprise. *Surprise at what, though?* He thought.

He felt a familiar prickling in his head. This Karak obviously didn't live by the same code of courtesy Permac had learned. He wished he had been trained to shield his emotions.

A small boy suddenly emerged from the next house carrying a tray. He peered curiously at the newcomers. Karak recovered his composure and smiled. The boy probably volunteered for this duty just so he could boast to his friends that he had seen the strangers first.

"Warel, what do you have there?" Karak asked.

"For you and them," the boy said. "Mother asked if you need her now, Mr. Moragh."

"Thank you," Karak said. "Bring it inside to Tayla."

"Your name is Moragh?" Permac asked, trying to sound casual.

Permac felt a wave of suspicious anger surge from Linsora then a burst of instant frustration, followed by anger. He knew she was aware that the people around them could read her emotions and that she could not control what she felt. Indeed, it was only with great effort that Permac controlled his own emotions. The man extended his hand to them. The offering of a handshake was meant to show that neither party held a weapon. Linsora's hands were both in the folds of her skirt.

"Yes. Moragh is my family name. It is an ancient line, going back to one of the original founders of Hakai. Is it one you know?" The man smiled at them. Permac abandoned courtesy and sensed Karak's emotions. Nothing but a sense of welcome, but tinged with the surprise Permac had noted. He stepped forward to take Karak's hand.

"No," Permac said, "not as a family line."

"Ah," the older man nodded. Permac wondered how much understanding that one word indicated. Karak of the Moragh line grasped Permac's hand with firm, hearty grip. He released Permac's hand with a nod and turned toward Linsora.

"Linsora Anselm? I'm pleased to meet you," he said.

With her left hand in a pocket clutching a small hand blade, she reached her right to him and shook Karak's hand in a cursory manner.

"Tayla said you weren't injured, but you seem to be limping," he said to Permac. "Warel's mother is a doctor. He'll bring her back shortly. For now, please come in. You must be hungry," Karak said, leading the way into the house.

The interior of the house presented as many contrasts as the exterior. The entryway was a hallway in the ancient sense: a public hall open to visitors, separate from the private quarters. Care had evidently been taken to make this area match the outside's impression of a mud and sand structure. The interior walls seemed to be rough stucco but shone with the same odd metallic light as the outside. What few decorations graced the walls seemed to be fabric, but these too glimmered. The cool, almost damp air was a welcomed relief from the heat of the desert outside. Permac didn't see any light source other than the daylight that filtered through the walls. He didn't see any doors, either. The middle of the room was filled with a large table, toward which Karak ushered them.

Tayla stood in a corner of the room, leaning casually against the wall, her arms crossed. The boy, Warel, stood next to her, staring at the strangers.

"Warel, go tell your mother to stop by a little later to have a look at our guests," Karak said.

"That really isn't necessary," Permac said, as the boy sprinted past, "I think I just bruised…"

"Nonsense, she's just next door. It's no trouble and might save you some later problems if there is an injury." Karak exchanged a glance with Tayla. "Please sit. If you'll excuse me, I'll help Tayla with the meal."

Karak and Tayla walked through an opening that appeared in the far wall. *More of that kagamite*, Permac thought. Something clattered to the floor in the kitchen, Tayla's high-pitched voice cried out. *Doesn't block out sound, though*, Permac thought. Karak murmured soothing sounds.

"What's going on?" Linsora whispered.

"Don't know," Permac said.

Karak emerged through the opening with several covered dishes on a tray. "My apologies. A spill in the kitchen. Nothing serious. Tayla will join us shortly."

The food was unfamiliar to Linsora and Permac - round pastries full of salty meat and vegetables. Not Khizaran, not Tokorellan - much like the people around them. Permac was relieved that they were being fed well, especially for Linsora's sake. Her appetite continually amazed him and she tended to be more amenable when she wasn't hungry.

Little conversation was exchanged during the meal. Tayla didn't return. Karak shrugged, as though the banging and rattling and muttering from the kitchen was a normal phenomenon.

"Well, Linsora and Permac, we receive few visitors here on Hakai, especially like you," he wriggled his clawed fingertips. "Tayla said you are mates. I understand that could pose problems. Still, questions remain." Karak cleared his throat, "We have standards of hospitality that I assure you will be met. However, the history of Hakai, both past and recent, is troubled and dictates caution. I can sense some reluctance on your part to be totally honest. And there is reticence on my part, as well. Understand that you are in my home, however, and I must insist that you tell your story first."

Permac risked sampling Karak's emotions, but sensed only serene honesty.

Karak said. "I must thank you first for the destruction of the other ship out there. Is that how you came to crash? Doing battle with them?"

Permac, for lack of a more imaginative plan, decided the only path to take was honesty. After a long moment of silence, during which Linsora didn't jump in with a version of their story, Permac took her hand and launched into his own.

"I'm afraid we can't take credit for that, Karak," he said.

"Oh?"

"Let me start from the beginning," Permac said. "Linsora and I met while serving on a Mercantile ship. As you probably know, it isn't easy for a Tokorellan to find a berth on ships, so I'm listed officially as Khizaran." He smiled at Linsora. "I told Linsora that I was Tokorellan and, at first, our relationship was, well let's just say it was stormy."

Karak grinned at them, "But love will find its ground, as they say."

"Yes, that's true. So, we Sealed the Oath with our captain's permission. Our ship was exploring a planet named Brachen." Permac paused to gauge Karak's reaction and noted a marked raising of the man's eyebrows. "You might know of it. Anyway, Linsora is an archaeologist. She found some pieces of glass that formed a star chart. We realized that our relationship would never be accepted by either the Mercantile or our families. We also knew that Brachen was where Tokor had landed just after he left Khizara – we found an old projection of Tokor, in fact. The star chart didn't lead to Tokorel. We thought it might lead to a place where we'd find welcome. Linsora thought it might lead to some answers about the Lost Fleet that vanished two hundred years ago. We bought that skiff out there from our ship's captain. And, here we are."

Permac was pleased. He had told the tale truthfully. As Moragh had said, not deception, just not telling everything.

"Remarkable," Karak said. "You are both either very brave or very foolish. Perhaps a little of both. But how did the other ship crash?"

As Permac's thoughts raced, trying to find a way to explain Moragh, Linsora spoke up, "Another Tokorellan we have met seems to be following us. After we crashed, he brought us to his ship and tried to convince us to go with him. We got away, but as his ship was taking off this other ship, the one that crashed, came along and got in the way. The other Tokorellan's name is Moragh, by the way. That's why we were startled to find that your name is Moragh, too."

"Moragh, you say? Is that his surname?"

"We only know him as Moragh," Linsora said.

"And he has gone?"

Linsora and Permac exchanged glances. "We don't know for sure."

"Remarkable," Karak said again. "Well, my story meshes with yours at some points. I do know of Brachen. My ancestors, the ancestors of all the people on Hakai, were there with Tokor. Most of the people who settled Hakai were part of the Khizaran fleet pursuing Tokor. I assume that's the Lost Fleet you mentioned. Tokor somehow had the means to create wormholes for ships to travel through. I admit, until we began to receive visitors, that part of the tale struck me as implausible. Somehow, both Tokor and the Khizarans arrived in this part of space, but how they did it...well, that was a mystery."

Karak refilled glasses with cold tea and passed around a plate of small sugary cookies.

"From what I understand of current technology, the wormholes Tokor could create lasted longer, but were more unstable. The Khizarans followed Tokor's path through one and ended up near Hakai. They established some settlements here, but continued looking for Tokor and a way to return to Khizara.

"Since you've come from Brachen, you know that the distance between there and Hakai could be covered in about a year with the ships the Khizarans had. We're told they had fuel sufficient for ten years of exploration. They were in their eighth year when they found Tokor on Brachen. They saved Tokor from an attack on Brachen. Do you know about that?"

"The image of Tokor we found on Brachen detailed the attack," Permac said between nibbles on a cookie.

"Ah, good." Karak touched Permac lightly on the shoulder. "Now Permac, you as a Tokorellan hold Tokor in high regard, so please forgive what I am about to say. I only relate what our history has taught. We are told that Tokor invited the Khizarans to join him. Some did. Some wanted only to return to Khizara. Some of Tokor's people wanted to return to Khizara, too. That surprises you, I'm sure, but after so many years with only more uncertainty in front of them, going home must have seemed attractive.

"Tokor promised to show the Khizarans the route back to Khizara. He outfitted their ships with his new technology and sent some of his people along to help with the navigation - I suspect they were people who wanted to return to Khizara. My own surname, Moragh, is that of a follower of Tokor who traveled with the Khizarans. Why they didn't demand the coordinates back to Khizara at that point, I can't say. Maybe they thought they could find it, maybe they fell under Tokor's influence, I don't know. But, they came back to Hakai to collect their families. Tokor had promised to meet them, replenish their special fuel, and tell them how to get to Khizara.

"When they arrived at the meeting place, they found only a solar system of uninhabitable planets, no one to meet them, and no idea where Tokor had gone. Worse, their ships were low on fuel. There was just enough of the wormhole fuel for a trip back to Brachen and a return to Hakai. On Brachen, they created the star chart in hope that Tokor would find it. Our ancestors came to believe that Tokor abandoned them. Once back on Hakai, they were stranded. Their ships had no fuel and there was no way to obtain more. They could only wait for someone to find them."

"Karak, Linsora and I have discussed our own versions of history. We've found that the facts may be the same, but rationales and motivations are presented from different viewpoints," Permac said. "The Tokor I have learned about is not someone who would have abandoned your ancestors."

"However it happened, Permac, my ancestors were left here with no means of space travel," Karak said with some bitterness. "We have had little regard for Tokor. On the other hand, we have similarly little regard for Khizarans, with my apologies to you, Linsora. My ancestral history also berates them for never sending anyone to search for them."

"They disappeared," Linsora said. "When Tokor and the Khizarans weren't heard from, it was assumed they had all died. 200 years ago, Khizarans didn't have wormhole technology either. Parties were sent out to search for them, but the wormhole Tokor and the Khizarans found must have dissipated."

"Probably true," Karak said. "Probably true. Nonetheless, ancient enmity is not easily overcome. It has become habit for my people to detest both Tokorellans and Khizarans."

"So where might that leave us?" Permac asked.

"Interesting question. Since, by virtue of your relationship you would not be accepted by either Tokorel or Khizara, my people may well embrace you as fellow outcasts."

"Huh!" Tayla appeared from the kitchen. She glared at Linsora.

"Tayla! If we are to join the Mercantile, we must…"

"Must what, father? Pretend we like everyone?"

"We must like or dislike on an individual basis only!"

The shimmer and the stucco of the outside wall vanished, revealing the sunlit expanse of desert outside.

Tayla said, "Mayra is here."

"Ah, Warel's mother," Karak explained. "We can continue after she's looked you over."

Mayra was a sturdy, dour looking woman. Any attempt Permac made to engage her in small talk or pleasantries was met with a scowl. She was the stereotypical Khizaran of Tokorellan tales. He remembered his mother's statement about Khizarans living in damp mud huts. All the buildings he'd seen on Hakai were a sort of stucco. 200 years ago, they may well have been mud huts. He wondered what the relationship might be in the tangle of histories.

With a grunt, Mayra completed her examinations. She walked to the place in the wall where the door was. The opening appeared and she strode out. Linsora and Permac waited, not daring to talk to each other, not daring to allow free rein to their emotions. Permac walked to the wall, but the door did not appear. Placing his hands on the wall, he could feel no door edge or handle.

As Permac walked away, the door appeared and Karak walked in.

"Mayra confirms what you said earlier, your injuries are minor and will heal. She does, however, advise rest and I for one am not inclined to argue with her," Karak chuckled. "I've lived next to her for fifteen years and don't recall ever seeing her smile. Makes me feel sorry for little Warel. At least his other relatives are friendlier. The suns are setting, let's sit outside and enjoy the evening. If Mayra looks outside, at least she'll see that you're both sitting down."

The outside air remained hot, but not as oppressive as it had been earlier. A sweet fragrance filled the air that, combined with the dry dust smell of the desert, gave the atmosphere a feeling of serenity. Permac sniffed the air.

"I know that smell!" He said, sniffing again. "It's chikara!"

"Yes indeed, and that's part of the end of my story," Karak said. "I'll have some chikara brought to us shortly."

They settled onto benches outside Karak's house. "Where was I? Well, my ancestors fared well here on Hakai. It has only been in my lifetime that Hakai was re-discovered, or revisited, by Tokorellans. They claim to have stumbled on us, but a great deal of suspicion exists about their intentions. Some Hakains believe they have known where to find us all along." Karak stretched, "But we now have ships and fuel again, so complaints have been few."

"You said your recent history is troubled. Does that have something to do with the Tokorellans and those others?" Linsora asked.

"Ahh, that answer is difficult. Our first Tokorellan visitors arrived, about ten years ago. Not until this past year have the problems begun. Every society has its misfits, those who prefer to take instead of work. We've never been immune from that, but recently, with the fast input of advanced technology, the misfits have become better armed and bolder. And perhaps more organized. We just call them the Others, people who are outside our society. I am the leader of this community. Leaders of all the communities meet regularly, presided over by each leader on a rotating basis. But without one leader, we've never been truly united. There is too much indecision regarding how to deal with the Others. To be honest, the role of Tokorellans in all of this is unclear."

"Is that where you learned to speak Merc? From the Tokorellans?"

"Merc...oh, Mercantile Standard," Karak seemed to stumble, "Yes, being isolated for so long, our language has evolved into something quite unique. Tokorellan has evolved as well. When the first visitors arrived, we were speaking different variations of Khizaran. Most confusing until we were provided with instruction on Mercantile Standard."

Warel pranced toward them carrying a covered basket. Skulking behind him was a small group of children, craning their necks to catch a glimpse of the strangers.

"Here's the chikara," Warel said.

"Thank you," Karak said, "Would your friends like to meet our guests?"

"Can they? Really?"

"Do you mind?" Karak asked Permac and Linsora. "You're a novelty."

Permac nodded and was surprised to see that Linsora had both her hands free to shake hands with each child. She crouched down to be at eye level with them, smiling and chatting. Permac's bruised leg didn't allow him to squat. Even if it had, he didn't think he would have. Children always struck him as somewhat alien creatures. Too much energy and untamed emotions. Linsora actually seemed disappointed when they left.

"I didn't know you had such a rapport with kids," Permac said.

"Did your mother tell you that the nasty Khizarans who live in damp huts would eat children? Little Khizarans have to come from someplace, too," she laughed. "Sorry. I do like them. All that boundless energy and curiosity. Wonderful."

"They do have energy," Karak sighed. "Here, Warel brought chikara. You will enjoy it Permac. I take it you've never had any, Linsora?"

"I've only had it once before. The Tokorellan who followed us here had some on his ship," Linsora said. "Permac has tried every fruit he could find trying to duplicate the flavor."

"Chikara is unique," Karak said. "Please, sit down and enjoy some."

Permac sensed an odd anticipation in Karak. He was tempted to stop Linsora from eating the chikara. Something felt wrong. They had eaten chikara on Moragh's ship with no ill effect. He could find no reason to stop her. The round, fist-sized fruit grew on vines and was a staple in Tokorellan cooking.

After it was peeled and the mass of seeds in the middle removed, chikara could be roasted, stewed, baked, fried, or eaten raw. Nearly every meal had some version of it. The plate in front of them had dewy pink wedges of lightly steamed chikara. Permac's mouth watered, he knew it would be sweet, just slightly crunchy and perfect.

He was on his fourth piece when Linsora, who had eaten five, gripped her head with a loud groan. The groan increased in volume. Permac sensed panic and confusion.

"Linsora! What's wrong?"

She screamed, "My head! Images. All over. Too fast." She slumped forward, holding her head.

Permac tried to influence her to feel calm.

"No," Karak said. "Don't send her anything more."

"More!" Permac shouted. "What do you mean more? What have you done to her?"

"I have done nothing," Karak said. "This will pass, but it might take some time."

"Do something! If you know what's happening, do something about it!" Permac grabbed Karak by his shirt and shook him. "If you have harmed her…"

"I have not. She will be fine," Karak said. He pried Permac's hands from his shirt. As though dismissing the situation, he turned to walk away. Permac blocked his way. Reaching into a pocket in his sleeve, Permac grabbed a small knife. Face to face with Karak, he held the point at Karak's neck. Karak was steadfast, unwilling to stem whatever was causing such pain to Linsora. He nodded toward Linsora. "You want to help her? Expand your conception of influences." Karak pushed the blade away.

Permac knew that both he and Linsora were being tested. He also knew he had been given no choice but to participate. He closed his eyes, concentrating on Linsora. He could not stop what she was feeling, could not calm her. She said something about images. What he felt from her was terrible and overwhelming. 'Images', she said. He had only sent emotions to people, never images. He tried to place a picture of a seacoast in his own mind – the kind of picture Linsora had described as her favorite place on Khizara. With effort and full concentration, he sent the image to Linsora. His sense of reality and place wavered. He lost all awareness of anyone around him other than Linsora. They were both on the beach, warm sun on their backs, cool ocean breezes on their faces. He could taste the salt of the ocean. He smelled the seaweed and acrid scent of rotting sea creatures. He heard waves lapping at the broad sandy shore, surrounding their bare feet with green foam then sucking the froth back out to sea.

Slowly, his focus returned. Linsora was slumped over. Her groans had stopped, but she remained with her head in her hands, breathing heavily. Permac was shaking and covered with sweat.

"Very well done," Tayla said, brushing past her father to stand between Permac and Linsora. "I think he can be trained after all, Father." She reached up and ran a fingertip across his cheek, "Purple really doesn't suit him."

Permac pushed her hand away with an angry swipe.

"If there is training to be done, I will do it." Karak said. With a sour look, Tayla turned on her heels and left.

Permac looked at Karak. Few people he had ever met made him angry. Fewer still were people he feared. He didn't like the combination. He didn't like that in two days two people with the Moragh name had the same effect on him, and both of them with vague references to some kind of training. "No one is going to train me to do anything. I am no one's puppet. My will is my own. No one, including you Karak, will be my keeper!"

Karak's gaze faltered. Permac thought he felt a twinge of apprehension. Slight and swiftly gone, but something to hold on to.

"Feel free to go inside when you are ready," Karak said. "The doors to your room will open for you."

Permac held Linsora until the suns set and many galaxies of stars shone above them. Every muscle in her body was tense and coiled for action. He cradled her head against his chest. Slowly, she relaxed and pressed closely to him.

"I liked the ocean," she said. "Thank you."

"So did I," he said, kissing the top of her head. "Let's go there. Let's live there forever and never think about history again."

"What happened?"

"Something to do with the chikara, I think."

"Maybe I'm allergic to it."

"I don't think it's that simple," Permac said. "Karak knew it was going to happen, he expected it. Then he sat back to watch how I would help you."

"And you did," she said. "I'm so tired, Permac. I can't try to figure this out tonight."

"Karak said we have a room inside. I don't think we have any choice tonight, but we'll find someplace else to stay tomorrow, even if it's back at the skiff."

Together they went inside and found their room. As Karak said, the door to their room opened for them. When it closed behind them, Permac felt a pang, but the door opened when he stepped back to it. He tried it several

111

times. By the time he threw himself on the bed, Linsora was already snoring.

In spite of his fatigue, Permac couldn't sleep. He walked around the room, tried the door a few more times, and finally stretched out on the cool floor. Permac flattened his spine into it to ease his tension. He ran his hand over the surface of the floor. *It's not a floor*, he thought. *It's dirt. Just hard packed dirt. It smells like home.*

He crawled into bed next to Linsora and drifted into a light sleep. Images of Tokorel floated through his dreams, the smell of the damp ground after a light rain. The smell of chikara. The ground and the chikara. He woke with a start. *The ground*, Permac thought. *Of course!* He leaned over and nipped at Linsora's neck. In her sleep she smiled and moaned a low growl. She turned and dug her claws into his neck and then his back. For the next hour, they were as quiet as any Khizaran couple could be. They fell asleep in each other's arms and rested peacefully throughout the remainder of the night.

Two shadowy figures spoke in whispers outside the house.

"Keep your voice down!" Karak hissed. "They're suspicious enough as it is."

"And you think they'd notice?" Gordek nodded toward the door that had resounded with growls and cries of pleasure just moments before. "Besides, this is your house. You're allowed visitors."

"In the middle of the night?" Karak asked. "I've told you what I know of them and I'm as intrigued as you are. They will suit my needs better than yours. You will not meet with them and that is my final word about it!"

"We had a deal!" Gordek muttered. "And she's Khizaran."

"NO!" Karak said, too loudly. He lowered his tone again to a whisper. "Permac may be able to help me. He has potential - of that I am sure. I am also fairly certain that he is not one who will be controlled with ease. The woman is a different story. She has latent abilities that could be remarkable if developed properly. Even before she had chikara, she had some awareness of being influenced. She told Tayla she could taste them. They must both be handled carefully. Do you understand? Carefully and slowly."

"I have no intention of manipulating them. I just need their help with…"

"I know what you need their help with and the answer is still no!" Karak set his jaw and narrowed his eyes.

"Karak, I have taken things slowly, as you requested. I have spent more time on this planet than I ever intended to. You have benefited from my presence, do not deny that. My small band has created the discord you wanted. My group and I will leave, then you can promise, and deliver, the end of the dreaded raids by the Others. That alone will get you the power you want. You don't need them." Gordek glanced toward the now quiet house, "You don't need both of them. Keep him. I'll take the woman."

112

"I don't think your interest in her is confined to archaeology, Gordek," Karak looked disgusted. "You're old enough to be her father!"

"None of your business, my friend. I just want my share of the benefits of our agreement."

"Have you conveniently forgotten about the stores of chikara you have on your ship?" Karak hated the man. He would welcome sending him away from Hakai, but he was not willing to let him take Permac and Linsora. They would be wasted with Gordek. Their talents prostituted. Or worse, Gordek just might achieve his goals with their help. Karak had his own goals in mind and they didn't include Gordek. He had told Gordek only part of what he knew of the visitors. Flooding the woman's mind with images had indeed been a test, but it was also a ruse. While she was occupied with new sensations, images of her own history were open to him, confirming what her name had suggested.

"I have not forgotten," Gordek said. "Have you forgotten the instructors I provided to teach all of you Mercantile Standard? The engineers for your ships? I'd say you're on the owing end right now."

"Gordek," Karak started, "it's late and I'm tired. I'm tired not only from a long day, but I'm tired of you. Now leave my home or I will have you removed by force. And if you or any of your party ever set foot on my land again you will not live long enough to boast of it. Is that clear?"

"You are making a terrible mistake, Karak. Mark my words."

"Threats?" Karak looked up. His eyes were narrow and his face hard. "I welcome your attempts to carry them out."

CHAPTER 13

The suns rose long before Linsora and Permac stirred. They found food on the table and all the doors open. Karak and Tayla were gone, as was their ground transport. Linsora suggested they rummage around the house, but Permac said there was no line at all between rummaging and snooping. Besides the general principle of respecting the privacy of their host, he didn't want to be caught in the act when Karak did return.

Warel stopped by several times with baskets and trays of food. Mayra might not be the most talkative or pleasant of people, but she was an extraordinary cook. Permac noted that none of the food contained chikara.

"Is there a place to wash clothes?" Linsora asked the boy. "I brought my things from the skiff, but I'd like to get the other ones cleaned."

"I'll take them for you," he said. "There's a place in town where we bring ours."

"We'll go with you," Permac said.

"Uhh, well, I ahh," Warel blushed.

Linsora hugged the boy. "It's okay, Warel. We're still tired anyway. When you come back, I'll teach you how to play backgammon."

Warel grinned and trotted off with the clothes trailing in the dust.

"He's not supposed to let us leave," she said to Permac.

"So I gathered. You like him, don't you?"

"Are you jealous?" she laughed.

"No more than you are of Tayla." Permac realized too late that his attempt at a joke was very much misguided.

"What do you mean by that?"

"Uhh, well, I ahh," he said.

Linsora poked Permac in the chest. "That's the same thing Warel just said. Okay, I'll admit that Tayla annoys me."

"Annoys you?"

"Yes. And the next time she touches you, I just might be annoyed enough to break her fingers. I think she has the same affection for me."

"Uh-huh," Permac said. He sat on a grassy patch of ground and pulled Linsora down next to him. "Well, I've been thinking about what happened yesterday. I don't have a complete explanation yet, but I do have an idea."

"Good, because I don't."

114

"The ground here smells like the ground on Tokorel. You've done enough digging in dirt, you must have noticed that different places smell different."

"I suppose so. I never thought about it much, though."

"Neither did I, but it hit me last night that this place smells like home. I've never been anywhere else that reminds me of home as much as Hakai. Not just the air, but the ground. It has the same color, the same texture, the same scent. And all of that has something to do with chikara."

"And the chikara had something to do with what happened to me yesterday?"

"You're sure you never heard of chikara on Khizara?"

"No. The first time I heard of it was from you."

"What about the smell?"

"I don't know, maybe," Linsora tried picture her home world. "Maybe in the country. My mother's land is in the country, quite a distance from the city. I loved going there. It smelled like trees and wild animals. Sometimes when the wind was right, it smelled like flowers."

"Is it anywhere close to where Tokor lived?"

Linsora looked surprised. "You know, the place where Tokor lived is fenced off. It's called the Forbidden Area and no one's allowed in. The far end of my mother's land borders it, though. She never took us there. Why?"

"Okay, Tokor was from Khizara, right? He developed his abilities there. On Brachen, Tokor said he trained the Khizarans. If he could train them, that means all Khizarans can be trained. Both Moragh and Karak mentioned something about training, too." Permac scooped up a handful of dirt and let it slide between his fingers. "I'm beginning to think that basic Tokorellan abilities don't have much to do with training or a genetic predisposition. I was never trained. I think it has more to do with something in the chikara. More to the point, something to do with the soil the chikara grows in. If Tokor was from the Forbidden Area on Khizara, maybe that's where the chikara grew – maybe that's why it's a forbidden area."

"Forbidden so that no one else would eat the chikara." Linsora, who had been reclining against Permac, sat up. "What about me, then? When I ate the chikara on Moragh's ship, nothing happened. And the Ghoranth – Tokor said he tried to train them, but couldn't."

"You didn't eat much of it, though. Last night, you had how many pieces? Four or five? Maybe you have to build up whatever it is in your system. On Tokorel, even babies are fed chikara. The Ghoranth?" Permac shrugged. "No idea. Maybe…maybe there is some genetic aspect to it."

"Hmm. None of the food from Mayra has chikara does it?"

"No, and I've wondered at that. Maybe she doesn't approve of whatever Karak is doing."

"What about the greens and salad, are there chikara leaves in them?"

"No, the leaves are toxic. The plant is called tejina, only the fruit is called chikara. We eat the fruit, but not the leaves."

"Animals and insects must eat the fruit sometimes. What happens to them?"

"Nothing. Only people are affected. We can send basic emotional influences to animals, but I've never heard of animals sending influences."

"Maybe we should visit Mayra," Linsora said. "When Warel comes back, let's ask him to take us to see her."

Mayra greeted them with her customary scowl.

"Mayra," Linsora started, hoping Mayra might react more positively to a female-to-female conversation. "We want to thank you personally for all the food you've sent. It's been delicious. I want to tell you, too, how delightful Warel is. I've enjoyed talking to him."

A brief flash of a smile crossed Mayra's face at the mention of her son. "You're welcome. I'm proud of him." She peered at her visitors, seemed to struggle with some internal conflict. Finally she said, "Come in please. I don't think you came here just to compliment me on the food and my son."

"Actually, you're right," Permac said as he and Linsora perched on chairs. The interior of Mayra's house was almost identical to Karak's. "You probably know what happened to Linsora yesterday. We think it has something to do with chikara - maybe with the ground the chikara grows in? We also noticed that the food you've sent today hasn't had any chikara. Forgive me, I know Karak is your neighbor, but I don't trust him to tell us the truth."

"Karak is my neighbor, not my friend," Mayra said. She sighed and fiddled with some ornaments on a side table. "You're Tokorellan?"

"I am," Permac said. "Linsora is Khizaran."

"I've only met a few Tokorellans and even fewer Khizarans."

Mayra studied their faces, waiting for a reaction. Linsora squinted. Permac blinked.

"You've met Khizarans?" Linsora asked.

"To be honest, I'm not sure. They said they were Khizaran. And, well…" Mayra looked around as though searching for some way to escape from what her visitors wanted to know. "…well, their abilities were…they had mental abilities like Hakans and Tokorellans, but at a limited level." She threw her head back into the cushiony back of her chair. "My dears, I don't know how or why you came here, but the answer to your simple question has layers of

116

complexity."

"How could Khizarans have…" Linsora began.

"As I said, it's a many layered story. You asked about the chikara. I'll tell you what I know because you've guessed some already. I'd rather you have the truth than conjecture and, unlike Karak, I don't like secrecy." Mayra paused. "Still, I should not be telling you."

"We don't want to put you in any danger," Permac said.

Mayra smiled. "You're in more danger from knowing than I am from telling. I don't know what you might do with the information. Hopefully, nothing. Hopefully, you'll take it, understand it, find a pleasant home somewhere and raise lovely children." She patted Permac's arm as her smile faded. "But, somehow I doubt you'll take that bit of advice."

Permac and Linsora perched on the edge of their chairs while Mayra refilled each cup with steaming tea. She settled into her chair. Steam curled around her face. Permac thought for a moment she had forgotten about them.

"Marya," he whispered.

"Yes, I know you're waiting. The best way is directly, I suppose. You said you suspect the chikara has something to do with what happened to Linsora. The mental abilities of Tokorellans and Hakans comes directly from chikara. The fruit has microscopic organisms in it. When you eat the fruit, you eat the microbes. They're harmless parasites and remain alive inside the body, lodged in various places, including the brain. I'm sure you don't want a full biology lesson, but Khizaran physiology is especially conducive to them. Once a certain level is present, the ability to receive and transmit emotions emerges."

"So I've been eating these things all my life?" Permac shuddered.

"Since before you were born, assuming your mother ate them," Mayra smiled.

"What about me, then?" Linsora's voice was tiny, breathed with dreadful hope that what she had heard wasn't true. "Last night…"

"Usually, people are fed chikara in slowly increasing quantities, starting with only a bite or two. You were allowed to eat as much as you wanted. The initial invasion of the organisms can be painful. I didn't approve, but Karak is powerful. What he commands, he gets." Mayra sniffed.

"It was more than painful," Linsora said, "There were pictures, images, falling on top of each other. I felt like my head was about to explode."

"Images?" Mayra leaned forward, "You didn't have any abilities before this?"

"No," Linsora said.

"Wait, you did though," Permac said. "You could taste something when you were being influenced. That's not usual. And your mother's land on Khizara bordered the land where Tokor lived. It's possible that you picked up some small vestige of the abilities just by being so close." He looked at Mayra for confirmation.

"It's possible," Mayra said. "But images. Those had to have been sent to you by Karak. But, still, for you to be aware of images at your stage of development – well, that's generally an advance skill. Can you send and receive images, Permac?"

"Until yesterday, I didn't think so. I'd never even heard of anyone doing it. I did send images to Linsora, though." Permac reached for Linsora's hand. He felt as betrayed as when he first saw the image of Tokor. "Mayra, this does make sense, but I've never heard anything about it. People on Tokorel must know this. How come I don't?"

"I can't speak for Tokorel, but here on Hakai the information is specialized, passed on only to those with a need to know. I suspect some dishonesty among the original settlers led to the secrecy. Tokor's people might have collected the chikara from Brachen without telling the Khizarans why. Then, once everyone had the abilities, it became something natural but knowledge of the microbes was passed along selectively."

"Amazing. Someone told me that people on Tokorel weren't being deceived, they just weren't being told everything. He was talking about something else, but if these microbes can be kept secret…" Permac gulped too-hot tea and winced. "The people I've seen here on Hakai – their eyes don't change color like mine do."

"That's where training comes in. Most people are content with whatever native abilities they have. But as with any ability, some people hone them to a higher level."

"So, once you have them in your system, they don't go away?"

"They seem to become somewhat dormant if time passes without ingestion of more chikara, but I don't think they ever go away," Mayra said. "Tokor found that the organisms could be transferred from one orchard to another. The story is that he had quite a large area on Khizara and when he left, he took both chikara and soil with him and started planting on Brachen. Once the plants are established, the microbes are found in the soil, too. Even the dirt is interesting. We use it as part of our building material. A small amount applied as paint or paste on the walls gives them a shimmering appearance. We call it kagamite. One of our villages uses a rather unique concoction. When viewed from a distance, you can't see the houses at all. The kagamite assumes the same properties as the surrounding landscape. It's almost as if the houses disappear. If you stay here a while, I'll take you there for a visit. Is it used on Tokorel?"

"I've never seen it," Permac said. "It's beautiful, though. I wonder if

118

different soils on different worlds allow for different properties."

"Mmm, could be."

"And the chikara came here from Brachen?" Linsora asked.

"Ah, yes. My ancestors didn't have any with them when they came back to Hakai to pick up their families. After they failed to meet Tokor, they went to Brachen to clear out all they could find of what remained of the orchards there. They returned to Hakai and planted here. They wanted to be ready for their eventual encounter with Tokor, so they could meet him on equal footing."

"I found a star chart on Brachen and the course was marked with plants Permac said he recognized as tejina. We found some unknown microbes in the plants."

"Sounds reasonable," Marya said. "They wanted to leave a clear message for Tokor about who had left the star chart and where they had gone."

"But they didn't find the chart. It was broken when I found it," Linsora said.

"Well, that's still a matter for discussion. Our first off-planet visitors were Tokorellan. How would they have known where to find us if they hadn't known all along?"

"And the Khizarans?"

"Ah, brought here by Tokorellans, my dear. I only know the politics of Hakai and even here alliances are volatile. I can only imagine what scenes are played out on a larger scale."

"And Karak is in the middle of it all," Permac said. "What's he up to?"

"Karak. He's our community leader, but he wants more. He's well on the way to becoming the leader of all Hakai. The recent attacks by the Others has given him a reason to call for more centralized organization than we ever had before, including a police force that's conveniently under his control. Now that we have space travel capability again, he has visions of leading Hakai to both Tokorel and Khizara."

"That's insane!"

"Ambitious, but not insane," Maya said. "He has contacts on both Tokorel and Khizara already. Rumor has it that his daughter, Tayla, has a Khizaran lover with political influence. He's feeling more and more secure all the time. But, personally, I believe he's more trusting of his allies than he should be. Anyone willing to betray their own homeland would most certainly not hesitate to betray Karak."

"It sounds like Tokorel and Hakai have a lot in common," Linsora said, not hiding her contempt for either one very well.

"We do. And I'm sure there's a lot we could learn from each other," Mayra said. "And I'm sure we'd benefit from official contact with Khizara as well. But the emissaries we've had from Tokorel have been frustrated by our lack of centralized government. What the leader of one village might agree to, the leader of another might not."

"So Karak wants to be the one making decisions for everyone, is that it?" Linsora asked.

Mayra nodded.

Permac wiped his palms on his jacket. His hands were sweaty and shaking. "His surname is Moragh. Do you know if others with that name are involved?"

"No. Why?" Mayra cocked her head. "I do know that the Moragh family was split at the time of Tokor. They left Khizara with Tokor, but some ended up here."

"Someone named Moragh has been following us," Permac said. "At least he's been following me. When we crashed, he met us out there in the desert and tried to take us away with him."

"Maybe you should have accepted his offer," Mayra said.

Permac and Linsora walked slowly across the grass to Karak's house.

"Why do you suppose Karak is interested in us?" Linsora asked.

"We conveniently landed in his lap," Permac said. "A Khizaran and a Tokorellan could be useful to him. Especially two who aren't pleased with attitudes on their home worlds."

"Only if we agree to work with him. He hasn't exactly done a lot to make us trust him." Linsora kicked at a clump of dirt. The thought of the tiny organisms she might have released into the air made her shiver. "Maybe we should have gone with Moragh. Maybe we shouldn't have come here in the first place."

"Are you, of all people, saying you regret something?" Permac chuckled.

"I'm allowed, you know," she said. "We found the Lost Fleet of Khizarans who didn't follow Tokor. We know what happened, more or less."

"We don't know why they didn't connect with Tokor, though." Permac shook his head, "I just can't believe that he simply abandoned them."

"From all you've said about Tokor, and from that projection, I have to agree. He's not as good as you've been told and he's not as bad as I've been told," Linsora said. "I just feel very small. The farther we go, the more we learn, the more questions there are and the worse the whole situation seems. I can't believe that Karak is a real threat to Tokorel and Khizara - Hakai seems so backward. If he has contacts there, who knows? Like Mayra said, it's not hard to find people willing to destroy a society to meet their own needs. No matter what kind of plan is for sale, someone will buy it. Look at us. We're subversive in a way, too."

Permac looked at her, raising his eyebrows.

"Does that surprise you? Or are you surprised it took me so long to realize that?" she asked him.

"A little of both. The whole affair on Carratia wasn't exactly lawful. I wouldn't call it subversive, though."

"We came here out of curiosity. Part of that was a desire to avoid the Carratians, I'll admit. But I think we both hoped to bring new information to both Tokorel and Khizara. Maybe to play a part in reconciling our worlds. That's no small thing. It's not a bad thing, either, but look at the histories of every world out there. How much chaos has been created by people who wanted to do something good?"

Permac wrapped Linsora in his arms, "A lot less than by people who just want to advance their own fortunes. We can't change what we've done. Look, we accomplished something on Brachen. The Carratians might not be as quick to dismiss artifacts once Haavens is done with them. It's the same thing now. We're picking up bits and pieces, like scattered artifacts. We just need to stay alive long enough to get the information to someone who can do something with it."

"What about Moragh's ship? Remember what Mayra said about the kagamite and the village that you can't see? Moragh's ship seemed to disappear, too. Tokorel doesn't have kagamite, no one here seems to know Moragh, but Karak's surname is Moragh. And did you notice how Karak hesitated when I asked him where he learned Merc? I don't think the Tokorellan visitors taught them everything, especially if they haven't been here much" Linsora rested her head on Permac's chest. "I feel like we've both stepped into a mound of chikara fertilizer."

They agreed not to let Karak know the details of their chat with Mayra. Late into the night, Permac woke to hushed voices and scuffling sounds in the main hall of the house. He rolled out of bed, pulled on clothes, and left Linsora snoring peacefully.

CHAPTER 14

Linsora opened her eyes. Bright light filled the room, filtered through the walls. She wasn't surprised when she turned over and Permac wasn't there. She stood up and stretched. Safe. She knew Permac was safe. He was coming. She didn't question how she knew. Life tasted light and airy. The wall opening appeared and a small fabric bag flew through, landing with a tinkling sound.

"Permac? What's this?"

She opened the bag. Inside were tiny jewels in every color of the rainbow. They smelled delicious. She licked one. Intense sweet fruit flavor, with just a hint of sour.

"These are wonderful! Where did you get them?" She felt buoyant, rested and peaceful. "Permac?"

"Good morning," he said, slightly out of breath.

"Morning. Where have you been?" Linsora asked.

"I woke up early and went into town…"

"They let you do that?" Linsora asked. "Did you run all the way?"

"Run? No. They have no reason to stop me. Where could I go? What could I do?" Permac asked. "I wandered around the marketplace. Everyone seemed to know that I was one of the visitors. They gave me some samples. Here, I brought you some pastries and meat." He unwrapped several packets. The aroma made Linsora's stomach rumble. She ate while Permac talked. "They said that I could barter services for food. I could help them with their new ships. We can live comfortably here!"

"What?" Linsora said, "Have you lost your mind? Look if we stay here, my eyes will be turning purple before long. You have to know I don't want that. I may love you, but I don't particularly love your abilities."

"Come back into town with me. Maybe you'll like it."

"Are Karak and Tayla back?"

"Uhh, no. I, uhh, haven't seen them," Permac said. "Have some breakfast then we'll walk into town."

Linsora shrugged. Permac wasn't usually out of breath after a walk and wasn't usually so obviously excited about much of anything. His even-tempered personality took most situations in stride. Still, she felt too good to worry about it. She ate, dressed, and followed Permac into the marketplace.

By the time they reached the village, the bag of candy was nearly empty. Dozens, possibly scores, of stalls lined the main street of the village. Instead of stores or shops, people on Hakai seemed to do business on a small scale, with family run stalls. Kids chased each other, people called to friends. *Not unpleasant*, Linsora thought.

"Can we get more candy?" she asked.

"Of course. We'll find some a little later. I want you meet someone first."

Permac ushered Linsora through the crowds, then turned down an empty side street. Around the corner, a door was open. Permac steered her toward it.

"Ah, welcome back. And you've brought Linsora. I'm Gordek." The man was as tall as Permac, perhaps twenty years older. His close-cropped hair was streaked with gray and his eyes did not seem like those of a man accustomed to smiling. He extended his hand to Linsora. Linsora offered her own, still sticky with residue from the last bit of candy she'd captured from the now empty bag.

"You are the suspicious one," Gordek said. He enclosed her hand in both of his.

"It's my nature," Linsora said coldly and yanked her hand away, leaving much of the stickiness on Gordek's damp palm.

"Well, I am the village historian. I understand you're an archaeologist. We might have many interests in common," Gordek wiped his hand on his shirtsleeve and threw on a cloak. "I have recently discovered some items you might find fascinating, in fact. It's just a short walk from here."

"Wonder if I could get some water?" she asked. The candy was gone but the sour undertone was more intense. Even spitting didn't get rid of it.

"There's a spring out there," Gordek said.

They trudged across the field between the village and some low hills, toward what looked like the mouth of one of several caves. The idea of entering a cave bothered her more than anything. The only other time she had been in a cave was on Khizara when she was young. She remembered feeling like the walls, all the masses of stone and earth over the cave, were closing in on her. Her friends had to carry her out after she fainted. Permac knew about her claustrophobia, why would he bring her to a cave, of all places. Linsora looked back toward the village. No one else was in the field.

"What brought you to Hakai?" Gordek asked casually.

"Didn't Permac tell you?" Linsora looked at Permac. His expression was bland. "We are mates and our families don't approve. We're looking for a new home."

"No," said Permac. "You can tell him the real reason."

The sour candy taste increased. She hadn't eaten any since they left the marketplace. She felt affection for Gordek, something like she had once felt for her father. Permac gazed at her, an expectant half-smile on his face. *Permac doesn't look like that*, she thought. *This Gordek's handshake was creepy. Too friendly. The sour taste...*

She casually stepped away from Permac. "Go ahead, Permac. After all, this trip was your idea."

"Yes, of course. But you are the archaeologist. You explain it so much better."

Linsora reached for a knife in the folds of her skirt. At the same time, she pivoted on her heels, planning to sprint back to the village. Everything about this was wrong. She launched herself forward, but Permac moved quickly to stand in her way. She shoved him, feinted right, and moved to her left. What little time that had taken allowed Gordek to grab hold of her arms. A sense of gray began to fill her awareness, a blanket dimming the field and her senses. She looked up at Permac. In the haze, his image wavered. He wasn't Permac. The sour taste filled her mouth. She shouted curses as complete darkness enveloped her.

CHAPTER 15

Linsora's head ached. Her body hurt. She was propped against the wall of a well-lit cave, her hands tied behind her back. The cave was humid and smelled of mildew. *At least it's big,* she thought. Someone was calling her name. She struggled to turn around. Three other bodies were on the floor not far from her, all of them with their hands bound. One was Permac.

"Linsora!" he whispered. "Are you all right?"

"What's my assistant's name?"

"What?" Permac looked at her like she had lost her mind.

"My assistant on the *Dominator.* What's her name?" Linsora was persistent.

"You mean Denub? Why? We're tied up and need to get out of here!" Permac grumbled.

"I needed to know it was really you. I had the displeasure of meeting someone who looked like you just before I was dumped here." Linsora looked around the room. "Do you sense anyone else here besides us?" she asked. "Is that Karak and Tayla over there?"

"I think so. I don't sense anyone else here," he said. "What happened?"

"I was going to ask you the same thing."

"Last night, I heard Karak and Tayla come in," Permac said. "I heard what sounded like a fight, scuffling. I went out."

"I didn't hear anything. Why didn't you wake me?"

"I never like waking you from a sound sleep, you aren't at your friendliest when you're drowsy," he said. "I thought I'd just poke my head out to see what was going on. I saw Karak and Tayla lying on the floor just before someone hit me. Next thing I knew, I was here."

"You never spoke to someone named Gordek?"

"No," Permac said. He scuttled across the floor toward her, "Here maybe we can get ourselves out of this before they... damn, someone's coming."

Permac looked towards the other side of the cavern. Linsora's eyes followed. Two men entered, Gordek and another man.

"Ah. You are both awake," Gordek said, "Ralain, untie them."

"You're the one I thought was Permac, aren't you?" She rubbed her wrists while Ralain untied Permac.

"Yes," Ralain said.

"It was an unfortunate means of introduction," Gordek said. "Karak would not allow us to talk to you. If I had tried to arrange a meeting with you openly, he and his people would have known about it and prevented it," Gordek said. "I intended only to get Karak and Tayla out of the way long enough to meet with you, but Permac here surprised us last night. We could only manage to take three and by the time we had secured them, the suns were up. We had to get you here quietly and make sure you didn't wander off while we made some arrangements."

"Well, you have all four of us here," Permac said. "Now what?"

"I can help you leave here," Gordek said, seeming pleased. "I'm Tokorellan."

Linsora scowled and planted her feet firmly, hands on her hips. Her jaw jutted toward Gordek. "You say that as though it was a positive attribute. You're not the first person to suggest we should leave Hakai. That's rather a compelling reason to stay. Except for Permac, I have not met one Tokorellan I would trust. I trust Permac with my life and my mind. I will continue to do so. But," and she indicated Gordek with an outstretched arm, "I do not trust you. And should I begin to trust you, the trust will be suspect since one of you probably placed it my mind. And I care little for your assurances otherwise."

Gordek stepped forward, Linsora held her ground. "I understand your hesitance, but…

"Hesitance?" Linsora laughed without humor. "I hope you know it's more than hesitance. I need some answers and I need them now."

"We may not have time right now," Gordek said.

"*I* have time. *I* have questions," she said. "Why should we want to leave Hakai? What makes it so dangerous? I have no great fondness for Karak and Tayla. I have no great fondness for Hakai. Permac and I no longer have a ship and we don't plan to stay on Hakai forever. But I do *not* like being told what to do. Not by them, not by you, not by anyone."

"We…"

"I am NOT finished, Tokorellan," Linsora barked. Both men stood silently, with Linsora leaning forward, the snarling, hissing center of everyone's attention. They seemed to be entranced by her show of contempt. She had avoided looking them directly in the eyes. She knew their influence did not depend on eye contact, but she found no reason to tempt fate. Looking into the depths of their eyes felt like looking into the eyes of a demon. As their silence continued, though, she did look. Nothing looked back. Their eyes held no recognition, no life. They seemed to be statues, but still warm and breathing.

"Permac!" She was startled to see the same expression on his face with one exception: his skin was sallow, his breathing short. He stood motionless briefly, then collapsed onto the floor. Linsora ran to him, felt for a pulse. His skin was cold but the pulse was regular. She didn't notice the shuffling sound behind her and yelped when a hand clamped down on her shoulder.

"Your turn," Tayla said. "And I will take great pleasure in doing it myself."

Linsora was squatting next to Permac. She spun on the balls of her feet, her elbow made sharp contact with the inside of Tayla's knee. Tayla cried out in pain and toppled backward to the dusty floor of the cave. Linsora looked up to see Karak disentangling himself from the ropes. She reached into her boots for knives, but Tayla twisted and grabbed a handful of hair, pulling her off balance and giving Karak enough time to reach them. He circled her neck with one powerful hand and pulled upward until she stood in front of him, gasping for air.

"I suppose I should thank you for distracting them," Karak said.

"Why wasn't I affected?" Linsora croaked. Her hands clutched Karak's at her throat.

"Your mind is still not completely developed in respect to what it could do. Not tuned to certain frequencies, shall we say. But feel fortunate in that. The power it required to stop them would have killed you. Nearly killed Permac, I'm afraid, but he'll recover. So will they before long."

"We should take him with us," Tayla stood over Permac.

"We can't right now. Do you know this place?"

"No, one of the caves we haven't checked yet," Tayla said. "There are hundreds in these hills."

"What Gordek has stolen has to be close by," Karak said.

Linsora's vision was dotted with specks from lack of oxygen. Karak tightened his grip on her throat and the specks swirled around until she was aware of nothing.

Linsora opened her eyes with a start. She had been overpowered twice in one day and didn't like it. She determined not to let it happen again. Permac was sitting up. Gordek and Ralain were rubbing their temples.

"I must apologize," Gordek said, stepping closer to Linsora. "We failed to monitor Karak and his daughter closely enough. I want to address all of your concerns, but Karak will return. We must be quick."

Linsora moved away from Gordek.

Gordek's expression of concern was replaced with something colder and harder. "I could have killed Karak and Tayla, but I didn't. Karak wants to control Hakai and thinks he can use you and Permac to help him. His vision is narrow and his plans for you are not benevolent. On my ship I have what I presume you came here to find – artifacts, records from the time of Tokor. You choose."

"Permac and I need to talk," she said.

"Do it while we're walking," Gordek said.

Gordek led the way and Ralain took up a position behind Linsora and Permac.

"Can you make any sense out of this?" she whispered.

"None. I'd rather travel with Moragh than these two," Permac said, tilting his head down toward Linsora. "I'm not thrilled to hang around Karak, either."

"This cave has to lead outside," she said.

"When it does, run. No matter what you feel, run. I don't think Gordek could keep up. The other one, Ralain, might."

"They might be more interested in getting away from Karak than catching us," Linsora said.

"I hope so."

The long cavern began to narrow, but not enough to make Linsora feel uncomfortable.

"Is that what you stole from Karak? The artifacts?" Linsora asked Gordek.

"Stole? No. I'm only taking what Karak gave me before he started to think he could have everything," Gordek said.

"Neither you nor Karak strike me as people willing to risk your lives for the sake of science and history," Linsora said. "What's so important about them? What's so important about us? Why are you so afraid of Karak?"

Gordek glanced back at her, "Do you ever have a normal conversation? You're either making statements or asking questions."

Linsora glared at him. She paused at a hole in the wall. The cavern was large enough, but the idea of going into a tunnel made her skin crawl. Permac took her arm and she tasted his sweet influences. She still didn't like tunnels, but at least she wouldn't have to be carried out.

"Keep walking," Gordek said. "Karak is powerful. The chikara on Hakai has remarkable properties."

"We know about the organisms," Permac said.

"Ah, not everyone does. Well, something about Hakai has resulted in a particularly effective strain. And some people just have a particularly strong native talent, like Karak and my friend Ralain back there," Gordek led them through a maze of tunnels. Each one led to a place where two or three other

128

tunnels forked off. Gordek stopped periodically to check for trail markers.

"As for the artifacts, both Karak and I believe they hold information about a place that has even more potent chikara. Someplace Tokor knew about. The artifacts were stored in these caves and, over time, were forgotten. Without space travel capabilities, it didn't matter to anyone. Now it does. I found them. I claim them. As for you two, well a Khizaran and a Tokorellan not known to be part of any political group could be valuable. You can go places, meet people that might not be open to someone else."

"We'd have to agree to do it," Permac said.

"Everyone has a price," Gordek said. "Everyone. Karak made an arrangement with me. I'd help him gain power here on Hakai - that was his price. I did that. He got greedy, though, and refused access to the artifacts after I found them."

The tunnel opened into a small cavern. Shards of broken pots lay strewn on the floor amid natural outcroppings of rock as tall as a man.

"We found heaps of artifacts in here," Ralain said.

"Where are they now?"

"On my ship, which is where we're going," Gordek pointed toward a tunnel on the other side of the cavern. "Behind those rocks. Hurry! Karak's coming!"

They were near the mouth of the tunnel when several people emerged from the tunnel they had just left on the other side of the cavern. Karak pushed toward the front of the party and pointed a long tube toward Gordek. Linsora pulled Permac behind the cover of the tall rock outcroppings.

Gordek seemed frozen.

Screaming, "No!" Ralain threw himself in front of Gordek just as a blue light flashed from Karak's tube.

Ralain staggered backward and fell to the floor. Part of the shock wave hit Linsora. She felt pressure in her head and a force great enough to slam her into Permac. She saw Ralain fall to the ground. Blood poured from his mouth. He was dead.

Permac pushed Linsora toward the tunnel.

"Linsora, run! I'm right behind you," Permac said.

Linsora had just entered the tunnel when a group of people running toward her forced her to step into Permac. They both stumbled back into the cavern. Gordek called for his people to fire on Karak.

Karak pointed the tube at Linsora. She threw herself to the side and pulled Permac with her. The blue flash ricocheted off the walls of the cave. Once more, they scrambled for the cover of the rocks.

"Those tubes, it's not an energy weapon, it's something else," Permac said. "Someone's coming. Help, I think. Not sure, but someone. Soon as he comes out on the other side, go to the tunnel and run. I'll be right behind you."

Some of Gordek's people were on the cavern floor, injured or dead. As were some of Karak's people. The generals, Gordek and Karak, still maintained positions behind what remained of their troops. Linsora peered around Permac and saw Tayla next to her father. The sound of running came from Karak's side of the tunnel. *One person, several running in unison, hard to tell.* Permac inched toward Gordek's side of the tunnel.

Linsora saw movement on Karak's side. Permac pushed her forward, told her to run. She reached for his hand. Warm, strong. The shelter of the tunnel was close when the cavern walls reflected another blue flash. Linsora was propelled forward, losing her grip on Permac. She stumbled.

"You!" Gordek yelled. "How…"

A white flash, a deafening roar. She dropped to the ground, unable to see or hear.

She felt her way along the rough cavern floor. As her vision returned, she saw an indistinct body sitting next to the tall rocks. She rubbed her eyes. Gordek clutched his head, rocked back and forth.

"Permac!" Her voice echoed. She called again as her focus returned. Except for her calls, the cavern was silent. No groans, no challenges, no excited breathing.

Permac lay on his back near the mouth of the tunnel they had run toward. In the center of the cavern more prone bodies littered the floor. Some slight movement on the far side, near another outcropping of rock caught her eye. She slithered along the floor toward Permac.

His eyes were open, but staring. "Come on! We have to get out of here."

She shook his shoulders. His head rolled to the side.

She tugged his hand, but the fingers were limp. She felt no pulse. "Permac! No!" Her screams rang against the cavern walls and returned to her as some kind of thin wail. "Wake up, damn it! Help me!"

She didn't see Gordek come up behind her. She felt him reach into a pocket on the sleeve of her jacket and grab a knife. She welcomed death. She lifted her chin, offering her neck. Instead of feeling the sting of the blade, she heard the hiss as her knife flew through the air coming to rest, embedded to its hilt, in Karak's forehead.

Gordek steadied Linsora. "I'm sorry. We have to go. Now."

"No! Permac needs help!"

"Linsora." Gordek gripped her arms and pulled her away. "He's gone. He's dead."

"He is not! No he is *not*! No!" She wriggled out of his grip and returned to Permac.

"Ralain is dead, too. We can grieve later." Gordek rose and waved toward his remaining allies, "You two. Over here! Help her get to the ship. Hurry!"

Linsora felt herself being rushed away from the scene of destruction. She glanced back at Permac's lifeless body. A blur of dark and light, tunnels and caverns, followed. On the far side of the hills, the tunnels ended in a blaze of sunlight. The suns were warm. Linsora felt no comfort. She felt no urge to run. She felt nothing. A space transport waited. Without protest, she climbed aboard.

The ascent into space always delighted Linsora. It meant the start of something new. The line between the atmospheric blue and the darkness of space was sharp. The line of goodbyes to those staying behind. Linsora never left anyone behind she regretted leaving. Except maybe leaving Khizara five years ago. Leaving her brother victorious. Leaving Kral. And now, leaving Permac. *Can't be.* She didn't notice the demarcation line. She only noticed the darkness and the sleek Khizaran battle cruiser the transport entered.

Gordek's light hand on her elbow led her through the sloping corridors to a spacious room toward the top of the ship. "If you need anything, just call."

"Wait!" Linsora knew that she was speaking, but the voice seemed to float from somewhere else. "Where are we going?"

Gordek looked at her. "Khizara." He looked a moment longer, waiting for any other questions, before he left the room.

Linsora slid down the wall to sit on the floor. She hadn't noticed the sour taste earlier, but she noticed now that it was gone.

Permac, she thought. *You can't be dead. Can't be. Can't be.*

She stared at her hands. "Where's the blood? There should be blood."

Her hands shook during the ship's first jump and didn't stop shaking when the jump was completed. The tremor took possession of her body. She was cold and no strong hands would ever warm her again. She drew her knees to her chin. What she later remembered of that night was gasping for breath between cries for someone who could no longer hear her.

CHAPTER 16

Cloaked, hooded figures lurked on the edges of gray landscapes in Linsora's dreams. When she turned to face them they would vanish, leaving behind the sound of laughter. Linsora chased the phantoms of Moragh and Karak and Gordek. In one dream she heard a voice behind her, taunting. One she had silenced in many dreams - one that had silenced her in many nightmares. One even her dream self did not expect to find in this context. She spun to face him and he did not vanish immediately. He remained long enough to smirk. Her half-brother Yokosh.

Linsora lunged toward him still screaming and awoke with a start. Cold dread made her stomach churn in her waking state as well as in the dream. The sound of her screams seemed to echo off the walls and return to her as hollow as the ghostly laughs. She reached out to Permac for comfort. The chill of the hard bed met her hand as memories of the waking horrors she faced flooded back. In her dreams, Permac had slipped away from her as he too chased the phantoms. He had promised --- no, even in her dream he had promised nothing. She had wanted him to promise that he would come back to her. He once told her she couldn't go off chasing phantoms alone. She had insisted she could. *Well, maybe I can, but I don't want to,* she thought.

She had no tears left. Her face felt stiff with the salty remains of those she had shed during the night. No need to wash them off. No need to feel anything anymore, except empty. Her mother didn't spend an undue period mourning her father, but then they had both lived long lives together. And her mother had died soon after her father, so perhaps she did mourn. Linsora had cried private tears at both of their deaths, she remembered, but never - *NEVER* - had she felt like this. There had always been hope, something bright and beckoning ahead. *Now, right now,* she thought, *there is nothing: no sadness, no anger, no prospect for joy, and most of all, no energy left to spend on anything.*

She closed her eyes and listened to the familiar soft humming of the ship. It reminded her where she was, but did nothing to comfort her. She wondered briefly what a Tokorellan was doing with a Khizaran ship, but she knew that nearly any kind of ship could be purchased given enough funds.

I should be content to think of Permac waiting to battle Moragh in hell. No, he'd be happier eating his chikara in some lovely afterlife place, she thought. *I never asked you which one you'd prefer, Permac. So much I never asked you.* She shook her head, trying to clear it before her entire body began to shake again. This Khizaran ship was small, much like ones she had served on years earlier. "I never told you about those years either, Permac," she muttered. She dug the claws of one hand into the palm of the other. Such a long time ago for everything - her brother, Khizaran ships, Carratia, the *Dominator*, Permac - but not much longer. She reached into a pocket for a long dagger and closed her eyes. The Khizaran suicide ritual was brief - a moment of preparation to dispel all regrets, a moment of farewell, a moment of ending. She didn't know what to expect in the afterlife. *Maybe I didn't ask you what you believed because I don't know what I believe*, she thought. *Well, no matter what anyone believes, what's there is probably a surprise. I hope I see you, Permac. That's the only hope left.* She felt warm, as though a soft blanket had been draped around her shoulders. *Is that you, Permac? Or is it adrenalin?*

She positioned the blade at her throat. The warmth intensified. Heat rose from her toes, through her stomach, and exploded in a blinding flame, engulfing her brain. An absolute, consuming rage tinted everything in her sight blood red. She barely noticed the sour taste in her mouth. A low keening rose from the depths of her lungs. Fueled by fury, the whine from between clenched teeth built to a loud, fully mouthed howl.

Linsora abandoned herself to the release. She picked up chairs and smashed them across tables. When no chairs remained, she pounded and kicked the tables until they lay in pieces. Nothing in the room was spared. Even the blankets were torn to shreds. She didn't hear the soft whoosh of the door opening.

Gordek stood poised to step inside, "I called for you, but when there was no answer, I thought I'd..." He surveyed the damage inside, noting the animal fury on the woman's face, her bruised and bloody hands.

"LEAVE ME!" she yelled, followed by a string of Khizaran epithets interspersed with the word Tokorellan. Gordek heard something solid crash against the door even before it closed. He remained outside her room, returning to the place where he had been leaning against the wall for some time. He smiled and nodded his approval.

Linsora hurled the leg of a chair toward the spot where Gordek had been. She stood panting in the middle of the ruins. One last unbroken slat from a chair caught her eye and she tossed it at the door with one last shout.

"Permac, I will kill your killers. And I assume your vow to take the life of Moragh. If I am to be left alive to feel, then I will feel only anger," she said. She had no gods who stood witness to her vows. She needed none.

She kicked some debris out of her way and decided she would demand new quarters from Gordek. He was nearby - she knew that. And he had sent the rage.

"I trusted you, Permac. I also trusted Kral. No, that was different. You didn't betray my trust like he did. Now, I can trust only my instincts. That's all anyone can ever do." Linsora felt a chill. She remembered Moragh. She had been only vaguely aware of both men on Moragh's ship. "He said something about the universe having eyes and ways to touch the mind. He said to beware of - of beggars, of the lowly, the obscured. He said something about running in circles, turning you inside out. Then he said to trust your instincts and your heart."

She was still breathing heavily from the exertion when her human half berated her ever so gently for the destruction. It also reminded her that she was taking on the responsibility for a great deal of blood. Her vow to kill Yokosh remained. Now Moragh. And would she rest while any of Karak's people remained alive? Might that not be too much for one person? She felt doubt fluttering about her resolve like gnats. Her hands tightened into fists and she concentrated on the wavering emotions, turning them back into a straight line of anger. Satisfied, she prepared to confront whatever lay in wait for her outside the door. She splashed water on her face and scrubbed it with a towel. One shard of the mirror above the sink remained in place, she stooped toward it.

Her face was pale, her hair a wild mess. Her eyes were red and...

"What..." Gordek had come back into her room.

"My eyes!" she whispered hoarsely, "My eyes are purple!"

"That's the natural progression of things." Gordek said. "You've been eating chikara. Even a focus on your own emotions might make your eyes change at this point."

"I don't want this!" Linsora shouted. With nothing left to break, she turned on Gordek. Her fists pounded on his shoulders, his arms, his chest.

He grabbed her wrists and sent calming thoughts into her mind. "You don't have a choice anymore. Accept it. Nurture it."

Linsora turned her head and spat on the floor. "I don't want your emotions. Do not - ever – use them on me again. They taste terrible."

Not all emotions tasted the same. Permac's were sweet, but those from Gordek left a lingering sour taste. She wrenched her hands from Gordek's grip and stepped back far enough to jab a finger toward him without making physical contact. "I hold you responsible for Permac's death. If you hadn't brought us to those caves, Karak wouldn't have attacked."

"You think Karak would have put up with either of you? He's...he was...used to having his orders carried out. He thought you and Permac both had remarkable potential. Maybe so, but he had little patience."

"And you have a lot? You sent that rage to me."

"To save your life. If I'd sent you happiness or tranquility, you'd have gone back to despair as soon as I left." Gordek folded his arms across his chest. Linsora thought he might be reaching for knives. In that same posture, she would have her hands on the hilt of at least one. She pivoted so that only her left side faced him, presenting a smaller target and allowing her right hand to find its own weapon. "I sent anger. The rage that caused this mess was yours. Suicides happen when there's no emotion left. I know Khizarans well enough to know that anger is the best way to keep any of you alive."

He's not going for a knife, she thought. *Maybe he doesn't even carry one. Maybe he thinks he doesn't need one. Permac didn't carry one until he met me. He's angry. He's trying not to show it. Am I sensing his emotions? No, damn it, of course he's angry. I just accused him of responsibility for Permac's death. I just hit him. Why work so hard not to show it? You're not very honest, are you?* She rolled her shoulders to relieve the tension of preparing for a fight that never happened.

"So I'm alive. Congratulations. Don't expect me to thank you."

Gordek's jaw moved from side to side. Linsora suspected he was used to having his orders obeyed without question, too. He and Karak must have been an interesting combination.

"You're alive. Permac's not. I regret that. I'm sorry for your loss."

"Are you?"

"I'm trying to be civil," Gordek hissed.

Linsora turned away. Maybe Gordek was being polite. Maybe. But he certainly felt no true regret that Permac was dead.

"I don't know quite how I'm supposed to act, Gordek. Too much has happened and none of it makes sense." That was the closest she intended to offer by way of apology.

"Of course. If there's anything I can…"

"No," she said. She didn't know what she wanted. Nothing. She wanted nothing and that option had been taken away. Death would have been a cowardly escape. She had lived alone most of her life and most of her life she hadn't minded. For a few months, though, she had shared her life with her opposite counterpart. She and Permac balanced each other. With the balance gone, she was left dangling, with nothing to reach for. *There's that nothing again*, she thought. *I told you not to take blood vows, Permac. If I did kill your killer, I wonder if I'd feel any better.*

"Linsora," Gordek spoke softly. Linsora realized she had been staring into space, into the great nothingness she felt. "I've had food prepared. At least have some tea."

"Sorry. I would like some tea, thank you."

They walked down the sloping corridor. Linsora tried to find something to reach for. *Khizara. We're going to Khizara.* "Did you say we're going to Khizara?"

"We should arrive in five days."

"You're Tokorellan."

"Yes. It's not difficult for a Tokorellan to blend into Khizara."

"I suppose not," she said.

The crew galley had been converted into a pleasant dining area. Linsora remembered the ships used by the navy as starkly utilitarian ships. Although this one hadn't been colored as Capt. Haavens' *Dominator*, the seats were comfortably padded and the tables spaced far enough apart to allow some small privacy while dining. She sipped the hot tea. *Easy for Tokorellans to blend into Khizara*, she thought. *Impossible for a Khizaran to blend into Tokorel. How many are there on Khizara? Tokorellans aren't being told everything. Khizarans know nothing.*

"How do you happen to have a Khizaran cruiser?" Linsora hoped it would sound like a logical enough question.

"Funds, pure and simple," Gordek stretched his legs out in front of him. Linsora thought he looked far too pleased with himself. "I provide commodities to those who want them."

"Without paying Mercantile royalties, I suppose."

"The Mercantile might not approve of all I do," he said.

"Weapons?" Her mind began to wrap around the ideas. "People?"

"People? I'm not a slave trader, if that's what you mean," he said.

"Tokorellans to Khizara is what I mean," she said.

"Toko…" Gordek looked confused, then he burst into a laugh. "I see. Yes and no. I've done it, but not on a large scale. Far too crude, Linsora. My business is based on subtlety and finesse. Much more effective than transporting an army."

"Weapons, then. Like those things Karak had. What were they?"

"Not weapons, either," Gordek said. He ran his thumb around the rim of his teacup, delaying his response. "Not like those. I don't know what they are or how they work. Nothing like I've seen, but intriguing. But, no, I'm not a weapons dealer, either. That's also far too crude. People who buy illegal weapons can't be trusted not to use them on the dealer."

"So why are you going to Khizara now? I don't think taking me home is high on your priority list." *You're far too impressed with yourself, Gordek. That's not an attractive trait. Not a smart one either. There's always someone better. The minute you think you're the best is when you let your guard down and some nobody can slit your throat.*

"To find something." Gordek sat up and leaned toward her. "And, with your help, I can do it."

"What makes you think I'll help you?" Linsora found herself leaning away from him.

"Like I said, I provide things people want. What is it you want?"

"Nothing you can get."

136

"You might be surprised."

"You think everyone can be bought? I just want to get on with my life."

"Do you? I've only just met you, but I think I can name several things you might want. You might want to be the one to find the origin answer. I can't give you that, but your own ship? A crew? Funding? That would be possible." Gordek said.

"What the hell are you looking for?" Linsora poured more tea. She pulled a small knife from her jacket and speared a slab of meat. Gordek didn't flinch when she produced the knife. *Maybe you are used to being around Khizarans*, she thought, *or maybe you're just arrogant. Either way you're dangerous — to yourself and to anyone associated with you. A ship and funding, sure. But if the price is being in your debt or on your payroll — sorry, no.*

"Something important," he said.

Linsora bit a chunk of meat and chewed. "It's not easy to negotiate when you're not telling me what your price is. How do I know you'd follow through with your end of the bargain?"

Gordek reached for a slice of meat. Linsora stabbed the same piece, positioning the blade between Gordek's fingers. Their eyes locked until Gordek slid his hand away.

"Reputation," he said, licking gravy from his fingers. "Defaulting on an agreement isn't something my clients would find impressive. And I don't think you're someone who'd suffer being cheated quietly."

"Dead people tend to be very quiet."

"But news of dead business partners travels." He reached for another bit of meat, nodding to Linsora first. "I can offer you a ship and funding with confidence that I can deliver. Do you know how to get back to Hakai from Khizara? Finding your Lost Fleet is one thing. Arranging a grand reunion…well, if you don't know where it is…"

"I know how to find out." She could contact Haavens. He'd still have the coordinates on the *Dominator*. Besides, weeks on board the skiff hadn't been wasted. She knew the coordinates well enough.

"You're resourceful, then," Gordek smiled. He traced a pattern in a tiny pool of spilled tea on the table. "How resourceful, I wonder. How… Khizaran, I wonder."

"What the hell does that mean?"

"You chose an education in archaeology, not military science. You've probably been away from Khizara for some time." Gordek dangled a piece of meat between his fingers. "You do have knives, but your features aren't typically Khizaran. And Khizarans don't have a monopoly on irritability. They just take ludicrous pride in it."

Linsora's vision narrowed to include only Gordek. He seemed relaxed. No muscles were obviously twitching with the strain of trying to look calm. He was challenging her. On Khizara, they'd already have knives drawn. As commander of this ship he had certain rights she respected. As a passenger on his ship, she wouldn't get far if she killed him, even in a fair duel. The piece of meat hung between his fingers. He examined it casually before dropping it back onto the platter. Linsora squeezed the handle of her eating knife. Handling food and putting it back on the serving plate was an offense no Khizaran mother tolerated.

"Funny, isn't it, that people like us more than Tokorellans," Linsora pushed her chair back and rose. "At least we're not rude and insulting."

"I'm not finished," Gordek stood, his chair tilted, then toppled backward to the floor.

"I am. You want a business partner? Find someone else. I'm not interested in what you're offering. What I want is Permac. Can you give me that?"

"I was making a point. If you're as Khizaran as you claim to be, you might be interested in knowing who killed Permac."

Linsora had taken a step toward the exit. She stopped without turning. Gordek spoke toward the mass of auburn hair that flowed in waves past her shoulders. The right shoulder seam of her jacket was torn. Her skirt was smudged with dirt from the cave. Her clothes were speckled with splinters and lint from broken furniture. The mess of her clothes fell around curves, some soft some muscular. Gordek stepped toward her, close enough that wisps of her hair tickled his chin.

"The man who entered the cave, the one responsible for that white light?" He said, his voice nearly a whisper. "I'm willing to wager that you'd like his name and how to find him."

Linsora spun on the ball of her foot. Her knuckles were white around the hilt of the eating knife. The sharp tip nicked Gordek's throat, just below the line of his close-cropped beard. A tiny trickle of blood spurted under the blade. His arms were spread, caught motionless in the act of reaching out to her.

"I'm better at this than you are, Gordek," she said, looking directly into his wide eyes. "How Tokorellan are you? Can you influence me fast enough? Don't forget I can taste it. One hint of that taste and you're dead."

"And you'll never know who killed Permac," he said.

"Anyone who'd use that kind of information as a bargaining tool isn't likely to give it up. I do your little task, and there'd be something else. And something else. And something else. What the hell kind of man are you?"

"Maybe the only man in the universe you can't afford to kill."

"Bastard!" Linsora moved the tip of the knife to the edge of Gordek's chin. With a flick of her wrist, she nicked the skin creating another trickle of blood before reversing the blade. She walked to the table and wiped the knife clean of blood and gravy. "That blast was meant for you, wasn't it?"

"If it had been, I'd be dead. I can't tell you why Permac was targeted," Gordek said. "I take it, then, that you're interested?"

Linsora thought his voice was maybe half a tone too high, maybe with a slight quiver.

"Same answer as before."

"Then I'll give you something for free. Remember the artifacts I told you about? The ones from Hakai?"

"The ones you stole from Karak?"

"They're in a cargo bay," he said. "Spend some time with them. See what you can find out about your Lost Fleet. We have five days. I'd hate to think you were bored."

Gordek's voice had returned to its normal deep pitch. Linsora noted a taunting note. *It's another challenge*, she thought.

"You wouldn't have taken them purely for their historical value, Gordek. What are you looking for?"

"Maybe I want to sell them. All the more reason for an archaeologist to examine them first, don't you think?"

You can't get me to answer your signal by bribery. So, you're trying something else. Five days. I have nothing to lose by looking.

"What if I said no?"

"Then I'd lock you in that ruin you created in your room."

"That ruin is as much your doing as mine," she said. "I'm sure you have crew. Get it cleaned up and I'll look at your plunder."

Linsora knew the layout of Khizaran cruisers and strode down the slope toward the cargo bays where she assumed the artifacts would be stored. Gordek followed some distance behind. At the locked doors, she waited. Gordek entered the codes and the doors opened to heaps of rubble that looked like Linsora's destroyed room.

Whole sections of walls stood on end. Scattered around them were books, papers, dishes – all sorts of general refuse created by society that someone thought valuable enough to save. Oddly, there were a number of large pottery urns – not the type of thing Linsora would expect from two hundred years ago. Even then, people used containers similar to modern ones. The back of Linsora's tongue registered sour and her emotions registered caution, a sense of advice to approach the artifacts with care.

"I though you'd be intrigued," Gordek said. He placed a hand on her shoulder, not a comradely clap or friendly pat. His hand lingered, soft and menacing.

Linsora pushed him away. "Do *not* test my emotions! Do *not ever* send me emotions. Do not – *not ever* – advise me how to do my work." Linsora faced Gordek, jabbing a clawed fingertip into his chest. "You are *never* to touch me again. You are to stay away from my mind. You are to stay away from me entirely."

Gordek sighed heavily. He turned as if he was about to walk away and then spun around quickly, extending his arm. The back of his fist met the side of Linsora's face. She fell back, stumbled and sprawled onto the floor. Misty gray haze filled her vision. She could almost feel her brain bounce against her skull. Blinking to clear her eyes, she focused on Gordek. The gray haze was replaced by red. Red surrounded him and would soon be the color he would lie in.

She reached into her boot for a knife and jumped to her feet. She took aim at Gordek's head. Suddenly, the knife felt as though it just come out of the forge. Searing hot metal burned her hand. She yelled and dropped it.

Gordek stepped forward, his hands tightened into fists. "Not all Tokorellans are as gentle or patient as your precious Permac. Don't push me. I command this ship and I don't tolerate Khizarans well. If you can't control your emotions, I'll control them for you. At the very least, you'll learn to control your tongue. And I'm better at *this* than you are." Gordek walked to a panel on the wall and spoke quietly before turning back to Linsora. "Examine all this. Go to any part of the ship for whatever resources you need. You'll be watched, your emotions will be monitored, and you'll be subject to my rules. I can't afford to have any of this destroyed. I can't afford not to know what information might be here. Do it as my partner, do it as my prisoner. Makes no difference to me. Do you understand?"

Linsora's reply was short and simple. She spat.

"You certainly have spirit," he said.

The doors to the cargo bay opened and two men entered.

CHAPTER 17

Linsora watched Gordek leave. Her hands were not blistered or burned. He had only made her think the knife was too hot to hold. Moragh had done the same thing to Permac. Permac refused to believe Moragh was Tokorellan. In Permac's view, vile behavior just wasn't Tokorellan. *Well, Permac, maybe now you know that evil lives everywhere.*

She was tempted to do absolutely nothing until she found out just who Gordek was. He had saved her life by killing Karak, but she felt no need to thank him for that. Gordek very likely welcomed the opportunity to take the other man's life. She had not been saved out of any kindness on Gordek's part.

The only thing that seemed certain was that she was not the rescued maiden nor was she his guest. But, the artifacts intrigued her. *Well,* she thought, *I don't have to tell you anything, Gordek. I don't know why we are going back to Khizara, I don't know what you hope is in this pile, but I will find out before you learn any more from me. And once we're there, I'll never have to see you again. If you know who killed Permac, someone else who survived that cave has to know, too.*

Linsora walked over to the pile of ruins lying in the cargo bay. She picked up a small book. The brittle, yellow paper began to crack. She set it aside, making a mental list of supplies she might need from whatever kind of lab the ship had. Old paper required special handling. Much of this was more than two hundred years old. It was probably old when Tokor or the Lost Fleet took it with them from Khizara.

She moved to a pile of dishes, glassware and pottery, most of it broken. She shook her head. Not a lot of care had been taken in loading any of this. She wondered if Gordek had smashed some of the pots looking for whatever it was he was looking for. She began to sort the items. Her focus was entirely on the task. When a sweet taste entered her mouth, she looked up, more than half expecting to see Permac smiling down at her. The only other people in the cargo bay were the guards slouching against the door

"Permac," Linsora muttered. "If I truly believed in an afterlife, I'd think you were haunting me. Maybe I've lost my mind."

The sweet taste remained as she sorted more household belongings. She felt warm and wondered if she was catching something. She glanced up, away from the guards. She had the prickly sensation of being stared at. Something moved near a section of wall.

She walked as casually as she could around the standing walls. No one. No movement. No breathing. Nothing.

She felt cold again. She felt empty, alone and small. "Just shadows," she said. "Shadows and hopes."

Linsora rubbed her eyes. She had been sorting artifacts for five hours. The large pottery urns all smelled musty. The inside surface was coated with dirty residue. These were probably used to transport soil containing the microbes from Khizara to Brachen, then from Brachen to Hakai. More than once, she wished she had protective clothing, at least gloves. The microbes were already inside her body, but the idea of them made her skin crawl. She picked up a small urn. She turned and headed toward the cargo bay door. The guards snapped to attention.

"Come on, you can't be afraid of me," she said. "Even if I did get away from you, where the hell could I go?"

The two guards looked at each other and shrugged.

"I just want to get something to eat. You do eat, don't you?"

Linsora pushed the door open.

One of the guards led the way, the other following Linsora. She realized that she was still carrying the urn. She held it up and looked at it. Something was scrawled inside, "…in full sun – low humi…wet no f…" Much of the writing was smudged. It wasn't inscribed into the urn, but written with some kind of ink. "…om near home…main loca…tejina…no fr…"

"Move along!" the rear guard said, pushing Linsora.

"No. Wait!" She tilted the urn toward the light. "I have to go back."

In the cargo bay, Linsora walked to the spot she had found the urn. In her sorting process, she had divided the piles into sections and sorted items in each section. There was no way to tell which items might once have belonged with each other. She blew dust from items in that particular section, peered inside other urns of all sizes, carefully opened brittle books.

"Did you help load this?" she asked the guards.

They hunched their shoulders almost in unison. By their sheepish half-smiles, she knew they weren't sure if admitting to it was good or not.

"Take me to Gordek."

"That was quick. What did you find?" Gordek sat at a table heaped with plates from old meals and crusted cups half filled with murky liquids. His hands were poised above the keys of a terminal.

"Quick? It's been hours!" she snarled. "I see your sense of cleanliness is as finely tuned as your table manners."

Gordek stared at her, his expression grim.

"I haven't found anything. I want to know how carefully the items were loaded. I'm not interested in finding anything for you, but I would like to make sense of what's in those piles. How I approach this depends on whether everything was just scooped up and moved or if it's in the same relative position now as when it was on Hakai. Those belonging to one person or family would probably have been lumped together. If they weren't moved carefully, I'll have to sort everything to find associations."

"What did you find – and note that's the second time I've asked. If you haven't found anything, I doubt you'd worry about associations."

"I don't even know what you're looking for," she said. "I'll have to sort everything, see if I can figure out what belongs together."

She turned to leave, but the burly guards blocked her way.

"Linsora!" Gordek roared. "I don't like having to ask a question more than once."

"Here's what I found." She tossed the urn toward Gordek. Caught by surprise, he fumbled and dropped it. The piece shattered into several large slices and hundreds of tiny shards.

Linsora took a step toward Gordek's desk. Both guards reached for her, holding her back. The instant fury she felt was disturbed by warmth, a gentle sense of warning, a sweet taste. An idea that this was not the time to test her will against Gordek's was on the edge of her awareness. If she tried, she had a sense that he would destroy her. Not kill her, but destroy her - and she didn't know quite what that meant. The warmth continued and Linsora looked around wildly for the source. It was Permac - it had to be.

The guards read her movements as an increased attempt to reach Gordek and tightened their grip. The warmth vanished. Her tongue prickled with bursts of sour. The room remained the same, but a sense of enclosure crept around her forehead like someone pulling a hood down over her face. Twenty spiders scuttled across her cheeks, pulling the rough hood tighter. *No spiders, no hood*, she thought. *Not real.* Her eyes were dry, with each blink her vision became more clouded. She struggled for breath. The space around her head was too small. The terrible dark closet Yokosh shoved her in. He slammed the door and leaned against it. He was bigger, stronger. She was only five. No air, darkness. He laughed until he snorted. *You're not Yokosh*, she thought. *You can't know this.* She inhaled in short gasps that made her head spin. No snorting Yokosh. Only Gordek calling her name.

"Linsora, pay attention to me," he said.

She stared at the tips of his boots. Darker now, only his voice and his boots and the stifling cage. His voice pounded in her ears.

"I advised you not to push me, Khizaran. If I thought it would do any good, I'd have the guards beat some sense into you." Gordek remained seated at the table. "I suspect you would die long before you'd consider behaving with reason."

Reason? Reason is knowing I'm not in a small room. Reason is not listening to you. Reason is taking a deep breath. I can't. Linsora's eyes shifted from green to pale violet. She concentrated inward, trying to regain control of her emotions. *How? I don't know how. I want to send you pain, Gordek. Is that an emotion? Damn. I don't know how. I can't...*

Sweetness tinged the sour burning her mouth. *Like lemonade, sour and sweet,* she thought. *Still too much lemon. A little more air, though.* She inhaled fully and lifted her gaze to Gordek's face. Beads of sweat dotted his forehead. He seemed to be struggling to maintain his control. Gordek rose and kicked a large piece of the broken urn out of his way. His breath was labored. He clenched and unclenched his fists.

Linsora didn't know if the pain he felt was what she had wanted to send him. *Probably not, I still don't know how. Are you here, Permac? You can't be, but you must be. What am I supposed to do?*

"Gordek," she said, her voice thin, "you want my cooperation. I think you need it. I don't know why. I do know that I won't give you anything until I find out why. We don't have to like or trust each other for that."

Linsora felt the sweet taste surge, then vanish. At the same time, Gordek seemed to recover from whatever he had been fighting. She knew she had gone too far for the moment, a small window of advantage had been opened for her and she had treated it like a cargo bay door. *What else could I say? That I'd help him? Just smile and agree with him? You know me better than that, Permac. Did you give me time to control my emotions? Did I waste it?* Her face still ached. The hood of enclosure still hung around her head. She was panting and as sweaty as if she'd run ten miles. *I still have my anger, Gordek; no one can threaten that out of me.*

Gordek wiped his forehead and took a deep breath. He looked at her curiously.

"You are right about one thing, I do need you. And about another, I do not need you to trust me. You have chosen to be adversarial, so be it. You are becoming stronger, Linsora, but never for an instant think you are stronger than me," he said. He moved from behind the desk, circling the guards and Linsora. He spoke from behind her, close to her ear, "And don't think that you can lie to me. If you trust nothing else, trust that your mind is and always will be open and available to me."

"You only read emotions. You can't pull my thoughts from me!" Linsora eyes were deep violet. She controlled the panic, but only with effort.

"I don't have to. Let me show you."

Linsora felt the air in the room become heavy, hard to breath. She fought against the guards just to get away, to run from the fear. It occurred to her that Gordek had not discovered her fear of enclosed spaces at all. He simply sent fear. She slapped her own label on it. The knowledge didn't help. As pure as the rage she had experienced in her quarters, now a pure deadening terror overcame her. All of her concentration was not enough to send it away. Then she heard Gordek speaking to her, one voice cutting through the anxiety. But he didn't offer comfort, he asked her questions and she felt compelled to answer them. She realized that he couldn't directly inhibit her will. An emotional overlay of fear was necessary, perhaps as a distraction. Still, she could not resist him and that added to the fear.

Gordek perched on the edge of the table, "Tell me, finally, what you found."

Linsora was taking deep, quick breaths, her eyes bright purple, every muscle in her body tense. She could not choose to remain silent. The words spilled out, "Instructions for planting chikara."

"And," Gordek nodded casually.

"Notes. Chikara won't grow in damp climates. No fruit. Won't grow on Khizara."

"Yes, I did know that. What else?"

"Something about Tokor. He was a botanist. Something about the tejina plants and books. Writing smudged."

"What about preparation? Where the tejina came from?"

"Nothing."

"Well, little Khizaran, that's what we have to learn. I will tell you that tejina still grows on Khizara. Know where?" Gordek teased. "Oddly enough, in what you call the Forbidden Area."

The information struck Linsora as significant, but she couldn't put the pieces together. Tokor's powers came from chikara. The fruit didn't grow on Khizara. The tejina plants did, but the leaves are toxic. *So what so what so what?* She thought.

"And I'll give you something else," Gordek shoved some plates away and fully sat on the table. "What I asked you is what I most want to know. Information on the source of tejina, where Tokor first found it. It's not native to Khizara. Tokor kept detailed records of what he planted on Tokorel. He had to have done the same on Khizara. No one has found his earlier books. No one has been into Khizara's Forbidden Area for nearly two hundred years. What better place to look for his books than where he lived? Who better to gain access to the Forbidden Area than an archaeologist, especially one bringing home information on the Lost Fleet?"

"You're insane," Linsora threw her head back, tried to grit her teeth.

"Insane to think that you'd help me? You're rummaging through the

145

artifacts now, aren't you? Think of being the first to explore the Forbidden Area - your name next to your father's in the history books, and not just as his assistant. As you can see, I've been busy, too."

Linsora gurgled what was supposed to be a laugh.

"Is there a problem?"

Linsora closed her eyes, "Can't stay on Khizara."

"Who can't?"

"Me." Linsora felt like her ears would explode from the pressure around her, from the weight pressing, closing. Her breath was shallow.

"Why?" Gordek asked. "You're hyperventilating. Tell me before you pass out or we'll have to do all this again."

"I'm going to watch you die a slow death one day, Gordek," she barely stifled a moan. If the two men weren't holding her up, she'd be curled in a ball on the floor. She wanted to hold her hands over her ears, her eyes, especially her mouth. "My brother. Minor member of the Prefecture. Tried to steal my property, nearly killed me. I challenged him. Lost the duel. Banished for ten years. I can visit, but not stay."

"Ah Khizarans," Gordek seemed to savor the tale. "When was this?"

"Five years ago. Yokosh has the land now."

"That's your brother? Yokosh Anselm? There's nothing about him in the record of your family."

"No, Khol. Half brother, my mother's son."

Gordek stood suddenly, surprise on his face. "Yokosh Khol? Yokosh Khol is your brother? Well, well. Karak failed to mention that." He wondered what else his former ally had failed to mention and what the implications of this tidbit might be. "What phantoms are in your mind, Linsora? Amazing the names people give to fear. You'll have to tell me one day."

He allowed the fear he sent to Linsora to intensify and watched pleased as she cringed from whatever occupied her psyche, then ended it.

Linsora slumped between the guards. She felt as though her body had been beaten, every muscle she had held tense now hurt. She stood of her own accord and fixed an expressionless stare on Gordek.

"I'll tell you while I'm watching you die."

"Will you? You talk a good game. You have the nerve to cut and draw blood. Not everyone does, you know. But to kill? That's a nerve few can muster."

Linsora remained motionless and staring. She didn't have to protest his accusation or honor him with an explanation. She had killed. Gordek lowered his eyes and shifted his shoulders, obviously regretting that particular taunt. Now he knew she had both the tools and the nerve to kill.

"How do you know Yokosh?"' she asked. "Of all the unlikely things I can imagine, that's near the top of the list, although you two are probably well suited to each other."

"We're not even in the same neighborhood, Linsora. I don't hold him in much higher regard than I imagine you do. How I know him? Well, maybe we can schedule an evening of tales."

Linsora tapped her foot. It was a tale she very much wanted to hear. But not enough to trade any of her time or stories with Gordek. *He wants to know who I killed*, she thought. *Well, let him continue to want.*

"Yokosh's in the Prefecture, have him get the permission you need," she said.

"He has no believable reason to go other than pure curiosity. The entire Prefecture has to agree to release the restrictions."

"And my dear brother tends to be more blunt than clever. Why tell me what you're looking for now? Why not earlier? What's changed?"

"As I said, I've been busy. My bargaining chest has grown. Seems you've managed to endear yourself to the Carratians so much, they're eager to find you again. Certain parties are quietly offering a tidy sum. Somehow I get the impression that your lifespan would be negatively impacted by that particular reunion."

"So either I help you or you sell me back to them? I thought you weren't a slave trader," Linsora said. She tried to sound unconcerned, but she couldn't readily see a way around this one. "You want Tokor's books. Why? What's in them?"

"Still asking questions?" Gordek smiled briefly, then slammed his fist on the table. His voice thundered, "*You* do not ask the questions. You only provide me with answers. That should be clear to you." He paused, seemed thoughtful, "The point is that you find all there is to be found from those artifacts. Who knows, maybe you won't have to convince the Prefecture to let you explore the Forbidden Area. And, as a measure of my magnanimity, once I have the answers I need, I can throw the Carratians off your tail and give you the name I'm sure you want."

Once Haavens reports to the Mercantile, the Carratians won't have any reason to want me. Linsora felt chilled. *Either that or they'll want me even more. Gordek said the bounty is being offered quietly. Maybe they hope that will keep me in hiding and silent. After Haavens goes public with my testimony, the Carratians will only have revenge as a motive. And they'll probably offer an even higher bounty.* She realized Gordek was talking.

"…have set up quarters for you in the cargo bay. You'll have all the time you need to work."

Linsora was barely aware of the walk back to the cargo bay. A cot, bedding, and small table with food had been set up near the artifacts. The guards left, but she knew they were just outside the door. Even though it had been hours since her last meal, she only picked at the food. She looked at what seemed to be a piece of fruit she had been nibbling. Chikara. She was about to put it back on the plate when familiar warmth touched her mind, very lightly as though from far away. With it came a gentle urging to eat. She bit into the fruit. *The last person who told me to eat was Per... no, not Permac. Ralain, masquerading as Permac. Ralain's dead. And Permac's dead. Is he, though? Are you dead, Permac? If you are, who's sending the influences? Not at all clear. Obscure in fact. Moragh said to beware of the obscured. They will send you in circles. Turn you inside out.* She laughed, sending the bitter sound into the far corners of the cargo bay and chasing away the warmth. *I've already been turned inside out. Is going back to Khizara the completion of a circle?*

She swallowed. Her father had been a maker of lists, a habit her mother often chided him for. She said that Terrans spent too much time considering the possibilities instead of taking quick stock and deciding. Linsora tended to use her mother's approach in daily life and her father's for work. She glanced at the mound of still untouched artifacts and decided all of this was work related.

She made mental lists of knowns and unknowns.

Moragh. Tokorellan. You were a passenger on Haavens' ship. You wanted to take us away from Hakai. You wanted to separate us. Probably not a friend. Definitely a big unknown.

Karak and Tayla of the Moragh surname. Dead. No, only Karak, I don't recall seeing Tayla's body, but then I didn't really look, she thought. *Hakains who want revenge on both Tokorel and Khizara. If Tayla is still alive, though, she might know who killed Permac although she didn't seem awfully fond of me. Feeling's mutual there. Gordek killed Karak with my knife, too. That's not something bound to make you want to help me.*

Gordek. Tokorellan. His people seem Tokorellan, too. You want to find information on chikara and you want it desperately. How the hell can you know Yokosh? That's just very odd. I don't think I want you to find what you want and I sure as hell don't want to help you do it. I sure as hell can't see a way out of it, though.

Permac. Tokorellan. What else? Why were you so important? Why do I still taste your sweetness? Do I just want to? Could you possibly be on this ship? I saw your body, felt no pulse. I want you to be here. More than anything, I want you to be alive. I want you here to help sort out the absolute mess I'm in.

Linsora stood and wandered to the heaps of artifacts. She was tempted to pick something up and throw it, but glasses could be replaced - none of this could be.

She stiffened and looked toward the far side of the room. The door opened and Gordek strode in.

CHAPTER 18

Gordek exchanged a cursory glance with Linsora and sat at the table. He popped a slice of fruit into his mouth. Linsora rummaged around in a pile of pottery, busying herself sorting them into those with writing and those without.

"You should eat something," Gordek said, still chewing.

"Are you worried about my health?" Linsora glanced toward him, curious that she felt nothing of him in her mind.

"Yes, actually," he gestured toward her with a bit of fruit, "If your eyes change color in the Prefecture, I don't think you'd remain healthy for long."

Linsora remained hunched over the pile of shards. That one point had not occurred to her. She thought she heard Gordek laugh. He had sensed her surprise. She looked toward him, anger rising again, and concentrated.

"Linsora!" He leapt to his feet, using her name as a reprimand. "Stop that! You cannot win! I came here to be conciliatory, accept at least that. Had I been through what you have recently, I wouldn't be inclined toward friendliness either." He paused, adding in a tone tinged with threat that struck her as more natural, "My allowances for you are limited. Remember that you cannot win. It's pointless for us to waste energy battling each other."

Linsora opened her mouth, planning to remark that she had plenty of energy to spare. Before she spoke, a sharp whip of, she wasn't sure what, brushed past her mind. It had the taste of Gordek and something that was not pain, but held the promise of pain. *I can't fight you,* she thought. *Not yet. But your pompous confidence won't last forever. That much I can promise both of us.*

She ground her teeth and kept her anger to herself.

Gordek sat down. He bit into something that looked like a Terran orange. Crimson juice ran down his sleeve.

"You can hold your tongue, then. That's much better," he said. He met the fire in her still-green eyes with a contemptuous smile. "I have to admit I was amazed to hear that Yokosh Kohl is your brother."

"Half-brother," she muttered. "I don't want to be any closer to him than I have to be."

"He speaks just as fondly of you. He never mentioned your name, though."

"He probably refers to me as the mutant half-breed," Linsora laughed.

"Actually, yes he does," Gordek said. "I like your laugh. In exchange for it, would you like one more amazing tidbit?"

Linsora glared. *Yes I do, but I won't give you the satisfaction of saying so. And don't count on hearing many more laughs, either.*

"Karak's daughter, Tayla, and your half-brother know each other, too. Know each other quite well. I introduced them a year ago. Lovely couple, as you can imagine."

"Tayla? And Yokosh? Gordek, the universe is a big place. I've traveled most of my life and haven't once met anyone who knew people I know on Khizara. Here's a tidbit for you, Gordek. When you're lying, make it as simple as possible."

"You don't believe I know Yokosh?" Gordek waved a slice a fruit. "He has a scar on his hip, another on his arm, from a fight you two had over your mother's property. He says he allowed you to live so that you could spend the rest of your life with memories of being defeated."

"He didn't allow…" Linsora began. "Never mind. So you know him. And I suppose if she's Yokosh's lover…"

"What?"

"Well, she didn't seem to like me."

"That someone doesn't like you is a surprise?" Gordek chuckled. "She and Karak were suspicious and alarmed that you'd found them. She thought Yokosh had let something slip about Hakai and you'd come to find out for yourself."

Gordek pushed the plate of fruit toward Linsora. "Now, as I said you should eat. We don't know precisely how your physiology will react. The results have been remarkable so far, but we need to extend them so that your eye color doesn't change. You also will require some training in the use of these new skills." He wiped his mouth with his sleeve, smearing some of the spilled juice on his face. Linsora imagined, with a great degree of pleasure, that the smears were his blood. His expression darkened at her covert insolence. "And you will learn some respect."

In a dramatic gesture, Gordek waved his hand. "Emotions are powerful, Linsora. You've tasted fear, try this."

Linsora tasted the sharp tang of sour and before she could react, was overcome by absolute weakness. Her knees buckled. She collapsed onto the floor, landing painfully on a pile of metal cooking pots.

"And then," Gordek said, "Just as quickly gone."

She stood and straightened her clothes.

"Did you torment small animals when you were a child, Gordek? Normal people, even normal Tokorellans, don't take pleasure in other people's distress. No wonder Karak hated you."

151

"And Karak treated you well? Even I wouldn't have fed you so much chikara."

"I'd think two depraved personalities would enjoy each other's company," she said. "Why did Permac's eyes change color? He was raised eating chikara."

"Tokorellan chikara. It's not nearly as potent as the fruit from Hakai." Gordek stopped smiling. Beads of sweat formed on his face, just as Linsora had seen earlier.

"Are you ill?" she asked.

Gordek stared straight ahead, not at Linsora, not at anything in particular. Linsora focused on sensing his emotions. She didn't quite know how. Sending emotions seemed easy enough. Everyone always sends emotions out - care, hate, tenderness, loathing. To a small degree, everyone is aware of them. In a crowd of people, you know when someone is staring at you and you can usually find their eyes. With Tokorellan abilities, concentrated doses could be sent to specific targets. Purposefully sensing emotions, though, that was different. Linsora cocked her head toward Gordek, and tried to relax her mind, clearing it as much as she could of all other input.

A wave of energy swept past her. It was as like standing at the edge of a fast flowing river. She could dip a foot in and feel the strength of the current. At the surface, it wasn't strong enough to carry her away, but if she waded in farther, she would be swept up. She wrenched her mind back to herself.

Gordek trembled. His eyes were wide, his face as pale as death. Odder still, and frightening, his eyes were purple. "It can't be you. You're not strong enough yet!"

"I wouldn't even know how."

Gordek didn't reply. He gripped the sides of the table, breathing heavily. His clothes were drenched with sweat and he had the appearance of a haggard old man. She reached a tentative mental toe into the current. Almost as quickly, she pulled back. The force was compelling, but far beyond what she could hope to enter and survive. Gordek groaned as the energy seemed to reach a crescendo.

Slowly, his breath returned to normal. "It would appear that you have a champion. I don't know where he is. Until I know more, you're safe."

"Who?"

He ignored her and rose slowly. "New quarters will be prepared for you," he looked around as if trying to find some stowaway lurking in the shadows, "You may come back here to work whenever you like, and you will be treated well." He emphasized the last part of the sentence. Gordek strode to the door, turning for one last look at the cargo bay. "That, Linsora, was power. Appealing, isn't it?"

152

Although the sounds of the ship's engines lulled her to sleep, the frequent jumps interrupted her dreams. She dreamed of Permac and their time together, of Moragh and his deceptions, of Gordek and his cruelty, and lastly of her freedom. When she awoke that morning, it was her loss of freedom and her feeling of helplessness that she thought of first.

Somehow, someone had sensed that she was awake and a meal was brought to her. Fried meat, crusty bread, some kind of deep pink jam, and chikara. Always chikara. Permac said she'd love it and spent what Linsora considered undue energy trying to find a substitute for his recipes. She admitted it was good, sweet and, when served raw, crunchy with only a little juice. She dipped a finger in the jam and tasted it. Very sweet intense chikara flavor.

"I wonder if the nasty little germs survive cooking," she said.

She wiped her finger on a cloth quickly. She didn't like the idea of the microbes. She didn't like the idea of having Tokorellan abilities.

"I do though," she said, sticking a finger in the jam again. "I wanted to send an emotion to Gordek. Whoever sent him whatever it was they sent him does have power and it is appealing. Damn appealing. Damn dangerous." She licked her finger. "Permac used it to win poker games. That's harmless enough. He said there are social rules on Tokorel about when it's not polite to check people's emotions. I don't think Gordek is worried about being polite. Way back when Tokor was around, he never told anyone where the abilities came from. Maybe he didn't know about the germies, but he did know about chikara. If he'd told Khizarans then... Maybe he tried to, who knows. Maybe his diaries would clear up what really happened."

She spread jam on some bread, placed a piece of meat on top and covered it with more jam and another slice of bread.

"Mm. The jam could use something hot to balance the sweetness, though." She chewed and brushed crumbs from her skirt. "If Khizarans find out about this now...no, it's when not if...will they want it? Will Khizara become another Tokorel? Will everyone everywhere have to guard their emotions?" She poked the air with the last bit of sandwich. "Tokor couldn't train those Ghoranth, though. Maybe not everyone is a good host to the germs. Lovely. That'll make Khizarans pariahs just like Tokorellans are."

She flopped back on the bed. Working with the artifacts didn't sound appealing. She wanted to blast loud music and lose herself in the rhythms of pure beat. Fiddling with the bedside console, she turned the volume as high as she could. She only heard the knock on the door when it had become an insistent pounding.

"Come in," she yelled.

Gordek entered. She didn't turn the music down immediately, taking a moment to enjoy his expression of distaste. "Good morning," he shouted. "I trust you slept well."

Linsora felt that she could look contemptuous now without fear of reprisal and did so with great satisfaction. She waited until the selection was over and turned the music off. She rolled off the bed lightly, ending up on the side away from Gordek. Picking up her jacket, she examined the tear at the shoulder with a shake of her head.

Gordek sighed heavily, "Yes, well, I would like to talk with you for a few minutes before you start your day." He closed the door behind him. "I never asked what brought you and Permac to Hakai. I'm curious."

"Seems like such a long time ago," she felt her guard dropping and remembered Permac, their innocent departure from *The Dominator* in search of, of what? She'd worn this jacket on Hakai and in that cave. Throughout her years of travel she hadn't collected souvenirs. *Carry a light pack and heavy memories*, her mother always said. She'd repair the jacket, though. It was all she had left of Permac. "We wanted to find out what happened to the Lost Fleet. We found a star chart on Brachen and thought Hakai might have some answers."

"Ah, Brachen is where you ran afoul of the Carratians." Gordek paced the short distance from one side of the room to the other. "Did anyone tell you about the star chart?"

"No, but…" Linsora wrinkled her brow, "But I knew something was there." She sat with a thump that would have made a less solid floor quiver. "I can taste influences, that's something I've heard is odd. When my father and I first surveyed the area around Pak-bor, he wanted to work on a hilltop, but I knew the habitation site was in the valley. I can sense the remains of ancient settlements. I don't know how. Same thing on Brachen, I just knew something was waiting to be found."

"And you'd never had chikara before you reached Hakai?"

"I'm Khizaran, what do you think?"

"So you don't know if someone was, perhaps leading you to the chart?"

"No. I mean, I don't know. Why?"

"For you to be the one to have found the chart and to arrive on Hakai when you did…" Gordek stroked his close-cropped beard and shook his head. "You obviously knew nothing about Tayla and Yokosh. I can't quite make sense of it, but I don't believe in coincidences."

"Do you think the man who killed Permac is involved? You said if the blast had been meant for you, you'd be dead. Why kill Permac?"

Linsora's voice broke. She turned away from Gordek and buried her face in the jacket with Hakai's dust and Permac's last touch.

154

"I want to know that nearly as much as you do." Gordek spoke softly. Softly, too, he stepped forward and stroked Linsora's hair. She jerked her head away and he grasped her shoulders. "Linsora, take comfort when you can. From anyone who offers it. Sometimes consolation is only that, simple with no expectations. Space is vast and cold and empty. There's too much loneliness. I am sorry for your loss. Right now, that's honest. Finding someone to share the darkness with is rare. Losing that person is worse than losing your own life. I know. I do know."

Linsora allowed his hold on her shoulders to remain. Allowed the moment of shared sorrow. Welcomed the comfort. Gordek did know and, perhaps, had not allowed anyone to comfort him. Maybe no one had offered.

The moment faded. Both Linsora and Gordek returned from their private grief to an uncomfortable present.

"Well," Gordek said, stepping back toward the door "Did you find your answers on Hakai?"

"I found the Lost Fleet." Linsora folded the jacket carefully. "But every answer creates more questions."

"And now? Still on a quest for answers?"

"Maybe. You say that like I'm a child looking for a lost pet. Truth can be as powerful, as…as your mental charms."

"Indeed so," he said. "Think about what the combination might mean. Truth and, as you put it, mental charms."

"I have a feeling the only truth you're interested in will result in your own advancement."

"What else is there? I mean that. If you did manage to find the truth with a capital T, and by some miracle managed to unite Tokorel and Khizara, you'd be regarded as something of a hero. That's not unattractive."

"It's not my intention," she said, although more than once she had questioned herself. The whole enterprise began as a lark with serious motives plastered on for the sake of propriety. "My purpose now is to survive."

"Mere survival is boring, Linsora. Remember the power you felt yesterday. Think of what you could do with just a small amount of that. And don't tell me you're not interested."

"I'm interested in the work I have to do today and I'd like to get started."

"You haven't asked who sent that power."

"I asked yesterday and didn't get an answer. I thought you didn't want me to ask questions, Gordek."

Gordek was between Linsora and the doorway. His lips forced a curled smile and he stepped out of the way. Linsora walked quickly down the corridor.

"You think it's poor dead Permac," he said to himself. "But you have no idea who was in that cave. You have no concept of his abilities. He still has the scar on his face. He wants to remember me. I'm going to ensure he never forgets me. On top of everything else, Linsora, you seem to be a direct path to him. I don't know how or why. It doesn't matter, though, does it? You're not immune to what I can offer, and the Forbidden Area is only the beginning."

Gordek watched her until she was out of his sight. He motioned to a guard who had been standing down the hall. "Keep an eye on her. Report any strange behavior immediately. And if she talks to anyone, or no one, you will let me know at once. Is that clear?"

During the next days, Linsora busied herself with the task of learning as much as she could about the people whose records lay before her. She looked over the mounds of artifacts and wondered how accurate a picture of anything she was likely to get from it. Gordek didn't care about historical accuracy. Most of the records Linsora had seen were ordinary household lists and official record keeping documents. There were also several more references to maps charting a course through space to "The Cornerstone." That was all they called it. Maybe the origin of the microbes Tokor found. That's what Gordek wanted.

Gordek paid cordial visits to the cargo bay daily. He listened to her reports, but no longer seemed to expect any grand revelations.

She had neither seen nor felt Permac's presence and started to question if she had, in fact, ever really felt that presence. A second, lesser sense of loss invaded her emotions, but she had been able to keep it in check. A small part of her still wondered, but the logical part of her continued to reassure her that Permac was dead. She saw it. Her eyes didn't normally deceive her. But she realized that she didn't actually *see* the event. She saw the flash, the second white light, then an apparently dead Permac on the cavern floor.

She had never spent much time making plans for her future. She had her work and there were always ships looking for archaeologists. She liked the work. She didn't expect to be the one to stumble on the great answer of humanoid origins. Just adding information was a satisfaction. The thrill of discovery, piecing together the puzzles of lost civilizations, restoring some of the past to contemporary memory – that was the motivation. And she had wandered for ten years. Her father had spent his entire adult life similarly wandering.

Toward the end of the trip to Khizara, she realized she couldn't get through the situation she was in just wandering. The artifacts sparked her interest. Khizara's Forbidden Area could hold a wealth of information about Tokor. Maybe enough to bring Tokorel and Khizara together. *That's a grand idea, Linsora*, she thought, smiling at her conceit. *Yes indeed, I will single handedly bring two cultures together. Maybe not. Maybe if I find enough, I can find some way to get back to Hakai. I have to find Permac – even if it is only his body. No one ever had a good reason to survey the Forbidden Area. Maybe no one ever even asked. Maybe now…*

She ate chikara and spent time with other crew members who coached her on the limited use of her new abilities. She could influence emotions without her eyes changing color, but only slightly. She would have to be very careful on Khizara. Any eye color change would be an immediate death sentence.

Just before the jumps that would take them into the solar system of Khizara, Gordek paid his daily visit.

"Still no information on any kind of preparation or the origin of chikara?" He asked.

"No." Linsora became busy jotting notes. Gordek followed her.

"I want you to go to the Forbidden Area on Khizara."

"You already said that. I already told you it was impossible."

"And I told you it might not be," Gordek's voice had lost its cordial tone. "No one has been there for nearly two hundred years. No records exist of any towns. Or of anything at all, in fact. Whatever the circumstances of Tokor's leaving, he did it in a hurry."

"I know, and you think he left books behind."

"I'm sure of it."

Linsora stopped jotting and faced him. "Sure? How can you be sure?"

"Tokor's books on Tokorel make reference to his original diaries and journals. One of his journals was on Tokorel, but it disappeared. The others have to be on Khizara."

"Maybe he left then on Brachen."

"Did you find much on Brachen that Tokor left? Only what they couldn't carry. No, his notes are on Khizara."

"And what makes you think I have any intention of helping you find them?"

"You're interested. You're an archaeologist," Gordek smiled. "Your father made a major find on Khizara. Pakron, I think?"

"Pak'bor."

"Yes. Don't you think that might make your argument for gaining access to the Forbidden Area stronger? Not to mention that you're bringing back information on the Lost Fleet."

"It might," Linsora said. His arguments were the same ones she'd been playing with. The idea of surveying the Forbidden Area was one of the most tantalizing she could ever remember having. And she did have a good argument for gaining access. She stopped looking busy and faced him. "Yes, I'm interested. And, as you've pointed out, I'm not interested in being handed over to the Carratians. Still, I'd rather take my chances than hand information over to you. You can't do anything to help me get into the Forbidden Area. If I do go, what I find belongs to Khizara."

"You wouldn't want to be exposed as a Tokorellan agent, would you?" Gordek asked casually.

"A what? I'm most certainly not…" Linsora started.

"No, you're not. But it wouldn't take much to convince your Prefecture of that, would it?" Gordek picked up a small plate and made a great pretense of examining it in detail. "I take it you're fond of your home world and intend to return permanently one day? If you're branded as a Tokorellan agent you'd be lucky to escape with your life. Any chance of a peaceful retirement on Khizara would vanish. And your reputation as an archaeologist? Well, no one likes a spy. Not to mention how utterly pleased your half-brother would be." He replaced the plate in the neat piles Linsora had created. "As you probably realize by now, I do not intend to spend my own retirement in obscurity. I have plans in place and operating. I have a wide-ranging network of associates – on Tokorel, on Hakai, on Khizara as well as within the Mercantile itself. I can call on any number of people to testify against you."

Linsora stared at him, too stunned to shout a protest.

When the Khizaran cruiser circled her home planet, Linsora didn't rush to a viewport to gaze at her homeworld as she usually did. This homecoming should have been triumphant. Should have been with Permac at her side. Should not have been one filled with dread and regret. Gordek escorted her to a smaller craft in another cargo bay. Before she boarded, Gordek said, "You know people in the Prefecture. Spin a good tale for them. Use your influence, so to speak. I'll do what I can to help. When you get to the Forbidden Area, I'll meet you. Be assured, I will meet you. And be assured I'll know what you're doing." He took her hand and began to raise it to his mouth, teeth bared – a Khizaran courting ritual, one reserved for the most intimate of lovers.

She pulled away and spat at him. "How dare you! When all planets leave the night sky and space is warm!" She glared at him and turned to board the transport ship.

I do dare. Not only that, I will continue to dare and I will succeed, little Khizaran, he thought.

CHAPTER 19

Khizara was not as Linsora remembered it. Five years had added embellishments to her memories. The avenues were not as wide, the buildings not as ornate, the city not as large as she recalled. She had compared all other cities to Khizara the capital, all other planets to Khizara the world and none had measured up. She had been determined to think of her home world as the best. Peering down on it from the window of her hotel room, she smiled. It may not be the absolute best, but it was still her home. She propped her feet on the windowsill and poured more ale into a glass. The Green Sea crashed onto the shore with unabashed Khizaran fury and Linsora closed her eyes to listen to sounds never heard aboard a ship.

She remembered the image Permac had sent her that awful time on Hakai after she'd eaten so much chikara. He said they should go to the beach, live there forever and never think about history again. *I wish we'd done that instead of…well, no, we did what we did. In the same circumstances, we'd do the same*, she thought.

The transport had arrived in the bustling port without incident several hours earlier. After only a few days of training, Linsora didn't want to have to use her new talents in public and was relieved that the badges provided by Gordek were current issue passes. The man at the arrival desk didn't even glance up at Linsora and the pilot. They were waved through the gate and entered the throngs surging amid the shops, food stalls, and ground transport vendors. The pilot had disappeared in the crowd, having agreed to meet Linsora in a week. He said he was going to pick up some extra currency by offering his transport for hire, but she suspected he would never be far from her. She bought some food, meat she could trust to be meat and not meat-shaped mysteries served on most ships, and leaned against a post. While savoring the aromas around her, she closed her eyes and opened her mind to sense whatever else might be around. One of her teachers had warned her about trying to do this, that the assault of emotions in a crowd might overwhelm her. She had tried it on board the ship with no negative effects, so she risked it here. Her eyes would only change color if she expended a great deal of effort to influence someone. Just sampling others' could be done quietly.

She enjoyed the sensations from the Khizarans. They felt familiar to her, tasted as right to her as the meat. A powerful burst of anger struck her moments before the sound of raised voices. Passion and sorrow combined reached her from a passing couple. Whatever her people felt, they felt strongly. No controls or limitations were placed on emotions here. No suspicion dampened their lust for everything. Linsora smiled. She felt free for the first time in weeks.

Gordek said he would know when I reached the Forbidden Area, she thought. *I could blend into Khizara, right now. Just wander off, never contact the Prefecture and, as Permac once said, go about my life. I'd never have any of the answers to all the questions, but I'd be free. Maybe free enough to find the answers on my own somehow, eventually.* It was a tempting thought.

She continued to eat and was just about to close her mind again when something flashed past. The last bite caught in her throat, making her choke and lose her concentration. By the time she had gulped down her cup of tea and was composed enough to sense those around her again, the feeling was gone. But she was sure. There was at least one other Tokorellan here and it was not her pilot. Her feeling of freedom vanished. This Tokorellan could be from any of the factions and could be one of Gordek's people. Linsora doubted that she would have been left completely on her own here. Not only the pilot would be nearby, others would be, too. Shadowy and obscure.

Well, she thought, tossing away the remains of her meal and her fleeting vision of running away, *I couldn't abandon all the questions anyway. I can't abandon the vows I made, for blood, for vengeance. I can't abandon Permac. If he's alive, I have to find him. And if he is dead, I have to know.*

She had made her way on foot to the best hotel in the city. Gordek had also provided her with ample credit. She took her time and wandered along familiar winding streets before entering the main boulevard running through the center of Khizara. Ducking into doorways or stopping to look over the wares of street vendors, she would sample the emotions of the crowds on the street. No other Tokorellan seemed to be present, but that didn't mean none were there. The array of sensations from all the people around her only gave her a headache. Once at the hotel, she ordered several ales, took them to her room and relaxed.

A warm breeze blew the curtains into the room. Linsora pushed them away and sat up with a groan. Too many Khizaran ales and too much on her mind. She punched in an order for tea and food, then stood gazing out of the window, admiring her home.

Khizara's land formed an incomplete ring around the center of the planet, making all of it tropical to semi-tropical. Lush vegetation ran right up to the emerald colored seas. Kral had told her, well he had told her many things, but she remembered he said her eyes were the color of the sea.

Kral. She hadn't really thought about him for years. He was Yokosh's friend. And he was more than that. She had nearly Sealed the Oath with him. And she had served on his ship. But his bonds to Yokosh were stronger than any he had to her. No, his ambition was more powerful than any affection he might feel toward anyone.

When the door chime sounded, Linsora jumped. She tried to sense who

160

was there, but her head only ached more. With one hand on a knife, she opened the door with the other. The waiter was probably used to this sort of greeting and only grunted when she took his card and entered the amount of his tip. She remained by the door as he placed the tray on the table. As she closed it behind him, her headache stopped. She was about to open the door to see who he was, but it didn't matter. They would be everywhere. She only regretted that her tip had been so generous.

"Prefecture schedule," she spoke to the terminal as she sipped the strong, bitter tea. It was hot. She had always preferred hers cold, but the rising steam helped to ward off the chill she felt about what she had to do.

"Good, you're in session this week," she said.

"Rephrase question," the computer stated in a dull voice.

"Schedule for Prefect Behazh," she replied. She had decided to meet with him first. He was a ranking member of the Prefecture, but more importantly he was an old family friend. *And*, she thought, *Kral's father*. If she could talk her way around him, she could do anything.

The schedule appeared on the screen. It was deceptively open, she knew most of his appointments would not be listed, but at least she knew he was in the city and working today.

She steeled herself for the next question, "Schedule of Yokosh Kohl."

So, he was in the city as well. She also checked the schedule for Kral. He was not in Khizara, but she did find that he was no longer simply a ship captain. He was commander of an entire fleet. *You've done well*, Linsora thought. *Standing with Yokosh was wise after all.*

She left the room and entered the busy city. She did not sample the emotions of the crowd again. She knew she was being watched.

The Prefecture was housed in the imposing structure at the center of the city. Guards surrounded the large building topped with five sharp points that rose toward the hazy blue sky. Linsora stood among the tourists admiring it. She picked up one of the information sheets thinking, as she always had, what a foolish waste it was to have these fluttering bits of paper so freely available. Anyone who wanted to know about the capital could pull the information up on a terminal. But, even Khizarans liked to go home with something in their hands, something free. She read it. She had read it before. Nothing had changed in five years. But, still, to her it held new significance.

The capital had stood on this spot for thousands of years. The actual structure had been replaced many times, having been destroyed by warfare, fire, or sheer age. The five spires represented the five bands of ancient Khizarans brought together nearly five thousand years ago by Pantokh. Originally there had been six spires. The sixth, which no longer existed, had represented the tribes led by Tokor. Linsora shuddered. He had led his people into a remote region and there plotted to overthrow the new Prefecture. Tokor and his followers attacked Khizara, setting the capital ablaze. The remaining five bands defeated Tokor. He and his followers escaped into space, pursued by loyal Khizarans. None were heard from again. A major Khizaran holiday celebrated the bravery of the Lost Fleet. What remained of the capital was demolished, the sixth spire forever destroyed. The expulsion of Tokor from Khizara was regarded as a Khizaran victory. To Tokorellans, the successful establishment of Tokorel was a victory.

And who will win this time, Linsora wondered

Linsora spat. She closed her eyes and allowed her anger to roll over the doubt. She was most angry at Permac for not being here with her. Angry at herself for not dying with him. Angry at fate for placing her in this position. She marched up the steps and entered the building, scowling at the woman behind the front desk.

"I will see Prefect Behazh," she said.

The woman raised her eyebrows, and scowled back. "You have an appointment?"

"Not yet. Tell him it is Linsora Anselm. He will see me," Linsora wished she were as sure of that as she sounded.

CHAPTER 20

The woman at the desk indicated surprise when she received the response that Prefect Behazh would indeed agree to see this Linsora Anselm. Linsora was a bit surprised herself that he not only granted her an audience, but an immediate one. Behazh, his face looking not much older than it had five years earlier, embraced Linsora in a warm hug. He had always looked ancient to her. His hair was white but glinted like sliver in the sunshine. He once told her that his hair only turned white after she was born, but her mother said he had been gray-haired since his early thirties. The creases around his eyes and mouth were deep. He was man prone to frequent smiles and genuine affection. Behazh held her at arm's length.

"I see you haven't learned to stay out of the way of people's fists yet," he gently touched the remaining outline of the bruise on her cheek, a reminder of Gordek.

Linsora smiled, "At least I'm in better shape than the last time you saw me."

The last time had been five years earlier, with Yokosh. After their mother died, her will stipulated that her land was to be inherited by Linsora. Yokosh would inherit land from his father, and so would not need their mother's for his support. Yokosh claimed that their mother's property, the land given to their mother by their grandfather, was his by virtue of his being the oldest male heir. He also asserted that when their mother had Sealed the Oath with a non-Khizaran, she had given up her right to bestow Khizaran property. It was an insult to their mother and a legally murky claim.

Before meeting with Behazh, he had goaded Linsora into challenging him to a duel. She fought with sloppy wariness, letting more than one opportunity to strike a deadly blow purposefully slip past. She didn't believe he would kill her. At that time, she didn't want to kill him. It wasn't about the property, why Yokosh wanted the land remained a mystery to her. She only wanted to address the insult. It should not have been a death fight. Over the subsequent five years, Linsora sometimes wondered why she had been angry enough to challenge him, but not angry enough to kill him.

Her defense was as sloppy as her offense and Yokosh acted. He would have killed her and not had to worry about legalities. Linsora remembered lying on the ground, blood flowing from the gash in her side. The wound was serious, but not life-threatening. She remained on the ground waiting for Yokosh to approach. Waiting for him to believe he could strike the killing blow. She was positioned to roll and strike her own killing blow. Then Kral stopped the duel. Kral was the witness. Yokosh's friend. Linsora's lover. He had volunteered for the job of being arbiter of the duel, being witness to the

the winner's win and the loser's death. And, as witness to a duel where death was not the stated goal, he could step in to stop it.

Linsora didn't know if he stepped in to save Yokosh's life or hers. He knew the loss of the duel without the loss of life would mean she would also lose many Khizaran rights since she had officially made the challenge, but the loss would only be temporary. Kral tried to tell her he knew she had fought at a level below her abilities, that he had seen her hold back, that she would not have survived. But, Linsora felt betrayed. Kral could have stopped the duel at any time. He waited until she was down and would be declared the loser.

Behazh decreed that the property belonged to whomever their mother gave it, but that Linsora could not claim it for ten years. During that time, it would be Yokosh's, an award to him for the terminated duel. But the duel never really ended. Her promise to kill Yokosh stood, probably as did his promise to kill her. She hadn't seen Kral or her half-brother since.

"I am surprised to see you," Behazh said. "I honestly didn't expect to for..."

"I know I have five more years to wait before claiming my property. And I know I can't stay," Linsora said, detaching from him. "I trust Yokosh is looking after it well."

"As well as you might expect," Behazh sighed. "If you want it to be of any value, you'll have to put some work into it - after you claim it."

"I'm not here to claim it," Linsora smiled. "That can wait."

"Oh. Well, then," Behazh sat and indicated a seat next to his. "I didn't notice your name on recent arrival rosters. Have you been back for long?" He spoke in a matter of fact manner, but a great deal of suspicion was implied.

"I arrived yesterday." Linsora walked to the window. She had to ask, but didn't want Behazh to read her face when she spoke his son's name. "How's Kral? He's a fleet commander now?"

"He's worked for it, Linsora."

She turned from the window, "Behazh, I didn't mean...I know as well as anyone that you don't become a fleet commander because of who you know."

"He was on his way to that position even five years ago. Yes, he stood with Yokosh and Yokosh has also gained power. Yes, they still associate. But this and the event of five years ago are unrelated. You've been gone five years. Coming home must make the unresolved issues fresher to you than to the other parties." Behazh peered at her from under bushy white eyebrows, just as he did when asking for the truth about stolen pastries when she was a child. "I expected, as did Kral, that when you recovered, you'd come back to us, continue your life."

"You think I ran away." Her voice was flat.

"Honestly? It's not an easy truth, this one, but yes. Kral was hurt. He saved your life the only way he could. The duel escalated to something he hadn't expected. Maybe Yokosh knew it would be a death duel. Maybe you knew. But Kral believed it was to settle an argument. As simple a fight as anything like that ever is. The first one down withdraws, you clean each other's blades, get drunk together, and go on. Yokosh, for some reason, hates you and I don't say that lightly."

"Kral's feelings were hurt? Kral stood with him!"

"Kral has known Yokosh longer than he's known you."

"He was going to Seal the Oath with me, Behazh! I would think that implies a stronger bond!"

"It does. As I said, he saved your life the only way he knew how. If he stood with you and stopped Yokosh, you'd have lost your land. Standing with Yokosh, he could stop the killing blow without penalty to you."

Linsora's eyes were hot, her hands numb and cold. "I know. I knew then," her throat was dry and sentiments she hadn't even wanted to think about came to life in a husky rasp. "I hated him. Kral, I mean. I knew why he did it, but I hated him as much as I loved him."

Ice clicked at the rim of a pitcher as Behazh poured water into a glass. Linsora gulped and held out the glass for more.

"And now?" Behazh asked.

"I don't hate him," Linsora smiled. "And I don't love him. I'm glad he's doing well."

"His hurts have healed. He Sealed the Oath last year, with Raminaa. New love has astounding healing properties," Behazh winked. "I can read you now just as I could twenty years ago, Lin. New love has healed much of your pain, too."

"Raminaa? I'd never have guessed that. Does her family still keep herds?"

"She's in charge of them now, in fact. Doing well at it."

"Just as I should have done? Stayed on my land, keeping the animals and raising children?"

"Linsora! You're who you are. Raminaa is happy on her land. Your mother never was, your father certainly wasn't tied to the land. Why should you be?"

"It would have made my life simpler."

"But not happier. Tell me about your five years away. Tell me about your love."

"What I have to tell you is not simple."

"With you, Linsora, it never is," he said, patting the chair next to him.

Linsora swirled the water in her glass. The plan of attack seemed reasonable while she was sipping tea in the hotel. All the arguments refuted, all objections neatly turned into advantages. Now, standing in front of Behazh, she felt like a child again. She remembered hiding behind her mother when this man, who had seemed old even then, twenty-five years ago, visited their household complex. She cowered when he reached out a hand to pat her shoulder. Then he smiled. All the severe lines vanished behind lively blue eyes and a wide grin. *You're not smiling now*, she thought. *You know I wouldn't be here for something trivial and you don't like it.*

She reached for his hand and gave it a squeeze, as though she was still a child telling Behazh about the exploits of her pet. He always listened with honest interest, as though her tale was the most important news of the day. He understood that, to Linsora, her tale truly was important and granted her the dignity of honoring her passion.

"My love is…was…was and is Permac. He's dead." Linsora waved the beginning of Behazh's sympathy away. "Before he was killed, we found the descendants of the Lost Fleet."

He didn't react immediately. He seemed to stare right through her. She thought he had become pale.

"How?" Behazh gripped her arm, a bit too firmly. She felt a slight prickle at the back of her neck.

"I thought you'd be excited," she said, pulling away.

Behazh ran his hand down her arm and took her hand. He smoothed her hair with his other hand.

"Behazh, what's wrong?"

"I don't know how you manage to find trouble, but you do it better than most," he said. "Not long ago, someone else was here saying the same thing."

"Yokosh?"

"Tell me your story first." Behazh shook his head, but Linsora sensed that her half-brother's name was the correct guess.

She wanted to stand and pace, to look down onto the rush of ordinary Khizarans three stories below. Behazh held her hand firmly, holding her in place until her story was told. She didn't dare influence him to trust her, even a slight change in eye color would be obvious and what control she had been taught required more concentration than she could muster now. She opened her mind to sample his emotions and felt nothing more than she would have guessed by looking at him – worry and concern.

"My story has nothing to do with Yokosh, at least not directly," she said. "But it does involve Tokorellans."

The lines on Behazh's face became deep furrows. His eyebrows met, becoming a single white line. They no longer gave Behazh the kindly look of a patient uncle. He had become the stern Prefect. Linsora followed the sudden swing of his gaze toward the door of his office, toward shifting plays of light and shadow.

"That is a name to be spoken softly," he said.

"It is now. Maybe not forever." She leaned forward, touching her forehead to his. She spoke in a low voice, a tone not easily overheard. "My love was a good man, Behazh. Kind and funny. He cared more for me than I can tell you. He helped me find the Lost Fleet. Behazh, he was Tokorellan."

She didn't allow time for his reaction. She told of finding the image of Tokor on Brachen, of the star chart. "We found the descendants of the Lost Fleet, Behazh! I know a lot about what happened to them, but not everything."

Behazh whistled. "You make my head ache, Lin. Do you have any idea what the implications are?" His grip on her hand had steadily increased during the telling of her tale until Linsora thought he might crush every last bone. He enclosed her hand in both of his, replacing the squeeze with absent-minded patting. "Of course you do, otherwise you wouldn't be here. You're right about Yokosh. He did tell me he might know something of the Lost Fleet, but he didn't say much else. You know him, he likes dangling sweet scented information in front of people's noses."

"When?"

"Three weeks ago. That would be just about the time you arrived on, what's it called? Hakai?" Behazh tilted his head, "Is there a relationship in the timing?"

"I would have said no a week ago," Linsora smiled. "Now, I'm not at all sure. Some people have told me that Yokosh has…well, let's just say ties to people on Hakai. I don't know if he's been there, though."

"Political ties? Or romantic? He's not known for making wise choices on either front."

"Most likely both."

Behazh breathed heavily, "Well well and well again. But you've been there. You have the location?"

"I can get it."

"Which means no. And," Behazh wagged one finger, "That also implies it might not be simple. I don't want you to take any risks. We've survived for this long without knowing where they are…"

"I do. And…" Linsora suddenly remembered Captain Haavens.

"And what?"

"The captain of the ship that brought us to Brachen, where we saw the image of Tokor, Captain Haavens has the coordinates, too." Linsora exhaled. "And much of the crew of his ship saw Tokor's image. That information may already be floating around the Mercantile."

"Too much, Linsora. Too much for me and for all of us." Behazh ran a suddenly damp hand across a suddenly damp brow. "I suppose you should give me the location."

"You sound like you don't want to know."

"In a way, I don't. Are they...I mean...I don't know what I mean, exactly. They're probably ordinary people?"

"Ordinary how?" Linsora took a deep breath. "Not ordinary in the sense of Khizaran ordinary."

"Neither of us is being clear. I was thinking that we have elevated the Lost Fleet to such a platform of integrity and bravery, it might be disappointing to find their descendants are people just like us after all. That they were just like us. What did you mean? I have a feeling it's not the same thing."

"No it isn't. Behazh, I've been through a lot in a short time. I've learned a lot. And there's so much more to be learned." Linsora tried to come up with some kind of explanation that wouldn't involve telling everything to Behazh, but truth was the only story she could think of. "Tokor's powers, the powers the Tokorellans have, comes from a plant. The plant is called tejina and, in a dry climate, it produces a fruit called chikara. Eating the fruit gives them the powers. The people on Hakai, the Lost Fleet descendants, have very potent chikara."

"So, the Lost Fleet people aren't ordinary Khizarans. They're more like ordinary Tokorellans, is that it?"

"Pretty much it."

She recounted the story of Tokor's departure from Khizara and how the Hakains were left behind. "They feel they were abandoned by Tokor and Khizara. Behazh, they've had visitors from Tokorel. It's only proper that we contact them, too."

"Linsora, you know what kind of reaction the Khizarans would have. Our heroes, our Lost Fleet, subverted by Tokor?"

"I had the same reaction. But if those Khizarans can influence emotions just by eating chikara, anyone can. Maybe Tokor knew any Khizaran could do it. Maybe he didn't. The projection of Tokor on Brachen indicated he didn't want to attack Khizara. That it was some impatient followers who did. And Tokorellan history says that Khizarans attacked Tokor! Behazh, let me go to the Forbidden Area. Tokor might have left records behind, something that might clarify how this all started."

Behazh's eyebrows separated into two entities and rose toward his hairline, leaving little forehead between the two. His hands abandoned patting Linsora's and rose to his face. He rubbed his temples, pulling his eyebrows back into a normal position.

"All this and you're asking to go into the Forbidden Area?" Behazh shook his head, indicating a definite negative.

"Someone has to, Behazh, and one day someone will. Why not us? Why not now?"

"Who better than you, is that what you mean?"

"I'm an archaeologist, I know how to investigate the Forbidden Area carefully. I know what the plants look like, too, so I can steer people away from them." Linsora was lost in the excitement of the chase, words tumbled from her list of arguments. "My father discovered Pak'Bor. I was with him. I have information on the Lost Fleet and new information on Tokor himself."

Behazh didn't seem to be listening. He rose slowly and moved to the window gazing down at the people, his people.

"None of this is small, Linsora. Pak'Bor was important, but the only impact was a few more pages in our history annals and a new place to travel on vacation. Each element of your information – the Lost Fleet, Tokor, and that plant – each one could change Khizara in ways neither of us can imagine."

"I know," Linsora joined him and leaned her head against his chest. "But if Yokosh has the same information I do, he'll use it."

"What about them?" Behazh pointed to the people on the street, hurrying toward lunch dates, rushing toward the Prefecture to watch the opening of the daily afternoon session, waiting on a corner for a friend. Ordinary. "How will they react? Not well, I imagine. Old beliefs don't surrender gently." He stroked Linsora's hair. "Even if you find that Tokor himself didn't orchestrate the attack on the capital, it won't change anything. People associated with Tokor did."

"Maybe not. Maybe Khizarans orchestrated it to get rid of Tokor."

"Would that be better?"

"It would make him seem less like a magician, less powerful. He'd just be someone with unusual knowledge who…"

"Who was persecuted by Khizarans. And it would make him even more of a heroic figure to Tokorellans. Maybe even to those Hakains. Whose side are you on?" Behazh punched one fist into the palm of his other hand. "I'm sorry, I didn't mean that. I've known your family all my life. I've known you all your life. You take a straight-line approach – problem and solution – without much worry about the implications of your actions to yourself. I've always found you refreshingly naïve about politics. You believe that everyone around you is as honestly motivated as you are. And that's gotten you in trouble more than once. You're not simply asking for funding now. Your brother seems to have inherited all the political savvy. He believes everyone around him is as duplicitous as he is, and in the realms of the Prefecture and the Mercantile, he's generally right."

Behazh stretched his arms, like he was reaching toward the heavens for some kind of answer. "Part of my alarm is personal. As intriguing as an archaeological survey to the Forbidden Area is, if I propose it to the Prefecture and they deny entry, my position will be forever suspect. I've spent a lifetime establishing myself as a reasoning and sensible intermediary. I could be painted with the brush of an old man who wants to make a big bright splash before his time is over. I'm not the only one holding the Prefecture to a reasonable line, of course, but I am a strong presence now. If I'm discredited...Linsora, you've been away for five years. You don't know the situation. It's becoming dangerous."

"How so?"

"There is a movement calling for increasing the military budget, increasing our forces. There are whispers about making a move to take over the Mercantile."

"People have always grumbled about the Mercantile, Behazh."

"This is more than grumbling. If we give Khizarans information on that plant, they might not be as shy about using it now as they were two hundred years ago. They just might begin to feel powerful enough to act on the grumbling. Added to that, if we give the worlds of the Mercantile a Tokor who is kind, benevolent, and a victim of Khizaran persecution, the grumbling from everyone about Khizaran aggression would re-ignite. The spiraling down into chaos from there makes my head spin."

"But Tokor didn't rendezvous with the Lost Fleet. He abandoned them. That doesn't make him look very benevolent. Haavens' crew will spread the story they heard on Brachen. We need to get the whole story out before people start to hear rumors." Linsora heard the twang of a whine in her voice. She felt like stamping her foot, putting her hands on her hips, and jutting out her jaw. *I'm acting like a ten year old begging for more sweets,* she thought trying to adjust her body.

"So we tell Khizara we've found the Lost Fleet, befriend the Hakains, offer our apologies for not finding them before this, and launch into an exploration of the Forbidden Area? What about the fruit?"

"If Yokosh knows about Hakai and the fruit, his friends, political and personal, know about it, too. If not now, then soon. Think of it as pre-emptive strike. Get the information out in a reasoned manner. Think of being on equal footing with Tokorel! Think of being aligned with Tokorel. Better to have them as friends than enemies. They've had years to establish usage. Culturally and physically. Better to have them work with us to learn how to use the fruit than allowing only a few to have it or learning it through trial and error."

"You do have grand visions," Behazh said, clapping Linsora on the back. "Grand visions come with grand problems and grand foes." He turned her around and stared into her eyes. "Have you eaten that fruit?" Behazh shook his head and placed a fingertip on her lips, "No, don't tell me. What I don't know I can't report. Still, I have a feeling there's a lot you're leaving out of your story."

Linsora felt like her stomach was about to turn inside out. She wished she could use all the influencing powers she had on her own emotions. "Some people believe that the records Tokor left on Khizara have information on the origin of the fruit, maybe something about a special preparation he used to make it more potent. If the books are here, they'd most likely be in the Forbidden Area. No one has been there since just after Tokor left. If we could find them and learn more about the fruit, maybe we'd be in a better position to negotiate with Tokorel and Hakai."

"We could use it to bargain with."

"Maybe. Just a survey of the Forbidden Area to see what might be there. Tokorel might be interested in information about the place Tokor lived, too, even if we don't find anything otherwise valuable. We've been afraid of Tokorel for two hundred years. Maybe the time has come not to be."

Behazh still held her gaze, but she sent feelings of trust to him. Just a little, maybe just enough to make him hear her words with less prejudice than he would normally feel.

"My dear, I believe you are sincere. No more than that. I cannot, for the sake of Khizara, believe more than that," Behazh said. "In the midst of all this, did I hear you say your mate was Tokorellan?"

"Yes, I said he was a good man. A man I loved."

"How did he die?"

"On Hakai. We were caught in some political tempest. I don't know how it could be possible, but people we met are the same people Yokosh knows. I didn't know it then, but they did. It all became violent and Permac was killed. I was..." *I was what? Rescued?* She thought. *Not really.* Behazh waited. "I came to Khizara with people interested in learning more about Tokor. People who weren't interested in the politics of Hakai."

"I won't ask you the origins of those you traveled with. This is already far too complex. All I can do is consider your request. A survey of the Forbidden

Area may well be overdue. At the very least, I will consider that portion." He walked to his desk, waved his hand over a panel then crossed his arms. Linsora knew his hands were on concealed weapons. She would have no choice but to accept whatever it was he was about to suggest. "I will need at least a day. The entire Prefecture must agree on entry to the Forbidden Area and my request will have to be convincing, if I make the request at all. Until then, you will be placed in protective custody."

"Behazh, I don't need that. I'm safe and..."

"And I will ensure you stay that way. Anyone with the kind of information you have is liable to be of interest to a variety of parties. Even if you have told no one else, the stars let secrets fall at their whim sometimes." Behazh cocked his head toward the door.

"The Prefecture's guest suite is the safest place I can think of for you. And, as I noted, you seem to have a talent for running into fists and knives." He opened the door to two heavily armed Prefecture guards, "She is to have no visitors, no outside contact whatsoever. Whatever she wants, procure for her - but examine it well. I want her returned here safely tomorrow."

The guard nodded toward Linsora. She exchanged a last look with Behazh before becoming the center of the small circle.

The quarters were more than comfortable, fitting for visiting dignitaries, with ample room for Linsora to pace. She thought about sending fatigue to the guards then leaving, but she had come this far. One more day. One more day and she'd have all the forces of Khizara to protect her and Tokor's secrets from Gordek. One more day. She asked the guards standing at attention at the doors about their favorite foods and placed a meal order including quantities of the best delicacies her home world had to offer.

CHAPTER 21

Linsora filled the large tub with steaming hot water, climbed in, and submerged. The psychic healing benefits of a hot bath had never worked for her. She felt none of her tension ease in the steam, none of her alertness diminish. The freedom she had tasted on her arrival in Khizara was gone, taken not only by the Tokorellans but now by a leader of her own home world. Behazh was concerned about her safety, she granted him that much, but he was more concerned about the safety of Khizara. *He sees me as a threat*, she thought. *The problem is, he might be right.* Tokor was a mythic figure to Khizarans, the embodiment of evil. If he were revealed to be benign, or even shown to be good, who would the Khizarans focus on as an enemy? Linsora had no doubt that her people needed an enemy - an outside force to unite them. *Perhaps*, she mused, *every society needs one. Maybe that's where the devils on so many worlds come from.* Khizarans had as varied a selection of religions as any race, most included a range of gods both good and bad. Her mother claimed to believe only in what she could report on and her father claimed he was happy enough to wait until he was dead to find out what the cosmic realities were. Consequently, Linsora had never made the concept of a god, with or without a capital G, part of her philosophy. *Good exists. Evil exists. No need to wonder why.* She closed her eyes and let the hot water lap against her chin.

From two rooms away, she heard a door swing open. The guards always knocked before entering. She climbed out of the bath, fumbled into a large robe, and retrieved a small dagger from her boot. She opened her mind and nearly dropped the dagger. She felt blazing fury. That alone was expected from a Khizaran, but this was a fury tinged with fingers of emotion being sent out to her. It tasted burned, unpleasant, and oddly familiar. She immediately placed barriers to it in her mind, as she had been taught. She could not yet control her powers well enough to disguise the fact that she had them and knew she was revealing herself to this person, but deemed that better than accepting the influences being sent her way.

Suddenly, she felt a wave of dizziness. She staggered but retained her grip on the knife. With all the effort at her command, she returned a sense of weakness to the trespasser. It was answered with another burst of a spinning sensation that sent her sprawling on the floor.

She heard the laugh first, then his voice. "So, sister, it seems you have picked up a few tricks yourself. But you're still not as strong as I am."

"Yokosh!" she whispered.

"One and the same. You can't begin to imagine how eager I was to see you when I heard you were back."

Linsora shook herself and stood up. Yokosh was at least a foot taller than she was, lean and wiry. Five years ago, he wore his sandy hair cropped short. Now he sported a longer tousled look, making his deep-set blue eyes more vivid. Linsora had to admit her brother was attractive, deceptively boyish and innocent. "You're looking well, evil living suits you."

"It does," he smiled graciously. "Better than clean living suits you, sister. You worry too much. It shows. Gordek tells me you never relax – that's just not healthy."

"Did he tell you I was here?"

"Oh yes," Yokosh plopped on the bed. "Amazing how you two met, isn't it?"

"I've met Tayla, too. She's nearly as delightful as you are," Linsora said. "I take it you know about chikara, too."

"That, and other useful substances," he pulled pillows from under the covers and scrunched them under his head. "And I've been exposed to more than you have, little half-breed sister, and for much longer. I always was and always will be stronger than you could ever hope to be."

"You know, I've spent a lot of time hating you. From now on I won't waste my energy," she pushed his feet off the bed. "You're just crude. Stronger and smarter don't go hand in hand, either."

A dagger of pain shot through her head. She held the bedpost for support.

"The great Tokorellan magic," Yokosh laughed. "Useful even to someone as stupid and crude as myself."

"You can't kill me here. What do you want?"

"I know why you're here and I don't like it. Information might be in the Forbidden Area, but it's been there for 200 years and isn't going away. If you find anything, it won't stay secret for long. We're not ready for that, not yet. Gordek is impatient."

"You're just afraid he'll get there before you do."

"And that he'll leave you alive to do whatever strikes you as a good deed," he said. "For some reason I cannot fathom, he wants to keep you alive. Do you have anything to eat?" Yokosh rummaged through a tray near the bed, helping himself. "Now that we know the information is in the Forbidden Area, we can go there anytime. We don't need you."

"Who's this 'we' you're talking about?"

"The 'we' is myself and other Khizarans who believe we've become far too fat and happy. The economy is sound, everyone feels safe and secure. The fire is being eaten away from Khizarans." He picked up a slice of toasted bread. "Just like this – it should be hot, not cold and limp. We have a superior ranking with the Mercantile. Little sister, we could have more than trading relations – we could rival the Mercantile. We could be the ones who set the rules and take a five percent cut of every transaction."

Linsora sputtered a laugh, "So you want to rule the known universe? Have your own economic empire? That's your vision of the new Khizaran fire? Somehow I don't think so. You want to ignite wars so you'll have a chance at glory. So you can have a reason to spill blood whenever you feel like it. That's the Khizaran fire you want, and it's appalling. And, by the way, the Mercantile takes three percent."

"Exactly. We'll take five and the members will be happy to pay the two percent extra for a guarantee of protection."

"I think that's called extortion, brother."

"Doesn't matter what it's called as long as they pay. The point is, the entire Mercantile is sloppy now. There are people like the Carratians who pay less than three percent by whining about high operating expenses. Imagine a force with the abilities of my people. We will sweep out of the stars – every major port at once, and take over."

"You're delusional. But, you know, I encourage you. I doubt you and your people will live long enough to regret any of it."

"You think so? You think I plan on doing this with ordinary weapons? Oh no no no! The ports will hardly be aware of us." He tapped the side of his head. "Think Tokorellan, little sister, think of mind control."

Linsora did think. She thought about the image of Tokor on Brachen and his mention of a weapon of peace. A weapon is a weapon, regardless of the intentions of its designers. In the hands of people like her half-brother, the end result would be far from peaceful.

"Gordek is part of all this? What a team you two make," Linsora granted her brother a withering smile.

"Many people are part of this. People in the Prefecture, people in the Mercantile, people on Tokorel. Want to know how I met your friend Gordek?"

"Gordek is most certainly not my friend and I don't really care how you met him."

Yokosh rolled off the bed, laughing. He pulled a pouch from his pants pocket and emptied it on the bedside table. Dried leaves scattered across the remains of the food. Yokosh chose several and popped them in his mouth. "Know what this is? Leaves of something called tejina."

"What did you say?"

"Ah, you've heard of it! You'll never guess where this came from!"

Yokosh chewed the leaves into a brown pulp and washed it down with a swig of lukewarm tea. "From our dear mother's land."

"My land?"

"Not yours yet. Not yours ever. Long before another five years have passed, you'll be nothing more than dust," he said, grabbing more leaves. "Did Gordek tell you he was not so politely asked to leave Tokorel after a run-in with some bigwig? A power thing and Gordek lost. He came to Khizara a few years after you left looking for tejina plants. Making sense yet? If you plant tejina in a dry climate, the plants bear fruit called…"

"Chikara."

"Very good! Tokor was a botanist. He was an explorer, too, and collected plant samples. One of them was this," Yokosh opened his mouth wide for Linsora to see the sludge in his mouth. "Along with it came the tasty little microbes. They're in the fruit and the leaves. Mostly the fruit. Even then, where the fruit grows makes a difference. But it's the preparation, the combination of tejina with something else, that we don't know. That's where the real power is. We don't know where Tokor first got the tejina, either."

"I thought the leaves were poisonous."

"They are if you eat them right off the plant. Gotta roast them first."

"You think you'll find the secret of this preparation in the Forbidden Area? Maybe the location of its origin?"

"Exactly. Tokor didn't know if he'd survive. He was a scientist. He didn't want the knowledge he'd gathered to die with him. So, it stands to reason that he'd have left something behind. He even left some tejina – he could have taken it all, you know. The microbes only get into the soil when chikara falls and rots. Why do you think the Forbidden Area is forbidden? I'm not the only one who thinks something interesting is still there."

"Why bother telling me?"

"I want you to have something to think about while you're dying," he smirked. "Or during your long nights with Gordek."

"As I said, you're delusional."

"Oh no. You see, Gordek has expressed a certain, shall we say, attraction to you. We have come to an agreement that I find most appealing. I am willing to let you go freely if you agree to Seal the Oath with our friend Gordek. He's assured me he can keep you quiet."

Linsora spat in his direction.

"I take it that means you'll think about it."

"I'll think about your death. I'll think about his death. I'll think about my own death before I'd Seal the Oath with him."

Yokosh grinned, "Oh, little sister, I find it such an amusing pairing, too. But, there is an alternative. In two hours, if you don't agree to Seal the Oath, you will be the subject of an interesting experiment. We have never tried to combine our mental powers in an effort to control someone. Up until now it had been considered too dangerous. But, we'll be willing to try it on you little sister. You're very expendable."

"Control me?"

"I will take you to the Prefecture this afternoon. You already admitted to Behazh that you've been in contact with Tokorellans. Yes, I know that, too. I have people everywhere, including people with good ears outside Behazh's office. I will present you as an ally of Tokorellans. You will have no chance to defend yourself, because you will have nothing to say. Gordek and I will control you. I will tell the Prefecture that after I discovered your treachery, your Tokorellan friends used their magic to silence you. For effect, I might even have your eyes change color. I can say you're trying to fight off their influence or something. Might cast a good deal of suspicion on Behazh, too. And the end result will be more fear of Tokorellans, easier funding for a stronger military force, and, not inconsequentially, your death. All of which plays into my waiting hands. Once my people have more power, we can go to the Forbidden Area anytime."

"If Gordek is so interested in me, why would he agree to help you kill me? "

"He has as little choice as you. This is my territory."

"Yokosh, there is no choice. I'd rather be dead, as I told you. Dead by my own hand or the Prefecture's is still dead and not sealed to Gordek."

"Two hours, then I'll be back with Gordek," Yokosh wiped his hands on the bed and gathered the dried tejina leaves back into his pouch.

She sat on the edge of her bed trying to avoid any portion of it touched by Yokosh. Her half-brother had gone through her clothes and taken all the knives he could find. Since she had just gotten out of the tub, he was even able to check her boots. He wanted to be sure her death wasn't a solitary affair he'd be unable to witness.

"Options, Linsora," she said to the empty room. "There has to be something. Has to be."

If I Seal the Oath with Gordek, I'll be alive, she thought. *Sealing the Oath and everything that goes along with it has to be consensual. I could…I wouldn't have to…*Her imagination supplied her with vivid pictures of everything she wouldn't have to do with Gordek. She shuddered. *I couldn't stop him. He could use his influences. He would use them. And he would lock me up when he wasn't using them. Eventually he'd make a mistake. Even he's not perfectly vigilant. How long, though? Years maybe. Even one hour is too long.*

She grabbed the plate littered with crumbs and bits of toast Yokosh had torn apart. She spat on it, raised it over her head and hurled it toward the slate floor. It shattered with a satisfying crash, splintered shards of the formerly fine china skittered in every direction. Linsora surveyed the pieces and chose an edge portion, round on one side, razor sharp on the other. It was cold.

I won't give you the satisfaction of watching me die, Yokosh.

For the second time in a week, she prepared herself. Her skin prickled with energy. She inhaled deeply, moving her attention away from that portion of the brain that cries out against pain, especially self-inflicted.

What will Behazh think? A little voice of preservation was not yet stilled. *He'll have to know that Yokosh was involved somehow, but he'll have no proof. Yokosh will have no proof for the Prefecture, either. Will he? He can't assemble any witnesses, not reputable ones, as fast as this. Could he make my eyes turn purple? I don't know how he could, that doesn't mean he couldn't.*

She tested the edge of the plate against her thumb. She winced as blood spurted across the white ceramic.

Why was this so easy last time? I'd have done it if Gordek hadn't sent the rage. She stuck her thumb in her mouth, playing her tongue over tiny flap of damaged skin, tasting salty blood. *I had nothing then. I knew Permac was dead. I know he's dead. If I'm dead, who'll stop Gordek?* Her thumb throbbed. *Funny how such a small cut can hurt so much. My death will stop Gordek. Without me, he can't get into the Forbidden Area.*

She stared into a middle distance, not focusing on anything but the dust motes in the air. Inhale, calm, exhale, count. Inhale. *Stop. No stopping now. No.* Inhale, count. *Make peace with your enemies. No, I condemn my enemies. I will die without making peace. Before, I had no enemies. I hated, but I had no enemies. There's a difference. No, I didn't even hate. I had nothing. Hate sustains. Despair is having nothing. Stop. Stop. Stop.* She shivered. Her feet on the cold slate were icy. Her skin still prickled, the tiny hairs raised atop bumps of gooseflesh. *No stopping. No stopping.* She brought the sharp end to her throat.

"Linsora. Stop!"

Only a whisper. Not a shout from Yokosh or Gordek. Only a breath floating on the air. *Only my mind.* She sensed someone. She thought she heard a drop of blood from her thumb splot on the floor. The skin around the cut was white, though, not bleeding. Tiny soft cobwebs seemed to catch on the goosebumps of her arms, like a soft cloak, warm, inviting peace and comfort. Salty blood, sweet blood. Sweetness.

A shadow moved in the far corner.

"Linsora, over here."

"Who are you?"

The shadow shimmered.

"Your assistant is Denub."

Through the flicker of shadow, Linsora thought she saw a smile.

"How?" she asked. "It can't be."

"No time. Listen. Not..." the murmur became a sigh became something that dissipated before it reached her. She felt glued to the floor, but leaned forward trying to grasp the slight vibrations in the air. "...alive. On To..."

"Permac? I can't hear you."

"What's wrong?" The whisper was stronger.

"I don't know, I can't hear you."

"Fixed that. With you, I mean?"

"Yokosh says if I don't Seal the Oath with Gordek, he'll take me to the Prefecture and accuse me of being a spy. They, Yokosh and Gordek, have some plan to control me. Don't know what or how."

The shimmer faded to a shapeless gray. Linsora could see dust motes floating inside it.

"Permac?" She took a step forward and reached out her hand. The air felt no different inside the haze. No heat of life, no cold of death. She jumped back when the shimmer moved.

"...ecture. Go there. We'll help."

"We? We who? Permac!" The ghostly shimmer faded and vanished, leaving the air still. She dropped the shard of plate. It must have made a sound when it shattered, but she didn't hear it. She still strained toward the dark corner.

I've lost my mind. I'm hallucinating. She laughed, *it might be interesting to Seal the Oath with Gordek, though, and make him live his life with a madwoman.* The corner didn't shimmer, maybe it never had.

Before Linsora had time to reconsider, Yokosh returned, accompanied by Gordek.

"I thought I had two hours," she said.

"Gordek here wanted to see his blushing bride," Yokosh said. He kicked broken china across the floor, eyeing the red-stained edges of some pieces. "Been away from Khizara too long, sister? Did you lose your nerve?"

"I didn't lose my sense, Yokosh. You never did think clearly enough to finish anything. This won't be any different."

"Bitch! If it's up to me to decide how you die..."

"That's enough!" Gordek pushed past Yokosh. "Linsora, I thought

179

Behazh might be able to ensure your safety, but your brother's nothing if not bold. His forces here are more extensive than mine. Unfortunately there was little I could do to prevent all of this. That does not mean we can't recover from it." Gordek paused, as though considering what to say within Yokosh's hearing, "We need your expertise in the Forbidden Area. Yokosh thinks he can find what he needs easily, I don't. We need information on the original source of tejina, how to prepare it. Tokor hinted at unlimited power!" Gordek was getting excited and began to talk faster. "Do you see what this could mean to us? We could control worlds, fleets of ships, entire civilizations! And you could be a part of it all - at my side"

"How lovely for both of you," Yokosh grunted.

Gordek glanced at Yokosh. The younger man winced in pain. His knees buckled slightly.

Linsora smiled. Yokosh was literally being brought to his knees without being threatened by a weapon or physical force.

Yokosh's bony left knee hit the floor. Gordek continued, "Just think, Linsora, you could remove anyone in your way."

Yokosh spoke through clenched teeth, "Gordek," he said, "if you do not release me, I guarantee that others who have far more power than I will hunt you down, and the only thing you'll be leading is the way to hell for the rest of your followers!"

Gordek looked mildly annoyed. "I may be many things, but I am not a liar. We have a deal, Yokosh, and I don't intend to go back on it."

Yokosh dropped completely to the ground, breathing heavily, and looked up at Gordek. "I will make you suffer for that." Yokosh stood and tried to salvage what little dignity he had left. "For now, Linsora has a decision to make. Let's go so that she can decide on her own."

Gordek looked once more at Linsora. "We will make a glorious team, you and I." He took her wrist, raised it to his mouth. Before his teeth touched her, he felt the stinging blow of Linsora's other hand slash his face. His look of surprise melted into a grin. "You are marvelous," he said.

"I couldn't remove anyone in my way, Gordek. I couldn't remove you." She wrenched her hand away from him. "Yokosh," she called. "There's no decision. I won't help either of you."

"By doing nothing, you have already helped me. I can't lose, dear sister." He turned to Gordek, "Keep your part of the bargain. You want to clean the blood off your face first, or do you want that as the last reminder of my sister's love?"

"Linsora!" Gordek's tone was scolding. "While you're alive, your promises are alive, your vengeance."

"Someone else gave me that chance five years ago. I'm not sorry I had the time, but I don't make the same mistake twice if I can help it."

"Can't you see what will happen if he takes you to the Prefecture? You'll be the first known Tokorellan agent on Khizara. No one will trust anyone else. It could result in political and social chaos."

"I thought that's what you wanted."

"It's what he wants. Karak couldn't see farther than taking control of Hakai. Yokosh can't see more than taking Khizara. They talk in larger terms, but their goals are local. Besides, it's not what you want. It's not what you'd like to be remembered for."

"Once I'm dead, I won't care, will I?"

"Don't underestimate my goals, Gordek," Yokosh said. "Especially when you can't see farther than her. Believe me, she's not worth the trouble. Let's get on with it."

Someone thinks she's worth the trouble, Gordek thought. He had not forgotten his encounter on board the ship with someone who most certainly had her interests in mind. *Fine,* he thought, *we'll do this. And we'll see how well you fare.*

"Linsora?" Gordek asked.

"Get on with it, both of you. And may you both live long enough to die slow deaths."

Linsora steeled herself for the attack. As on Gordek's ship when she dipped her mental toes into whatever attacked Gordek, she felt a swift river of energy. This time, she couldn't choose to pull back. The very essence of her self was in front of a tidal wave tumbling out of control. The crest of the wave broke and crashed down on her, then pulled her inside. At that point, her mind was no longer her own. Two other minds occupied the space in her head. She was imprisoned within her own skull, caught inside the wave of mental energy. She felt no pain, in fact she felt very little of her own body. Her awareness, however, was not dimmed making it that much more frustrating. Mental strings tugged at her, forcing her movements. With each step, she renewed her vow of vengeance on them both. She was aware of the constant combination of tastes, Gordek and Yokosh, sour charred meat.

One foot in front of the other, one breath after another, heartbeats ticking away the last moments of her life. Linsora walked between Yokosh and Gordek down service hallways leading from her room to the Prefects' private chambers. Gordek guided her with one hand firmly in possession of her right arm. Yokosh's hand was at her left arm, but it felt like he was only touching her with his fingertips, as though some kind of disease might transfer between them.

Permac said I should let them take me, she thought. *Permac's dead. He knows my assistant was Denub. I know that's the question I asked him on Hakai. Am I really such a coward? I'm alive because I chose anger over death on Gordek's ship. I'm alive now because I chose to grab onto a tiny hope of staying alive. I'm not that important and if I was dead, I'd be less important. If I had slit my throat, they'd both be stuck with empty hands. Maybe not Yokosh as much as Gordek, but they wouldn't have me to use. Being killed in the Prefecture isn't the same as killing myself. Not the same at all. I'll die without my reputation. Everything I've ever done will be tainted. This can't be right. What have I done?*

Linsora had attended sessions of the Prefecture, but only in the visitors' gallery. Even her relationship with Behazh hadn't granted her access to the hall behind the Prefects' seats. Where the public Prefecture chamber had decorations considered ornate by Khizaran standards – from the mural on the ceiling showing Khizara's five spires standing in relief against a stormy sky, to the dozens of hand-sewn tapestries on the two side walls, to the gleam of highly polished woodwork on railings and doors – this back room was dingy. Raw unpainted plaster was pockmarked with reminders of Prefects' tempers - some had kicked the walls, some had punched or gouged the walls with knives. No decorum was required here and no rationale existed to repair what would only be damaged again.

"Wait here," Yokosh whispered to Gordek. He straightened his spine into a dignified stance and composed his expression – changing the hard edge of self-satisfaction into stunned sorrow. He didn't quite succeed. His blue eyes sparkled at the prospect of his half-sister's ruin.

Linsora's experience with influences was that they were temporary. Whoever sent them had to be physically close and the effect was fleeting. *If Yokosh has to speak to the Prefecture, how can he maintain his control on me?* The answer came with shuffling behind her and a new taste. The sour charred meat became tinged with something like the heavy yeast flavor of fresh bread. Not unpleasant by itself, but the combination was making her sick. She felt too tired to think about any regrets or any plans.

"Yokosh," Gordek sounded alarmed. "We have to stop this. Look at her. We can't regulate our influence without equipment. It's too much."

"You afraid she'll pass out before they kill her?" Yokosh said. "I'm just afraid she'll die before they have a chance to execute her. I only need a minute."

The burned meat taste faded when Yokosh entered the noisy public chamber and returned when he opened the door on a silent chamber moments later.

"Fellow Prefects, observe what her allies have done to her. They cannot be trusted even to treat their own well." Yokosh steered Linsora into the chamber ahead of him. He left her standing at the edge of the speaker's podium in the middle of the room, between the Prefects and the gallery. "When I learned she had returned to Khizara and was in Behazh's custody, of course I was concerned. I found her at the Prefecture's guest suite. The guards slumped on the ground. And…"

"Yokosh!" Behazh's voice boomed across the chamber. "How did you know she had returned? How did you know where to find her?"

"Do you accuse me, Behazh? Do you think I could do this?"

"I asked a simple question. We, all of us here, are aware of the history between you and your sister." Behazh was standing.

"She's not unknown to people who work in the Prefecture, Behazh. She was seen. I was informed."

"And when she was taken to the Prefecture guest quarters, these people followed?" Behazh shook his head, "I must re-visit my security measures."

"Security against what, Behazh? What did she say that made you take any kind of security measure at all?"

"The simple security of my privacy, Yokosh," Behazh said. "The visitors I receive are no business of yours. The disposition of those visitors is no business of yours until I announce it to the Prefecture. The conversations I have with visitors is most certainly no business of yours. How many other Prefects are your people monitoring?"

The wash of the stream around her made the voices seem distant. *I could push out of it, maybe enough to…enough for my eyes to change color. That's what he wants. If I don't try, he'll fail. He can't out maneuver Behazh.*

"I didn't come here to argue security, Behazh," Yokosh's voice had become low, deep and dangerous. "I came here to reveal a spy. Someone you obviously trusted. When a ranking Prefect is putting his trust in spies, I think that is my business."

"A spy for whom?" Behazh's voice matched Yokosh's in intensity, but Behazh exhibited only calm assurance. "You need to train your own spies better, Yokosh. If they reported the entire conversation, you'd know you're not fighting from a strong stance. If they only reported on a certain few words they heard, then you have been misinformed."

"Just look at her! The guards I found, they're here. They weren't overpowered physically. Let them speak," Yokosh gestured toward the back of the chamber. Two sheepish looking guards stood with unhappy body posture.

Behazh smiled toward the men, "Gentlemen, come forward. We will hear you."

The two men took a place next to Yokosh on the podium.

"Gentlemen, I have known you for many years and trust you with your attention to duty," Behazh said. "Feel free to speak honestly. You have done nothing wrong."

"Thank you, sir," the taller man rubbed his clean-shaven head. "We were outside the guest suite, on your orders, and, I can't explain it sir, but we just became sleepy. More than sleepy. One minute we were awake and the next thing we knew, we were on the floor with Prefect Yokosh rousing us. I'm sorry, sir, I don't know how…"

"And you saw no one? No one had visited the guest suite?"

"No sir, we were ordered not to allow anyone to enter."

"Thank you," Behazh said. He turned his attention to Yokosh and nodded. "And your explanation?"

"My explanation rides on what was heard in your chambers. My half-sister admitted to you – outright and with no apology – that she has Sealed the Oath with a Tokorellan! Who but Tokorellans could make the guards sleep in an instant? They tried to destroy us once. They have found a way back into our society! Through her!"

The silence of the chamber burst, as though all sound had been held inside a bubble that rose to the ceiling and popped, releasing shouts of disbelief, cries of treason directed at both Linsora and Behazh, roars of sheer amazement, barks of others calling for order. The two guards left the podium and joined rank with other guards who formed a protective line between the Prefects and the gallery.

Linsora felt Gordek release her arm. She was alone, on the gallery side of the guards. *How long does it take to die if a hundred people attack? If you're going to send help, Permac, now would be a good time.* She could see Yokosh, his smirk. *I'll die cursing you, brother. There has to be some good in that.*

Yokosh reveled in the chaos he had created. He called half-heartedly for calm and order, turning first toward the gallery then toward the Prefects. On his last turn toward the gallery, though, he stopped. He seemed to search the faces of the people who were leaving their seats, forming small tangles of bodies moving toward Linsora. He glanced toward her, then scanned the crowd again. He gripped the podium and threw his head back, his face contorted in pain.

Linsora couldn't see, the world was suddenly blanketed in absolute black. The waves of energy in her mind wavered. She felt as though a hand had punched through the weight of the waves, beckoning to her, offering to pull her toward the surface. She couldn't take the hand, but she was being pulled along. The mental release of the surface was close. Linsora added what push she could. Before breaking the surface, the punishment of the surf surrounded her. Crashing inside her head were Gordek and the other person, a yeasty sour taste, and someone else, something sweet, too sweet. She tasted bile rising in the back of her throat. She wanted to scream, to make one last gesture of some kind before her head exploded.

With an audible whoosh, she was above the surf. Gordek and the yeasty taste were gone entirely. Whoever offered her the lifeline was cleaning out the unwanted sewage. Linsora did scream – in relief, in outrage, in exhilaration. She could see. She could move. She ran to the podium where Yokosh was bathed in sweat, he held onto the podium with white-knuckled hands.

"Listen to me!" she shouted. "Listen to me. If you look for demons hiding in shadows, look here. Yokosh not only consorts with the Tokorellans, but has their powers as well! He is the one who held me silent."

The gallery swirled with people moving from one bunch to another, those in the back bumping into those in front.

"Listen to me!" she shouted again.

Movement and noise stopped before Linsora realized it, her ears rang with echoes. All the bodies clustered together seemed to sway. Linsora risked poking her mind toward Yokosh. She felt the powerful stream that had flowed toward Gordek on his ship.

Someone in the front of the crowd moved, a woman's shrill voice called out, "Kill them both!"

"Stop!" Behazh pushed his way through the cadre of guards. "There will be no sentence without proof and there will be justice. Let her speak!"

Linsora felt Yokosh's fury, his burned meat taste intruded on the sweetness, leaving her feeling alternately trapped and released. But nothing sour, no indication that Gordek remained either assaulting her, helping Yokosh, or even helping with the assault on Yokosh. She trembled, but Yokosh vibrated, shaking the podium. His concentration was being split between attempts to regain control of Linsora on his own and fighting through the stream of mental energy assaulting him. As he lost his sense of range and exceeded his personal safety zone, his eyes changed from blue to bright purple.

Linsora pointed at Yokosh. "There's your proof. Look at his eyes. Are these the eyes of a Khizaran?"

The Prefecture guards rushed forward, only to stop short before laying a hand on the Tokorellan demon.

"He told me he can only influence one person at a time. Even his hold on me was temporary," Linsora called. "He can't stop all of you!"

The guards approached Yokosh, slowly at first then in a rush as though speed would counter any mental influencing. They held his arms and legs. They carried him, fighting and yelling, out of the Prefecture chamber.

When Yokosh's shouts faded, the silence of the Prefecture was absolute. The Prefects and spectators seemed to have stopped breathing. Linsora realized that all eyes in the chamber were on her. In a very un-Khizaran manner, she blushed.

Behazh joined Linsora on the podium.

"Prefects!" he called, "Until today we knew Tokorel only as a distant and vague threat. What encounters we had were on other worlds, never here. It seems we were sadly mistaken. For two hundred years, we have feared them." The Prefects rumbled. "Hear me out! Yes, feared them! We had no defense against them. We choose to ignore them instead and that is the terrible truth. We can no longer afford to pretend they are distant." Behazh's voice thundered, "We share ancestry. As not all Khizarans are good, we must no longer assume that each and every Tokorellan is evil."

"Behazh," a Prefect shouted, "How do we know who is Tokorellan? How do we know that she isn't? That you aren't? How do you know that I'm not?"

"Daria, I appreciate your concerns. The basic truth is we don't know. But we can not, I repeat, can not begin to distrust everyone. We would destroy ourselves faster than any enemy could! Listen, many of you know Linsora. You knew her mother Behlat and her father Robert Anselm. Eighteen years ago, Behlat, Robert and Linsora found Pak'bor, still the oldest known settlement site on Khizara. And recently - listen well to this - she discovered the fate of the Lost Fleet. I trust her. You need to know that she visited me earlier with a most unusual request. In light of what occurred here today, I believe we should give her our full consideration. What Yokosh tried so desperately to prevent might be in our best interest to encourage. I will let her explain. I ask you give her the courtesy of your attention."

CHAPTER 22

While Yokosh's interference set the stage for Linsora very nicely, his defeat held the seeds of his possible success. The only contact between Khizarans and Tokorellans was the occasional brawl at a port of call. Tokorellans were more mythical than real to Khizarans, allowing Khizarans to heap on them every evil attribute in the Khizaran psyche. The members of the Prefecture had known Yokosh for years. He was as ordinary a Khizaran as they were, in fact he possessed more than his share of some qualities considered typically Khizaran.

Linsora repeated to the Prefecture the explanations she had given Behazh, although severely edited. The projection of Tokor, finding the star chart to Hakai, meeting the descendants of the Lost Fleet, and her hope of adding some truth to history in the Forbidden Area. She made no mention of chikara. Behazh was far more diplomatic; he would have to make the decision on how and when to introduce that information. She considered pointing an accusing finger at Gordek, but she still didn't know the location of Hakai. She still didn't know the name he promised to reveal. Besides, he had done nothing she could prove. She hoped the resources of Khizara would be enough protection.

Linsora spoke with a passion she usually reserved for work. Except for the Carratians, most people were swayed by her enthusiasm for uncovering the mysteries of the past. But since her time with Permac, her passion included more than work.

"Prefects, one of Yokosh's accusations is that I Sealed the Oath with a Tokorellan," she glanced at Behazh. He smiled and took her hand. "That part is true. Please! Listen! As I told Behazh, he was a good man, he was funny and caring. He could influence emotions, but never once did he use his abilities in an evil manner. He died on Hakai, the place where the Lost Fleet settled. Behazh said not all Khizarans are good and not all Tokorellans are evil. The same is true for the descendants of the Lost Fleet." She looked around the gallery and the rows of Prefects. Everyone likes a love story, especially a tragic one, but she couldn't tell if they were moved or simply too stunned to react.

The Prefects requested time to deliberate and filed out of the ornate chamber into the plain rooms in the back. Linsora felt exposed standing on the podium. She knew she was the object of gawking attention from the gallery visitors, who had by now re-taken their seats. She wanted to face them, to scan for someone familiar, but facing them would invite questions she didn't want to answer, maybe couldn't answer.

No one had asked how she broke out of Yokosh's hold on her. No one asked where Hakai was or how she had met her Tokorellan mate. Eventually, they would, though.

Someone had helped her. *Maybe Permac? He said there'd be help, and there was. But the taste was too sweet. Is it you, Permac? Where are you? I don't know what's going on. I don't know where Gordek is. Probably not still here at all. Maybe with Yokosh gone, he'll be gone, too. I don't know where Hakai is. I don't know the name of whoever killed Permac. Are you dead, Permac? Yokosh knows where Hakai is, though. Has to be some way to find out from him. Has to be some way to get back there to Hakai. Has to be some way to find your body, dead or alive, Permac. Who helped me here? Not necessarily a friend. Could be an enemy of Yokosh. Could be an ally of Gordek. Not necessarily a friend. Can you influence the Prefects? And if so, which way would you go? I want to go to the Forbidden Area, I admit that. Maybe I've convinced myself just by arguing for it. If the Prefects refuse, that'll be the end of it. If I told them everything, they would refuse. If if if. I want to go, I hope I can. And I hope…*

The Prefects filed back into their side of the chamber. Linsora noted that some were red-faced and grim, some looked calm. None of them looked pleased. None of them looked like they had been influenced to feel generous. By a slim margin, they had agreed to grant her a month to survey the Forbidden Area. Supplies and manpower would be provided, whatever she needed. Strict security and reporting protocols would be established.

As she stepped down from the podium, she felt a light breeze in her mind that tasted like the spray from waves on the Green Sea. Not the feel of Permac, and certainly not Gordek. She felt pleased, as though she had been congratulated. In a far corner of the Prefecture, hidden from Linsora, a man leaned against the wall, his arms folded. The slight smile on his face was interrupted by a scar that ran down the length of his cheek from just beneath his left eye, toward his mouth and ending at his jaw. Another bruise, by now a dull purple, marked his neck.

CHAPTER 23

Linsora spent what remained of the day with Behazh, making lists of supplies and talents she would need to take to the Forbidden Area. Having been away for five years had put her out of touch with former acquaintances. She assembled a small crew and put them to work contacting others. For four days, the crew expanded and worked feverishly. Another day, and they'd all be in the Forbidden Area. Linsora hadn't seen or felt Gordek. For the first two days, she had taken every private opportunity to sample the emotions around her, but felt only Khizaran passion. No prickling at the back of her skull indicated that her emotions were being monitored. No comforting sweetness or answering whisper.

She realized that her abilities were local and specific. She couldn't read or influence anyone who was not near her, and probing into a generality left her frighteningly drained, as though all power down to her very life force was flowing into a bottomless, whirling void.

She abandoned her efforts. She worked, wolfed masses of Khizaran meat washed down with masses of Khizaran ale as though the intervening five years had never happened and she was again gathering a crew for an exploration of Pak'bor. By the time the stars filled the sky on her last night in the city, she was satisfied, happily alone in her mind, and contentedly snoring.

Linsora wiped a hand across her forehead. It was harvest season and not as hot as it would have been a month earlier, but still a full two months before any sane person would embark on an archaeological survey on Khizara. Linsora always thought that when the air temperature was the same as a person's internal body temperature, it should feel comfortable. Instead, it felt like her insides were leaking out, trying to find some unknown point of internal/external parity. Everything looked like it was steaming, including the people.

She had arrived in the Forbidden Area three days earlier and spent the time organizing everyone. The crew found some buildings just inside the barriers of the Forbidden Area, but two hundred years had rendered them too fragile for use. Pre-fabricated huts were erected for living and office spaces. The largest hut was reserved for displays of maps. Linsora had printed copies of old ground maps, geo-thermal maps, and more detailed surveys relayed from space. Another crew was engaged in low flights over the area, pinpointing all areas of obvious occupation and creating more maps.

This was the second survey day. Based on the older maps, she had chosen to set up their camp near what appeared to have been the last village occupied by Tokor's people along what must have been their final exit route. If anyone had decided at the last minute to leave records behind, this would have been an opportune spot. Besides, Haavens had been right, there weren't many Khizaran archaeologists. Linsora wanted to start her crew on a less critical site so she could train them. She laid out a grid around the village and assigned everyone a sector. On the first day, she led the gaggle of her crew, pointing out what to look for. Today, they were in pairs.

She walked, her head down, looking for anything. Maybe a discolored area in the soil, maybe a spot where more vegetation grew or a spot where less grew. All such areas were noted. She hoped the others were being as diligent about not disturbing anything. Bhreagh walked next to her, a capable woman and pleasant enough companion. She was solidly built, tall and square and muscular, with the swarthy-toned skin of someone who spent her days outside in the sun. At twenty-four, she had only been out of the Navy for a year and, not having decided on a career, had spent her time engaged in day labor. Linsora found her quick witted, attentive to details and pleasant company. With a bit of training, she would make a fine archaeologist.

The Forbidden Area was larger than Linsora had imagined. It bordered not only her mother's property, but that of ten other families. She made a mental note of this - those ten families were likely to have tejina leaves and, possibly, be allies of Yokosh.

Her mind wandered as she walked. She was looking directly in front of each footstep, not at the landscape around her. Bhreagh's warning was a soft, "Watch out there," and Linsora didn't hear it. Her foot slipped in the soft dirt at the edge of a long hill. She wobbled, trying to regain her balance but only managed to catch hold of Bhreagh's outstretched hand. They were both off balance and Linsora slid over the edge. Both women tumbled down the slope. At the bottom, they sat up and watched as one of their packs plummeted down after them, sending lunch flying in all directions. They looked at each other and started to laugh. The more they laughed, the funnier it all became.

"No wonder they call this the Forbidden Area!" Linsora managed to blurt out, before they were both reduced to helplessness again.

"Oh, are you okay?" Bhreagh finally asked, wiping her eyes.

"I think so, but my sides hurt," said Linsora. "You okay?"

"Yes. You know, that's the first time I ever saw you laugh. You really should smile more, you know!" Bhreagh punched Linsora in the arm.

"You're right. I used to, not sure what happened," Linsora realized she had become bleak lately. She really needed to have more fun. "Well, let's see if we can find any of our lunch. I'd hate to have the Tokorellans come back and find our garbage all over the place."

"Yeah, no telling what they'd do," Bhreagh ended the comment with a soft curse, directed toward Tokorellans generally.

Linsora carried several packets of food in her skirt and was making her way toward what looked like a bottle when she felt it. Nothing was being sent to her mind. She felt what had once been the familiar sensation of having found something. She picked up the bottle and continued a few meters beyond. The ground looked no different, not really. But something was underneath, waiting for her. She was tempted to call Bhreagh over. Give her some training on the spot and have some help clearing the brush away. Instead, she looked around trying to commit the location to memory.

She wasn't sure how to handle her discovery. She wanted to know what was there before telling anyone, if she did tell anyone at all. As they ate lunch, Linsora decided to make her way back after everyone else in the camp was asleep. She knew no guard would be posted in the camp, since any breach of the outer walls of the Forbidden Area would set off alarms all over Khizara. She had scheduled two more days in this location. *Should be enough time*, she thought. *I can afford to be sleep deprived for one of them.*

When the only sounds were snores and deep breathing, Linsora made her way back to the hillside. She performed a quiet excavation by the dim light of a shaded lantern. The outlines of a box were visible when the moon rose. The box was still firmly wedged in the soil when the moon was at its height. Only when the sky was brushed with the first rays of crimson did she pull it free. The box was disappointingly light, but sturdily constructed. She knew she should wait until she was in a secure environment before opening it, but the luxury of following the strict procedures her father taught her was just not available. The hinge creaked as she opened it, then broke. Inside were papers, carefully wrapped but dangerously brittle. She touched them, could feel the weight of the two hundred years that separated the author from her and decided she owed it to whoever left it to treat this treasure with care. She would have to bring them back to her office. She would need time to examine them. And she would have to tell Behazh about them. Once more, her options were whittled down to none.

CHAPTER 24

A figure in a long cloak strode through the darkened midnight streets of the capital city of Khizara. Few others were around and those who noticed the figure pretended not to. In the days since the Tokorellan had been arrested, fights had become more common than usual and strangers were being avoided. It had not yet reached a point where strangers were challenged on sight, for now avoidance especially in the dead of night was enough.

The sound of footsteps echoed against the sides of the imposing Prefecture building. A narrow sloping alley led to the door of the prison. The figure paused and watched as the guard at the door turned, unlocked the door, then stood still next to it. The same was repeated for each of the three guards inside. None of them seemed to notice as the long cloak brushed past them.

Yokosh was lying on a cot in an otherwise empty cell. Since he had been dragged from the Prefecture, he had spent every waking moment cursing Linsora and cursing Gordek. Although the force that had sent him from his half-sister's mind was unknown to him, he couldn't help believe it belonged to someone in league with the other two. He vowed to have the blood of both. He was also surprised that he was alive at all. No one dared question him, perhaps no one dared come close enough to execute him either. The cell was periodically flooded with forced energy beams. When he regained consciousness, he found trays of fresh food. If there were guards around, none were close enough for him to influence. When the door did open, he sprang to his feet, his mouth gaping in surprise.

The cloaked figure entered the cell, "You are a fool, Yokosh. An absolute fool. And with that expression on your face, you even look like a fool. I wonder why I love you."

Yokosh reached for her hand, raised it to his mouth. When he bit the soft flesh of her palm, she growled softly. "Tayla, you are the last person I expected to see here - and by far the most welcomed."

"My father is dead. Gordek killed him with your sister's knife," she said, handing him a cloak. "Kral is waiting for us with transport, but we have to hurry."

The message from Behazh surprised Linsora. She had slept late, claiming a headache and planned to contact him later.

"Linsora, I have some rather disturbing news," Behazh said. "Yokosh has escaped. All the guards were found in something like a catatonic state and he was gone."

"The only thing that surprises me, Behazh, is that it took so long!" Linsora said. "We don't have many defenses against talents like his. I don't find the news disturbing, though."

"I do. You know as well as I that he will try to kill you."

"Yes, but not here. He's probably not even on Khizara anymore," Linsora was getting impatient. She didn't want to be called back to the city yet. "Besides, Behazh, how would he get past the outer defenses? I don't think..."

"I can't take that chance," Behazh sighed, "Linsora, I have access to information and people not generally available to Khizarans. I, too, know people with - well, shall we say, talents. If Yokosh is on Khizara he may try to use his talents to attack you. I am sending someone on the next ground transport to protect you. He will explain more when he arrives."

"No, Behazh. I don't need..."

"Linsora, don't argue with me. I'm not telling you to trust this man with any information. I do believe, however, that he can protect you from your brother."

Linsora wondered why this man with talents hadn't been used while Yokosh was still in prison. She wondered why Yokosh was still alive.

"Fine, I'll expect him then," she said. "And I also have some news for you."

"Bhreagh!" Linsora called out to her assistant when she heard the low hum of the ground transport, "Go meet them. I'll just be a minute. Take them to the guest hut."

She quickly cleared the desk. The original documents were stored in the vault. She purposefully scattered her notes in careless order in the top draw. Behazh claimed to trust whoever it was he sent, Linsora didn't feel quite as generous.

"Bhreagh!" she called again, then mumbled, "Damn, where is she? For days she hasn't been more than a meter away and now when she could actually be useful she's not here at all."

Linsora sighed and left her office. The outer door banged into someone who blocked her way. Linsora gave the door a shove and a curse. Bhreagh stumbled to the side. Her hands were raised and the woman nodded toward the transport. Six uniformed Khizarans stood in an arcing line. Each one carried several weapons, fully charged and pointed toward the row of huts. Linsora opened her hands and moved slowly across the yard.

"Far enough," snarled one of the guards to her.

"Idiot!" Linsora snarled back, "I'm the one you're supposed to be protecting here."

In purposeful defiance of the weapon he now trained on her, she placed her hands on her hips instead of raising them. She was about to attempt sending a wave of nausea to the guard when she noticed movement inside the transport. Several more people emerged. They were in civilian clothes, armed only with hand weapons that were still holstered. She didn't recognize them, not their faces, not exactly. Still, she felt a familiarity. She opened her mind, something she hadn't done since leaving the city. The emotions whirled around her from all sides. The guards were Khizaran, that was clear. The others, though, were oddly blank to her. *Yes, I have seen you and I do remember where*, she thought. That should have prepared her, but when the last figure appeared at the top of the transport ramp, Linsora was startled. His weapon was not holstered, but pointed directly at her. She concentrated briefly, but sensed only the same blankness she had from the others who had been aboard the ship that brought her to Khizara. She concentrated again, this time to calm her own fear. No one was sending it to her. After all that had happened, the sight of Gordek striding toward her was enough to cause it; fear was the last emotion she wanted him to sense from her.

"Don't look so surprised. I told you I'd meet you here," he said.

"I am no longer surprised to see you anywhere, Gordek. Although I admit to some curiosity about how you happen to be here." Linsora gestured to the array of weapons being aimed at her and couldn't resist a sneer. "Why do you need all this? Have your wonderful powers been damaged? Or are you just afraid to use them?"

Gordek's expression was grim, "Don't talk, Linsora, and don't think. Your mouth and your arrogance will one day kill you. Take me to your office." He took her arm and shoved the point of the gun into her back.

Once inside, Gordek held her arm loosely as he kicked the door closed and holstered the gun. He grabbed her arms, pinning them to her side. With a swift, defiant move, her knee found his groin. His face dissolved into folds of contorted agony. He released her arms as his knees buckled. Linsora reached for a knife, but Gordek recovered quickly. He grasped her wrist. Pulled her back to him. His face still registered pain. Linsora felt him trembling. He twisted one arm behind her back and forced the other to his mouth. When he bit the side of her clenched fist, she opened her hand and clawed at his face, drawing blood. Gordek offered a weak laugh. He spun her around and slammed her into the wall. Holding her wrists behind her back with one hand, he pulled her hair with the other. She felt his hot breath on her neck and began to yell a string of Khizaran curses, while her foot found his knee as she mule-kicked back at him.

He stepped back, grabbing his sore knee with one hand and drawing the gun again with the other. He growled, his voice low and husky. "I could take you right now, with or without mind control. Believe me, I find the prospect very appealing. But I have lived with Khizarans long enough to know what actions require blood vengeance. Rape is certainly one of them. If I had you like this, you would spend the rest of our time here trying to find ways to kill me and not doing what you're here to do. I cannot afford that."

Linsora faced him, a knife in each hand. "Can't afford or just can't, Gordek? Touch me and the rest of your time alive won't be long enough for you to worry about anything."

"I just want you to remember who is in control. It is not you. It is not Behazh. And it is not your mysterious guardian, not any more." He limped forward and, ignoring the blades, shoved the gun under her chin.

"I will explain, in a moment. First, I want to give you something else to think about. You know I can send you pain, fear. Well, I can also send you this."

Linsora sensed the taste of Gordek entering her mind. She screamed in frustration and disgust, then stopped and inhaled sharply. Mixed with the sense of Gordek, was the most exquisite sense of pleasure she had ever experienced. Her throat was dry, her breathing reduced to a series of gulps for air. Every nerve ending was on fire and she wanted more. Her knives clattered to the floor. But the taste of Gordek remained, just enough bitterness to allow her to retain a slim hold on her sensibilities.

"No," she pushed the words between clenched teeth. "Now not, not ever. Not even for this. It is meaningless."

"Sometimes, when tempted with it often enough, pleasure for its own sake is meaning enough," Gordek said. "I can offer you more than Permac ever did - and don't think he didn't send you enhancements as well."

"Permac didn't need to send 'enhancements'," she snarled, trying to pull her thoughts into a defense.

Gordek laughed again, then Linsora felt the fire fading. He was gone from her mind, but she felt more disappointment at the loss of the fire than she wanted to admit. It was tantalizing. It was beguiling. Gordek couldn't sway her with threats or with pain - he knew that. But she had fewer defenses against such an indulgence of sensation.

Her eyes closed as her mind felt the last tingle of sensation fade away. When she opened her eyes, she stooped to collect her knives, ignoring the gun still pointed at her.

"I asked you before why you need that," she said, still breathing heavily.

"Sit down over there and keep your hands in sight," he said. When she didn't stir, he repeated in a tone offering no room for argument, "Sit down."

Gordek maintained a distance from her as she walked across the room and settled into a desk chair.

"Better. I said I would explain. Yes, I am the protector sent to you by

195

Behazh. Amusing, don't you think? I have been quietly acquainted with Behazh and some other members of the Prefecture for some time. He knows I'm from Tokorel. When you told him you had contacted Tokorellans, he was alarmed. He thought you might know of his relationship and bring the authorities crashing down on him. Interesting, Karak had the same reaction to you."

"Is that why he put me under guard?"

"Probably. For your safety and his own peace of mind. Don't look so crestfallen. Your Behazh is almost as honest as he presents himself to be. A little influence goes a long way among Khizaran minds," Gordek noticed Linsora stirring and aimed the gun directly at her head. "I would like you to hear this. I can knock you out then continue later, if you'd like."

"I don't have to listen to you insult my people," Linsora said.

"Insults? More like truths, how you interpret them is up to you," Gordek lowered the gun. "Look at the Khizarans - and I don't put you entirely with them; you have more sense than most. But just look - hostile, aggressive, with minds geared only to the mechanics of war. Minds innocently open to any emotion."

"Not true, Gordek. We have engineers, poets, artists, and we can feel emotions freely, with no fear of them being overheard and no doubt about their honesty. I don't think that makes us less than you."

"It makes you weaker. Your own experiences show that, don't you think?"

Linsora tensed. She was ready to leap from the chair but made do with gripping the arm of the chair until her knuckles were white. "Don't try to couch your desire to take over Khizara in terms of your dislike for our aggression. Wherever you come from, you're the same. Only your methods are different."

"Perhaps, but it is, to use your word, meaningless. A desire for power accompanied by strength has won many a war. Strength wins. Winners write the histories and create the rationales for the battles. The losers are always wrong and it doesn't matter what either side really stood for. The upper levels of war are filled with economists and strategists, there's not much room for morality."

"Just how much do you want? It's not just Khizara, not even Tokorel. There are no gods, Gordek, you cannot be one."

"You don't have to be a god in order to be perceived as one," he said. "But, let's not discuss philosophies. I don't believe you know who your benefactor is. You think it's your Permac, don't you?" Gordek sputtered a laugh. "Whoever it is, that person is powerful. But since there are no gods, all power has limitations. His strength is short lived, at least for now. He did not

196

push me out of your mind in the Prefecture. When I sensed his presence I left. I have no great allegiance to Yokosh and seeing his fall gave me nearly as much pleasure as it gave you. Obviously, I still achieved my ends."

"Is that why you helped him escape?" Linsora asked. "So that you could be sent to save me from him?"

"No, he blundered through his own escape. As long as his stupidity results in benefit to me, he is useful enough. He is not as powerful as he thinks he is. He just might prove to be most useful as a prize for you, Linsora. Think of that."

Gordek held up his hand, to stop Linsora from interrupting him. "You have a talent, perhaps related in part to spending time on your mother's land. You know, somehow, where artifacts are to be found. You amazed your father. Yokosh told me the story about the time when you were quite young and on a survey with your father. You argued with him, insisting that he sink a test pit in the valley. From experience, he knew that most ancient settlements were on hillsides, but delayed the survey to run a test since you were so insistent," Gordek smiled broadly, "And I can only begin to imagine what an insistent Khizaran twelve year old must be like, up against a Terran father. That's when he found Pak'bor - one of the oldest settlements yet discovered on Khizara. He made his name from that and his fortune. You knew it was there. You've done this repeatedly. If anyone can find what this area has to offer, you can."

"And my prize, as you put it, would be Yokosh? He's not worth the price," she mumbled.

"Your prize would be power enough to do whatever you want with Yokosh or nearly anyone," Gordek said. "You can choose your own prize."

"As long as it fits within your greater schemes."

"Of course. You wouldn't be here at all without me. Would you rather have been left with Karak? I don't expect thanks, but I do insist that you not give yourself more credit than you are due in all of this." Gordek was becoming impatient with the woman and her refusal to comprehend the simple concept that she was an appealing tool and one he would gladly have by his side, but a tool nonetheless. "At hand, however, are your discoveries. The source of Tokor's power is here. He started here, lived here. I'm not aware of his having passed along any information about just how he became who he was."

"Maybe for a good reason, too. I don't think Tokor would approve of you, Gordek. He may have wanted to keep this source of power out of the hands of people like you," Linsora kept her voice low. She was expending a great deal of energy remaining still when every instinct screamed at her to attack him.

"I'm sure you're right," Gordek said, nodding to her. "But secrets are like honey in a paper bag - eventually they ooze out. Tokor is long dead. His followers have had two hundred years to capitalize on whatever it is they do know and have done nothing. The time has arrived for that to change. And, like it or not, you will play a significant part."

"What if I choose not to cooperate, Gordek?"

"That, too, is beyond your control. You want to know as badly as I do. For different reasons, to be sure, but I don't think you could ever walk away from this." Gordek seemed thoughtful, then continued, "Whatever you find has no place to go but between us. You have no place to go but here. No one will interfere with your work. And no one will interfere with my purposes. Which brings us to your guardian.

"Many of those on the transport are like me and we have agreed upon yet another little experiment. Whether we have the opportunity to perform it also depends upon you. Your champion seems to be attracted to any use of mind control directed toward you. Possibly even any sort of threat that results in strong emotion from you. Either way, he's not always present and you are the only one who can call him. None of the others will influence your mind and even I will only do so selectively. If you do your job, you will not be the least threatened. If you decide to be difficult, well, we have these. We won't kill you - just stop you temporarily. I know you're familiar with the after-effects of being knocked out by one of these: not disabling, but not without some discomfort. Since it happens quickly, you will have no time for a strong emotional reaction. If your guardian insists on stepping in, however, my colleagues and I will combine our powers. We will deter him," Gordek looked directly at Linsora, "And if he continues, we will destroy him."

"What does that mean?" Linsora asked.

"Summon him," Gordek taunted, "And I'll show you."

Linsora remained silent. If she could have summoned him before this she would have. She had tried. She had peered into every dark corner, examined every shadow, turned at every whisper. The two days she spent in the city after the incidents in the Prefecture, two days of mental searching, had left her exhausted. By the time she arrived in the Forbidden Area she had given up trying to reach Permac. Now she would have to avoid reaching him, at all costs. Just what the ultimate cost might be, she couldn't even begin to guess.

Gordek allowed the triumph that he had finally found in his bargaining point with the woman to enter his voice, "Well, Linsora, you have no comments? A pleasant change, I must say. Perhaps you can learn after all when it is wise to be silent, as long as you also know when it is wise to speak."

Linsora looked down at the floor. He was going to ask about the papers. She had told Behazh only that she found them, not what was in them. Would Gordek believe that she had found as little as she had? She decided not to wait to be asked.

"Gordek, you must know that I found some papers," she glanced at him long enough to see the victory in his eyes and she gripped the chair with renewed force. He had done nothing to warrant blood vengeance, he was clever enough to avoid that, but the sheer force of her hatred made her wish for his death. No - more than his death she wished for his suffering. Death was too quick and clean. He would not always win. If she was forced to be part of his ascendancy now, so be it. But she would one day be part of his fall. "I'm afraid they contain very little. I would prefer that the original papers not be disturbed any more than they have already, but you may look at them."

She would have loved to fight him even on this and felt the crush of defeat deadening her voice. She knew he would hear it as well and that would add to his pleasure. *I will choose my battles wisely, Gordek,* she thought. *I will play my cooperation by my own rules.*

"I found them buried next to what had once been a house. You can still see the foundation lines. Apparently they had been purposefully buried quite a while before Tokor and his people left. It will take specific tests to determine just how long they've been there." She heard Gordek's foot tapping on the floor, he was becoming impatient with the drawn out explanation. She would go on, just a bit longer. The trick would be knowing when to stop. "The house seems to have been remote, maybe a hunting cabin or camp. There's no settlement around it that we could find, but Bhreagh and I only did a cursory survey. Still, a larger settlement must be within easy walking distance to… "

"Get to the point," Gordek interrupted, his voice tense, "I don't care about the archaeology."

"The point is that the archaeology is important and the papers are important, just not to you," she said. She waited long enough for Gordek to raise the gun toward her. She wanted to bring him to the point of difficult decision, whether or not to pull the trigger and knock her out for half an hour before continuing. The gun was steady and Linsora thought she had delayed long enough, "Gordek, they're love letters. They say nothing about the politics of government, only the politics of families."

Gordek stared at Linsora for a very long moment. "You will not toy with me, Linsora. I have neither the time nor the patience for it. That is something else you must learn." With the twitch of one finger, he fired. The force pushed both Linsora and the chair backwards, leaving her sprawled, unconscious on the floor. "And you will learn, Linsora, if it takes the rest of your life and if the rest of your life is only two weeks, you will learn."

Linsora knew she was lying on the floor. She could feel what would be a bump on the back of her head and who knew how many other assorted bruises from the fall. Gordek had left her just as she had fallen, her legs still draped over the fallen chair. She opened her eyes and stifled a groan as she gathered up what seemed too many limbs that didn't want to respond. Still, she had to know how far she could go. Only once you know what the limits are you can test and extend them. This one headache was a small price for knowing what Gordek's annoyance limit was.

"As I said, Linsora, if you are difficult you will be stopped," Gordek said to her as she stood and righted the chair. "I believe that what you found are simply love letters. Next time, tell me directly. Understood?"

Linsora's head hurt too much to reply with banter. "I understand my job is to find what the Forbidden Area has to offer. You, Gordek, you must understand that my job is to perform an archaeological survey. If you choose not to understand how that works, then shoot me again, but with full power. Today I have work to do here, in the office. If that displeases you, too bad. Right now, you are in my way."

She took a deep breath and briefly concentrated to calm her own emotions. No matter what Gordek did, she had to keep all feelings of peril out of her mind. Whoever had helped her didn't deserve Gordek's attention.

"And I will continue to be in your way," Gordek snarled. "Tell me what work you will be doing here."

Linsora's resolve to maintain her composure slipped. She clenched her fists at her side and turned toward the desk. "Maps, Gordek," she hissed. "We're here one more day. I have to determine which of these villages to examine next. If you'd like to be useful, go join one of the survey crews."

"I can wait," he replied, settling comfortably on the far side of the room.

CHAPTER 25

Linsora circled the room, comparing old and new maps. When she left the office to get medication for her aches, Gordek followed her. She made several trips outside, to other buildings in the compound on various pretexts, knowing Gordek would be roused from his seat to accompany her. Her campaign of wary annoyance had begun. That he was well aware of it delighted her.

By mid-afternoon, Linsora had determined where the main village was likely to have been. The settlement wasn't any larger than other villages, but it was centrally located and seemed to have more permanent structures still standing. It would be a half-days' walk, and Linsora called the team together at dinner.

"I may have found the main location. Tomorrow, we should bring along whatever we need for several days and make our way there." She turned to address Gordek, "I don't want the ground transport disturbing anything so we'll walk. Your people will have to carry whatever they need for several days as well. We can find water along the way, and I expect the rest of the area is just as lightly forested as this one, so it won't be a difficult trip. But they need food and bedding. I hope you're prepared. We don't have a lot of extra supplies."

"I appreciate your concern," he said with a slight bow. "We'll be ready."

During the walk the next day, Linsora stayed close to Bhreagh. They talked, laughed, and seemed in every way bound for a picnic. Occasionally, Linsora stole a glance at Gordek, smiling at his every scowl. She found she was enjoying the camaraderie with Bhreagh. She had not had the opportunity to chatter aimlessly with a friend since - well she couldn't remember since when. Not since that long trip in the skiff with Permac. And before that, probably years.

Soon after their break for lunch, Linsora began to feel the pull of discovery. *Maybe this is it,* she thought, *maybe this is what I've been destined to find.* And she chuckled at the irony of the time spent wandering in space when the object of her search bordered her own property on Khizara.

The advance team leader came running back to her position, "Linsora, I think we've come to what's left of the walls around the town!"

"Let's go in," she said.

They fanned out, each making note of the dimensions and extent of the walls. Linsora assigned the coordination of all the data to Bhreagh and made her way toward what appeared to be the center. *Someone could spend a lifetime here,* she thought wistfully, *and still not find all that is buried. How can I find the most important thing in just a few days? If we could find Tokor's office or his home, that would be the most likely place to look.*

"Gordek," she strode to him, "Whatever we're going to find will be here. There's not much time left before they close this area again. Your people can finally make themselves useful by going back to the compound and bringing everything here in that transport. Just be sure to leave it well outside the walls."

Gordek bristled at Linsora's tone and at the orders she issued. She had been pressing her advantage but he would allow her to continue. For now. Later, she would know the full extent of his wrath. She would be his or she would die. He forced a slight smile and nodded. Their eyes locked, challenge meeting challenge. When his smile became real, hers faded. He crossed his arms, leaned against a slender tree and watched her as she turned to walk across the expanse of what had once been a bustling town, possibly Tokor's home, before issuing orders to his people.

Two more precious days passed and Linsora had another headache. So much was calling to her. She was amazed that no one else noticed it, not even Gordek seemed to hear the impulses left by all the hundreds who had been here. Each one was faint, but the sheer number of them was becoming overwhelming. This morning, she determined to try a different approach.

When she had opened her mind generally in the capital city, she felt like she was being drawn into a vacuum. Without a point of focus, the energy just dissipated. If she could open her mind here, though, maybe she could find out where the strongest impulses came from. With any luck, the strongest would be Tokor's. Being the leader of this community, he had the most at stake. Gordek assigned no sense of responsibility to power, but Linsora thought that Tokor probably did. When he left he didn't just fly off with a small group of soldiers. He took entire families.

She gritted her teeth to ask Gordek for help. She wanted him to make sure she didn't overextend herself. It would mean having him in her mind, it might mean opening the door for Permac, but she could see no way to avoid it.

Linsora loaded Gordek's five shadows with packs full of food and water for the day, all the gear she might need and a good deal of gear she knew she wouldn't need. The first sound she had ever heard from them was a series of grunts as they trudged along with their loads. Bhreagh and a small contingent of Linsora's crew brought up the rear. With Gordek's help, Linsora was able to filter out some of the weaker 'voices' and concentrate only on the strongest. She stopped in a residential area outside the remains of a house. The street had a toothy appearance, several bleached-white house walls up to four meters high punctuated by gaps where only rubble was left. Linsora closed her eyes. She didn't hear voices, just felt tugs.

Three streets. Four. Five. At some houses, Linsora would tour the perimeter, pausing to clear her head and, when out of sight of her crew, spitting in an attempt to get Gordek's sour taste out of her mouth.

She pointed toward the middle of the eighth street to a large house with gaping holes where window and doors had once been.

"Something there, maybe." She walked around the outside of the house. In the back was another small building surrounded by shattered glass. "Looks like it might have been a greenhouse. I want to look around more." She turned to Gordek, "You can stop helping me now." Linsora waited for Gordek's influence to leave her mind. But it remained. "I said, you can stop now!"

"I like it here," he replied. "I think I'll stay a while longer." The leer on Gordek's face made Linsora sick to her stomach. She hoped that he felt her disgust.

"At least make yourself useful, get me a broom and a shovel."

She swept glass into little piles outside the outbuilding. Nothing unusual on the ground. She stepped inside the skeletal framework that had once held the panes of glass, still sweeping.

"Hmm, I'd expect to find at least a few broken pots if this was a greenhouse."

Square stone tiles lined the floor. Weeds poked up between most of them. Linsora knelt to brush at the dirt with a small whisk. Using the handle, she tapped on the tiles. Scuttling around the floor on her knees, brushing away debris as she went, she tapped from one end to the other. Less than halfway back, along an adjacent line of tiles, the tap produced a hollow ring.

Gordek suddenly withdrew from her mind. He must have been waiting for an indication that she had found something.

"What is it?" He ran to her side and looked at the spot that Linsora was examining.

Linsora stood and whirled towards Gordek. "I don't know. I won't know until I remove these stones. Carefully. I need a team over here. Don't be impatient; and DON'T stay in my mind again without an invitation. Why don't you just..."

Her words trailed off as Gordek once again filled her mind, filled her being with exquisite pleasure. She was unable to focus her eyes. She was short of breath. Her knees became weak and she almost fell to the ground. Everything was spinning.

She could hear Gordek through a hazy veil, "Compelling, isn't it?" His laugh echoed in her head.

She collected herself and stood, shaking and defiant. "Go away. Leave me alone. Let me do my work."

"You will call your champion. You'll have no choice. He will come to your aid and then I'll be rid of him forever. Have no doubt, it will happen." With that, he turned to leave. He stopped and without looking at her said, "Do your work. Find what we need to know. I will be watching." He walked just far enough to be away from her but stayed near enough to be seen - and felt. His five all too solid shadows, who were now sweating profusely in the humid warmth, sat with him.

Linsora called for Bhreagh. "These tiles, here, aren't just laid on the ground. There's no vegetation coming up between them. I think there's something underneath. Let's pull them up."

"Are you all right?" Bhreagh asked.

"I'll be fine. I will be fine." She added the second sentence in an effort to convince herself. She knew the time would come.

As crew members swept the floor, Bhreagh and Linsora wrote numbers on each cleared tile and recorded the placement on a chart. They recorded images of the entire floor and structure.

"Work your trowel between each slab. Try not to chip the stone. Who knows, someday they might reconstruct all of this in a museum."

"Maybe they'll have a picture of us next to it!" Bhreagh put her arm around Linsora and called for another image to be recorded.

The stack of stone tiles grew slowly. They began with the tile that was easiest to pull up. Digging and loosening adjacent tiles they finally removed one that had been placed next to a wooden frame. Linsora felt Gordek's intense interest, but true to his word, he kept his distance. Bhreagh chipped away the mortar between the next tiles. Four tiles had been laid on top of a small metal door, the edges a corroded orange. Linsora pried the door open with the edge of a trowel and peered down into a gaping black pit. Gordek stood next to her.

"Get me some light," she ordered.

Gordek scrambled back to the packs. In other circumstances, Linsora would have found his willingness to obey her amusing. She shone the light into the hole.

"Some kind of storage cellar. There's a staircase leading down." *But,* she thought, *I can't go down there. I'd freeze.* "Bhreagh, take the light and go have a look."

"I'll go," Gordek said.

"No you won't. Bhreagh knows enough not to disturb anything. You don't."

204

"Why don't you go?"

"I want to stay here to take charge of anything she might bring up. I don't trust you to handle that carefully, either." She smiled, pleased with her explanation. "Be careful, Bhreagh. The stair looks sturdy enough, but it's old."

Bhreagh descended slowly. Linsora shivered as the top her head disappeared into the cellar.

"It's smaller than the dimensions of the greenhouse," Bhreagh called. "There are shelves along the walls. Some broken pots. Oh, some tools, too." A shuffling sound and a sneeze. "Lots of dust and dirt. The walls are lined with stone, but the floor is dirt. Something on a top shelf over here. Boxes. Metal boxes."

"Can you get them?" Gordek asked.

"Wait. Bring down more light and record it all before moving anything. You've waited this long, Gordek, another half hour won't kill you."

Ultimately, Linsora could delay the inevitable no longer. Bhreagh handed up the equipment first, then the three metal boxes. Other than being coated in dust, they were in excellent condition and unlocked. Whoever left them either thought they would never be found or didn't care.

Inside each box, nestled in brittle paper wrapping, were large leather bound books. Linsora carefully blew dust from the cover of one. The scent was that of a private room in a library, musty and tantalizing. She gazed at the book, wondering what terrible mysteries it held.

"Open it!" Gordek breathed on her shoulder.

"No," she said. "Not now. It's nearly dark. We need to get back to the camp."

Gordek said angrily, "I've waited your half hour. I've waited years. Open it now or I will do it myself!"

Linsora handed him the box. "Take it," she said, "since you are obviously the better archaeologist and know how to handle this without causing damage to the pages, the binding, the ink. You certainly must know the precautions to take. Here." She stood, arms outstretched, waiting for Gordek to take the box. She felt him touch her mind. He knew she would happily hand it over to his hasty destruction. He took a step back.

"All right," he said, "make your preparations. I will be present for every page turned. If I find you've opened the books without me, well..." He flourished his hand toward the ever-present lurking men.

Linsora felt her stomach sink as Gordek herded her back to the ground transport.

CHAPTER 26

Everyone in the camp followed Linsora and Gordek to the transport. Gordek made sure that only the two of them went inside. She pulled on heavy gloves. They looked awkward, but actually provided a very delicate touch. The gloves created a thin force field between the glove's surface and any object being held, cushioning the pressure according to the amount an object could safely withstand. She placed each book under scanning equipment and a three dimensional image appeared on the table next to it.

Linsora riffled the pages of the first book to free the edges of dust and break the bonds time had formed between the pages. The paper was high quality that had weathered well. The pages didn't stick together. Perhaps the author had taken care to allow the ink to dry on each page before starting the next. The metal box had effectively kept munching insects away. Still, the book was old and Linsora opened the heavy cover with care.

She realized she and Gordek had both been holding their breath when the first page revealed was blank and they exhaled nearly in unison. Another turn, and the title appeared handwritten in a bold script, *Journal of Tokor, Volume 2.*

Linsora pulled her gloved hands away.

"I've satisfied my part of the bargain, Gordek," she said.

He stared at her, blinking. Linsora thought he might even be salivating in anticipation.

"My part was to find the books. I've found them. Before long all of Khizara will know what's in them, this isn't exactly a private enterprise. But you'll read them first. You can take off and use whatever information is here before anyone else does," she said. "Before that, though, I want what you promised. The location of Hakai, which I'll pass on to Behazh immediately, and the name."

"We'll read the books first."

"No."

"You know what I can do."

"Go ahead. At the first sour taste, the first mental prickle, these books will be dust. Three books, all positioned under scanners that can carefully read them or, set properly, pulverize them." She waggled a gloved finger over the control pad. Permac had tried to teach her the fine art of poker bluffing. With a Tokorellan, the bluff might not be possible, but she hoped Gordek wouldn't take any chances. The scanners couldn't destroy the books, but no one else was in the room to contradict her.

Gordek licked his lips. His eyes darted from the books to her still wagging fingers.

"Well done," he said. "For the moment."

"Over there," she pointed to the direct communication link between the survey party and Behazh. "And be accurate."

She watched him hunch over the terminal and enter the coordinates. As he straightened, she directed her mind toward his. She hoped she'd detect any deceit. She felt anxiety and anger. He didn't like being trumped.

"I trust you as much as you trust me," she said. "We're not done. I get the name, you get the books."

Gordek took his place next to her and forced a smile. "You think the name will do you any good?"

"I won't know until I have it, will I?"

"His name is Moragh. He has a scar on his face," Gordek traced a line on his own cheek. "I've had the marks he gave me repaired. He chooses to keep the ones I gave him."

Linsora felt the blood leave her head and pool somewhere in her feet.

Gordek cocked his head, "You know him?"

"Maybe," she said. "So he was aiming at you! Who is he?"

"As I told you before, if he had been, I'd be dead." Gordek waved at the books. "As for who he is? Well, that wasn't part of our agreement, was it? Can we proceed?"

Linsora flexed her fingers and began turning pages. *He saved us once. He could have just taken us with him on Hakai. I don't think he really wanted to. He knew you were there, Gordek, he must have. Why would he kill Permac? Maybe he was really aiming at me?*

She had turned the first half of the book's pages without reading them. *Did you want to find this as badly as Gordek does?* She began to read. Although the pages remained sturdy, the ink varied in quality. Some entries were clear, others faded and barely visible. She noticed that Gordek was hunched over the book, his nose inches from the page.

"Just don't drool on it," she said.

Tokor wrote of his return to his childhood home in the town of Yakto after completing his university studies. No mention of plans to take over the government, no mention of politics at all. Tokor's primary interest was botany. When the progression of Tokor's life reached the point where be began travels, Gordek perked up. Like most scientists, Tokor kept detailed lists of what he collected from each region of each world – description, chemical composition, the conditions that existed at the collection point, the results of any experiments done at the site, mode of transport for each sample, where and how it was handled once back on Khizara. For several of the edible plants, Tokor also included his favorite recipe. The lists went on for pages and pages. Linsora turned the pages with the same speed and care as the ones on history, pretending interest in botany.

"Scan for tejina on each page," Gordek said.

"Are you sure? He might not have called it that originally. You said it has to be combined with something else."

"Do it!"

Page after page of notes followed with no mention of tejina or chikara. The journal contained information on what Tokor deemed the most important of his discoveries. Many of the plants Linsora considered native to Khizara had been brought to her home world by Tokor. She realized he must have distilled the information in this book from his exploration logs, which would be much more extensive.

"Maybe there's nothing here, Gordek."

"Keep going. There has to be."

Volume 2 ended with no satisfaction for Gordek. The cover of the books gave no indication which volume was inside. The next book they opened happened to be Volume 1.

"I don't need to read the details of Tokor's puberty," Gordek said. "Get the next book."

Volume 3 continued more lists of plants. Toward the end of the book, the log entries ended with a blank page, followed by another blank page. The next page contained one word, "tejina" written several times, some clear, some with lines drawn through, as though Tokor was debating whether to include it or not. Following was not the usual format of properties and handling, but straight text.

"I have left the prior pages empty as I have not yet determined the wisdom of including the information they would have contained. My discovery of tejina has had consequences more disastrous than I could have ever imagined. Certainly more than I ever intended. Now that I have the luxury of time to consider, I wish to leave information that may be of some use to Khizara. The previous pages detail those plants that flourish on Khizara and how best to cultivate them. Also included are details on plants that have flourished with genetic manipulation. Care has been made to insure that imported plants do not supplant native growth. Everyone knows the agricultural disaster that occurred when Terran wheat was introduced to Paros. If the plants I've detailed thus far are not in cultivation when this book is found, they may be safely produced. I cannot tell what my reputation might be when this is found, however. Will I be known as a botanist or a rebel? I'd prefer the botanist label, but I despair of having that renown. Nonetheless, the plants I have listed are safe, easily cultivated, and excellent sources of food and medicine. Trust that or not, it is the truth.

"Regarding tejina. I will say that I found the plant on a planet with a dry climate. How I found it and where it is, I will not reveal. The planet had no native sentient population to observe or question. My observations on tejina's native planet were that animals eat the fruit but not the leaves. There are no universal toxins, by that I mean there is something that eats everything. A poison to one species is nutrition to another. I observed no insects or animals eating the green tejina leaves. I emphasize that they must not be ingested. Once dried, however, insects – both locally and on Khizara – feast on them as on other vegetation.

"Since mammals ate the fruit with no ill effect, I took it upon myself, as always, to try it. I must say it was delicious. Once the tough outer peel is removed, the pulp can be eaten raw or cooked in any manner of ways.

"Upon eating the fruit the first time, I experienced headaches and muscle cramps. I thought it might not be suitable to a Khizaran system. Since I remained alive, I ate once more. The second time, there were no ill effects. As I ate more, I began to realize I could sense the emotional state of those around me. And, not long after, I knew I could influence their emotions. The only side effect was that my eyes became violet. This unusual manifestation was not easily overcome."

"Not much of this is new," Gordek said.

"It is to me. Be quiet and read."

The book detailed how Tokor found that chewing the dried tejina leaves produced an immediate sensation of satisfaction. The members of his crew who chewed the leaves without eating the fruit experienced only a limited ability to influence and sense emotions. Those who did both, however, had abilities far superior to those who did just one or the other.

"Among those who have eaten both the fruit and dried leaves, the intensity of their abilities varies. However, only the preparation process results in superior abilities." The ink became faded during this paragraph and only a few words were visible. "...concerned about...mental state...oils...incurably unst..."

"What's that say? He's talking about the preparation!" Gordek reached out for the book but Linsora intercepted his hand.

"Don't touch! Maybe the image can be enhanced later, but *do not* touch the paper! Shall I go on?"

Gordek grunted.

"The samples I brought back to Khizara bore no fruit. Only in a climate-controlled environment, where the humidity is low, is fruit produced.

"I had hoped to share my discoveries with all Khizarans. I had hoped to awaken another sense. I believed that an addition is always good. Maybe it can still happen one day, I don't know. The reality is that the addition is only good if it's accepted. If only some people have it, it becomes an unfair advantage. And, going down the line, the advantage is hated by those who don't have it.

"No, that's not the whole thing, either. The ability to read and influence emotions is odd enough to be mistrusted all by itself. The purple eyes made us stand out, made us easy targets, made other people not want to have them despite the good that comes with them. It didn't take long, what, maybe ten years? Wild tales about the evil people with purple eyes sprang up. I was removed from my seat in the Prefecture and removed from my home. We are all here, in this prison. Life is pleasant enough, but it is still a prison."

At this point, the quality of the handwritten text changed. The careful handwriting that had taken time to produce was gone, replaced with a scrawl that had a hasty appearance.

"Rumors abound. No one knows what the truth is, but we cannot afford to ignore them. More than one report has reached us that the Prefecture is sending an army to destroy us. May the gods of my ancestors forgive me, I have approved a pre-emptive strike. Today we'll march on the city. With our minds and our weapons, we will take over the Prefecture. We will make them understand the value of our abilities. We will make them accept our abilities and us. We will share our abilities with them whether they like it or not."

The next pages stuck together. When Linsora managed to separate them, she saw brown smears all over the page.

"It's blood."

The smears blotted some words, but it could still be read. "Time is short. We must leave Khizara within hours. Our attack was expected. I think we were lured to the city. I think the rumors of their attack on us were false, but started by them to force us to make the first move. I think we surprised them by not being slaughtered. We killed many of them. They killed many of my people. My wife is dead. My brother is dead. At least my children and my sister are safe. Before leaving the city, I saw the Prefecture building in flames.

"Us and them. We are all Khizarans, there should be no distinction. One day there will be none. We have control of the port now and people are boarding ships. As soon as we are all gone, I'm sure they'll mount a pursuit. I hope I'm more correct about the wisdom of leading my people through space than I was about the wisdom of going to the city. I have trusted my instincts before, all I can do is the same once again.

"I am having all the tejina packaged. I have ordered the destruction of all the greenhouses. I intend to take all of it with me. I will not leave anything that might result in the same disaster again. If any remains, eat the chikara, chew the leaves, I don't care. The abilities might be useful to the populace - as

I intended them to be. The preparation that extracts the essence to its highest degree I will take with me, possibly to my grave. I will take my full logs with me.

"I am not a man prone to visions. In fact I have always mistrusted prophecies. But I have had, not exactly a dream, not exactly a vision. Words that play over and over in my head.

"The universe has eyes and ways to touch your mind. Beware the lowly and the obscured. They will make you run in circles and will turn you inside out. Trust your instincts and your heart. I see the six spires of the Prefecture, then no spires. I see five spires on Khizara, one spire somewhere else. The six spires will be separated, but I see the six spires re-growing after they are all destroyed again. Six spires in each of four places – I don't know what that means. There will be war. I may be seeing something in the future, it may be something that I have been destined to prevent. My energies will be devoted to ending bloodshed. No more wives and brothers need die in senseless conflict. I have seen the war, though, in my head. I don't know if the re-growth and expansion of the spires can happen without the war. Some way must be found. I will find it. The war is ushered in by a mix of blood, the taste of...I don't know of what, I get the impression of a taste.

"Enough, it is not important and I should not have wasted time setting it all down. Ending this, I want to say to you, the Khizarans who have found this, that I love Khizara and the Khizaran people. I will do nothing to destroy you. I will work for unity."

CHAPTER 27

Linsora closed the book softly. The scanning instrumentation had created copies so the contents of the books could be accessed any time without further disturbing the originals. She busied herself with replacing the books in a vacuum vault and checking accuracy readings on the instruments. She spent more time looking busy checking other systems on the transport. The slow reading of the books had taken all night. Linsora listened to the first calls of dawn birds and stifled a yawn. Gordek was silent.

"Hmm, looks like a storm is brewing." Linsora touched a screen showing a satellite view of Khizara. A large whirling storm cell moving from the Green Sea toward the mainland was slowly overcoming the map.

"Tokorel."

"What?" said Linsora.

"He took the book to Tokorel."

"Seems so."

Gordek's fingers played over the controls. He read the section on tejina again. He kicked a chair out his way, left the transport with a slam of the door. Bhreagh rushed in.

"Well? Our friend Gordek is in a state. He and those lunks are head to head out there. They're supposed to be here to protect you, right?" Bhreagh walked to the console. "Somehow I don't get a protected feeling around them. They're creepy. Hey, can I read the books?"

"Go ahead. It might change your opinion of Tokor, though." Linsora glanced outside. "They are creepy, aren't they?"

Bhreagh scanned the pages. "You know, if the Mercantile gets hold of this, I can see them offering a Travels of Tokor tour."

Linsora laughed, "With you as the grinning poster girl. You do have visions of fame, don't you?"

"Sure, why not? Maybe we can be a team."

"I think I'd like that."

The door burst open. Gordek glared at Bhreagh. "You're letting her read it?"

"As you said, Gordek, secrets are like honey in a paper bag. Eventually they leak out. Are you afraid Khizarans will flock to Tokorel if Tokor is no longer regarded as a monster? Maybe you should go into the greenhouse business. Somehow, I don't see you as a tour guide."

Bhreagh stifled a laugh.

"A tour guide?" Gordek shook his head. "I'd like to talk to you outside, Linsora. Privately."

Bhreagh shot a glance at Linsora. "Uh, Linsora, we should prepare a message for Behazh. I'm sure he…"

"Yes. Would you see to that?" Linsora didn't know what Gordek was up to, but as cold as it made her stomach feel, she was in no position to refuse. As she left the transport, she turned to Bhreagh and mouthed a silent *thank you, don't worry.*

Gordek steered Linsora through the clearing where the transport was parked, past a small stand of trees into a meadow. His little gang of five was waiting.

"Ah, I wondered where these comedians went. We're done, Gordek. Our bargains are satisfied. I have a lot to do."

She felt a prickle at the top of her head.

"So do I. And our bargain is far from satisfied. You lied about destroying the books. Clever, I'll admit. You have your end but I don't have mine."

"I agreed to find Tokor's books, that's all."

"And there's at least one book still waiting to be found," he said. "We have to go to Tokorel. Most of Tokor's records are in museums, but one of his books has been lost. Maybe hidden. I need your help to find it. Even when I was in your mind earlier, I didn't experience what you did – how you found Tokor's house."

"Me? Go to Tokorel? You can't be serious. He didn't say where the origin planet of tejina is, but we can plot the other places he went. Maybe find a general region. It shouldn't be that difficult."

"Did I ask you for your consent?" Gordek sat on a fallen log.

"That faint section can be enhanced. I don't have the analysis equipment here, but if you wait…"

"One paragraph? I don't think a few lines will hold the answers. You don't either," Gordek said. "I'm not a scientist and even those I know haven't come up with whatever it was Tokor did. That's the secret to his power. And I need to know the location, for reasons you can't even begin to guess."

"You think you have hidden motivations? Greed just oozes out of you, Gordek, that's not something you even try to hide," Linsora spat toward his feet. "How do you expect to get within a solar system of Tokorel? Your ship is Khizaran."

"You're wasting time. Don't worry about my Khizaran ship. We will get there." He picked up a handful of weeds, examined them. "On Tokorel there are fields of chikara. Even the weeds smell sweet." He planted a steady gaze on Linsora. "We will go there. That is not the issue. The current issue is that, as I have said, I have certain legal problems. In order to land, I will need to be stealthy. To accomplish that, I cannot have whoever your champion is around to interfere in any way. If he knows you are there, he will know I am too. So, here and now, little Khizaran, you may have a chance to see him – for the last time."

"I won't help you call him." Linsora tried to step away, but couldn't move her legs.

"You didn't want to go down into the cellar. I recall that in those caves on Hakai, Permac was calming you. I didn't know why at the time. Now I do."

Thousands of feelings ran through Linsora, one after another after another. She felt as if her body and mind were about to be ripped apart. The barrage stopped and she could once again move.

"I regret, truthfully, the necessity of causing you distress."

The taste of Gordek washed over her. She was enclosed, her senses encased in a small dark space, getting smaller. She was being crushed, slowly.

"It's not real!" she screamed.

"Real enough," Gordek said. "That's what matters."

She was aware of stumbling back toward the edge of the meadow. She tripped on something and fell. Curled into a ball, she tried to calm her breathing. The darkness around her was profound, no light, no edges, nothing to focus on. Nothing but the weight of the darkness. Pressing on her chest. Squashing her limbs. Her stomach turned inside out. She rolled to her knees to vomit. Her head was compressed in a vise. Can't run. Can't breathe. Can't die. She rocked and moaned, completely enveloped by her presence in hell.

"Close the door."

The voice was clear and strong. She heard herself say aloud, "What?"

Gordek looked toward the woman who was now distracted by something. He motioned to his comrades to prepare for battle and watched.

Linsora heard the voice again. It was Permac. "Imagine a safe, bright, warm room. No one has access but you. Picture the door. Imagine with all your strength that you are walking into that room. Now turn and close the door. You have now closed your mind. You are safe. Don't open the door until you hear from me again." The voice left.

Gordek and his five companions gathered in a circle around Linsora. Gordek motioned, and they began to concentrate. He heard a voice. The same voice that Linsora heard. Only it wasn't kind and gentle but filled with wrath. "Gordek, it ends here."

Gordek and his five men directed their thoughts toward Linsora. "Yes, it does end!" Gordek laughed out loud. "You have limits. You can't protect her and fight all of us. Try! Stay and fight! At the end of this you will be nothing!"

Linsora huddled in a corner of her imagined room. The iridescent purple walls glowed with light. No sound other than her pounding heartbeat. She was still on her knees in the meadow. Stray weeds tickled her ankles. The taste of Permac, comforting and sweet, was strong. She brushed the weeds away and saw her hand running along the sparkling green of the floor. The combination of sensations was delightful, intriguing. She stood up.

Gordek watched the slender Khizaran woman walking around the perimeter of a square in the meadow. He deflected the thoughts sent to him by Permac, moved them away from any portion of his brain that would accept them as reality.

"Bring her back to us," Gordek said, nodding to his companions.

Linsora stopped walking. The Khizaran symphony she had created for her enclave stopped. For an instant, she saw green grasses under her feet instead of the solid green sparkles of her room. For a moment, the feel of Permac fluttered.

Gordek noticed the wavering influence and prepared for the next assault. Too late, he became aware of another influence. He whirled toward the woods behind him. Something caught his attention just before a flash of white light blinded him. A cloud of buzzing insects seemed to fly past, stinging and prickling as the mass of their bodies, tiny legs and wings, rushed over. Through his closed eyes, he saw the flash of light again. Four more. Each one accompanied by another wave of pests. He knew they weren't real, but convulsively waved them away.

"Gordek! Over here!" The voice was not in his head. It was physical. He looked into the meadow. The five men he had relied upon to help him, five men with abilities he knew to be nearly as great as his own, were lying on the ground. Gordek approached each one. They were all dead. He turned toward the forest, toward where he thought the blasts had come from. Shimmering in the dappled sunlight stood an image of Permac Sudé.

"You couldn't have done this alone," Gordek said.

"Maybe, maybe not. Do you care to test me?"

Inside the room, Linsora heard Permac. "Open the door." Her eyelids fluttered as she focused on the real world around her. The bodies of Gordek's henchmen were close to her. Surprised, she took a step back. Gordek was staring at something. She followed his gaze and saw Permac.

"You're alive!" She ran toward him. He held up one hand.

"Not too close. We will be together soon, I promise you. But not now."

Gordek turned and looked at Linsora. "Are you so sure? We both know Permac is dead. Anyone who can do that," he pointed to the five dead men, "can present any image he chooses."

"Perhaps I am dead, Gordek. And who would know better than you? You never intended to take me with you on Hakai. If Karak hadn't attacked us, you'd have killed me yourself. And what if I am dead? What if I am a phantom you can't kill?"

The image of Permac laughed.

"Or, alternately, if I am dead and not able to influence you, then it must be that Linsora has developed abilities far beyond what you know."

Gordek clenched his fists. He gathered all the mental energy he had, so much that his eyes turned a deep violet. As he did, a shimmering green fog enveloped Linsora. Gordek's energy was reflected off the fog and bounced back to him, striking him with equal strength. He landed on his back with a thud, at Permac's feet. He reached for an ankle to pull this man to the ground, but his hand passed through it.

Gordek struggled to his feet. "What are you?" he asked the image in front of him.

"More than you'll ever know." Permac answered. He tilted his head. Gordek dropped to the ground. He choked.

"No," Permac said. And the influx of emotions stopped. Gordek slumped to the ground. "I will not take your life."

"Will not, or cannot?" Gordek struggled.

"You will pay for all you have done."

Linsora stared at Permac. There was hatred in his eyes. The months they had been separated had changed him. If it really was him. "Permac, where are you? On Khizara? I saw you die on Hakai. What about Moragh?"

"I was injured, not dead. Right now, physically, I'm on Tokorel."

"Impossible!" Gordek said

"Not at all. Think about it, if you'll pardon the pun," Permac chuckled. "You can think about anyplace, let's say Brachen. You can imagine it fully – the sights, smells, the feel of the place. Your thoughts are there even when you aren't. In the proper state of mind, you can project your consciousness there. Essentially be there."

"It takes more than a proper state of mind. If it was that easy you could maintain your presence. You can't, can you? Even now, the image is becoming faint."

"You've been away from Tokorel for a long time. If you want me, if you want to know what's been developed, come to Tokorel. If you threaten

216

Linsora in any way between now and the time we meet, your life will end. I swear it."

Permac shimmered, Linsora could see through him. "I love you," he said. "Carry that with you until we meet. I'll be with you now and always." She felt the warmth of his words enter her mind and savored the taste. He pointed to her hand, lifted his own wrist to his mouth, and made a biting motion. Then he smiled and was gone.

CHAPTER 28

Linsora stared at the empty space where Permac's image had been. She held her wrist and could almost feel the pressure of his teeth. She remembered pleasure and joy. *That's what Gordek will never understand*, she thought, *the joy.*

"How sweet," Gordek muttered.

Linsora ignored him. She didn't want her memories interrupted. But she wasn't allowed that small luxury. Gordek had come up behind her. Just as in her office, he spun her around and took her in his arms. The taste of Permac faded, replaced by Gordek. The joyless pleasure he sent filled her mind. She tried to retreat to the safe room Permac had given her but found the sensations too impelling to abandon. She concentrated on keeping part of herself aware of Gordek as the ecstasy increased. Her body was limp against Gordek's. His mouth was at her throat. His hot breath in her ear. His hands were everywhere. When he withdrew from her mind suddenly and just as suddenly released his hold on her, she fell to the ground.

"Filthy bastard! How DARE you!" she shouted.

"Yes, I dare," he said. "Perhaps for the last time, but right now I do dare. He is very powerful. I will grant him that. But the effort he expends to send his influence and image is tremendous. He was tiring when he disappeared. If you were truly being threatened, I have no doubt he would return. If I tried this after he had rested, I have no doubt he would return. But right now, yes I do dare."

Gordek took a step away from her then paused. "As I said, all power has its limits. I have spent my life finding the weaknesses of powerful men and I will find his." He turned toward her, "And you, little Khizaran, seem to be his greatest weakness. He just can't resist rushing in to protect you, even at great cost to himself. And your weakness? You did little to resist me just now. You can still choose. You can still have power, pleasure. He never answered your question about Moragh, did he?"

"The only power I want is whatever it would take to cause you suffering. And my reaction to the feelings you sent has nothing to do with you. Even if you arranged it so that those feelings never stopped, if you so much as blinked while sending them I would kill you," she said. "You cannot possibly expect me to see any sort of choice where you are concerned."

Gordek smiled.

"You have crossed the line. Now blood vengeance does apply," she whispered.

Gordek laughed, "You intend to kill me? Just as you intend to kill

Yokosh? He remains alive, if I recall correctly."

Linsora leaped to her feet her hand holding a small dagger. As she was poised to throw it at him, she felt a faint warmth, a light taste, accompanied by a hazy notion that she might still find Gordek to be useful. *All right*, she thought, *I won't kill him now. But I will answer some of his insults.* With a smooth motion, she flung the knife toward Gordek and watched as it pierced his shoulder. He cried out in surprise and pain.

"Would you like to meet those I have killed?" she said, walking toward him brandishing a larger blade. "I could easily arrange for that right now. How long does he have to rest? A day? An hour? Just how daring are you? Fight me now Gordek, fairly, without mind games, and I won't call to him. That or leave me alone."

Gordek winced as he pulled the small blade from his shoulder. He tossed it at her feet. "Now is not the time for testing," he said.

She stopped and kicked the knife away, "I do not want your blood unless it accompanies your death."

Gordek sighed then bowed slightly, "Then we are at an impasse."

"No. You are at a distinct disadvantage," she turned away from him. Maybe Gordek would be useful. Someone didn't want him dead, at least not yet. "Don't follow me and stay out of my sight until I call for you."

Linsora strode back toward the ground transport. By the time she saw Bhreagh, her spirits were soaring. Permac was alive, without any doubt this time. She didn't know how or why, but he was alive and waiting for her.

"Linsora? What happened over there?" Bhreagh asked. "We saw flashes of light…"

"Quite a lot. Gordek will need some medical attention and you'll find five large pieces of garbage that need picking up," Linsora said.

Bhreagh placed her hand on Linsora's shoulder, "I seem to keep asking you if you're okay. Are you? You look different."

"This time I really am fine," Linsora looked at her friend. She wanted to tell her all about Permac but realized it would take longer than all day to convince Bhreagh that a Tokorellan could be anything but evil. "Bhreagh, I just learned that the man I love, who I thought was dead, is actually alive. I am more than fine!"

Bhreagh grinned, gave Linsora a friendly punch in the arm, then folded her arms around the smaller woman, "I wish you happiness!"

CHAPTER 29

Linsora paced the interior of the ground transport. She walked around it. She read Tokor's book again. Her high spirits faded as the sun rose higher in the sky and the full impact of all the recent information became clear. Tokor's book might heal the years of distrust between Khizara and Tokorel. It could also spark outright war between them. If she couldn't talk to Bhreagh about Permac, how could she expect the Khizarans as a whole to look on Tokorellans with anything but fear and hatred? It would take time and careful handling of the information. It would have to start with Prefect Behazh. She trusted him, above all others, to take a reasoned approach.

Then there was the Forbidden Area itself. Only a few days remained of the month the Prefecture had granted her here. There was so much to be learned from this place and not only about Tokor; but she could spare no more time for all the tantalizing details of life two hundred years in the past. Someone should begin the job, though. Maybe even Bhreagh. That too, would have to start with Behazh. He would have to believe that the tejina plants had been totally removed and that nothing here posed a threat to Khizara.

But some of the plants were here. Yokosh had them. Maybe some that had grown outside of Tokor's area or some that had been missed. Or some that were purposefully left behind. She had not spoken to Behazh about her brother after he was arrested. Or rather, Behazh had not spoken to her. Either the Prefect did not suspect her of knowing anything about how Yokosh obtained his powers or he knew a lot more than he let on.

Linsora kicked the side of the transport viciously to vent her frustration. Every answer came with its own set of new questions. The only thing she had in common with Gordek was the hope that the answers would be here. *I don't know what I hoped for*, she thought, then laughed at herself. *I hoped to reunite two races by proving their ancient history was wrong. So, it's wrong. So what?* She sighed. *Maybe reuniting one Khizaran with one Tokorellan will be a start.*

Several hours passed before Linsora made her way across the makeshift encampment. Clouds obscured the bright sun and the light breeze of the morning had become a stiff wind. Gordek was slouched in a chair, oblivious to the dry leaves and sand blowing around him. He did not look up at her approach. "Well?" he asked.

"It seems we must both go to Tokorel," she said.

"And what makes you think I'm still willing to go back?"

"I think you have to. Your ambition is stronger than any sense of personal safety. If you had been scared off, you wouldn't be hanging around here now."

"Your sense of personal safety isn't well developed, either. We have more in common than you're willing to admit."

"Would you like a matching wound in the other shoulder? Don't twist everything. It gets really tiresome," she reached up to keep her hair from blowing in her face. The motion made Gordek flinch. He more than half expected her to send another knife his way. "You want to go to Tokorel to find this mythical book that holds the secret of ultimate power. Do you know how stupid that sounds? It's something out of a fairytale. But, you're determined. I want to go to Tokorel to find Permac. That's a lot simpler."

"Is it? Sounds like a reverse fairy tale. The beautiful maiden braving dragons to save her lover. Are you so sure the image we saw was really Permac? If he's alive, why can't he come here? Why can't he meet you someplace? Calling you, a Khizaran, to Tokorel? It's like calling the beautiful maiden into the dragon's den."

"Are you trying to talk me out of going? Or trying to find a reason why you can't go?"

"Oh not at all. I do need your help to find the book. I'm just trying to allow a ray of reality to fall on you. Scoff all you like, but I do care about you for more than the obvious reasons. I'd hate to see you disappointed to find your Permac is really just some old hag of a man in a lab who's playing with his new toys."

"I'm not buying your concern, Gordek. Who else but Permac would risk his life to help me?"

Gordek thought about the other influence he felt during the encounter. Someone else was close, maybe at the edge of the forest. That's where the flashes of light had come from, not from Permac even though he took credit for them. *It's a long trip to Tokorel,* he thought, *whoever was in the woods won't be on my ship.*

"Assuming I still intend to make the trip to Tokorel," Gordek said, "How do you plan to get Behazh's approval to make the trip. He'll want to keep you close. No one knows where Yokosh is, after all. And you can't exactly tell him about your visit from Permac, can you? If he sends anyone to Tokorel, it would be an official party of ambassadors. It would not be you."

"Don't you think I know that?" she spat back at him. "I can't just leave Khizara without telling him, though. I owe him. I can't have him spending resources trying to find me. He'd worry. Worse, he might regard my leaving as suspicious."

"He's not your father."

"He's the closest thing I have to one." She shifted her weight, hating what she had to ask him, hating that he already knew. "I will need your - your influence with Behazh to approve my going."

Gordek made a sound, something between a chuckle and a cough. "Let's see, that's the second time you've asked for my help. And for this, what do I get?"

"Nothing, Gordek. Not from me, at least, if that's what you mean. You get to remain alive to face Permac. You get to spend a few more weeks with your vain hope of destroying him and your empty visions of grandeur," she said. "If that isn't enough, fine. I will make my own way to Tokorel. Then both Permac and I will find you."

Gordek stood. He towered over the small woman but didn't notice her stature. He could feel her cold assurance even without touching her mind. "Contact Behazh then," he said. He put a hand on his bandaged shoulder and looked beyond Linsora toward the direction of the Green Sea. "Maybe we can even get out of here before the storm hits."

Linsora glanced in the same direction. A wall of white moved steadily toward them, flanked by swirling, angry black clouds. She smiled. It had been five years since she had felt a Khizaran storm. Her home world may not be the grandest in the universe, but Khizaran storms were the most exhilarating she had ever experienced.

"What's wrong, Gordek?" she asked, "Do our storms scare you?"

Gordek's expression was as black as the distant sky. If he reacted to her mocking tone as he wanted, she would be writhing in pain. Instead, he said between his teeth, "They should scare you as well. Being inside a stone building during a storm is one thing, but there's not much protection here."

Linsora shivered as the temperature suddenly dropped. The camp would probably end up scattered across the Forbidden Area if the storm came through at full force. Still, she threw her head back and laughed.

"Make yourself useful, then. Get everyone to gather up their things and take shelter in the ground transport." She felt the slightest twinge of Gordek's thoughts touch her mind, the faintest of warnings. She didn't care. Whatever he might do to her in the future was worth being able to harass him now. She turned, still smiling, and walked toward the transport fully aware that he sensed just how smug she felt.

The wind blew Linsora's hair into a halo around her head and whipped her skirt around her legs. Maybe that's what caused her to stumble. Maybe it was the blast of emotion that struck her mind as she approached the vehicle. It wasn't Gordek; the taste was light, clear. It didn't have the warmth of Permac. She knew it, though. Somewhere, this taste had come to her before. She stopped and looked around wildly. The other members of the team rushed past her carrying supplies and personal belongings into the transport. There was no one she didn't recognize.

The feeling was scolding. She was being reproached for feeling smug. She

222

returned her own angry blast. *No Tokorellan will teach me manners*, she thought. *Gordek deserves what he gets now, and I am more than deserving of giving him just a taste of what he gave me.*

She remembered the taste. The same she experienced in the Prefecture gallery after she was granted access to the Forbidden Area. Linsora looked toward the forest surrounding the camp. Someone was out there. The taste intensified, along with a sense of intense curiosity. She opened her mind but felt only the familiar emotions of those she knew. The taste faded, but the curiosity remained.

"Who are you?" Linsora called, but the words were muffled by the light rain and fog.

A boom of thunder startled Linsora. The sound masked the low rumble of a small ground vehicle driving away from the encampment. The sole occupant concentrated on the panels in front of him as he deftly avoided the limbs of trees that had already fallen in the storm. His intensity accentuated the deep lines of a scar that began beneath his left eye, curved toward his mouth and ended at his jaw.

CHAPTER 30

Linsora stood outside in the howling wind and driving rain until trees began to fall around her and was drenched by the time she entered the transport. Bhreagh rushed up to her with a blanket, clucking that she should know better than to stay outside for such a long time.

"Thank you," Linsora said, wrapping the blanket around her shoulders. "It's been a long time since I've seen a storm like this. Isn't it wonderful?"

"Yes! I always have so much energy during one," Bhreagh laughed. She poked an elbow into Linsora's ribs and whispered as she nodded toward Gordek, "Even makes that one look attractive!"

Both women burst into loud, sputtering laughter.

"Can we still contact the city?" Linsora asked when she had recovered.

"I think so, " Bhreagh said. "Voice might be questionable, but the data ports should be fine."

"I'll be in the cabin, then. I need to have some privacy for a while," Linsora said, to Bhreagh's nod.

The transport rocked as lightening struck the ground close to it. The crash of thunder was joined by the sound of a large tree toppling onto the roof. It's impact jostled the sturdy car enough to let everyone inside know they wouldn't be going anywhere for a while when the storm was over. Linsora cursed to herself. Her fingers played over the console, trying to contact Behazh. Bhreagh was right, too much interference for voice communications, but she could still connect to the main Khizaran systems. She sent a message to Behazh saying that the party would return to the city as soon as they could. Bhreagh had already sent the text of the books.

Linsora pulled up a map of the Forbidden Area and the lands adjacent to it. *You, whoever you are, want me to be curious. I am, but about what? Where am I supposed to start? Haven't I done enough damage already?* Once more she noted that ten families owned the property around the Forbidden Area. She recognized their names, mostly because her mother's property was among the ten.

She issued another request. After an hour she had learned that the same ten families had held title to the properties for generations. Most of the families had minor Prefecture positions, but not at the same time. Linsora didn't know what she was looking for.

"Okay, lets try something else."

She asked for the most fertile areas immediately surrounding the Forbidden Area to be highlighted.

224

"Fertile for _____ " the screen displayed.

She groaned, and typed, "Broad leafed plants."

The entire area was highlighted. "Of course it is. This is farmland. Okay, how about degrees of fertility for broad leafed plants that don't like moisture?"

Varying bands of color covered the area.

"So, the fertility and rainfall combination varies. So what? How about over time?"

She requested a two hundred year progression of fertile areas. "Again," she said. After she had run the same display four times, she sat back in the chair and ran her hands through her still damp hair. The storm raged outside. The transport shuddered occasionally and the pounding of the heavy rain sounded like some ancient god was drumming his fingers on the roof. Linsora didn't notice. She ran the display one last time, watching how the fertile area shifted eastward, then westward again, accompanied by a shifting concentration of dots representing members of each family who held minor Prefecture posts. The fertility had moved into her property only recently and Yokosh held a minor position. The property held by Yokosh's father, who had also held a minor Prefecture post, was at the current eastern edge of fertility.

"That's why he's so desperate for my land!" she pounded her fist on the table. *You wanted to be sure you had a place to grow the tejina and your father's land was becoming incapable of supporting it*, she thought. *While our mother's land was just entering a fertile period.*

And in the middle, an area that had been continually fertile for the entire two hundred years, was curiously devoid of anyone who ever had anything to do with the Prefecture.

Linsora leaned forward, staring at the screen. "Expand area six," she fumbled entering the command with hands that had begun to tremble. It was there, in the middle of the middle. The town of Yakto. Still a little nothing of a village, but it was Tokor's birthplace.

"I have to go there," she said to herself. "And I cannot let Gordek know anything about this."

She didn't know what she expected to find, but she had learned to trust her hunches. No, not hunches, instincts. That's what Moragh said to Permac, "Trust your instincts." With her eyes closed, and for the thousandth time, she wished Permac was with her. A smile crossed her face. *Maybe you are.*

Outside, the storm's intensity grew. Lightning struck every several seconds. Several strikes hit the transport craft. Someone read the control panel, "The winds are up to 175 kph."

Debris struck the transport frequently. On the wayward side of the vehicle was a shielded observation port. Linsora and several others went to watch. The darkness of the sky belied the fact that it was late afternoon. The lightening gave an eerie strobe effect to the objects flying by. The greenish rain glowed with the phosphor falling from the upper layers of the clouds. Evaporation was so intense and rapid from the Green Sea that many minerals were brought into the clouds. Phosphorous, which caused the Green Sea to be green, would make up a large part of the cloud. Linsora remembered how the clouds would glow at night when the huge summer storms formed. Lightning flashed. Some of the more recent raindrops glowed from the brief light, and then faded into the darkness again.

A bolt of lightening hit a nearby stone. The resulting explosion sent pieces of the rock flying in all directions. A large, heavy chunk came crashing through the observation port. Seven of those watching were struck. "Close the shield!" someone shouted, and the heavy metal curtain dropped to cover the hole in the side.

"Good thing no one was hurt worse than this," Bhreagh said, handing another roll of bandage to Linsora. "Just a lot of cuts. The eye is just about over us, that'll give us some time to see if we can fix the window."

Linsora dropped the bandage. "Yeah. How long do we have? In a storm like this, I mean?" At top speed, Yakto would be an hour away.

"A couple hours, maybe three. Depends on how the eye hits us. Why?"

"Nothing," Linsora wrapped a cut arm distractedly. Her patient yelped as she pulled the bandage too tight. "Oh, sorry. Hold still, I'll get it." Bhreagh shot a glance her way. "Before you ask, Bhreagh, I'm okay. Actually, I was thinking of making a quick trip out to see that the site of Tokor's home is still secure. I know we covered it all up, but those stones had been mortared. Now the cellar only has a creaky door and some tarps."

"Uh huh."

"You game for it?"

"You're crazy, but sure. The transport only has room for two, though."

"I know," Linsora said softly.

CHAPTER 31

Bhreagh made the preparations for their short excursion and broke the news to Gordek. He protested, but not strongly. Linsora might enjoy the storm, but even she wouldn't want to be out there in a small transport once the eye had passed. She needed him to get her to Tokorel. Running away wasn't likely.

"You're sure you want to do this?" Bhreagh asked as they drove away from the camp.

"Positive."

"What's up? I mean really. Don't say 'nothing'. You know as well as I do that the site is secure." Bhreagh veered around a fallen tree. "Nasty out here."

"Being cooped up with Gordek was more than I could stand. A couple hours away from him for any reason is worth the effort."

"And…"

"Okay, here it is. I have to get to Yakto and I have to get there without Gordek. When you mentioned the eye of the storm, I saw that as the only opportunity I'd ever have. I know that doesn't make sense to you. I promise I'll explain it all someday."

"Well, I believe that. I believe you'll tell me all about it, too. So now what? I don't know where this Yakto place is."

"I do. Tokor's house is on the way, let's stop there and check the site anyway."

"Anybody ever tell you you're too honest for your own good?"

"Actually, yeah," Linsora remembered Permac saying something like that. "Bhreagh, do you trust me?"

"Sure. I'm driving around in the eye of a storm with you!"

"I mean, my basic nature."

"Just what do you mean? Yes, I trust you. I like you."

"I don't like leading you around with the promise of telling you everything someday." Linsora took a deep breath, "The man I told you about? The one I thought was dead? Bhreagh, he's Tokorellan."

Bhreagh slowed the transport. "I don't have a snappy reply to that one. There has to be a good story behind it, though."

"Oh, there is." Linsora braced herself in the lurching vehicle and told her friend about Permac, how they met and some of their experiences. She left out mention of Moragh and the fact that she'd eaten chikara. "And that's it."

"Gods of my ancestors, you have had a life, haven't you? How do you know he's alive?"

Linsora shifted uneasily, "Somehow he has access to something that allows him to project himself here. I know it sounds like fantasy. But Gordek tried to make him, I don't know, use up all his energy back there before the storm. Bhreagh, I saw Permac – or an image of him."

"How do you know it was really him?"

"It has to be! It just has to be."

"Then it is," Bhreagh took one hand off the wheel and punched Linsora in the arm. "Hey, if Gordek tried to sap your Permac, is he…?"

"Uh, yes, he's Tokorellan, too."

"I'm not surprised. There's something very creepy about that man." Bhreagh sped through the streets of Tokor's former home. The houses had been through two hundred years of storms and whatever damage they sustained in this one was minimal. "Here we are."

"Okay, let's just do a quick check to see if the tarp is in place."

"We won't have much time to spend in Yakto if you want to get back to the transport before the storm hits again. Do you know someone there?"

"No. Actually, I'm not sure. I'll stay there. You can tell Gordek to come get me after the storm has passed. That'll give me a day or so."

"Oh, he'll love that one!"

"I'm sorry to do that to you," Linsora said. "But I can't think of anything better right now."

"That's okay, he won't be able to do more than grumble and he does that anyway."

"The tarp is pulled up a little over there," Linsora pointed. "Hold this end and I'll pull it from that side."

Linsora walked around the edge of the tarp. Wind and drizzly rain swirled around her, whipping strands of hair across her face. The team had covered the entire floor of the old greenhouse and secured the edges with the stone tiles they had pulled up. She saw puddles of water on the tarp, but nothing to indicate water might have gotten underneath. A blast of wind suddenly swept from behind her. A loud cracking sound made her jump and look toward the sky. A few clouds directly overhead, but not the kind to produce lightening. She reached the far end of the tarp. At the other side, Bhreagh was on her knees arranging the stone tiles at her end of the tarp.

"Okay, grip your end and I'll pull," Linsora called into the wind.

As the two women pulled, Linsora heard another crack. She placed a tile on the stretched tarp. She stood, about to check another edge, when movement caught her eye. As if in slow motion, an ancient tree in the yard was surrendering to the ravages of the storm. The trunk tilted, seemed to hover, and with a mucking sound pulled its roots from the mud and toppled over.

"Bhreagh! Move!"

The woman chose to fling herself in the wrong direction. She rolled into the path of falling tree. Linsora ran across the tarp.

"Bhreagh! Don't move! Are you okay?"

"That's my line!" Bhreagh said.

"I'm not joking!"

"I know, sorry." Bhreagh stretched. "I think I'm okay, I don't hurt and my arms and legs work. The main part of the tree missed me, but I'm tangled up in the limbs. This one here is on top of me."

Linsora tugged on the tree trunk, pushed it. She broke branches. She crouched next to it and tried to lift if as she stood. Her hands were full of splinters, but the tree wasn't moving. The branches it settled on were bending, sinking into the mud. A thick limb pressed heavily on Bhreagh's chest.

"Is there anything in the car? Any kind of tools?"

"No, we took everything into the transport in case the car blew away."

"Rope?"

"I don't think so."

"Damn it!" Linsora kicked the tree. "Wait, didn't you say you saw tools in the basement where we found the books?"

"Yeah." Bhreagh's breath was shallow.

"Maybe I can find something there to pry this up enough for you to get out. Hang on. You hear me? Hang on. I'll get you out!"

"Uh huh."

Linsora threw the tarp away from the greenhouse floor. She pulled up the creaky metal door and stared into the black hole. The opening seemed like the jaws of some dreadful beast from the uninhabited jungle continent on the far side of Khizara. People sometimes went there to hunt. A lot of them never came back.

"Permac, if you can hear me, I need your help now!" It was as close as Linsora had ever come to a prayer. She waited a moment, then a moment longer. No sweet taste filled her. No calming influence. Only the sound of the wind and the roar of terror in her ears and Bhreagh's gasping breath. The tree was settling in the mud, pressing more and more on her friend. "I can do this!"

She fished a small light from her pocket and stepped down into the hole. The wooden steps groaned. Each step felt brittle. Each one a sharp tooth waiting to close on her ankles. Eight steep steps and her head was still above the rim of the hole. The ninth step brought her entirely into the darkness. She tilted her head up, toward the open sky. The stairs had no railing. She shone the light down onto the last three steps.

"Come on, just breathe. Just a few steps," she said aloud.

The light was dim. She focused only on the yellow rays. Three steps and her feet touched the dirt floor. Linsora shone the light around the walls. Something metal glinted on a shelf to her right. She felt pressure in her ears, on her lungs. Darkness closed around her, constricting her heart.

"No!" she said softly, "Not now. Get the tool."

She reached out to the nearest shelf and propelled herself forward toward the glinting metal. The roar in her ears increased. She grabbed two of the largest objects on the shelf and stumbled back to the stairs. Climbing out into the light was easy. The rain was cold and wonderful. She felt giddy and the urge to laugh was uncontrollable.

"What's funny?" Bhreagh gasped.

"Me. I'm funny." Linsora wedged the metal pole under the tree. "Let's get you out first. I'll try to prop the tree up. Can you wiggle out?"

"Not yet, but I can breathe again." Bhreagh shoved branches aside and slithered away from the tree limb that had rested on her. "A little more. Okay, hold it." She slid along in the mud until she was free of the tangled limbs.

Linsora released the pole and the tree sank back to the ground.

"Whew, that was something!" Bhreagh stood up. "Look at me! I'm covered with mud now."

"You're all scratched up, too," Linsora said. "Maybe you should stay in Yakto with me."

"No, I'm alive. Nothing's broken. A few scratches are a lot better than being stuck under that tree when the rest of the storm hits. Thanks." Bhreagh shook leaves and small bits of wood from her clothes. "Looks like we'll have to replace the tarp, though."

"Won't take long, you sure you're okay?"

"I'm sure!"

"Okay, first I want to put these tools back." Linsora said. She had managed to go down there once to get the tools. She had survived. No ugly creature from a bad dream had eaten her. She hadn't been crushed. She had to

230

do it again. "You start to secure the tarp. I'll be right back."

The dark hole was as dark as it was earlier. Linsora took a deep breath and walked down all twelve steps quickly, following the yellow light. She placed the poles on the shelf and stood in the darkness. She didn't like it, would never want to become an explorer of caves or other nasty dank places, but she had survived.

"I did it, Permac. I don't know if you knew I could, or... Well, maybe the danger wasn't enough this time. Or..." She didn't dwell on alternatives. "The point is, I did it!"

She stomped on each step in triumph. The fourth step from the top, however, didn't appreciate her victory. It broke as her foot made contact. She lurched forward, her arms splayed over the rim of the opening. Pain shot to her brain from her leg, her vision blurred.

"Bhreagh!"

"What happened?"

"The step broke. My leg. Something's wrong."

"I'll pull you up. Grab my hands."

Linsora's left leg hung where the step had been. Her right leg bumped against something. It took all her concentration to banish the image of something down there tugging on her, trying to pull her down. Any twitch of her right leg brought new pain, memories of old pain, red flashes of screaming flesh and dark monsters blurred her vision. She tried to find something solid to put her left foot on, to help boost her body up. The toes of her left leg found the tip of the next step. With a shrill cry, she pushed up while pulling on Bhreagh's hands.

A cool cloth was on her head. Bhreagh's face was inches away.

"Linsora," Bhreagh spoke softly. "You passed out. I think your leg is broken. Don't talk. I'm going to put something around your leg and get you to the car. Don't worry, I'll be sure the tarp is secure, too." The woman grinned at Linsora. "What a team we are, huh? I guess we can't be trusted out alone together at all!"

CHAPTER 32

Bhreagh tore a limb from the fallen tree to use as a splint and cut pieces of both their jackets into strips to bind it. She tried to have Linsora hobble along with her support, but finally carried her piggy-back to the car and wedged her into the passenger seat.

"All I have for pain is some stuff I use for headaches. It'll help a little. Don't run away, I'll see to the tarp and be right back."

Linsora couldn't find any position that was close to comfortable. She stared at the leaves blowing past. The trees were bending farther in the wind. All the delays had eaten into their window of time to make the trip during the eye.

"Okay, it's all set. I closed the trap door and set the tarp up. I'll have the step fixed when the storm is over. Probably have the originals removed and put in something new."

"Good plan."

"Well, how far is Yakto from here?"

Linsora gave Bhreagh directions through the town to an overgrown road. The ground vehicle bumped over ruts and all too often left the road entirely to avoid fallen trees or sink holes.

"Sorry for the rough ride," Bhreagh said. "This thing will go almost anywhere, but I don't want to get stuck in a mud pit. We're out of the Forbidden Area. Wonder if alarms are going off anywhere? Maybe the storm cut the power. Looks like the trees end just ahead. It's getting darker. I hope that town pops up before long. The wind is really picking up."

Bhreagh continued a chain of patter. Linsora gripped the sides of the seat and muttered a series of uh-huh responses.

"Hey, there's a town ahead. I can see some lights and buildings."

"Must be Yakto."

"Even if it isn't, that's where we're going. The rain's starting again."

The little village looked deserted. All the windows of the two story houses and shops were shuttered against the storm, all doors firmly closed. Bhreagh activated the search beacon on the car's roof. Red and green strobes accompanied a high pitched wail. The forest car was designed not to get lost.

"This thing is designed to be seen from space. I hope it can get through to someone here." Bhreagh drove slowly through the town, circled a few side streets. She was making a second pass along the main street when a door was flung open.

232

"What's wrong?" A young man, maybe early twenties, with a dark mustache and close-cropped hair ran through the rain. "What are you doing out in the storm?"

"We're not in the storm, not yet," Bhreagh said. "My friend here has a broken leg. We need medical attention."

"Damn!" The young man stared at the pale face of the passenger. "I'm the doctor on duty, I'll take you. The storm will be back before long."

"Get in. I'm Bhreagh, this is Linsora."

"Rento. Go down two streets, make a left. There. See the third building? Go around the back."

"That's your hospital?"

"It serves well enough. I'll get the door, you can drive right in."

"Hey, Linsora, we're here."

"Good." Linsora raised her arm and gave Bhreagh a weak punch in the arm.

Rento stood at the door, beckoning them inside and shaking water from his soaked clothing. He rolled a stretcher to the side of the car and, with Bhreagh's help, lowered Linsora onto it.

"You don't look at the peak of health, either," Rento said to Bhreagh, indicating all the scratches.

"Take care of Linsora first." Bhreagh peered into the room full of medical equipment, but seemed less than willing to step into it. "Uh, you need any help?"

"No, you can wait here, I won't be long," Rento said.

"Good. I don't like medical stuff." She reached out and gave Linsora's hand a squeeze.

The medical facility was small, but seemed very well equipped. Glass fronted cases held multi-colored bottles of ointments and medicines. Sinister looking tools of the medical trade hung on the walls and some, attached to cords, were suspended from the ceiling. Rento wheeled the stretcher toward a gleaming box in the middle of the room. A clear bubble jutted from its side. He adjusted the open end of the bubble so that it covered the broken leg. Linsora had suffered injuries throughout her life and recognized the bubble machine as an injury analysis device.

"What's that one for?" She pointed toward another larger but equally gleaming box behind the bubble machine. The larger one had an opening in the side that would accommodate an entire body.

"I'll determine the extent of your injuries here and, with any luck, that one over there will repair the damage." Rento moved the bubble over

Linsora's leg. The machine hummed. Rento placed his hand on a pad.

"Hmm, I haven't seen one like that before."

"Uhh, new design," Rento turned knobs and made adjustments. "It's a clean break, just the tibia – your shinbone. I'll wheel you over there. Looks like this isn't the first time you've broken something, there's some scarring around your ankle. The mender is different than the ones you've been in before. It works well, but isn't painless. With your permission, I'd like to have you asleep."

"Go ahead. As long as I wake up again, I don't mind."

She waited for the press of the anesthetic injection against her arm. She felt nothing. The only sensation was a tingle and the taste of a sea breeze before she was asleep.

"Linsora," Rento was wheeling her away from the medical equipment.

She struggled to sit up, but Rento gently pushed her back down. He had draped a gray blanket around his shoulders like a cloak. Another gray blanket covered her.

"Just rest for a few minutes."

"How did you do that? Where's Bhreagh?"

"Bhreagh refused to be treated. I did check her injuries, but none of them were serious. She said your companions wouldn't believe her if she returned without some evidence of your adventure. So, scratches and all, she left. There was plenty of time for her to get back safely before the storm. I gave her directions on the quickest way back to your camp, too. The procedure took several hours, if she had waited she wouldn't have been able to get back and she didn't want everyone to worry. She insisted on my personal assurance that you'd be well taken care of and that we'd have you contact her as soon as the storm passed."

"She's a good friend," Linsora said. "I haven't had many like her."

"She cares for you a great deal." Rento pulled the ends of his mustache and adjusted the blanket. "You can sit up if you like. If you're up to it, you can try your leg. Should be okay now."

"Already? Usually takes a week of hobbling around after the bone mender. Was it that minor?"

"Actually it wasn't minor, it was well and truly broken, but, uh," Rento looked uncomfortable, "But our technology is, lets say, different than what's generally available. I can explain it, if you'd like."

"No, I wouldn't understand. Something about molecular synthesizers and restructuring? Never did lean toward that brand of science."

"Well then, I can tell you that your leg is probably even better now that it

234

was before. We took care of some old scar tissue, too. Not the scar on your side, though. I know some people prefer to retain their scars. A sort of battle souvenir."

"Thank you. That is one I want to remember. Can I get up now?"

Rento nodded. Linsora swung her feet to the floor and tested the formerly broken leg. Except for the memory of pain that caused her to step gingerly, it felt fine. Something was wrong with all of this, despite Rento's mild mannered demeanor. There was something she recognized, something familiar but out of place. She returned to the gurney and perched on the edge like a caged beast waiting for the opportunity to spring.

"Which leads me back to my original question. How did you put me to sleep?"

Rento sighed. He sat in a chair next to Linsora's gurney. She tasted the sea breeze, felt a tingling at the back of her neck.

"I think you know," he said.

She opened her mind toward the young man and felt nothing. Not calm assurance, not concern, not worry. Just nothing, as though he wasn't there at all. He fidgeted with the mustache again. Linsora threw her head back, bits of wood from her hair fluttered down onto her mud-caked pants. She smelled the parts of the forest that clung to her clothing. She smelled ...that was it, the smell.

"You have some here, don't you? There's chikara. I can smell it, that's what's familiar. The scent is on my leg." She stood and walked around the room, sniffing. "That machine, the bone mender, smells like chikara. Who are you?"

Rento sighed again. "It's all a long story and you'll have to talk to Pera." Rento held up a hand to stop another barrage of questions. "She's my aunt. For now, we're both stuck here until the storm has passed and you need rest. The bone mender, as you call it, generally leaves people feeling fatigued."

"What now? Will you influence me to sleep again?"

"No. Your own body is going to insist on it. All I'm doing is trying to help you. I didn't invite you and I didn't plan on spending the day holed up here. You're not the only one allowed to be irritable."

Linsora felt her face reddening, "Well, it's a draw then. I don't mean to be cranky, but, well, my story is a long one, too."

Rento offered his hand, which Linsora willingly shook. He led her to a sparsely furnished room.

"It's not much, just a bed."

"It's all I need. I do feel tired," she said. "And Rento, thank you."

"Don't mention it."

Linsora sniffed the room. The only chikara scent came from her leg. Her mind could sense no other influences, she could taste nothing. Rento knocked and brought in a small tray with a teapot and some pastries.

"In case you're hungry. I'm afraid I don't have any clean clothes here, but there are plenty of blankets. There's a shower over there, if you'd like. Rest well."

She sniffed the tea and the food, but it was normal Khizaran fare – hot tea and small meat-filled dough cakes. After eating, she pulled off her muddy clothes. Her right boot was probably still sitting on top of the tarp at Tokor's home, and the clothes were probably not salvageable. She pulled the knives out of their hiding places, and stacked the clothes on top of them, with the exception of one that she tucked under the pillow of the cot.

She stepped into the shower. Hot water flowed brown with mud from her hair. The heat made the scar on her side itch. The reminder of her fight with Yokosh was oddly comforting, a constant in all the flux of her recent weeks. After much longer than she usually spent in a shower, she dried off and surrounded herself in two blankets. They were soft against her skin and smelled fresh, not fruit-like at all. The skin on her hands puckered around the splinters left from her attack on the tree and the bits of wood caught on blanket fuzz, but that too was a reminder – this time of a triumph over her own worst fear.

She curled up on the narrow cot, lulled by the sound of the renewed storm crashing against the roof. She dreamed of the ocean, cool sea breezes on a hot day, waves pounding boulders into sand, waves lapping at her feet. And waves lapping at Permac's feet. Both of them on the beach, warm and safe.

CHAPTER 33

The taste of the sea lingered when she opened her eyes. She could sense someone close by. A plate of fresh food was on the small table.

"Rento?"

He opened the door. "Right here. The storm is over. I've contacted your camp. Someone called Gordek is even more irritable that you." Rento offered a small smile. "But I confirmed Bhreagh's story and told them you wouldn't be able to travel for two more days. That's how long your leg would normally take to heal. They're packing up and will meet you back in the city."

"Two days," Linsora took a cup of hot tea from Rento.

"You can go back before then, if you like. But I think your long story and ours, here in Yakto, will take some time." Rento stood. "My aunt sent some fresh clothes for you. They may not fit, but at least they're clean. I can have yours cleaned, if you think it'll do any good."

"Thank you. Don't bother. I don't think they'll ever recover from all that mud. These will be fine."

"I'll be outside, then. My aunt is eager to meet you."

Linsora showered again and tried to pick some of the splinters from her hands. The clothes were designed for someone taller, but then most Khizarans tended to be taller. The boots were soft leather and comfortable. She tucked her weapons away in the several pockets Khizaran clothing generally had. There was no comb or brush. She ran her fingers through her dry but definitely unruly dark red hair.

"All set."

"We can walk to Pera's. Her house is just down the street. You can stay with her. I think you'll find her guest room more comfortable than the hospital."

The walkway along the road was puddled and decorated with splatters of mud from house yards. Linsora didn't sense anyone else around, although she saw movement of people inside the now-opened windows of houses. Most villages in Khizara consisted of groups of houses, family compounds traditionally separated by land for gardens or grazing animals, now more commonly by space for the family's vehicles. These rows of houses all facing the street reminded Linsora more of the home arrangement on Hakai than anything Khizaran.

"Rento, I know you can sense and influence emotions. You know that I can, too, although to a more limited degree. Why don't I sense anything from anyone else around here? It's eerie."

"Pera will…"

"Pera doesn't have to tell me everything, does she?"

"I suppose not, but it is part of the long story," Rento glanced at her. "Okay, one thing then. We can, essentially, hold our emotions in private places."

"You can shield your emotions?" Linsora remembered that Moragh was surprised that Permac had never learned to do this.

"More or less. Here we are." Rento held the door for Linsora. She entered a house that looked much the same as other houses in the village. Two story, brick, with a small yard in front and a fence separating the front from the back. The air outside was after-storm humid, the house was welcoming dry warmth. Linsora smelled a fire burning some kind of fragrant wood.

"Pera?"

"In here, by the fire."

Pera was older than Linsora, probably close to what her mother's age would have been. Her hair was red hued, frosted with wisps of gray. Her face looked like a smile generally adorned it. Her blue eyes were the same as the ocean on some worlds. Again this reminded Linsora of her mother.

"I take it this is Linsora? Welcome, my dear." Pera enclosed the smaller woman in a full hug. Linsora stiffened. "Please sit down and warm yourself. Rento, would you get some tea for us, please? In the special pot, if you would."

Rento stared at his aunt, "Are you sure? I mean…"

"I am." Pera spoke with the authority of someone who was not to be argued with. Linsora liked that, especially in a woman. "Well, how is your leg? Rento told me…. What's wrong?"

Linsora was staring at her. "I don't mean to stare, but you seem familiar somehow."

"Just as I should!" Pera winked. "I know your mother's name was Behlat. And you father a Terran, was Robert Anselm."

"How do you know that?"

"Your name isn't unusual, so I couldn't just have accessed the census records and found a likely Linsora. Nor has anyone asked for your surname. And, I assure you, your friend said nothing about it."

"You could have checked for a Linsora with green eyes."

Pera laughed. "I could have. I'm trying to establish that I know you and not from census records. When Rento told me your name, I asked a few more questions. It was your name and the green eyes that made me recognize you. We met a very long time ago, when you were a child."

"Impossi..."

"Not impossible. You have not even begun to hear what you will deem impossible." Pera's voice had a sudden hard tone. "Please listen. We are related. Your mother was my cousin. Not so impossible, her land is just a few miles from here. Right?"

"I suppose."

"When you were very young, your mother brought you here. You were quite ill at the time. Perhaps you don't remember."

"Vaguely. I must have been around four. I was sick and traveled somewhere with my mother. She let me sleep with her and eat anything I wanted, including lots of sweet icy stuff. I remember that."

"And where does that lead?" Pera bent forward to poke at the fire. "My dear, I could tell you everything, but you wouldn't believe me. You have to put the links together."

"Links? What links?" Linsora felt her frustration rising along with her voice. She had just met this woman. The hug and the familiarity it implied made her wary. "I don't want to be rude, but I don't like riddles. I can accept that I came here when I was young, that you and my mother were cousins. The name of this place sounded familiar to me. If I wanted to guess, I wouldn't have had to come here!"

"Think about it." Pera's tone was firm but cordial. "Rento told me a little about you, I suppose I have an unfair advantage. If all the links don't present themselves, I'll tell you more. Why don't you start with the reason you came here? I don't think the broken leg was the primary motive, you could have had that tended to anywhere."

Linsora decided to take the tack she had originally planned.

"I found Tokor's book in the Forbidden Area."

Pera stopped poking the logs.

"I found three of them, in fact. You didn't know that?"

"No."

"They said precious little, in case you're worried. But they did mention that Tokor found the tejina plants somewhere and that they only bear fruit in a dry climate. Most houses in the Forbidden Area had greenhouses, probably for climate control. I'd bet a year's pay that you, and other people here, have greenhouses in your back yards, too."

Pera sat back. "You'd win your bet."

"I smelled chikara in the hospital. My…uh, I know someone who's very fond of the scent of chikara. I've learned to recognize it. And, yes, I've eaten it."

Pera raised an eyebrow.

"Tokor mentioned he was from Yakto originally. I did some research and discovered that the fertility zones for tejina have been shifting regularly ever since Tokor left, but the region around Yakto is in the middle and has remained fertile all the time. Tokor also said his sister lived in Yakto. I'd hazard a guess that she didn't leave with him. How am I doing?"

"Amazingly well."

"Thank you." Linsora took a turn poking the embers in the fireplace. Sparkling red and gold scrapings from the main log fell onto the ashes. Linsora felt sparks of insight flashing and dying as fast as the embers. "So, she and others continued growing tejina and chikara in the greenhouses and maintained a low profile. No one from this region has ever held a Prefecture post, which is unusual." Linsora didn't want to put the next link together, but it was unavoidable. "Since you live here, you have Tokorellan abilities. Since my mother is related to you and visited here, does that mean what I think?"

"It does. And more. She knew of and ate chikara." Pera smoothed a strand of stray hair into place and brushed a bit of ash from her skirt. "Linsora, both she and I, and of course you, can trace our bloodline back to Tokor himself."

Linsora smashed the poker against the log. Amid a cloud of ash and sparks, the charred log broke in half. She turned toward Pera, still holding the poker, just as Rento returned with a tray. Linsora tasted the sea breeze and felt her anger draining away. She retrieved what she could of her own emotions and shot a wave of anger back at Rento.

"Stop it this instant!" Pera commanded. "Neither of you will play at mind games here. You have a right to be angry, Linsora. And you, Rento, have every reason to be alarmed. That's that and let us go on from here." Pera adjusted her skirts. "Rento, please bring in the tray."

"You can't expect me to sit quietly and have tea when you've just told me I'm related to Tokor, do you? Damn it! Do you expect me to believe you?"

"I told you there was much you'd consider impossible." Pera poured a cup of tea. Steam surrounded her face. "There is ample proof I can show you later. Just try to digest the ideas for now. When you came here, and it was only once, Behlat did not think you would live. For some reason we're only beginning to determine, female children of Khizaran and Terran parents become ill and die before their seventh birthdays. There haven't been many such Sealings, between Khizarans and Terrans I mean, so the pool of data is small. Male children fare better. When you became ill, you couldn't hold down any food, she brought you here in desperation. She knew we had been investigating medical technology."

"Like your bone mender?"

"Bone mender? Oh, yes, the synthesizer. Yes. But at that time, we were nowhere close to having such tools. I did what I could." Pera took a sip of tea. "I fed you chikara."

"When I was four?"

"The sweet icy food you remember was chikara. You improved - you healed. With no side effects we could detect except for one."

"I could taste influences."

"What?" Pera's tea cup tilted. Hot tea spilled onto her lap. She stood suddenly, the teacup clattered onto the carpet. "Taste? No no no. What I meant was that you felt enclosed by influences. They frightened you. Another child learned of this and sent you a feeling of enclosure on purpose. You were hysterical for some time."

"I hope he was buried alive," Linsora snorted. "I've had claustrophobia ever since."

"It was, uh, I don't know if should tell you," Pera picked up the teacup. "It was your brother, Yokosh."

Linsora threw a cloth onto the carpet and ground her foot on it to soak up the spilled tea. She started to laugh.

"He must have been around seven. Even as a child he was evil. Did he inherit it from his father? I wonder what that man was like."

"I never knew Yokosh's father. He was a landowner, quite wealthy. Died in a duel, I hear."

"Yokosh's father's land was fertile for tejina back then. So, Yokosh's father knew about it," Linsora was putting more unpleasant links together. "And Yokosh has had some degree of the ability all his life? He could have…I mean before the duel…do you know about our duel?"

"I did hear of it."

"He could have influenced me somehow to be angry enough to make the challenge. Not to wait for the Prefecture hearing about the land." Linsora felt her past spinning around her, suddenly making more sense. She remembered how Yokosh's influence, the taste of charred meat, was familiar. How often had she tasted it during her childhood? How many more indignities did she owe him? "And my mother gave her land to me on purpose. She knew it would be fertile for tejina and that Yokosh's wouldn't be. Did she want to keep Yokosh away from a ready supply of it?"

"Perhaps. She was wise and insightful. She cared for your brother as much as she cared for you, but I believe she saw too much of his father in him. As I mentioned, Rial, Yokosh's father, was killed in a duel. He was not only hotheaded, but overly confident in his own powers both with a knife and influences. Behlat never gave either of you chikara, except that once when you were ill, so I have to assume Rial was responsible for introducing Yokosh to it."

"You don't have a relationship with the other chikara landowners? I'd have thought…"

"Thought that we'd have some sort of unholy alliance?" Rento said. "No, we prefer to live quietly here in Yakto and conduct our research."

"I think the ship has gone on without you," Linsora said.

"What do you mean?"

"I mean that there are political alliances among the chikara landowners. I mean there are organized groups out there who want to do just what Tokor failed to accomplish – take over Khizara! While you're here happily isolated and innocently researching, people are using and misusing your oh so secret and precious chikara and you don't have any idea! On top of that, you're sitting here with medical tools that could help everyone and who knows what else. You think people will be happy to learn that you've had this and haven't shared it?"

"The medical technology depends on chikara," Rento growled back. "You think Khizarans would accept that? If we share any of the benefits of chikara, we end up sharing it all. We'd end up like Tokor, dead or exiled."

"Like I said, the ship has launched. Chikara is already out there, and it seems like only people with personal agendas for power are using it. What the hell do you plan to do, come blazing out of the back country with loads of chikara for everyone like rescuing angels?"

"Stop again, we are losing the point of our discussion here," Pera settled back into her chair with a fresh cup of tea. "Have some tea, both of you."

Linsora swirled hot tea in her cup and ran a finger around the rim. The cup shimmered. She glanced toward the teapot. It had the same deep green glaze as the cups, the same watery gleam. A small picture painted on the side seemed to ripple, like fields in a breeze.

"It's just ordinary tea," Rento said.

"The tea might be, but the teapot isn't," Linsora said. "I've seen that kind of effect before. Kagamite?"

"Well, you see, everything is complicated. If you mean the glaze, we don't call it kagamite, but it is made from soil around the tejina plant. Everything is complicated. Chikara, like anything, has benefits and detriments. No one can control how any individual will use it. One man will use a knife to hunt for

242

meat, one will use a knife to kill in order to take another's meat. You must know that proverb. If everyone has a knife, some will still kill to take meat, but they'll have to think about it. I believe that the more people who have access to chikara, the greater the chance of preventing its misuse. And that, in turn, depends on a general acceptance of chikara, something that's coming but not yet here."

Linsora felt Pera staring at her. "And most Khizarans will react like me, is that what you're saying? "

"Yes. I have no desire to be a killed messenger or a martyr. If we brought the message any earlier than this, or even now, we stand the chance of being killed, as Rento said. Then, once chikara is in general use, as it will be, must be, we'd be hailed as a fallen heroes." Pera shook her head. "Not a role I relish."

"Either that or all our research would be thrown onto the funeral pyre with us. I don't relish that, either," Rento added.

"Exactly, so we must wait," Pera said. She poured another round of tea into each cup and settled into her chair. "Our research has determined there is a portion of the brain where the ability to influence emotions resides. All people possess it. Let that sink in, not just Khizarans, everyone. Think about our hands. All people have fingernails - ours are different. All people have this area in their brains – ours is different. Khizarans, more than most people, thrive on strong emotions. We have theorized that there is small scale emotional influencing among everyone all the time. Since Khizarans all have a native ability to detect it, we thrive on strong emotions all the time. They serve to overpower the lesser ones. Does that make sense?"

"We enjoy strong emotions because they are our own, not emotions sent by anyone. That makes sense." Linsora gulped her tea, "And it makes sense, too, that when strong emotions started to be sent, by Tokor and his people, that the reaction against that would be extreme."

"Exactly. It triggered a sense of familiarity. Receiving mild emotions was something everyone experienced but people weren't really aware of them. Sending emotions isn't something to be done casually. It takes discipline and training. Just now, for example, you felt angry and the emotion you sent to Rento was anger. The end result would have been two angry people. A sense of emotional detachment is needed. When you feel anger, the emotion you send must be the balance to anger. You see?"

Linsora nodded.

"Bringing this back to you, we have theorized that something about children of Terrans and Khizarans results in an unusual structure of neural pathways. The emotional sensing portion of the brain seems to be blocked until a certain stage of brain development is reached. Then, sometime before age seven in girls, it opens suddenly. The influx of emotions at that point also affects other portions of the brain, causing an inability to digest food. It's fairly complicated. In males, the pathway opens later in life and the relationship between digestion and the emotional sensing is less intense."

"And what does chikara do?"

"It seems to make the emotional part of the brain more stable. Reins it in, essentially." Pera gazed into the fire. "What we have found from autopsies on mixed children who didn't survive was that the neural pathway, especially in females, is unusually configured. Understandably, we were curious to see what that would mean. And, in your case, since your mother had the microbes in her blood, some had entered yours even before you were born. That may have helped you respond to the chikara when you were four."

"Why didn't you keep me here then?" Linsora asked, thinking about her life and how blissful it might have been to have spent it here instead of in the turmoil dotting her past.

"Because even at four you were Khizaran," Pera smiled. "Many pieces fit together to result in you. But, at the basic level of emotion, you were Khizaran and always will be. We didn't know when or how or even if those neural pathways would be activated further. Trying to keep you here would have been like trying to keep a kaibu as a pet. We only hoped that if you somehow became aware, you would find us again."

"Kaibu. Funny, my mother used to call me that sometimes. She said I reminded her one sometimes, small but fierce. I always thought they looked cute."

"I think you enjoyed the comparison."

Linsora looked around the room. It reminded her of her mother's house, familiar and comfortable. She hadn't thought about her mother or her childhood much lately, other than during conversations with Permac.

"You're right, I don't think I would have been content here."

"Just as you wouldn't be content to stay now." Pera placed a hand on Linsora's arm. "Yes, you could stay if you wanted. Arrangements could be made."

"I can't," Linsora said. "My life has taken me too far, and there's still a long way to go." The warmth of the room suddenly became stifling. "Can we go outside? I would like some air."

Beads of humidity glistened on Linsora's face, made her hair fluff. She breathed deeply, aware of the sweet scent of chikara.

"My mother never told me any of this. I wonder why?"

"She wanted you to be Khizaran, not someone who felt she had to hide."

"What about my father? Did he know?"

"I don't think so. They were so very fond of each other. Do you know how they met? He was doing a survey not far from the city. It was about a year after her first husband died. She was a journalist and joined the survey team for a season. She never left."

Linsora sat on the front steps. "If one person can influence another without being detected…"

"Your mother didn't influence your father to love her. Influences wear off. If the love wasn't there, it couldn't be forced." Pera picked weeds from a bed of herbs next to the house. "Although…do you know why your father came to Khizara in the first place?"

"Not much archaeological investigation had been done before. It was a whole planet full of opportunity."

"Certainly so. And rumors had long circulated among portions of the archaeological community that Tokor's books were still somewhere on Khizara."

"He came here looking for the books? The ones I found?"

"It's not beyond imagining that your mother first associated with him to steer him away from finding them. Whether she influenced him in that regard, I can't say. But I do know that they were genuinely in love. You know that, too."

"Well, I just wondered," Linsora said. "I wish I could remember what my mother's influences tasted like. I'm sure she must have influenced me now and then. Funny, everyone's taste is different, unique. I'd like to imagine hers as clean and sure, like strong tea. Pera, you were startled when I said I could taste influences. Why? You're not the first person to find that odd."

Pera's head whipped around. "Not the first?" She picked several more weeds, and with a resigned sigh, sat next to Linsora. "As I said, you are the first female child of a Terran and Khizaran to survive that we know of. And, you were born with some microbes already in your system. Your neural pathways are unusual. Your mother told me you could sense ancient voices at archaeological sites. That's how you and your father found Pak'bor and that's part of how your brain is configured. No one else I know can do that. People must leave part of themselves, bits of electrical energy, I don't know, that you can pick up. Detecting emotional influences as a taste, that's also different. When did you become aware of this?"

"Before I ever had chikara, well except for what I had here. When… I mean my…" It was her turn to sigh heavily. "My mate. He is Tokorellan."

"Oh my," Pera said. "Is it that Gordek fellow Rento spoke with?"

Linsora spat into the soft earth, "Sorry. No, most certainly not Gordek, although he is Tokorellan, too. Most definitely certainly categorically not Gordek."

"Then who… how?"

"Time for my long story," Linsora said. She told her entire tale to Pera, not leaving out the portions she had when telling the story to Bhreagh. By the time she brought the story to her arrival in Yakto, the sun was low and the humidity chilling.

"So the people on Hakai use the tejina soil on their buildings? Interesting. And this Moragh person seems to have used it on his ship? Also interesting. We've found the properties of the tejina differ depending on the climate, as do the properties of the soil. Hakai must have ideal conditions. If the climate is too damp, no fruit is produced. Too dry, the microbes don't become well established in the soil. Perhaps that's why the soil isn't used on Tokorel, it may be too dry. When the plants produce fruit in dry conditions and humidity is allowed in after the fruit drops, the microbes are at their most potent."

"And you use the soil only on pottery?"

"We don't have enough of it to slather on the walls," Pera said. "Most certainly not enough to coat a ship." Pera stood and folded Linsora in her arms again. This time, Linsora accepted the embrace and offered a return hug. "We both have a lot to digest. Rento is an excellent cook and I can smell something wonderful. Let's eat and talk about something less intense. The last time I spoke with your mother, she said they were heading to a site here on Khizara. You must have been around twelve then."

"Pak'bor?"

"Yes, we lost touch after that, but I remember all the excitement surrounding the find. The oldest city on Khizara? What a find that was."

Even Rento managed a smile or two during the animated discussions of past family tales during the evening. And, Linsora had to admit, he was an excellent cook.

CHAPTER 34

"I'm afraid you'll have to be satisfied with my cooking today," Pera said as Linsora stumbled toward the morning table. "Rento is a doctor and people have all sorts of injuries from the storm."

"I don't think Rento cares much for me." Linsora ate bread, some cold meat and more tea in shimmering cups.

"You're Khizaran and direct."

"So is he."

"But he was raised here, not with most Khizarans."

Linsora swallowed her reply with more bread and tea. Pera implied she didn't care for Khizarans even though she herself was one. Early on Gordek said not all Tokorellans were as gentle as Permac. *Permac is the only Tokorellan I've met who is gentle*, she thought. *At our base level, we're Khizaran. Being Khizaran and being all that implies isn't bad any more than being Tokorellan is bad Be careful, Pera, your prejudices are showing.*

"I'd offer to help cook, but I'm not good at it either," she said, draining her cup. "This is delicious. Is there anything else I can do to help you here?"

"I'd say you could spend the day relaxing, but I'm not sure you know how to do that. Your mother could never sit still, either," Pera cleared the plates from the table. "Well, then, let's take a walk and see what the storm did."

Fallen branches littered the spacious back yard of Pera's house. Linsora busied herself spreading them neatly. In a week they'd be dry enough to stack for firewood. Sturdy metal plates protected what Linsora knew was the greenhouse.

"Pera, I noticed that Yakto isn't set up like most Khizaran towns."

"In family groups? No and I admit that's one element I miss," Pera said. "But the realities of raising families with chikara, and doing so in secrecy, makes the family houses difficult. It's simpler to teach children the intricacies of influencing and sensing emotions in a small household than in a large environment."

"Tokor's village was arranged like this one, so were the towns on Hakai." Linsora remembered Permac said that he was raised in a small household. She had thought it sounded lonely.

"But there's no reason why Khizarans can't continue to live in family compounds, even after chikara is brought into use. It will all take a great deal of adjustment."

"Adjustment. People don't adjust easily. I suppose I've adjusted to tasting and feeling influences, though," Linsora threw a small stick across the yard. "Last night we talked about my tasting influences, but you never told me why you reacted like you did. The man I told you about, Moragh, was surprised, too. You seem disturbed. Why?"

"Well, as I said, it's not normal. I've never heard of it before and I suspect it has something to do with your brain structure. Most people who are aware of being influenced feel it as a prickling sensation, a light tickle. Do you feel that?"

"Sometimes, mostly I experience a taste."

"Your neural pathways must translate the influences to the taste receptors somehow," Pera pulled leaves from a branch before placing it on a pile. "You said you don't know who this Moragh is? I don't either, and that's the truth. But he must be, how can I put this, he must be someone close to an inner circle of power." Pera sat down, wiped her forehead. The Khizaran sun was fully blazing, creating an aromatic steam from the remaining puddles. "I told you that we can trace our line of descent back to Tokor's sister. Certain, um, information, legends have been passed down through the years. You said you read Tokor's books, was there anything about a vision or prophesy in them?"

"Something about words that kept going through his head," Linsora stopped her work.

"Well, it seems Tokor had a dream, I don't know, maybe a vision. I can't say I believe in such things, but I'll tell you what was passed on to me by my mother and you can decide for yourself. It's become a poem, recited to me when I was a child. I recited it to my own children.

"The universe has eyes and ways

To touch your heart and mind.

Beware the lowly and obscured

Whose soul with bile is lined.

They'll make you run in circles,

They'll turn you inside out.

Always trust your instincts

To see you through, throughout.

Six to none to five to none

Between not six but five and one.

A taste in mind and on the tongue.

A mix of blood and wars begun.

Then two uniting in the sky

Will five and one to six apply.

Six by four to multiply.

Makes one, makes one, makes one, say I."

Pera had closed her eyes to recite the poem. Possibly in reverence, possibly to remember all the words. Linsora sat down next to her.

"That sounds familiar, I think my mother may have said it to me when I was young."

"That's likely, although she was even less a believer in visions than I am, so she may not have put much emphasis on it. Do you see how it could be applied to you? The *taste in mind and tongue* part especially."

Linsora stared, not sure if she should laugh or be outraged. "Pera, you can't believe this applies to me. It can't. I'm not some embodiment of myth."

"No you're not, no one ever is. You're an archaeologist, you study cultures. You know that all through the ages, in every culture there are tales of heroes, saviors who fit the description of some prophesy," Pera leaned forward. "In every one, the time has been right for something to happen and someone happens to fit the description of the prophecy. If circumstances weren't right, that person would still have been there, would still have done the same things, but wouldn't have been seen as anyone special."

"I'm certainly nobody's definition of a hero," Linsora said, spitting. Humor was fast surrendering to outrage now. "What's the rest of it again? The spires, he saw six then none then five. Like the Prefecture building."

"No, five and one. Five on Khizara and one somewhere else, perhaps Tokorel."

"Mmm, then the taste line, and five and one to six. Sounds like a unification. None of that is farfetched."

Pera took Linsora's hand, "No, but think about the preceding lines. *A mix of blood*, you're Khizaran and Terran. *Two uniting in the sky will five and one to six apply.* You and your Permac Sealed the Oath in space."

Linsora pulled her hand away and strode around the yard, coming back to where Pera was still seated. "You sound like you believe it all. How many people have Sealed the Oath in space? Permac and I aren't the first. I'm not the first Khizaran of mixed parentage, either, Terran or otherwise."

"As I said, circumstances might make it seem more than it is. Any other time, your heritage, what you've done, wouldn't attract attention."

"So at what point did I walk out of my own life and step into this mess? I think I was shoved into it and I can claw my way out." Linsora caught a fleeting expression on Pera's face that was not the least bit reassuring. "My mate once said anything done can be undone. So can all of this." Linsora didn't feel nearly as sure of that as she tried to sound. " The last part, then. *Six by four to multiply*. What the hell's that?"

"Did Tokor's book mention Cornerstones?" Pera's tone was a measured and mild as ever, but Linsora noticed some strain. The woman's hands were tightly clenched together in her lap.

"No."

"Another tale then. His waking vision, the one he planned, was for Khizara to be the first Cornerstone of an eventual four seats of power. Four Cornerstones encompassing all known space, presiding over eras, perhaps a forever, of peace and prosperity. Six spires on each of the four Cornerstones. He wanted his followers to be part of every society, to guide each turn of history until ultimate and universal peace was achieved. I know, it sounds fuzzy and utopian, but I think he believed it possible."

"It sounds like meddling, to me. On Brachen we saw that projection of Tokor. He said something about that. He said if he'd been successful we'd know about him. He said he was working on something to make all warfare obsolete."

"Part of his plan, his waking dream. If this Moragh was startled at the fact that you can taste influences, he must know the prophecy. Perhaps he is a descendant of Tokor as well and perhaps he's playing with circumstances to make it happen."

"There's Khizara, and Tokorel, and Hakai. Gordek is looking for the place tejina came from originally. Could that be the fourth?"

"Could be. As I said, it's an old legend." Pera smoothed her skirt. "He, Moragh I mean, may have tried to separate you, but he wanted to take you somewhere. He wanted to know where you were. I have a feeling you, and your Permac, might be useful to his dreams. He seems, though, to have had your best interests in mind."

"How? By making me think Permac was dead? By throwing me to Gordek?" Linsora's voice thundered. "I don't want to be protected. I don't want to be useful to Moragh's dreams, to Gordek's dreams, or to Tokor's. I only want my own and I don't even know what they are anymore. I don't want some kind of universal peace where everyone is being influenced into some kind of near catatonic bliss. I want people to feel what fire they have. I don't want any part of any of this."

"And who the hell do you think you are to sidestep your destiny?" Rento

250

appeared at the gate to the yard.

"Destiny? I don't have one. I have choices. So do you." Linsora stood to face him.

"And you'd choose what? To disappear into history? To be nothing? You could take hold of this and…"

"If you're not content to spend your life here, then get the hell out. I get the feeling you're more Khizaran than you want to admit. Do something else. Don't try to soak your Khizaran fire with Tokorellan platitudes. Don't wrap me up in some Tokorellan destiny you only think you want."

"You question my integrity?" Rento's face was red. Linsora could have sensed his fury even without the benefit of microbes.

"You question mine? You question my acceptance of the great words of the great Tokor? Question away, you'd be right. I don't struggle with my decisions." She stepped toward him, her hands in pockets where knives hid. This is how challenges started. "You question yours, though, don't you? You're not at all sure that what Tokor had in mind is so benign. He was Khizaran, don't forget that. Conquest is conquest no matter how you get there. You like your chikara. You like what it can do for you personally, and for your medicine. I think you like the power of having it to yourself, too. I think you're afraid you might not be up to the challenge of keeping your power once everyone has chikara. Well, don't plan to ride to power behind me. I'm not going there."

"What about your father? You think he would want you to walk away? He came here looking for what you found. You think his intentions were so pure?"

"You have no right to accuse my father of anything, Rento! Did you ever even meet him?" Linsora had a knife in each hand. Rento had a knife in each of his. Linsora saw his shoulder drop, followed by a very slight forward tilt of his upper body. She angled her body to his, balanced on the balls of her feet, flexed her knees.

"This, Rento, is the Khizaran fire," Linsora hissed.

He made a sweeping pass, feinting with the longer knife, hoping to get in close with the shorter. She pivoted into him, blocked his left hand's thrust with her right, and pushed him off balance. Hot pain set her teeth on edge as he swiftly recovered and sliced her shoulder. He drew the first blood, not always an advantage. Linsora shouted, came up under his arm and sliced his forearm.

Although death was not intended in this kind of fight, both participants accepted it as a possibility. At the end, they would be cut and bloody, but there would be no lingering doubt. Winning a fight didn't mean you won the argument, only the right to have your side respected. And you, in turn, respected your opponent for defending his side. Respect begets respect. No drawn out discussions. No polite bow. No retiring to let the issue fester. No playing with words. No settling tomorrow. When it was over and adrenaline rush faded into a warm feeling of accomplishment, you might help your opponent up, or be helped up. You would be forever bonded by the ritual of mutual respect. You would clean your own blood from your opponent's knives and he would clean his from yours.

Pera edged out the way of the two engaged in their spiteful dance.

Shouts and curses rang out, time stilled into a sense of slow motion unreality for Linsora. Rento seemed to telegraph his every move, only to surprise her with something unexpected. Still, she inflicted as many hits as she received. She heard her heavy breathing and the scrape of her feet on the ground. Her muscles burned. Her hands were gummy with blood, but she didn't know if it was hers or Rento's. She wasn't aware of any pain from cuts, pain would come later. Rento moved forward. Linsora angled slightly left, then just as quickly moved right. Rento missed the sudden change, lost his balance and slid forward on a patch of mud. He landed hard on one knee. This was the killing point. Had she wanted to, the polite cuts and feints would have ended with a more lethal stab. Linsora had reached this point before, had shoved her opponent down onto his stomach, leapt onto his back, and delivered a final slice to the man's throat. He was a thief and would have killed her. She remembered the horror and victory she felt when that vile man's blood spurted over her hand. Hot sticky life draining from a cold shell. This fight with Rento was not one for death. She threw her knives down, indicating the end.

"That was uncalled for," Pera glared at both of them.

Linsora pocketed her knives. She and Rento would clean the blood from them later.

"Well done, Rento," she said, offering her hand. "Is your knee okay?"

Pera laughed, "Maybe I have spent too much of my life sheltered here. How can you both be cut and bleeding and you ask about his knee?"

"Cuts are minor, they'll heal. Landing that hard on your knee, though, can do a lot of damage."

The three of them caught some of ridiculous sense of her statement. All three laughed. Hearty, loud, raucous laughter of relief, of power, of naked emotions completely un-reined.

CHAPTER 35

The hotel room glowed with the rosy hues of morning. The air had the stale smell of the city. Linsora wrinkled her nose. A month in the jungle had spoiled her.

She, Rento and Pera spent their last night together by Pera's fire drinking not tea, but some lovely and potent drink Pera made from overripe chikara. Pera suggested that might be a good way to introduce chikara to Khizarans, but she wasn't sure if the microbes survived the high alcohol content. Rento drove her back to the city before dawn laden with presents from Pera. The new cuts on her arms and hands throbbed nearly as much as her head. She wished she had taken Rento up on his offer to heal them when he checked her leg in his mender.

Her role in the Tokorellan rhyme was far from resolved. Rento's belief in her destiny remained. He apologized for insulting her father, but not for his belief that she was sidestepping what could be greatness. Over and over, she told Rento how she had chosen no role of any sort. The more she protested, though, the more she questioned. She could have made other choices. She could have simply stayed with the *Dominator*. She could have gone with Moragh. She could have killed Gordek. *Damn you*, she thought, *Gordek and Moragh both. At least I know who Gordek is and what he wants. Distasteful, but honest.*

Linsora pulled the covers over her head. A link was missing, she had let something pass. Rento was a puzzle. His anger at her refusal to march into history was overblown. *As a Khizaran, even one with access to chikara, he should be sympathetic to me*, she thought. *He should realize that I want my fate to be my own. Still, there he was, defending Moragh. Saying I should regard him as a protector, someone with the best interests of both Khizara and me in mind. If he knew Moragh, he might not be so quick to defend him.*

She struggled with the covers, pulling them away from her face, and sat up. "You do know him, don't you, Rento. Pera does, too. She has to. Except for tasting influences, not much of what I said surprised either one of you. Kind, solicitous, helpful, and lying." She reached onto the table next to the bed ready to grab whatever unfortunate object first met her hand to throw at the wall. "Every answer I get comes with eight more questions." She touched something round and cool. It was a teapot. Just like the one Pera used in Yakto. Linsora placed it gently on the bed then reached over again for an ordinary glass. She hurled it across the room but barely noticed the crash as it shattered. Her attention was on the teapot.

The field of flowers painted on the side looked like the landscape surrounding Pera's house. As Linsora gazed at it, the flowers began to sway as though a light breeze had swept them. Clouds rolled lazily across the sky in the scene. Kagamite. Linsora lay back on the bed and closed her eyes. She could almost hear the late afternoon hum of insects, birds, and rustling foliage. She remembered the scent of the tejina plants.

A knock on the door brought Linsora to her feet. She concentrated and then smiled, rushing to open it. Bhreagh stood there with a tray of breakfast.

"Linsora! How are you?" the woman asked. "I had a message that you'd returned and thought you might be hungry."

"Thank you! I am hungry in fact."

"How are you? Your leg…." Bhreagh looked puzzled. "Your hand! You didn't have that cut last time I saw you."

Linsora thought about affecting a limp. Usually in the case of a fracture, her leg would have been immobilized for at least another few days. Not knowing how many more times she would have to do this and against her better nature, she turned back into the room while sending assurances of her health to Bhreagh. She didn't think she exerted enough influence for her eyes to change color, but she couldn't take any chances.

"Oh, it wasn't as bad as it looked," she said. "They managed to put me back together in just a few days. My hand, well, that along with my shoulder and several other places. I've been away from Khizara too long. Was too quick with my tongue and not quick enough with my feet."

"Got it." Bhreagh shrugged, she'd never been in a fight, but knew well enough how they happened. "Well if I ever break anything, I'm going there. Their doctors sound better than ours."

"How long have you been in the city?" Linsora changed the subject. "Is everyone here?"

"We only got back late yesterday. And yes, Gordek is here too," Bhreagh said with an acidic look. "It took us a whole day just to clear the debris off the transport. Let me tell you, Gordek was not a lot of help. Even after we got the message from, what's his name, uh Rento, Gordek still made himself very unuseful."

"He hasn't seen Behazh yet, then."

"No. But Linsora, didn't you notice the city when you got in?"

"Notice? What do you mean. I arrived very early. I didn't see much of anything," Linsora said.

Bhreagh whistled in surprise, "Well, you must have been sleeping! There are soldiers everywhere, and only soldiers. There's a curfew. No one is allowed on the streets after dark. Can you imagine? And during the day crowds are prohibited. I went out for a walk this morning and was stopped at the corner - they asked where I was going, why, and even asked to see my ID. I only went a few blocks before it got tiresome and I came back. I guess that's the whole

254

purpose, though, to keep people off the streets."

"Why? What happened? I talked to Behazh two weeks ago and he didn't say anything about this."

"Well, seems that once word got out that Yokosh was a Tokorellan agent, or something, people started wondering who else was Tokorellan. I mean, they look like us. They could be anyone. There were duels over even minor disputes and two Prefects were killed last week. No one trusts anyone else. We have no way of telling who is Khizaran and who isn't."

Linsora went to the window and peered down on her city. No one wandered the streets; no traffic snarled at the corners. It was eerily empty, except for the armed soldiers standing in pairs at each intersection. The sad part was only Tokorellans would have access to everything now. A normal Khizaran who couldn't influence the soldiers would be stopped and sent home.

"I hope Yokosh hasn't won," she muttered. This was just the kind of situation he had been hoping to create. A distrustful chaos.

"Well, I have to see Behazh. Bhreagh, I'm going to ask if the investigations in the Forbidden Area can be continued. Would you like to be in charge? You know the basics of archaeology, at least enough to excavate carefully. As long as you make detailed notes of everything, whatever you find can be studied later."

"Of course, I'd love it. What about you, though? Why can't you do it?" Bhreagh asked.

"I have something else to do for a while."

"Ah, I know. The man you thought was dead? Well, that's enough reason for me," she punched Linsora on the arm, a gesture of friendship Linsora had become used to from her friend. "I hope you find him well."

"Thank you. So do I," Linsora smiled. Her smile faded as she thought of Permac. He was alive. He had to be.

Another quick rap at the door and Gordek burst in.

"Well, I'm pleased to see that your leg is better, Linsora. I was concerned about you."

"Yeah, I'm sure you were," Bhreagh sniffed, placing herself between her friend and the man she thought of as creepy. "The injuries weren't as serious as I thought." Gordek didn't respond. He stood with his hand on the open door, inviting Bhreagh to leave. Linsora watched the staring contest between them, but she didn't sense any influences flying. Gordek must not think Bhreagh worth the effort.

"Bhreagh, if you have things to do, I'm fine here. Thanks for the food," Linsora said.

"You sure? Okay then, if you will excuse me, I think I'll try to take a walk again. At least the soldiers are pleasant."

"I'll contact you before I leave and let you know," Linsora said.

"Let her know what?" Gordek asked when Bhreagh had gone.

"Whether or not she can continue to work in the Forbidden Area."

"Why? Do you think Tokor left something else?"

"Gordek, what remains there is information on how people lived two hundred years ago, what they ate, what their houses were like, what they believed in, how they…"

"Yes, yes, fine. We have, however, found what we went there for. I have scheduled a meeting with Behazh in an hour. I've already spoken to him, and planted some ideas." He looked at Linsora carefully, "One day you must tell me all about the mysterious town in the jungle with miraculous cures. I'm not as easily - assured shall we say - as Bhreagh that the injury was minor." He pointed to her hand, "What's that? Bhreagh didn't say anything about any other injury. Run into someone you couldn't charm?"

"You always surprise me, Gordek. How can you be so incredibly rude, so incredibly suspicious, and so incredibly self-centered and still remain alive."

Gordek snorted a laugh, "You should know by now, Linsora, it's purely because of those qualities that I am alive."

As he turned to leave, his eyes fell on the teapot. His eyebrows arched. Linsora wished she had hidden it.

"I see you brought back a souvenir. Interesting," he said. He reached out to touch it, but Linsora scooped it off the bed. After an uncomfortable moment, he walked toward the door. "Well, we should leave in an hour for that meeting."

"Gordek," she called to him. When he stopped, she didn't know what to say. "I'll be ready."

CHAPTER 36

The streets of Khizara were nearly empty. The mid-morning haze swirled around scattered food stalls. The only customers were soldiers taking a break, not the usual throng of tourists outside the Prefecture. Linsora thought it looked like some plague had swept through the city, leaving only dust behind. Two Navy officers with stony expressions opened the transport doors. Linsora and Gordek were escorted into a side door of the Prefecture. The echo of their footsteps in the empty corridors followed them to the Prefect's office.

Behazh looked wearily at the two. He nodded to Gordek, noticing the scratches on Gordek's face and Linsora's pointed avoidance of the man who was supposed to be her protector. A fresh bandage swathed her hand. He would remember to be more guarded about Gordek in the future, though. He seemed to recall thinking the same thing before in fact. He shook his head and embraced Linsora.

"You worry me. Every time I see you, there's a new bruise."

"Sorry. I'm usually a lot more careful. No need to worry. I'm still alive."

"Well then, much has happened, as I'm sure you've noticed," he said.

"Yes, Bhreagh told me a little," Linsora said.

Behazh offered seats to his guests and Linsora explained what had been found in the Forbidden Area. She began with the cache of love letters, emphasizing their importance to the study of Khizaran history. She could sense Gordek's impatience at hearing all of this again and ignored him. Only the slight tapping of his foot against the leg of a chair served as a constant reminder that he wanted her to get to the point. The tapping ended when she began to explain about Tokor's book.

"Behazh, the book is undoubtedly Tokor's. Its age is right and so is its location. More than that, it seems to have been left purposely. He wanted the book to be found," she said.

"Probably just as well it wasn't found earlier," Behazh said. "It would have been destroyed. Time can dull some enmities." He gestured toward the window and the empty streets below. "And, then again, sometimes not."

"Maybe this can help, Behazh. Tokor's point wasn't to take over Khizara. If we can somehow get information out to the people," Linsora followed Behazh's gaze outside. "It might help if people know that Tokor's abilities aren't magic, that everyone can have them."

"Either help or make people ever more distrustful of each other." Behazh drummed his clawed nails on the tabletop. "Linsora, history may be skewed, but the point is that the abilities developed by Tokor are still potentially dangerous. The allure of power is strong. Can we believe that all of his followers are as altruistic as he was? Tokor is gone and we have no idea what his people want today. Obviously, as with your brother, some of them do want Khizara. Some may want even more, but we just don't know," Behazh rubbed his forehead. Linsora sensed that he had a headache and was about to send relaxed feelings to him, when she felt Gordek in her mind and a sense of warning. She realized Behazh's headache was the result of Gordek's influence. A misplaced attempt to help their cause by giving Behazh a disadvantage. She hoped Gordek would know her disgust and disapproval, but she knew he probably wouldn't care.

Behazh continued, "There is even talk of invading and destroying Tokorel. In effect finishing what was started years ago."

"Behazh! We would lose! You must realize that," Linsora said. "We can't fight them with ordinary weapons."

"I know that," Behazh boomed. "But not everyone chooses to believe it. As long as I am a Prefect, I can prevent it. But, I don't know how long I can hold this position."

"If we go to Tokorel, maybe we can bring back, I don't know, maybe teachers or people to help Khizarans learn to use the chikara, learn how to grow it," Linsora wanted to carve the smirk from Gordek's face. "Behazh, it makes me sick to think about that, too. But it'll happen anyway. Better to lead people into chikara use properly than to let them learn by trial and error. The minute Tokor found it, it was inevitable that we'd all have it."

"I know. And I agree. And I'm no happier about it that you are," Behazh paced back and forth in front of them, "I will send ambassadors to Tokorel. Gordek has suggested that you would be an appropriate emissary and I agree. You found the books. It would be fitting for you to present them. And you, having had positive experience with at least one Tokorellan, have less generalized suspicion. I am making Tokor's books available to the public, but I'm increasing the security around the Forbidden Area. I don't want the entire population rushing into it to collect plants. Maybe with enough information, we can start to return to normal." A look of sadness passed across Behazh's face, "Whatever normal is. I suspect that the definition of normal has changed forever."

"Behazh, I'm sorry, so sorry, if I've caused this. I never intended…"

"Don't ever – EVER – blame yourself for any of this. As you said, it was inevitable, we just happen to be here as witnesses. I suspect that Yokosh acted earlier than he wanted to due to your presence, but he would have acted. And, given his own time line, things might have been much worse for Khizara."

"Thank you," Linsora didn't feel reassured. She had examined the past few months trying to find the point of no return, the place where a different decision might have led to a different present. But she couldn't see any point in the past where she would have chosen a different path than the one that led her here.

"Gordek has offered to take you to Tokorel in his ship and we will provide a Khizaran escort. In fact, Linsora, you are not unfamiliar with the commander of the fleet I am sending," Behazh said. "I regret having to put you in this position, but he is the best I have. I trust you will maintain your sense of propriety."

"I don't understand," she said.

"You will."

Behazh opened the door to his inner office. A Khizaran Fleet Commander strode into the room. Gordek was astonished, not by the officer, but by Linsora's reaction. She rose to her feet slowly, a snarl of contempt on her face. The officer bowed stiffly to her, then stood quietly next to Behazh.

"Kral!" Linsora spat at him. "Behazh, you know of his association with Yokosh! How can you trust him!"

"Linsora!" Behazh said, "As I said, he is the best I have. He is my son. I trust him and so must you."

"I will trust you, Kral, only as long as you remain on your own ship," she said. "If you do not, then trust that I may yet make good my promise to have your blood."

The officer's deep aqua eyes glinted with thinly veiled rage. "You never did promise to have my blood. Only Yokosh's. If you would like to make that promise now, I will not refuse you the pleasure of trying."

Kral and Linsora stood ramrod straight facing each other. They easily slipped into the formal language of serious challenges. The code was ancient, the language ceremonial. It served to indicate the gravity of the challenge, leaving no question of whether or not the killing blow would be taken.

Linsora took a step toward the tall, muscular man. Behazh stepped in front of her. "There will be no blood spilled in the Prefecture," his voice was hushed, but shook with fury. "He is right, Linsora. You have no quarrel with him."

"He was Yokosh's second. Yokosh is not here. Therefore, he serves his master still and must stand in his place," she said, looking around Behazh at the man with whom she had once planned to Seal the Oath.

"I answer to no master but the Prefecture," Kral spat back. "You, however, once answered to me, and are still under desertion charges. Do not insult ME. You do not have that right."

Gordek had been silent during the entire audience with Behazh. He cleared his throat and rose to stand behind Linsora. "I once warned you that your mouth would get you killed. Offending a Fleet Commander is a perfect means to that end. Remember that we have much to accomplish."

Linsora spun around to face Gordek, "You - stay - out - of - this," she hissed. "I insult no one who does not deserve the honor, including you."

Gordek smiled at her. She knew he was thrilled to see her angry at someone other than him. She wished she had killed him when she had the chance and wondered what possible purpose was served in keeping him alive.

Kral had moved to Behazh's side and after a whispered exchange, the older man held up his hand, "This is ENOUGH! Linsora, I am giving you without argument what you came here prepared to plead for. Do not make me reconsider. I am prepared to allow some limited access to the Forbidden Area for purposes of historical study. Khizara is on the verge of civil war. The more we know of the ancient followers of Tokor, the less mysterious they will be. Maybe they will be feared less as well."

He looked at the three people in the room and sighed. "Your personal disputes cannot be allowed to affect whatever hope there is to settle matters. I especially do not want two Khizarans to arrive on Tokorel ready to kill each other. That would only confirm the worst of what they must believe we are like. Linsora, you and Kral will resolve what is between you and you will do it now. It is long overdue. Take what time you need, but settle it."

Behazh motioned to Gordek, "We will leave them here. Gordek, please come with me, we need to make arrangements for the ambassadors and whatever supplies your ship will need."

Linsora and Kral received a final stern glance from Behazh before they were left alone. They heard a click as the door locked. It might have been to assure their privacy, perhaps their safety, but neither of them believed that. They knew it was to prevent either one of them from walking out on the discussion.

Linsora turned toward the window. She gazed out on the empty city square and opened her mind. She tasted the roiling, quickly shifting emotions of a Khizaran. Kral was not someone she was prepared for. Nor did she expect the emotions she felt from him: anger, yes, but also sadness and affection.

Kral broke the silence, "Linsora. It's been five years and I don't know what to say to you. This is not exactly how I envisioned meeting you again. I am glad to know that you're alive, though."

"Indeed, Kral," she said, turning back to him. "I'm glad that you're alive, too. You seem to have done well. Fleet Commander is impressive." She held up her hand at his darkening expression, "And I know you earned the position, Kral. You always were a fine officer. Maybe there's just too much to be said."

"No. We can't pretend nothing was ever between us, either good or bad," Kral said. "You could have won the argument with Yokosh. The Prefecture would have taken your side. I told you that. I thought some sort of compromise could be reached." He smiled at her, "But you always did try far too hard to be Khizaran and Yokosh, well, he's Yokosh. You two could never agree on anything, much less a property settlement. I should have realized that. By the time it all came down to a duel, I chose to be there as witness so I could stop it before either of you were dead. Linsora, you fight well but I somehow knew you would be killed."

"I know that. I knew it then. But that didn't make it any easier," she said. "I felt I had been abandoned and betrayed. I didn't think you really wanted me back on your ship when it was over, either. I left Khizara soon after."

"I did send someone to recall you to the ship, but I never filed desertion charges. I suppose I was relieved in a way that you were gone, but Linsora you weren't the only one to feel abandoned."

Kral walked across the room to join Linsora at the window. She noted that he still moved with a grace uncommon to most Khizarans.

"That's it, then? A handful of words after years of hurt and it's over?" Linsora said softly. "Time does make a difference. Two hundred years ago, no one would have listened to Tokor's words. Five years ago, I would not have listened to yours. I wonder if Khizara and Tokorel can ever end up standing at each other's sides in peace?"

She looked up at Kral and returned his smile. He reached for her hand. Their fingers intertwined. He raised their hands to shoulder level, then turned them so that the back of her hand faced him. It was more than a handshake, more than the treaty accord this gesture usually signified. But still, less than a promise between lovers. Each one noted the scars on the back of the other's hand, the reminders of the Oath Sealing ceremony. He brought her hand to his mouth and lightly bit her wrist, as she bit his. They exchanged regretful looks for what might have been.

"I hear that you have Sealed the Oath, with Raminaa," Linsora finally said.

"And you? Do I know your mate?"

"No, but you may meet him."

"Oh, he's with you?"

"No," she paused, wondering how Kral would react. "He's on Tokorel."

Kral whistled softly, "I see the line between Khizara and Tokorel is becoming more blurred all the time. Just as well I suppose." He squeezed the hand he still held, "I'll do what I can to help you get back to him. It's the least I can do."

Linsora turned to the man whose deep blue eyes held only honesty. "Thank you. I did love you, you know."

"And I loved you," Kral replied. Then he smiled, "You were a damn good Science Officer, too."

They moved closer - she on her toes, he bending - and didn't hear the door latch unlock as they kissed.

"It seems they have settled their differences," Gordek snarled, with a combination of amusement and jealousy.

Linsora stepped back from Kral. She felt her face flush and wished she could stop the rising color. She tried to smile pleasantly at Gordek, but her face refused to cooperate. All she could muster was a withering look in his direction.

"Some differences are easier to resolve than others," she said, almost to herself.

Behazh did smile broadly at the two. He clapped his hands together, "Well, this is a good omen, then. Perhaps you won't mind that the plans for your trip have changed somewhat," he said.

Linsora shot Gordek a look. He had done something, influenced Behazh to make the plans suit him better. She knew there was nothing she could do.

Behazh continued, "Sending an entire fleet to Tokorel right now would not only be uncalled for, it would raise suspicions. It is better to send only one ambassador, someone familiar with Tokorellans, someone who will not send automatic feelings of enmity. That would be you, Linsora. No, don't protest - not yet, there's more. I have also decided to send only one ship as an escort. You will go with them, Kral, and your fleet will wait here. If the Tokorellans are not welcoming, we risk only your ship and not the entire fleet. And, as I have said, you are the best I have - the most likely to return either way it goes."

"Sir, the fleet should accompany us at least to within communications range. They can wait on this side of the last jump," Kral said. He didn't like the new arrangements any more than Linsora did.

"No, the Tokorellans would know. The last thing we want is to appear threatening," Behazh said. "The fleet will wait here. That's final."

Kral squared his shoulders and nodded curtly. Linsora gazed at Behazh. He no longer had a headache. In fact he seemed to be quite pleased with himself. She could barely prevent herself from accusing Gordek of bringing on these changes. She noted Gordek's smug look. With effort to send only what would not make her eyes change color, she sent a stab of pain his way. She was pleased to see him flinch. The return blast she had expected didn't happen. Just the taste of Gordek, just a hint of the terrible fear she knew he could send.

"We have begun all the preparatory arrangements. If any of you have matters to attend to, you have until late afternoon when both ships will be ready," Behazh said. "Linsora, you may tell Bhreagh that she and her party can return to the Forbidden Area anytime, but to check with me first. She is to report in to me weekly, at a minimum. You haven't damaged Khizara. You've opened doors for us. There may be some difficulties ahead, but this all had to happen eventually. I'm glad to be part of it." He wrapped her in his arms again, making her feel very little to be responsible for so much, "Good luck, bring us back a world of new allies."

As the three left Behazh's office, Gordek took Linsora's arm. She tried to wrench away when Kral strode up between them. Without actually pushing Gordek, he dislodged the older man's hold and took Linsora's hand. She clasped it and hoped he felt her gratitude.

"Gordek, we will meet you at the debarkation port in three hours," Kral said firmly. Without waiting for a reply, he steered Linsora toward the waiting military transport leaving Gordek standing alone, his fists clenched at his sides. Linsora knew she would probably pay a price for these affronts, but whatever the price was, it would be a bargain.

"Kral, I want to thank you for…" she began once the transport was moving through the streets of the city.

"No need," he said, closing the door between them and the driver. "Linsora, I - well, I have been - I mean…" He stared out of the window, then exhaled loudly. "I have been in touch with Yokosh over the years. I have used some of those leaves he chews and have gained some small measure of his abilities. For some reason, what I have is limited. I can sense emotions, but cannot influence them. Let's just say that Gordek is not someone I care to leave you alone with."

Linsora stared at him, her mouth hanging open.

"If I could offer you transport on my ship, I would," he said. "I don't think Gordek will permit that, though."

"I wonder if there are any Khizarans left who don't have Tokorellan abilities," Linsora finally said. "The lines between us really are blurring, aren't they?" They were silent as the city sped past them. When they stopped in front of the hotel, Linsora asked, "You've been in contact with Yokosh you said. Recently?"

"If I lie to you, you'll know it. So I can only ask you not to ask," he said. "I have matters to attend before we leave, but I'll pick you up here. By the way, that cut on your hand. Gordek?"

"No, he doesn't fight honestly."

"Another story you'll have to tell me someday."

"Kral, I hope life can be simple for both of us again someday," she said as she stepped out of the transport. "Give my best to Raminaa. Tell her that her choice of a mate was wise."

Linsora spent the next two hours trying not to be alone. When Gordek stopped by her room, she was busy making plans with Bhreagh and indicated she would continue to be. She didn't even look at him when she said they would have time to talk later, on board his ship. She didn't want to think about that time.

She did think about Kral and all the other people she had met on Khizara. Of them all, only Bhreagh was an ordinary Khizaran. Even she would soon be changed. If she worked in the Forbidden Area long enough she was bound to be curious about the plants. She would try various concoctions of unusual plants and probably end up making herself sick. Linsora desperately wanted to save her friend from what she now regarded as the Tokorellan infestation of her people. It was, however, far too late. The minute Tokor had made his discoveries, in fact, the wheels were set in motion and could not be stopped. It was inevitable that all Khizarans would ultimately have some of the Tokorellan magic.

"Bhreagh, I have something to give you," Linsora said before leaving to meet Kral. She unwrapped the teapot from her scant bag of personal belongings. She held it and could almost feel it warming in her hands. "This is rather unique, for your use only and only in private. I know you'll want to find some of those plants mentioned in Tokor's book. Well, they are called tejina and the plants on the side of the teapot will show you what they look like."

Bhreagh took the teapot and turned it over in her own hands. As she examined the scene on the side, her eyes widened and she nearly dropped it, "Linsora! The field of flowers is moving! How does it do that?"

"It just does. I'm not sure exactly how, though."

"This is very strange. In fact, much of the time I've spent with you has been strange. But, I have enjoyed it."

"You know, I have, too," Linsora smiled. "I'm almost sorry to be going."

"Will you be back? I want to meet that man of yours," Bhreagh laughed.

"Ha! You have to find one of your own, my friend!" Linsora laughed back. "I don't know when, but I will be back. You may be a renowned archaeologist by the time I do. We may both be old and gray, but I will be back. Take care - and as someone keeps telling me, trust your instincts."

Bhreagh gave Linsora one last punch in the arm before leaving.

An hour later, Linsora walked toward Kral's waiting transport. She savored the scents of her home world and sent a vow to return to it out on the brisk evening breeze.

Made in the USA
San Bernardino, CA
27 February 2014